BREA

The gleam in Ruel's blue eyes mocked her, as if he were capable of reading her thoughts. "Tell me you aren't interested in being kissed by me."

"I'm not. Not at all." But her words were breathless and held little conviction.

She could almost hear his silent amusement. His fingers tightened on her arm, giving her only a second's warning of his intention. Her hands came up to spread across his chest but were trapped there as Ruel gathered her inside the steel band of his arms.

Julie made no attempt to fight, nor did she avoid the mouth seeking out the softness of her lips. His kiss was far more tender than she had imagined and she knew that he was holding back because of her, not wanting to frighten or intimidate her. Yet the fierce sensuality that emanated from him was a force to be reckoned with . . . and in less than a minute, she had forgotten about Frank entirely. Ruel knew what he was doing.

from "Kona Winds"

Don't miss any of Janet Dailey's best sellers

ALWAYS WITH LOVE *** AMERICAN DESTINY ***
AMERICAN DREAMS *** BANNON BROTHERS:
HONOR *** BANNON BROTHERS: TRIUMPH ***
BANNON BROTHERS: TRUST *** BECAUSE OF
YOU *** BRING THE RING *** CALDER PROMISE ***
CALDER STORM *** CAN'T SAY GOODBYE ***
CLOSE TO YOU *** A COWBOY UNDER MY
CHRISTMAS TREE *** CRAZY IN LOVE ***
DANCE WITH ME *** EVE'S CHRISTMAS ***
EVERYTHING *** FOREVER *** GOING MY WAY ***
GREEN CALDER GRASS *** HAPPILY EVER
AFTER *** HAPPY HOLIDAYS *** HEIRESS ***
IT TAKES TWO *** LET'S BE JOLLY ***
LONE CALDER STAR *** LOVER MAN ***
MAN OF MINE *** MASQUERADE ***
MAYBE THIS CHRISTMAS *** MISTLETOE
AND MOLLY *** RANCH DRESSING *** RIVALS ***
SANTA IN A STETSON *** SANTA IN MONTANA ***
SCROOGE WORE SPURS *** SEARCHING FOR
SANTA *** SHIFTING CALDER WIND ***
SOMETHING MORE *** STEALING KISSES ***
TANGLED VINES *** TEXAS KISS *** THAT
LOVING FEELING *** TO SANTA WITH
LOVE *** TRY TO RESIST ME *** WEARING
WHITE *** WHEN YOU KISS ME *** WITH THIS
KISS *** YES, I DO *** YOU'RE STILL THE ONE

Published by Kensington Publishing Corporation

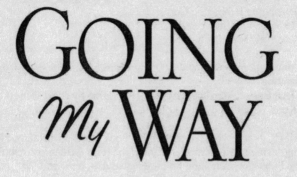

GOING
My WAY

JANET
DAILEY

ZEBRA BOOKS
KENSINGTON PUBLISHING CORP.
http://www.kensingtonbooks.com

ZEBRA BOOKS are published by

Kensington Publishing Corp.
119 West 40th Street
New York, NY 10018

All Kensington titles, imprints and distributed lines are available at special quantity discounts for bulk purchases for sales promotion, premiums, fund-raising, educational or institutional use.

Special book excerpts or customized printings can also be created to fit specific needs. For details, write or phone the office of the Kensington Special Sales Manager. Attn.: Special Sales Department. Kensington Publishing Corp., 119 West 40th Street, New York, NY 10018. Phone: 1-800-221-2647.

Zebra and the Z logo Reg. U.S. Pat. & TM Off.

ISBN-13: 978-1-4201-3221-2
ISBN-10: 1-4201-3221-0

First Mass-Market Paperback Printing: July 2005

10 9 8 7 6 5 4 3 2

Printed in the United States of America

CONTENTS

THAT BOSTON MAN

CHAPTER ONE

The din of the newspaper office was steady, telephones ringing, the clatter of computer keyboards and raised voices creating an unceasing hum of activity. With headphones on, Lexie Templeton barely heard it. She sipped from the paper cup of black coffee she held in one hand and then nibbled at a half-finished Danish pastry in the other.

Carbs and caffeine, the breakfast of champions. Okay, not. But she needed it. She put a different CD in her Walkman and cast a glance at her coworker Ginger Franksen, also her roommate and friend, who was ranting about something. At twenty-two, younger than Lexie by a few years, Ginger had yet to figure out that life wasn't fair and she tended to complain a little too much about that not exactly earthshaking fact.

She was definitely the fresh, Midwestern, annoyingly innocent type. Lexie sometimes felt a little like Ginger's mother.

She studied the slim, blue-jeaned figure pacing by the cubicle where they sometimes met. Ginger's long and beautiful corn-silk hair flowed past her shoulders and she wore very little makeup. She didn't need it, having that all-American look of pure honey that gathered men like bees. Lexie had no doubt that was what Ginger was going on about. She'd heard all about her roommate's current on-again, off-again romance in the last few weeks.

Ginger's obvious agitation made Lexie nervous and when she was nervous, she didn't eat. She set down the pastry in her hand and slipped the headphones off her ears.

Another sideways glance caught the amused but tolerant look of the third member of their group. Shari Sullivan, whose office was across from the cubicle where they were now, was considerably older than both of the others, but no one seemed to think of her as a mother figure. Shari was chic, sophisticated, always dressed to the teeth, and her blonde highlights were a work of art, created by Boston's most sought-after hairdresser.

Despite Shari's hard-bitten glamour, Lexie often felt sorry for her. Shari wanted more than anything else to be thought of as young, and she just wasn't. And she hadn't made the defining career move to a corner office, even though she worked longer hours than anyone in the newsroom.

They were definitely an incongruous threesome. Lexie had often wondered exactly what unseen thread tied them together. Obviously there was something; they met each morning for coffee, Ginger coming from her lowly position in the sports department and Lexie from her fast-rising post in political news. Shari did soft features on society and style, and wrote a gossip column as well.

She came out of her office just as Ginger was winding down. ". . . and Bob was so angry because I wasn't in when he called last night," Ginger said with a dramatic sigh.

Lexie wrapped a paper napkin around the rest of her Danish pastry and tossed it into the wastebasket beside the desk. "I suppose you apologized for going out to do your laundry," she said dryly.

"Well, I was sorry that I wasn't there when he called," Ginger said.

"Honestly, Ginger,"—exasperation riddled Lexie's response—"how can you let yourself become a doormat for that man?"

"I am not a doormat," came the protest. Even Ginger seemed to realize that as defenses went, it was kind of lame. "He wanted to talk to me and I wanted to talk to him. We just didn't make the connection, that's all. But that has nothing to do with my problem. What Bob is really upset about is this weekend. I can't make up my mind whether I should go with him to Cape Cod or not, and I'm afraid if I don't go, he'll ask someone else."

"Let him," Lexie declared in disgust. "And if you can't make up your mind, he may not be the right guy."

"What do you mean?" Ginger asked.

"If he really knocked your socks off, you wouldn't hesitate."

"True," Shari murmured.

Ginger picked at a cuticle. "But I really like him. I mean, I really, really like him."

Lexie only shrugged. "Why?"

"That's not a very nice question. You don't like him, I guess." Ginger pouted.

"Maybe you just don't like men, Lexie," Shari observed in the husky, insinuating voice she had perfected over the years.

Lexie shot her a look. "Spare me the armchair analysis, thank you very much. I like men just fine. When they're not being totally aggravating. You should have been with me yesterday when I interviewed that new candidate for Congress and heard him explain why he doesn't have any women holding responsible positions in his campaign."

"Besides on their backs," Shari said snidely.

Lexie snorted. "Don't think the distinguished candidate could handle that. He's got to be a hundred and five."

"Is he that really ancient rich guy with the polka-dot bow tie and matching suspenders I saw on the news?" Ginger asked.

"That's him. He even gave me that old song and dance about the difficulties of a single woman traveling in the company of so many men and, blah blah, the problems of a married woman leaving her husband while she's on the campaign trail." Lexie swirled the lukewarm coffee in her cup and decided not to finish it. "I couldn't believe I was hearing that crap. It's like nothing has changed."

"For a man of his generation, it probably hasn't," Shari pointed out. "He probably has a little wifey at home in a chiffon apron serving up cocoa and cookies."

"I think he divorced that one," Ginger, an avid reader of tabloids, said. "He has a trophy wife who's a lot younger. But she doesn't do anything but shop."

"Thanks for the news flash." Lexie wasn't ready to stop grumbling. "Why is it that a man is never asked how he manages to combine marriage and a career successfully, but a woman always gets that question thrown at her?"

"Excellent point," the older woman agreed with a throaty laugh.

"And speaking of careers,"—Lexie warmed to her subject with a vengeance—"if a woman makes more money than a man, it's still news. Did you see that article on it in *Time*?"

"It's a pity we can't convince men they can make

money having babies," Shari offered in a dryly amused voice.

"Isn't it, though?" Lexie murmured, impatiently brushing a lock of titian hair from her forehead. "No matter what men say, they secretly want a woman to do it all so they can put their feet up and watch football."

"But some men don't even like football," Ginger said. "So I don't think that's true."

"Believe me, it's true," Lexie continued. "Men want women to soothe their furrowed brows, to pander to their insatiable male egos, to tell them how great they are in bed, and our reward is the so-called pleasure of their company." Her gaze strayed to the tear sheet in Shari's hand, a photograph of a man dominating the page. "And he's the worst of the lot!"

"Rome Lockwood," Shari said with obvious admiration. The candid newspaper photograph didn't do the man justice, but Lexie had seen him too many times in person to be deceived by the picture. She had never met him personally, only observed him at political functions. That had been enough.

Lean, dark features. Jet black hair styled with rakish carelessness above the wide, intelligent forehead. Dark eyes, with a knowing light in their depths as if he knew the power of his attraction. And the photographer had caught him with a disarming smile on his sexy mouth. More than once Lexie had seen him work all that potent masculine charm, smoothly and subtly and successfully.

"Yes, Rome Lockwood," she repeated. "God, that sounds like a made-up name."

"It isn't. And he isn't a politician," Shari remarked. "So how did you happen to meet him?"

"Political functions often become social functions," Lexie answered, again with a trace of contempt. "And no A-list party, political or social, is considered a success without Rome Lockwood. Have you ever seen him with the same woman twice in a row?"

Shari thought for a moment. "Can't say that I have. No one has even come close to hooking him yet, although a lot have tried—desperately. Which may be why his little black book is rumored to have so many names. He probably finds safety in numbers."

"If I were Rome Lockwood, I'd be worried," Lexie observed.

"Why?" Ginger looked at the photograph, which Shari held up for her. A glimpse of the man in the picture made her add, "He's hot. He'll never have to worry about getting a date."

"He should worry that some of his many women might get together and compare notes. I'm sure he finds safety in numbers because it conceals the fact that he isn't man enough to keep one woman satisfied."

Her caustic statement was greeted by silence from Ginger, but Shari cackled with glee and reached for a scratch pad and pencil. "That's priceless, Lexie!" she declared. "May I quote that in my column?"

Lexie hesitated, then shrugged diffidently. "I don't care."

Shari hurriedly wrote it down, despite the rings cluttering her fingers and long nails polished a fashionably gaudy red. "Can't wait to hear the buzz. Everybody will be talking about this column," she said, smiling with feline satisfaction as she read over what she'd jotted.

"I think that's a horrible thing to say," Ginger accused. "You're probably just jealous, Lexie, because you aren't one of his dates."

"You're way off base." Lexie gave her roommate a pitying look. "But I do know his type. There'll never be just one woman in his life. He's always going to have to prove

what a stud he is by stringing out a long line of conquests. The disgusting thing is that so many men envy
him."

"He's kind of like Donald Trump," Ginger agreed
breathlessly.

"Well, not exactly," Lexie said. "Even I have to admit
that Rome Lockwood is a *lot* better looking than The
Donald. And much, much sexier. And that's definitely
his own hair."

"No wonder other men envy him," Shari laughed.
"He's what they all want to be."

"Lexie, a lot of women just love Rome Lock-wood,"
Shari began.

"A lot of women are fools," Lexie replied. "They cher-
ish fantasies that they'll be the one to catch him."

"And why not? What's wrong with a few fantasies?"
Shari argued. "He's tall, dark, and handsome, not to
mention filthy rich."

"And he's a born Casanova." Lexie put the lid on her
takeout coffee and placed it in the wastebasket.

"And you're a born cynic." Shari smiled.

"I prefer it to being a born innocent," she retorted,
straightening up and glancing at her watch. "I'd better
be getting back to my desk. Stan will be wondering where
I went," she said, referring to her editor.

"I'd better go, too," Ginger said. "See you later, Shari."
She followed Lexie as both of them left the cubicle opposite the older woman's office. "Hey, neither one of
you said what you thought I should do about this weekend. Should I go with Bob?"

"I can't tell you whether or not you should go," Lexie
frowned. "It's your decision, Ginger, not mine."

"I don't feel right about going," the girl sighed, flick-
ing her long, straight blond hair away from her collar.

"Then don't go."

"But if I don't, Bob won't ask me out anymore."

"He's not the only Bob in the world. Trust me on this, Ginger. You will meet many more Bobs."

"Easy for you to say. But it's not that easy to find a good Bob."

Lexie laughed. "Who knows? A bad Bob might be a lot more fun."

"Hm. Guess you don't deserve your reputation for being a prude."

Lexie shook her head. "I'm not. Just a workaholic. I don't actually have time to date anyone, good or bad."

Having been blessed with a pretty face and a striking combination of red hair and blue eyes, not to mention a toned body she'd worked hard to achieve, Lexie didn't lack for invitations. She even accepted one now and then. But she really wasn't interested in a committed relationship with anyone at this point in her life.

"See ya later," Lexie said, as they reached the hallway where they would separate to go to their different departments.

Ginger gave her a sheepish look. "Um, I'm meeting Bob after work. So it'll be a lot later."

"What about supper?" They rotated the responsibility for buying takeout food but they rarely cooked.

"Don't get anything for me."

"Okay. Whatever."

Lexie's cubicle was barely distinguishable from the rows of others just like it. A computer and keyboard had pride of place, but a a drift of printouts and memos half-covered the telephone. The file cabinet, desk, and a huge stack of back issues fenced in her chair. As Lexie squeezed through the gap between the desk and the short file cabinet, the man at the cubicle opposite hers glanced up. Ralph Polasky was a staff reporter twenty years her senior, and inclined to laziness.

"You're back," he observed. "Mike was here a minute ago looking for you."

Lexie had expected her brief absence to be noticed. Very little escaped Mike Farragut's attention. The little wheels on her chair squeaked as she pulled it away from the desk.

"What did he want?"

Her coworker shrugged. "Just asked where you were. I told him I thought you'd gone out for some coffee."

"I can imagine his reaction to that."

Ralph Polasky smiled. "You know Mike. He said something about time being money, and why didn't people take advantage of the sludge-in-a-pot that management provides, and so forth."

"Did he actually call our fabulous free coffee sludge?"

"No. It was just the usual speech."

Lexie nodded and sat down. The phone rang at Ralph's desk and he answered it, then cupped a hand over the receiver. "I forgot. I think Mike left something on your desk."

He returned to his call as Lexie quickly skimmed through the papers scattered haphazardly over her desk top. One practically leaped out from among the others, demanding her attention. It was the story she had just written and turned in to Mike not more than an hour ago. She sighed when she saw what was left of it after Mike's ruthless red pencil had gone over it. She leaned back in her chair and began reading through the changes and corrections.

After reworking the story, she e-mailed it to him and got back an almost instantaneous okay. Words of praise were the last thing Lexie expected from him, and she didn't receive any. But his follow-up e-mail announcing that he was giving her a byline on the story was ample reward.

The following afternoon, as she was leaving for the day, she passed Ralph Polasky in the hall. He'd been out on assignment all day and was just coming in to write up the story.

"What are you trying to do?" he asked. "Make a name for yourself?"

She laughed, guessing he had seen her story with her byline in the morning edition of the newspaper. "Jealous?" she teased. The elevator doors were just closing and Lexie hurried to beat them. "Don't work too hard, Ralph," she mocked as she slipped inside the elevator.

The good mood didn't last long. Ginger was at their apartment when Lexie arrived home. She was still in the thralls of indecision about spending the weekend with Bob. Lexie simply couldn't sympathize with her roommate's dilemma, but it was all Ginger wanted to talk about. She discussed it while fixing dinner, and after dinner, and brought it up again when she was washing the dinner dishes. By then Lexie's patience had worn thin.

"I don't care what you do, Ginger!" Her hands were on her hips, a damp dishtowel clamped in her fingers. "Either make up your mind or shut up. I'm tired of hearing about it!"

Her roommate's guileless face was incapable of concealing anything. The hurt that Lexie had caused was clear. Tears glistened in Ginger's eyes and her expression reminded Lexie of a puppy that had just been scolded severely. Without saying one word more, Ginger turned from the sink and dashed to her bedroom.

"Damn," Lexie breathed, and tossed the towel on the

kitchen counter. She was acting like an insensitive bitch, though she was angry at feeling guilty for speaking the truth.

Ginger remained in her bedroom for the rest of the evening. Twice Lexie walked to the door to apologize and make peace. Each time she was kept from knocking by the realization that Ginger was indulging in a childish sulk and by the feeling that she had been right to demand that Ginger make up her mind.

The next morning Lexie was dressed and walking out the door when Ginger finally came out of her bedroom. Lexie paused, wondering whether she should make a comment about the previous night or let the matter rest.

Finally she chose the middle ground. "The coffee is made. I'll see you at work, I guess," she said as she walked out the door.

She didn't see Ginger again until midmorning, when she glanced up to find her roommate standing by her cubicle. Blusher had been applied to pale cheeks with a heavy hand, and Ginger's eyes seemed unnaturally bright.

Oh, now for the drama, Lexie thought. Here it comes.

"I've decided that I'm going to Cape Cod with Bob this weekend. I thought you'd like to know." Ginger's announcement had a defensive, almost challenging ring to it.

"Bob will be happy to hear that," was the only comment Lexie made.

Personally Lexie thought her roommate was making a big mistake, but she kept it to herself. Ginger was already aware that she didn't think much of Bob. There was no need for Lexie to voice her disapproval and put more of a strain on their relationship.

"What time will you be off work tonight?" Ginger asked after a second's hesitation. "I thought I'd get a pizza."

"That sounds good," Lexie replied. "I don't think I'll be late. I'll let you know if it looks like I will be."

"Okay. Talk to you later." Ginger walked away, her mouth curving into a brave smile.

With a sigh, Lexie turned back to her computer. Some women just had to learn the hard way that men and romance weren't the be-all and end-all of existence. Luckily Lexie had avoided that stage. She'd known that since childhood.

"There you are, Lexie." Shari Sullivan's familiar voice interrupted Lexie's thoughts. "Just the person I was looking for."

She glanced up in surprise. Although she often stopped by Shari's office, the older woman rarely, if ever, came to hers. Lexie had always suspected that it was a case of status. When a person had their own column, less established reporters came to call on them and not the other way around.

"You were looking for me?" she said with some curiosity.

"Yes, I was." Shari glanced over Lexie's shoulder and looked at the partially written story on her screen. "Do you have a few minutes or are you under a deadline for this piece?"

"I almost have it wrapped up. I can spare a few minutes," Lexie said. "What is it?"

"Your comment about Rome Lockwood created quite a sensation."

Lexie gave the older woman a puzzled look. "My comment?"

"The one I quoted in my column the other day about Rome Lockwood not being man enough to keep one woman satisfied," Shari reminded her.

It had completely slipped Lexie's mind. "Oh, yeah," she said, nodding. "Major reader response, huh?"

"More than major." A faintly smug smile curved the scarlet mouth. "I was at a party last night and everyone was talking about it. And the calls and e-mails I got about it are just amazing."

"Really."

"Mm-hm. What I need now is another quote like that to keep generating the interest."

"You mean, from me?" Lexie laughed. "I'm sorry. I wish I had a ready supply of them but that one came out of the blue.'

"Surely you can come up with another," the blonde coaxed.

"Honestly, I wish I could. But I can't." She shook her head apologetically, half-amused by Shari's persistence.

The columnist wasn't deterred. Resting her oversized Chanel handbag on the low cubicle wall, she took out a pencil and notepad. "I won't give up so quickly. Rome Lockwood is news any time and when people mention his name, they're going to mention my column in the same breath," Shari insisted.

Lexie sighed. The woman had the tenacity of a bulldog. A very well-dressed bulldog.

"Tell me something about the women he's seen with," Shari prompted.

There was a helpless shrug of her shoulders as Lexie tried to comply. "I don't know anything about them. They're just your usual assortment of rich girls, Europeans who got lost looking for New York, a couple of Bryn Mawr graduates just for their smarts, and an occasional model."

"Why do you think he's so popular? Why is he regarded as such a catch?"

"You said it yourself. He's handsome and rich and single. Of course, without the money, he wouldn't be such a big deal," Lexie qualified.

"Without money, what would he be?" Shari asked.

"Oh, I don't know," she answered, not even trying to think hard. Total superficiality was what Shari wanted anyway. "He'd be something like a—like a gigolo, I guess."

Shari's pencil flashed across the paper.

"He's considered a very shrewd businessman." Shari glanced up from her notepad.

"Really? All he does is manage the family's holdings. His father made all the money. The only thing Rome Lockwood has to do is spend it," Lexie said casually. She wished silently that Shari would go away and let her get some work done.

"I'm told he's made astute investments." Shari's tone held a note of argumentativeness.

"And I bet the CEOs, or the wives of the CEOs, of the businesses Rome invested in told you that. They wouldn't accuse him of making unwise investments, would they?"

Shari's eyes lit up. "You mentioned wives. Corporate wives."

"Don't start, Shari. Please don't start. I was just trying to make a point."

The gossip columnist seemed not to hear that. "Do you think that Rome Lockwood is able to exert unfair influence in that way? Does he respect women or does he just use them?"

"I really wouldn't know."

Shari chewed on the end of her pencil. "I wonder if he's ever been slapped with a sexual harassment suit."

"Oh, I'm sure he's the type who believes in equal opportunity," Lexie said wryly. "Although I imagine his version of it is that he'll go out with a blonde, brunette or redhead." Her phone rang and she picked it up, missing the flashing smile of satisfaction from Shari as she answered it. "This is Lexie Templeton."

The classily dressed blonde stuffed the pad and paper back into her handbag, whispering, "Thanks a lot. See you later." With a wave of her beringed hand, Shari left her take the call in private.

If it hadn't been for one of the other staff members, Lexie wouldn't have known that Shari had quoted anything of their conversation in her column, which wasn't exactly front-page material. Lexie read her own pieces but not much else; she didn't have the time. But her casual remarks to Shari were apparently prime stuff, meted out as tidbits over the following ten days, snagging the columnist plenty of readers anxious to see if she said anything about Rome Lockwood.

After a few days Lexie's comments about the man became a source of gossip even within the newspaper. A few members of the staff thought she was going too far, but mostly the reaction was just good-natured ribbing that Lexie took in stride.

The little café next to the building housing the newspaper's offices was crowded when Lexie entered it a little past noon. There were a lot of familiar faces among the customers since its nearness made it the logical lunch spot for reporters.

"Hey, Lexie!" one of the guys who usually worked the police beat called. "What's the latest word on Rome Lockwood?"

She just smiled and shook her head, red-gold locks dancing around her neck. "Read Shari's column and find out for yourself, Hank. I'm not going to give you an exclusive."

The others at his table laughed and began talking among themselves. Lexie's attention had already been diverted back to her original problem, finding an empty chair in the crowded restaurant. Then she saw a man motioning her to join him—Gary Dunbar, a feature writer for the paper, a quiet man she had dated and had lunch with occasionally in the past. She made her way across the room to his table and the empty chair opposite his.

"I was about to decide I'd have to order a sandwich to go and take it back to the office." Lexie slid into the chair with a grateful smile. "Thanks for letting me join you."

He half rose politely out of his chair as she sat down. A lock of baby-fine brown hair fell across his brow and he self-consciously pushed it back into place. There was a gentle strength in his tanned but slightly ruddy face and Lexie was suddenly reminded of how much she liked him.

"I was going to stop by your desk to see if you were free for lunch," Gary said.

The waitress stopped, handed Lexie a menu, and automatically filled the cup in front of her with coffee before hurrying on. "It's probably a good thing that you didn't," Lexie replied, opening the menu to glance at the list of offerings she almost knew by heart. "I was on the phone. If you'd waited for me, we wouldn't have found a place to sit."

"It's usually full during the lunch hours," he agreed.

A hamburger platter, fries on the side, was set in front of him and the busy waitress turned to take Lexie's order. "I'll have a bacon and tomato sandwich, butter instead of mayonnaise, on white bread not toasted," she requested. With a curt nod, the woman was gone and Lexie returned her attention to Gary. "Go ahead and eat," she prompted. "Who knows how long my order will take? There's no reason to let your food get cold."

Gary hesitated, then reluctantly began to eat his hamburger. Between bites, he said, "You're creating quite a stir around town."

"You mean about Lockwood?" She sipped her coffee.

"You're being pretty hard on the guy, aren't you?"

"I just call it the way I see it." Lexie shrugged, indifferent to the vague criticism in his words, then smiled. "Besides, it sells newspapers."

"And makes a name for Shari Sullivan, who already possesses an inflated sense of her own importance to journalism," he remarked.

"She works hard at her career and has for some time." As far as Lexie was concerned, she was stating a fact and not defending her friend. "She's earned the right to some recognition." A plate was set in front of her by a rushing waitress. "Just a minute," Lexie called her back and returned the plate with its sandwich. "I don't want the bread toasted."

The waitress accepted it with a grimace of impatience and a look that said Lexie was being fussy.

"Do you know, I've never had the nerve to do that?" said Gary, a wry smile tugging at the corners of his mouth.

"Do you mean send food back when it wasn't the way you ordered it?"

"I never have," he admitted.

"As long as I'm buying the meal, I'm going to get what I pay for," she declared firmly.

"You should."

Within minutes, the sandwich was set before her, this time made the way she had requested it. By then, Gary was finished with his meal, but he had another cup of coffee while Lexie had her lunch.

"What's on your agenda this afternoon?" he asked.

"I have to go straight from here back to the office to write up the senator's press conference held this morning," she answered. "Nothing new—just the usual promises. He's coming up for re-election. How about you?"

"I have an interview at one-thirty with a woman artist who's been hailed as the next Grandma Moses. She's eighty years old and sounds like a character," Gary explained. "I talked to her on the phone. She sounds more full of life than I am, and I'm one-third her age."

"Does she live here in Boston?" Lexie had finished her sandwich and was sipping at a fresh cup of black coffee.

"No, in Concord."

Her blue eyes rounded. "It's nearly one now. You'll be late if you don't hurry."

He glanced at his watch in surprise, irritation thinning his mouth. "I lost track of the time."

Both lunch checks were lying on the table. As Gary reached to pick them both up, Lexie tried to beat him to it.

"Don't worry about that, Gary," she insisted. "Lunch today is on me."

"No, I'm buying." Both checks were in his hand as he straightened from the table. "I invited you to join me, remember?"

"You bought me lunch the last three times." She didn't mention that they had only lunched together three times in all. "It's my turn."

"No." Gary slipped a tip under his plate for the waitress.

"What gives? Since when does a man refuse free food?"

"Lexie, I don't ask a woman to join me and then make her pay for her own lunch." His ruddy complexion was steadily darkening with embarrassment. "Come on, don't make a scene."

"I would hardly call asking a couple of questions making a scene—" Lexie stopped when she realized that the people at the next table were looking curiously at her and Gary. Compressing her lips tightly together, she managed a stiff and ungrateful, "Thank you for lunch, Gary."

"That's better." He winked and started for the cash register. "Let's get together this weekend. I'll give you a call."

Lexie didn't respond. She wasn't absolutely sure that she would pick up that call. This little episode had grated on her for reasons she didn't quite understand. Maybe it was just because she didn't like Gary all that much and didn't want him to pay for her lunch or anything else.

"Men," she muttered.

"You said it, honey." The waitress paused beside her table with a coffee pot in her hand. "More coffee?"

"No thanks."

"It seems like you can't live with a man and you can't live without one," the waitress commented.

"There are times when I think I could," Lexie stated. "Live without one, that is."

"Hey, take a little advice from one working girl to another. If you can find someone to buy your lunch, don't argue. Just hand him the check."

Lexie just smiled and nodded.

CHAPTER TWO

The minor disagreement over lunch had left a bad taste in her mouth. Lexie tried to push the memory to the back of her mind, but it kept drifting into her thoughts. Her inability to concentrate on the story she was trying to write was even more annoying.

The notes in her ThinkPad weren't stringing together into a story the way they normally did. In the last hour, since she had returned from lunch, she had spent more time scrolling through old e-mails and deleting the spam than she had writing.

"Would you tell me where I might find Alexandra Templeton?"

Lexie's cubicle was toward the front of the room and she heard the inquiry being made to one of the reporters near the door. The male voice was vaguely familiar but she couldn't place it.

"Lexie!" the reporter called as she turned. "There's someone here to see you."

An amazing hush seemed to spread across the room. Lexie recognized the man walking toward her desk at about the same time that everyone else did and the blood froze in her veins for one stunned second. She watched Rome Lockwood cover the distance between them in swift strides. There was a relaxed arrogance about him; he was tall and lean, exuding a male presence that drew every eye in the room.

Tension rippled through her. Lexie knew why he was here to see her. If she didn't, the hard blackness of his gaze would have informed her that it wasn't a social call. When he stopped in front of her cubicle, he offered no disarming smile to soften the chiseled firmness of his mouth.

Lexie would have been less than honest if she didn't admit that the sight of this exceptionally good-looking man stirred her pulse. But what was true for a man was true for a woman. You could be physically attracted to someone without liking him or what he represented.

As he towered in front of her cubicle, Lexie was aware of the raking scrutiny of his gaze, going over her from the curling thickness of her red hair to her smoothly sculptured chin. It gave her the feeling that she had been dissected as analytically as a frog in a science lab.

"You're Alexandra Templeton?" he asked. His low voice was controlled and even, as was his expression.

"Yes."

He tossed the latest edition of the paper on her desk, opened to Shari Sullivan's column. "Just to confirm, I mean that Alexandra Templeton. The one who seems to know so much about me."

Something in his tone made her nervous. "How did you get past security?" she asked.

"I know the owner of the building. He told the gorillas in uniform downstairs that I was an okay guy. You don't seem to think so, though."

Her peripheral vision caught the approach of Mike

Farragut, her assignment editor. He was a Hollywood image of a harried reporter, clothing rumpled, in need of a shave, an unlit cigarette always in his hand waiting for him to find the time to go outside the building and smoke it. Which he never did, insisting that not having the time was the same as quitting.

Alexandra was grateful either way, because he was coming to her rescue right now. Or, more correctly, to the newspaper's rescue.

"Mr. Lockwood," Mike greeted him, switching his unlit cigarette to his left hand to shake hands. "Is there anything I can do for you? Mike Farragut's the name."

"No, thank you. I merely wanted to speak to Ms. Templeton," was the smooth reply.

"I see." Mike appeared to be in no doubt about the subject Rome Lockwood wanted to discuss with Lexie. He glanced at her pointedly, his squinting eyes asking a different question from the one he voiced. "Are you free?"

The unfinished article on her computer screen gave Lexie an excuse but she didn't choose to use it. Lexie felt no compunction to hide from this man. Granted, there was a rather intimidating air of authority about Rome Lockwood but he wasn't her employer.

"Sort of. I can spare Mr. Lockwood a few minutes." Her tone was cool and deliberately condescending.

"Hmm . . ." Mike's gaze swept the staff room, aware that the meeting between the two was the focal point of everyone's attention, even if everyone was pretending not to notice a thing. "Want to use my office for your discussion?" he suggested tactfully. "It's a little more private."

"Sure. What do you think, Mr. Lockwood?" Lexie challenged.

"Whatever you wish, Ms. Templeton." The knowing

glint in his eye seemed to mock her desire not to have an audience for their meeting, as if he anticipated she would come out second best.

That ruffled her fur, but Lexie concealed her feelings, rising from her chair to walk around the desk. Although tall herself, she still had to tip her head back slightly to look at Rome Lockwood.

At close quarters, she was also aware of how physically fit his lean, muscular frame was. There was a vague fluttering in the pit of her stomach. No man had a right to be so sexually attractive, she thought in irritation.

"This way." Lexie took the lead in showing him to Mike's private office. When the door was closed and they were isolated from the others, she turned to confront him. "What exactly did you want to speak to me about?" As if she didn't know.

"I'm curious," he began. He appeared infuriatingly relaxed and in command. "I don't recall meeting you before. Perhaps you could enlighten me as to where and when it was."

Rome Lockwood remained just inside the room while Lexie walked leisurely to the front of Mike's desk and turned around, leaning backward against it and resting her hands on its top.

"We haven't met before," she informed him. "I have seen you at several functions I attended as a reporter, but we have never spoken to each other."

"We have never met before," he repeated. "Yet according to what you've said in the paper, you claim to be an authority on me."

"I have never claimed to know you personally, Mr. Lockwood," Lexie corrected him. "Only your type."

"Which is—unless I've missed one of the columns—a predatory rich guy with the skills and charm of a gigolo, minus any sense of fidelity, whose business acumen is questionable. How am I doing so far?" He held his head high in challenge, his half-closed eyes not veiling the intensity of his gaze.

When he put it that way, her offhand remarks—cut and edited by Shari for maximum shock value—sounded like a character assassination but Lexie wasn't going to retract any of it. He had no right to put her on the spot. "You have an excellent memory," she said blandly.

"Well, well." His tone was acid. "At least you have one good thing to say about me."

"I'm sorry if you find my opinion objectionable but there it is." It was worded as an apology but it wasn't offered as such. It came out more like an ultimatum: take it or leave it.

"I do find it objectionable," Rome Lockwood stated. "because you don't know me, Ms. Templeton."

"I don't care to know you. It's sufficient that I know of you," she retorted.

"Meanwhile, your opinion of my so-called type continues to be printed in a widely circulated newspaper." The grim set of his features indicated his displeasure.

"I can't do anything about that," Lexie shrugged. "You'll have to speak to Shari Sullivan. She's the one who decides what goes into her column. I'm certain she would be more than willing to print any rebuttal you would care to make—"

"I have no intention of giving credence to your comments by making a public response to them," Rome Lockwood interrupted sharply, his pose of calmness cracking a little from the hot anger beneath.

"That's your decision." She remained calm, although that determined set of his jaw revealed a side of his character that she had not thought existed. "If my comments bother you, or strike a little too close to home, take it up with Shari. She prints them, I don't."

"Your opinion doesn't bother me in the least," he stated. "I've been called worse, I suppose. Unfortunately, there are members of my family who are hurt by the accusations you've made about me."

"How selfless of you." Her honey-coated response revealed that Lexie didn't believe for an instant that Rome Lockwood was concerned about the feelings of others.

An unamused smile curved his mouth, a shadow of the charming one Lexie had seen him bestow on those he favored with his presence. Still, she felt a fleeting wisp of its magic, compelling and very male. Luckily she had been acquired a useful immunity to the effects of charm, especially since she worked in a media business.

"Too bad I can't pay you the same compliment," Rome said. "But I just don't think that selfless is a word that applies to you."

"As I said before, Mr. Lockwood,"—Lexie ignored his taunting comment—"if you have any complaints about Shari Sullivan's comment, you'll have to go to her."

"I make it a rule never to deal with a middleman when I can go directly to the source," he said.

"Middleperson," Lexie corrected.

"And you're Shari Sullivan's source," Rome continued with hardly a break.

"So what are you saying?" she challenged. "You want me to stop voicing my opinion or . . . what? You'll sue me or the paper or both for slander?"

"If I contemplated taking legal action now or in the future, my attorney would be speaking to you right now, not me."

Sighing, Lexie leaned more fully against the desk. "Then I'm afraid I don't understand what you're hoping to accomplish by seeing me."

"I had hoped," his voice was dry, "that I might be able to reason with you."

"Change my opinion of you, you mean." Laughter danced in the blue lights of her eyes. That would never happen.

"Maybe," he conceded. "At the very least, I wanted to set the facts straight regarding the allegations you've made about me."

"Which ones?" Lexie asked, enjoying her moment of power over him. "Was it the comment I made about your money? You did inherit it from your parents, didn't you?"

"Yes."

"And your job—if it can be called that—consists of managing the family holdings, doesn't it?" she retorted.

"It can be more difficult to keep money than it is to make it, you know," aware of her implication that his job was an undemanding one.

"Why? Have you made some bad investments?" Lexie countered.

"One of your comments seemed to say as much."

"What I said was that some of the opinions expressed on that particular subject might be coming from people whose companies you invested in. Therefore, their saying that you are remarkably astute in business matters could be made simply in the interests of their own self-preservation." Her eyes rounded with false innocence. "I can't be responsible for someone else's interpretation of that."

"Of course not," Rome agreed cynically. "You put in all the right qualifying words, didn't you? Might, some, could be. And you slide right off the hook." His narrowed gaze added "like a worm" and Lexie's fingers curled tightly around the edge of the desk top.

"I believe," she continued, trying to stay relaxed and not let his unspoken jab tighten her voice, "that I also made a reference to your, uh, playboy image."

"What a dated word. Makes me think of Hugh Hefner doddering around in his monogrammed bathrobe."

She gave him a big, bright, if-the-bathrobe-fits smile. "There are too many witnesses for you to deny that you have quite a variety of dates."

"Because I'm not man enough to make one happy," he said, reminding Lexie of her comment.

Looking at him, he seemed all man and undoubtedly expert at all the ways of satisfying a woman. A sensual heat flamed through her body before Lexie could check it with the reminder that his image was false. She wasn't about to fall into the embarrassing trap of trying to defend that statement.

"You must admit that you have a long string of conquests." She didn't change from her original theme.

"Assuming, of course, that I conquered them," Rome countered.

"Please, Mr. Lockwood." Lexie forced out a disbelieving laugh, uncomfortably aware of how fake it sounded. "Don't try to give me that old story that they were all just good friends. Next you'll be trying to convince me that you sleep alone, waiting for the right woman to come into your life."

He shook his head. "Am I on trial here? You sound like an overzealous district attorney."

She folded her arms across her chest and didn't dignify that with a reply.

Rome smirked at her and continued, "Your Honor, we ask that you find the defendant guilty of . . . dating in the first degree. Off with his head."

"Very funny. But you'll never convince me that you're a virgin."

He gave her a look she couldn't quite read. "I wasn't aware that you were even interested in the answer to that question. Are you?"

"Am I interested or am I a virgin?"

He laughed out loud and Lexie realized, too late, that he had trapped her very neatly.

She glared at him. "Shut up."

"You walked right into that one. I would apologize but if you don't have to, then neither do I."

Lexie glanced away, not willing to let him bait her again. "The truth is you've done more to perpetuate macho myths than James Bond ever did."

"I didn't know he was a real person. Is he in Boston? Seems like Shari would be spreading the news." He imitated a gossipy woman's whisper as he continued. "*Which sexy British secret agent is sampling our famous chowdah? Buy tomorrow's paper to find out.* That's what it's all about, isn't it? Selling papers?"

"No." Rome was right, of course. But she wasn't about to admit it. She stared him down, unwilling to give in or show the faintest suggestion of a smile. But the expression on his face as he looked at her softened to something very like appreciation.

"May I make a suggestion?"

Lexie shrugged and tapped her foot impatiently.

"If you wine and dine me, then Shari will have proof that I really am a gigolo."

She looked him up and down. The view was very nice from where she stood. But she kept her tone measured. "Are you asking me to buy you dinner, Mr. Lockwood?"

"Yeah. And by the way, I hate chowdah. I hate anything with clams in it."

She suddenly wanted to tell him that she hated clams, too, but she forced herself to focus on what he had just said. "Okay. So I take you out and pay for everything to prove that the column's allegations are actually true. What's in it for you?"

Rome smiled broadly. "The pleasure of your company."

"Yeah, right. You don't really want to go out with me."

"Are you chickening out, Ms. Templeton?" Rome taunted. "Would you like some salt and pepper for seasoning while you eat your words?"

"No!" Lexie flashed.

"Then do we have a date?"

"Ye-es," she said, much more slowly.

"What time will you pick me up?"

She had a disquieting vision of her old car lurching around Back Bay, where his rich family had probably lived for generations. It was almost funny when she thought about the suavely handsome Rome Lockwood sitting in the passenger seat as the car crow-hopped down the street.

Mustering all her poise, Lexie asked, "Does seven o'-clock work for you?"

"Yes."

"I'll pick you up at seven, then." Lexie straightened from the desk, anxious to be out of the room and away from him so she could gather her scattered wits and plan what she was going to do. "If you'll excuse me, I have work to do."

As she started to brush past him to the door, he said quietly, "Would you like my address so you'll know where to pick me up?"

The crimson flush in her cheeks nearly matched the color of her hair as she retraced her steps to Mike's desk for pencil and paper. "Write it down for me, please," Lexie asked stiffly and handed the pen and paper to him.

His dark eyes were still laughing at her. Great crinkles at the corners, she noted with chagrin. She was doomed. It was a relief when he turned his attention to the paper and wrote the information in bold, slashing letters. Rome tore the paper with his address from the pad and handed it to Lexie.

"Don't lose it," he mocked.

She would have loved to put a match to it and destroy it, but that wouldn't change the pickle she was in.

"I won't." She slipped the paper into her pocket and returned Mike's pencil and pad to his desk.

"You may find that it's not that easy to manage a gigolo," Rome offered.

"How hard can it be?" His eyes crinkled up again at her unintentional gaffe, and Lexie wanted to kick herself. "I mean, how hard can it be to take someone out to dinner? Why do men make such a big deal out of everything they do?"

"Were you a born man-hater?" he inquired with a curiously amused look.

Talk about a leading question. Lexie decided to answer it seriously. "I don't hate all men—only certain types." Rome Lockwood had to know what category he was in.

Without waiting to hear whatever reply he could come up with to that, Lexie opened the door leading to the staff room. The low chuckle that came from Rome Lockwood's throat was more grating than anything he could have said.

Again they were the focal point of all eyes when the newspaper staff saw that they had reappeared. For a short distance, her path to her desk and Rome's path to the exit were the same. Her expression was deliberately closed so the others would not pick up on the less-than-successful aspects of the meeting, by her standards. Since she walked slightly ahead of Rome Lockwood, she didn't know if his amused triumph was apparent on his face.

At the point where their paths diverged, Lexie quickened her steps while attempting to maintain her composure. Mike Farragut had commandeered her desk in return for his and stood at the sight of them. Lexie knew she would have to field a lot of probing questions from him—to satisfy his own curiosity as well as the company's interest in the outcome.

She was bracing herself for that when she heard Rome say, in a voice that was unnecessarily clear and carried to the farthest corner of the hushed room, "Don't forget—this Friday evening at seven. I'm looking forward to our evening together . . . Lexie." The conscious use of her first name made Lexie seethe with silent indignation.

She turned and smiled sweetly. "I won't forget . . . Rome." Her voice projected just as far as his.

Rome didn't seem offended by her attitude. In fact, there was a distinct twitching around his mouth, as if he was controlling laughter. Lexie felt her temper rise, but he was already striding toward the exit door.

"Did I hear right?" Mike claimed her attention.

"You heard right," Lexie answered, her jaw clenching to keep her emotions under control.

The unlit cigarette between Mike's fingers had shredded and he absent-mindedly brushed bits of tobacco from his clothes as he gazed into Lexie's face.

"Maybe I didn't understand what I heard," he said. "Do you have a date with him on Friday?"

"Yes, I do." She was gritting her teeth so tightly that they hurt.

"I'll be damned," he muttered. Then louder, "I'll be gawdamned!" Mike started to laugh, a rollicking sound, as he turned to the now intensely curious staff. "She's a witch," he declared to them, "a gawdamned, red-haired, genuine Salem witch! She's got Rome Lockwood eating out of her hand. She goes into my office with a man who was upset by all the things she was saying about him, and when they come out, she's got a date with him!"

"Why don't you put an announcement in the paper,

Mike?" Lexie grumbled, sure he was going to run down the halls shouting the news to everyone.

He put his arm around her shoulders and gave her a bone-crunching hug. "You deserve a bonus for this, Lexie, Rome Lockwood has some influential friends. We were all expecting heavy pressure to put an end to the way Shari has been bandying his name about with your insults. But you just wrapped him around your little finger."

"It wasn't quite like that," she protested, both at his praise and the painful embrace.

Others began to gather around, bombarding her with questions, asking how she'd done it, what she'd said . . . it became impossible for Lexie to deny she had done something fabulously wicked. Nobody believed her. Finally she just gave up and let the storm of enthusiasm rain over her.

In the midst of it all, Shari Sullivan appeared. "Honey, I just heard that Rome Lockwood was here to see you!" she exclaimed. "What happened? Was there a big scene? What did he say?"

For the first time the others fell silent, eyes gleaming, giving Lexie a chance to tell Shari of her triumph, such as it was. "He indicated he wasn't pleased with the items that had been appearing in your column about him."

"Hell! Get to the point!" Mike barked. "She has a date with him this Friday."

"What?" Shari's poise slipped as she stared at Lexie in dumbfounded amazement. "Is that true?"

"Yes," Lexie nodded. It was impossible to explain with everyone telling what they thought the story was.

Finally the columnist shooed the others away and sat Lexie down in her chair. "I want you to tell me about it just the way it happened," she insisted, drawing up a second chair and leaning eagerly forward.

"I would rather forget the whole thing," Lexie protested, tension hammering at her temples.

"Don't be silly," Shari frowned impatiently. "This is going to make a terrific wrap-up for the story."

"Don't you dare put my date with Rome Lockwood in your column!"

"Why not?" The other woman bristled, then immediately changed to a reasoning attitude, appealing to Lexie's reporter instinct. "Just think of the lead-in. 'Feuding reporter and sexy tycoon settle out of court—with a kiss!' It'll be sensational, honey."

"There was no kiss. He had no plans to sue. I don't care how sensational it is, you aren't going to print a word of it." Lexie held her ground.

"If I don't, one of the other papers will," Shari reminded her. "I've made you and Rome Lockwood news in this city. Someone will see you together. Why let someone else have the story?"

Shari's logic defeated Lexie. "Okay, okay," she conceded. "But I don't want anything in there about the meeting today and what was said between us. And nothing about our date, other than that we were seen together."

"You can't be serious!"

"I am." said Lexie. This time nothing would budge her. "No one else will have that story. Only Rome Lockwood and I are going to know what we said to each other, and that's the way it's going to stay."

"But the date . . . Surely you can phone me some details Saturday morning so I can get it in Sunday's paper," Shari wheedled.

"Listen, Shari, this date is going to be a disaster."

"No date with Rome Lockwood is a disaster. It's more like a dream come true as far as half the women in this town are concerned."

Lexie realized there wasn't any way she could tell the older woman the true story of what happened. Shari's sole interest was in furthering her reputation. She couldn't be trusted to keep anything juicy out of her column. Lexie didn't object to Shari's knowing, but she certainly didn't want it appearing in print.

"That's all you're going to get from me, Shari," Lexie stated. "You'd better be satisfied with that."

When further cajoling and pleading and reasoning didn't elicit more information from Lexie, Shari accused her of not being a true friend, a plot designed to make Lexie feel guilty, and left in a huff. Lexie sighed and turned back to the notes she had taken at the press conference that morning.

When she went home to her apartment that evening, Lexie thought she had left the furor of Rome Lockwood's visit behind her. But her roommate, Ginger, was waiting eagerly for her arrival, filled with questions about the rumors that had so swiftly circulated on their networked computers.

"Yes, it's all true," Lexie nodded helplessly. "Rome Lockwood did stop by this afternoon. I did talk to him. And I do have a date with him this Friday night. End of story."

"You really have a date with Rome Lockwood!" Ginger sat down in the nearest chair, long corn-silk hair swinging about her shoulders as she shook her head. "Lexie, that's awesome!"

"Far from it." Lexie kicked off her shoes and sank into the only other easy chair in their small apartment. Wryly she noticed how the strain between Ginger and herself had been temporarily lifted—at least on Ginger's part—because of Rome Lockwood. The man's name seemed to be magic. Black magic was probably closer, Lexie decided.

"How can you be so down?" Ginger protested at Lexie's disgruntled air. "You should be jumping for joy. I would be."

"What about Bob?" Lexie wished she could bite off her tongue. She and Ginger had gotten along so well until Bob had come on the scene, so why had she brought him up?

"Bob is different," Ginger retorted defensively. "But Rome Lockwood . . . he's a celebrity. Almost a star. Who wouldn't be excited about that?"

"It depends on the circumstances."

"What aren't you telling me?" Ginger tipped her head to one side in a frowning study of Lexie's grim expression.

"That it isn't as wonderful and glorious as all of you seem to think it is. This date . . . we trapped each other into it." She sighed heavily.

"What?" Ginger was confused.

"Rome was upset about the things in the column," Lexie began at the beginning. "He had a mental list of my quotes. When we came to the one about him being like a gigolo, he suggested that . . . well, things got out of hand at that point." She straightened in her chair and leaned forward. "If you tell Shari this, I swear I'll move out of this place."

"What is it? I won't tell. I promise." Ginger crossed her heart in a child's promise, her eyes widening.

"At lunch today, Gary wouldn't let me pay for his lunch. It got me to thinking—"

"What does Gary have to do with Rome Lockwood?" her roommate demanded.

"Nothing. But he was being annoying about it, and I wasn't in a very good mood when I got back to my desk, and then Rome showed up. He said—he got me all con-fused, if you really want to know. But he pointed out that Shari's allegations—meaning my quotes—just weren't true."

"Is he going to sue?" Ginger asked, wide-eyed.

"No. But he made this really weird suggestion."

"Tell. Tell!"

"He said if I wined and dined him, then Shari's column would be true. The gigolo part of it, anyway. I think he just wanted to see if I would ask him out."

"Did you?"

"Yes. He accepted, even though he despises me and I hate him. So that's your grand date that everyone is buzzing about."

"You're kidding!" Ginger breathed.

"I only wish I were." Lexie raked her fingers through her long red hair and leaned back in her chair to study the ceiling. "I have to pick him up at his place at seven on Friday."

"Where are you going to take him?"

"I don't know." An impish smile curved her mouth. "How does McDonald's sound for dinner? And a movie at the tenplex later on? I'll treat him to a giant vat of popcorn."

Ginger giggled. "Extra butter, right?"

"Sure. And then I take him home. Can't you just picture Rome Lockwood in my banged-up Honda? He's so tall."

"Lexie, you wouldn't!" Ginger exclaimed in horror.

"Wouldn't I? I'd love to cheap out and show him how the peasants live. To tell you the truth, that's about all I can afford." She frowned.

"I can lend you twenty bucks," her roommate offered. "Haven't you got some cash squirreled away somewhere?"

Lexie nodded. "I think so. And I haven't maxed out my plastic yet. I was trying not to, so I could buy a ticket to London when the fares go down."

"You really wanted to go," Ginger said sadly.

"Well, it looks like I'll have to postpone London until next year," Lexie laughed but not very enthusiastically. "This year I'm going to spend it on Rome."

CHAPTER THREE

With the second earring fastened, Lexie stepped back to survey the results in the mirror. Shimmering coppery-red hair framed her oval face and cascaded in curls to her shoulders. A little eyeshadow, and a touch of muted claret gloss on her lips, and she was done.

The jersey silk of her dress was silver-gray, its style elegantly simple, clinging softly to her figure without molding it in a bold display. A necklace of antique silver circled her throat, its scrolling design studded with turquoise. The earrings matched it, the blue of their semi-precious stones winking through the loose curls of her red hair.

Lexie touched a finger to the pulsing vein in her neck that betrayed the anxious state of her nerves. She took a calming breath and tried to make herself relax. The tension didn't leave.

"You look awesome!" Ginger exclaimed from the doorway. "Where did you get that dress, Lexie? I haven't seen it before."

"I bought it for the occasion." The dryness in her mouth coated her voice as she turned away from the mirror to pick up her matching shawl of silver gray. "I decided if I was going to splurge on this evening I might as well go all the way."

"And the jewelry—I've never seen you wearing that necklace before."

"A gift from my father." Lexie had kept it tucked away in the folds of her lingerie in a dresser drawer, but it had seemed appropriate to her to wear it tonight.

"Aren't you excited?" Her roommate's innocently beautiful face was wide-eyed with imagined anticipation. "I know all about the circumstances, but aren't you just a little bit excited?"

"I'm dreading it, if you really want to know," Lexie said as she picked up her evening bag. Pausing, she thought aloud, "I wonder if Rome Lockwood has ever been stood up."

"You wouldn't!" Ginger gasped.

"I wish I could," Lexie sighed wistfully and walked from her tiny bedroom, not much bigger than a large closet.

"Are you leaving now?" Ginger followed.

"I have to if I want to be at his place by seven. I doubt if I'll be very late coming home tonight."

"Bob said he'd call me tonight, so I may not be here."

"See you in the morning, then," Lexie offered in goodbye.

"Have fun!"

That idea made Lexie's mouth twist in a wry smile as she left the apartment. Her small car, freshly washed and buffed, was parked outside of the aging building. The interior of the old Honda was vacuumed and spotless. Except for the dented and rusting fender, Lexie thought it looked better than it had in months, though it wasn't in Rome Lockwood's luxury class of transportation.

Nor did its appearance fit her extravagant plans for

this evening: dinner at one of Boston's poshest restaurants, followed by drinks at an equally posh club featuring live entertainment. It was going to be an expensive evening. Lexie freely admitted that she was doing it to impress Rome.

The narrow, twisting streets of inner-city Boston didn't permit Lexie to drive fast. A taxi would have been a better bet, but her short supply of cash wouldn't allow it. Turning a corner, she slowed the car as she neared the address Rome had given her.

Squeezing her car in a parking spot between a Mercedes and an Infiniti, Lexie switched off the engine. "Not the company you're used to keeping, is it, Honda baby?" Okay, now she was talking to cars. She was seriously losing it.

It was a shock to discover that her legs felt weak when she stepped out of the car. Lexie silently wished the evening was already over. It soon would be, she consoled herself and squared her shoulders.

She mentioned Rome's name to the doorman, who tipped his hat and said that Mr. Lockwood had been expecting her and that she was to go right up.

In front of his door, she punched his buzzer and waited. It felt strange to be standing outside a man's apartment, picking him up for a date, but Lexie wouldn't have admitted that for anything. When there was no answer, she pushed the bell again and waited.

It suddenly occurred to her that Rome Lockwood might have changed his mind. Anger flushed through her at all the effort she had gone to and the wretched anxiety of waiting for Friday to come. She had joked about standing him up only to have it happen to her. She started to spin away from the door when it opened. Her lightning-blue glance flicked sharply to the lean, dark man who stood there.

His hard male vitality seemed to reach out and ensnare her. A smile of apology that was forming on his mouth was arrested for a scant second as his gaze darkened mysteriously in a sweeping assessment of her.

There was something much too admiring about the look and it curled her toes with its sheer sensuality. It was a fleeting sensation, replaced by a formal, polite expression as Rome opened the door wider to admit her.

"Come in," he invited.

Lexie hesitated, letting her pulse settle to an even pace before entering his apartment. She knew how sexually appealing Rome Lockwood was to women—to her—but she wasn't intimidated by it. Being forearmed, she knew she would not be so foolish as to take any attention he paid to her seriously.

She let her senses register his physically disturbing state. The white of his shirt, only half-buttoned, contrasted with the natural tan of his skin. There was a sheen of dampness to his jet dark hair, so invitingly thick. The fresh and heady scent of a deliciously musky aftershave came from the smooth jaw line.

"Sorry, but I'm running late," Rome said. "I hope you don't mind waiting a few minutes. Make yourself comfortable." He gestured toward the array of chairs and sofas in the spacious living room. "There's liquor in the cabinet. Help yourself."

"Thank you," Lexie murmured, suddenly realizing she hadn't spoken until now.

With a slight smile, Rome moved away, promising, "I won't be long."

Alone, Lexie began to focus her attention on the luxurious surroundings. She wandered into the living room, decorated in earth colors. It was tastefully simple yet bold, as masculine as its occupant. Lexie suspected almost everything she saw had been chosen by a woman, someone probably in love with him who had instinctively provided him with a background suitable for his image. But a sultan's harem would have been more in keeping with his true character, Lexie decided.

Moving to one of the sofas, she sat down to leaf through a business magazine lying on the coffee table. The political news Lexie knew and the rest she wasn't interested in. Finally she flipped it shut and glanced at her watch. How much longer would he be, she wondered. Waiting was hell on her already frayed nerves.

Five minutes stretched into ten. Restlessly, her fingers worried the smooth turquoise stone in her necklace. In agitation, she rose from the table. She refused to pace and walked instead to the liquor cabinet where an ice bucket, glasses, and bottles sat.

The clink of a cube in a squat glass sounded loudly in the overwhelming silence of the room. Lexie splashed in a scant measure of gin and filled the glass with tonic water. Wrapping both hands around the fat glass, she turned and lifted it to her lips. Over the rim, she saw Rome walk in, looking devastatingly handsome in an expertly tailored black suit that intensified his dark good looks.

"Ready?" she asked, angered by the breathless catch in her voice. There was no way of denying the physical effect he had on her, but Lexie had hoped to conceal it. Averting her face, she turned away to set her barely touched drink on a tray.

"Yes, but there's no rush, is there?" His low, modulated voice was just as unsettling as his presence. "Since you haven't finished your drink, I'll join you."

"All right." Lexie smiled stiffly, not wanting him to see how anxious she was to leave and have this evening come to an end. With apparent calm, she watched him pour a shot of single malt Scotch over ice cubes in a glass like her own.

The glittering dark eyes gave her a sideways look. "Waiting is hell, isn't it?"

"I beg your pardon?"

He turned to face her, the corners of his mouth deepening in amusement. "I'm referring to rushing around to arrive on time only to have your date make you cool your heels in the living room. It's a frustrating experience, isn't it?"

Nerve-wracking, Lexie could have said but she suddenly understood the meaning of his words. "You deliberately made me wait for you. I don't think gigolos do that."

"This one just did."

"Why?"

"Well, not on purpose at first. I had some important phone calls just before you arrived and I—"

"Lining up your next clients? I understand the scheduling gets tricky in the gigolo business." That was a nasty jab but he pretty much deserved it.

"No." He smiled amiably and took a sip of the drink in his glass. Evidently he saw no reason to explain his dawdling. He actually seemed pleased that it had annoyed her.

His assessing gaze skimmed Lexie from head to toe and back. It was not so much a stripping look as it was caressing. Her skin quivered in reaction to the pleasant but brief sensation.

"I'd forgotten how beautiful you are, Lexie," he commented.

"Oh, please."

"Don't like compliments?"

"Not from a gigolo. Especially a fake gigolo." She took a final sip from her drink and set it down. "I made dinner reservations for eight o'clock. It's seven-thirty now. We should be going."

"Of course." He downed his Scotch and placed the empty glass near Lexie's.

Retrieving her handbag from the sofa, she led the

way to the door, waiting while Rome locked it behind them. Her car was parked at the curb and she walked half a step ahead of him toward it. He had to guess which it was; the old Honda looked so out of place among all the other, much more expensive cars. But Lexie certainly wasn't going to make any apology for her mode of transportation.

She unlocked the doors from her side and watched him slide in before getting behind the wheel. He was really close to her in a car this size. She had to look over her shoulder to back out and his face was just about kissing distance from hers when she turned her head. *Oh my.* She didn't miss the sight of his muscular thighs, clad in dark, expensive fabric and spread apart on the lighter-colored upholstery of the front seat. *Oh my oh my.*

Luckily, Lexie didn't embarrass herself by brushing against him accidentally. The little car was on its best behavior and Lexie concentrated on her driving, thereby eliminating conversation. Still, she was conscious of his gaze, which strayed to her often during the drive to the restaurant.

"I hope you approve of my choice," Lexie said when they arrived, not really caring whether he did or not.

"It's one of my haunts," said Rome as an attendant took the car to park it for Lexie. "Or did you check and find that out?"

"No. I have better things to do." She returned his sideways glance with a sparkling look of battle.

The interior of the restaurant was almost intimidating elegant. A stiffly formal maitre d' stepped forward to greet them, automatically smiling with pleasure, which was quickly replaced by a concerned frown.

"Mr. Lockwood, I'm terribly sorry, but I don't have you on my reservation list. I'm sure if you can give me a few minutes I'll have a table for you," the man promised.

"The reservation is in my name," Lexie said before Rome could respond, and the man drew back in surprise. "Templeton."

The maitre d' cast a questioning glance at Rome, who was suppressing a smile with difficulty. "That's correct, Charles. Ms. Templeton has the reservation in her name."

As the man turned, Lexie saw him steal a glance at his reservation book lying open on a walnut podium, to ensure that it was the truth. The look he gave her when he escorted them to a table plainly said he found it odd that the great and powerful Mr. Lockwood didn't seem to be in charge.

A waiter was at their table almost the instant they sat down, filling the crystal goblets with ice water and inquiring, "Would you care for a cocktail before ordering?"

Casually Lexie asked, "Would you like one, Rome?" and immediately regretted it when she saw the waiter purse his lips. He too seemed to think that she had no business being here.

"No, thank you," he refused, his gaze mocking her attempt to intrude into his privileged world.

It only made her all the more stubborn. "We don't care for a cocktail," she informed the waiter, addressing him in the third person just to be annoying. He darted a glance at a passive Rome Lockwood as he handed each of them a menu.

"The wine list, perhaps," the waiter suggested, offering it to Rome.

"The lady will choose," Rome replied, gesturing to Lexie, who gritted her teeth at his patronizing tone.

She accepted the wine list from the disapproving waiter. Her knowledge of Rome Lockwood was sketchy, picked up in bits and pieces from what she had heard and seen. Too late Lexie remembered that he was considered something of a connoisseur of wines. She knew next to nothing about them.

"Is there a particular wine you prefer?" Lexie asked the question only to conceal her ignorance.

It was as if those knowing dark eyes were aware that she was squirming inwardly. But Rome just shook his head. "No. Whatever you choose I'm sure will be excellent."

Lexie wanted to scream in frustration. She guessed what he was doing: letting her make a fool of herself. In public. Nice guy.

The wine list was formidable, with foreign vintages that Lexie had never heard of. She only hoped that a restaurant such as this would not have bad wine on their list.

"A white wine," she murmured, narrowing the choice. "Something domestic, I think." Something she could read was what she meant, but she defended it by lamely joking, "To improve our foreign trade deficit." She gave her choice of a California chablis to the waiter in what she hoped was a confident tone.

He nodded and withdrew. Neither the waiter nor Rome betrayed by expression whether her choice was a respectable one. The dinner menu, at least, was no obstacle course to be overcome, but the prices made Lexie blanch. She hoped her credit card wouldn't be declined when the time came to present it.

The waiter returned with the bottle and uncorked it in silence. Since the choice of wine had been hers, he poured the sampling taste for her when he served it. Ill at ease, Lexie went through the motions of approving it. As far as she was concerned, it tasted very good, but she was hardly an expert. Her uncertainty must have showed in her expression when Rome took his first sip.

"Very good," he assured her.

But his approval only made her cross. "You must have figured out that I know next to nothing about good wine."

"A good wine is one whose taste you like," he explained indulgently. "Do you like the taste of this one?"

"Yes." Her answer was curt and defensive.

"Then it's a good wine. Don't worry about it."

But she was and it irritated her. Lexie had pictured herself making brilliant and witty conversation over dinner, but everything she said sounded stilted and forced. The meal was delicious but for all the pleasure it gave Lexie, it could just as easily have been hash. By the time coffee was served she felt miserable, but Rome seemed to be enjoying himself at her expense.

When the waiter brought the check on its miniature tray, he naturally started to set it in front of Rome, but was forestalled. "I'm the lady's guest tonight," Rome explained.

Lexie didn't know who was more embarrassed, she or the waiter, as he set the tray before her. She seethed at the wickedly laughing glint in the dark eyes watching her from across the table.

The waiter did try to ease the situation by joking with Rome. "You made a bet and the lady lost, I see."

"You could say that," Rome agreed.

Lexie did some swift mental calculations. She had just enough cash to cover the bill and tip, plus the cover and minimum at the club, and there would be no chance of making a faux pas with a declined credit card. She took the money from her evening bag and placed it on the tray, flashing an angry look at Rome as the waiter left.

"Thank you very much," he said. "It's a pleasure to be taken out to dinner by a beautiful woman."

"No compliments. I mean it."

His gaze flicked downward to the rounded shape of

her breasts under the clinging material of her dress. "Would you prefer that a man not see how attractive you are?"

"Not necessarily," Lexie admitted. "But I want him to recognize that I have a mind, too, the same as he does."

"Well, I haven't known you long," said Rome, "but I did notice you have a mind. Anything else while we're on the subject of your wants and needs?"

"You don't have what it takes to satisfy my needs, Rome." She avoided the black infinity of his eyes as she slipped the shawl around her shoulders. "Shall we go?"

In answer, Rome uncoiled his long length from the chair.

CHAPTER FOUR

When they arrived at the nightclub Lexie had chosen to fill the rest of the evening, Rome gave her a sidelong look as they approached the entrance. "This is going to be an expensive evening. Are you sure you can afford it?"

"You know, I would never ask a man that question," Lexie smugly pointed out. "It would be like asking if he was tall enough. Or if he had—"

"I get it," Rome interrupted smoothly. His crooked smile acknowledged that she had scored a point. "Sorry. Didn't mean to insult you." He inclined his head in a mocking bow of remorse.

Lexie couldn't help smiling in return, briefly allowing herself to be taken in by his charming ways, succumbing to the force of his magnetism. Inside the club they found an empty table just as the featured singers took the stage.

Placing the money for their drinks on the table, Lexie acknowledged but only to herself, that her wallet had thinned more quickly than an overweight person on a starvation diet. Maybe Rome had been right in asking whether she could afford this lavish night on the town. He probably had a fair idea what she earned. In a way she hoped he felt guilty that she was spending so much money.

Studying his profile on the sly from under her lashes, Lexie didn't detect any sign of guilt as he watched the group performing. She realized he probably wouldn't feel guilty. He was just too self-involved.

The entertainment negated the need for conversation. Nothing was demanded of Lexie, except to applaud at the conclusion of each song. She began to relax for the first time since the night's beginning. She didn't know whether to give the singing group credit or the wine at dinner followed by the drink in front of her.

When the group left the stage for a break, Lexie commented, "They're very good."

"Yes, they are," Rome agreed.

"You've probably seen them perform before, but this is my first time."

Rome swirled the drink around the ice cubes in his glass, watching it, an inwardly amused look in his expression. "Lexie, if I spent as many evenings out as you believe I do, how did I happen to have tonight free? A Friday night?"

His gaze caught and held hers. "I . . ." Lexie faltered "I was lucky, I guess." She recovered quickly.

"Or maybe you hoped I had other plans and would have to say no."

"Before I did anything, I found out whether or not you were busy tonight.," she reminded him.

"So you did." he agreed. A dance combo had taken the place of the singers. As they struck up a slow melody, Rome glanced at the dimly lit dance floor, then back at Lexie. "Aren't you going to ask me to dance?"

This passive-aggressive routine was getting old. But she actually did want to dance with him. Both rose simultaneously but Lexie led the winding way through the clutter of tables to the small dance floor, illuminated by a changing kaleidoscope of colored lights. In a relatively clear area of the floor, Lexie turned. Rome stood in front of her, hesitating, a devilish gleam in his eyes.

"Do you want to lead or shall I?" he asked.

"You lead." Lexie managed a tight smile, annoyed at the way he had taken so many opportunities to tease her. "I wouldn't want to be accused of stepping on your toes."

Rome laughed, a pleasant sound that shivered down her spine, making Lexie once again intensely conscious of his attractiveness. When he took her hand and slid his arms about her waist, Lexie felt an electric current shoot through her. It added a new tension to her finely strung nerves. She knew she was unnaturally stiff in his arms but she didn't want to risk coming into closer contact with him at the moment.

"Relax." His low voice spoke in the vicinity of her ear. "Enjoy the music."

If he had asked her to enjoy anything else, Lexie would have ignored him, but she let the languorous beat of the music carry her away. She allowed herself to be drawn closer until she felt the brush of his jaw and chin against her hair. The music swirled about her, evoking its own romantic spell.

One arm was on his shoulder, her hand resting near the back of his neck. The other arm Rome folded to hold still against the black lapel of his jacket. A sensation of intimacy flowed through Lexie and she arched away from his chest, tipping her head back to warily search his face.

There was a musing curiosity about the look he gave her, oddly warm and gentle. "I always thought redheads had green eyes. But yours are really blue," he said absently.

But Lexie didn't want compliments from him, knowing that they came too easily. "Like limpid pools?" she mocked.

"I hope I would have been more original than that." His lazy smile was warm.

"I'm sure you would," she agreed, but hardly in praise.

"Are you Irish?"

"On my father's side," Lexie admitted.

"Me too, but on my mother's side."

"Black Irish, of course." Her gaze touched on the raven darkness of his hair and eyes.

"Of course."

"Rome!" a female voice declared in sheer delight. "I didn't know you were here tonight. Where are you sitting? You must join us."

Half of the words were said before Lexie could turn her head to see the chic blonde dancing with a disgruntled-looking partner. The man was plainly unhappy to see Rome. He was attractive in a bland, unassuming way but Lexie knew he didn't have a prayer against Rome Lockwood.

"Hello, Stella—Andy," Rome greeted both of them, but responded to none of the woman's questions.

The pressure of his hand at the back of Lexie's waist would have guided them away from the couple but the song ended, making it impossible.

"You can't have been here very long," Stella declared, "or I would have noticed you. Or maybe you've been hiding in some dark, out-of-the-way corner?"

Her cold gray eyes were turned on Lexie, radiating jealousy. The petite blonde inspected her and didn't seem to like what she saw. Lexie felt her monetary worth being assessed, the hard gaze stripping her silver dress for the status of a designer label. She wasn't bothered that the blonde couldn't find one.

"We arrived in time to catch the show," Rome admitted.

"I just can't keep up with you!" The blonde laughed, a brittle sound. "Another new girl! Well, introduce us and get it over with."

His sideways glance took note of Lexie's veiled amusement before Rome complied. "Lexie Templeton. Stella Van Wyck and Andy Crenshaw."

"Templeton?" The blonde's partner frowned in surprise at the name. "From the newspaper?" he added in disbelief.

"The same," Lexie admitted, realizing he had made the connection.

Stella was not nearly as quick, only the prompting word "newspaper" provided the clue. "From the newspaper?" she repeated, and darted a wide-eyed look at Rome. "You don't mean she's the one who's been saying all those nasty things about you."

"The one and only," Lexie said before Rome could confirm it.

"And you're here? Tonight? With her?" Stella looked at Rome as if he were crazy.

"Why not?" The arm that had been resting lightly at the back of Lexie's waist increased its pressure as Rome glanced at her, a mocking glint in his eyes reserved strictly for her, it seemed. "I've met the enemy and she's mine."

"Hardly," Lexie denied the claim in a cool voice, and heard him chuckle.

"I've heard that women will do anything to get you to notice them, Rome, but this one"—Stella favored Lexie with a contemptuous look—"really went over the top. But it obviously worked. She's here with you tonight."

The color drained from Lexie's face at the completely false accusation that had been leveled at her. She felt the silent speculation in Rome's gaze. Before she voiced

62 *Janet Dailey*

any denial, the band began playing another song and the four of them either had to dance or make room for others crowding onto the floor,

"Excuse us." Rome's arm was pushing her away from the dance floor.

They were halfway back to their table before Lexie attempted an indignant correction. "I didn't do any of that to attract your attention, Rome. If I wanted to chase a man, my approach would be much more straight-forward."

"I'd like to see that—your straightforward approach," Rome added with a wink.

At the table Lexie turned to confront him. "You don't believe me," she said. "You think I said all those things and asked you out because I wanted you. Your overin-flated ego probably thinks every woman is just dying to be with you. Well, I'm not! You don't interest me at all."

"I believe you." But his look was one of total amuse-ment, eyes glinting with laughter at her little speech.

"Then you won't object if we leave." She was still furi-ous, but his acceptance forestalled any more discussion. "It's time this evening ended."

For Lexie, the drive to his apartment was made in smoldering silence, but Rome seemed carelessly re-laxed, which only added to her annoyance. There was a parking space at the front curb and Lexie whipped the easily maneuverable small car into it.

Both hands on the wheel, the engine running, Lexie turned to him. "Here you are, delivered safe and sound. Nighty-night."

"Nighty-night, huh? Mm, I love baby talk." Rome smirked at her but he didn't move, his arm draped ca-sually along the back of the seat. "Aren't you going to walk me to the door? I know you think I'm not smart enough to find my way home."

"I never said that, Rome."

He shrugged. "Even so. I just can't get enough of you. Walk me to the door. Or you'll have to kick me to the curb."

He was having a lot of fun at her expense. Lexie glared at him.

"Don't tempt me." She switched off the engine and pushed open her door, stalking around the car to meet him as he climbed out of the passenger side. Lexie didn't trust herself to say a word until they reached his apartment building.

"I've seen you this far," she declared tightly. "Is that good enough?"

"Thank you." He nodded with fake politeness. "I would invite you in for coffee or a drink but it's only our first date and I wouldn't want you to get the impression that I'm easy." The corners of his mouth were twitching at the effort of keeping a straight face.

Lexie drew in a breath and held it. "I wasn't planning to tuck you in, baby boy."

Rome grinned openly as she turned away. "Wait a minute." He caught at her arm. "You're forgetting something."

"What now?" Lexie demanded in exasperation.

He arched an arrogant brow. "The good-night kiss."

"Oh, God!" It came out in the angry exhalation of a breath. "Do you honestly think for one minute that I'm going to kiss you—that I want to kiss you?"

"Just thought I'd ask. What's your answer?"

"Hell, no. You've been laughing at me all night."

"I hear you." Rome let go of her arm.

"Good. I'm glad!"

"But it is routine," he continued. "The romantic climax of any date seems to be the kiss at the door. For all I know, Shari Sullivan has a photographer stationed behind those bushes, ready to capture the great moment."

"She doesn't!" Lexie snapped.

"There's always so much emphasis on the first kiss. So much is expected to happen with it."

She wanted to smack him. Rome was doing it to her again, reeling her in like a fish on a hook, the barbs sinking in so she couldn't wiggle off. All she could do was squirm.

"Kissing shouldn't be taken for granted, though." His tone was thoughtful. "But timing is essential—when to make the move. And there's the problem of not bumping noses or heads. Should the kisser be gentle and sweet, or passionate, sweeping the kissee off her feet? If my technique is going to be discussed in tomorrow's column, I may need a few pointers."

Lexie didn't feel like doing him or Shari Sullivan any favors. But a kiss was just a kiss, and she couldn't resist the temptation to see how Rome Lockwood did it. He seriously pissed her off but she might never have this chance again.

It wasn't easy to take the initiative, especially when he wasn't offering any assistance. First of all, she didn't know where to put her hands. Finally she rested them on his wide shoulders for balance as she rose on tiptoe.

Her breath caught when her lips touched his firmly molded mouth. Its warmth and pliancy were a revelation as she kissed him, aware of his hands moving to her waist. Lexie was also aware of the intensity of her sudden response to his nearness, and cautious wisdom drew her away.

"Not bad," Rome murmured. "Let me show you how I like it."

Before she could say no, the hands at her waist were pulling her back, arching her against him while his descending mouth took possession of hers. With sensual skill, Rome demonstrated his mastery of the art. A warm, wonderful confusion was totally enveloping Lexie, leaving her defenseless.

Her hands were spread over his shoulders, fingers half-raised in a paralysis of surprise and bewilderment at her reaction. Her mouth was mobile beneath his, allowing his pressure to part her lips. Rome deepened the kiss, making her hunger for something more.

She was shaky inside when he ended the kiss. The sweep of her lashes veiled the look in her eyes, but the breath she had been holding was released in a revealing sigh. Despite all that, she moved firmly away from him, realizing that she was not as immune to his virile attractiveness as she had believed.

"Good night," she said, glad that her voice was steady. The absence of his touch broke the sexually charged spell.

"Sure you don't want to come in?"

"No way." Lexie shook her head vigorously.

"Well," Rome paused, a half smile crooking his mouth, "thank you for a very interesting evening. Tell Shari I said hello."

"I'm not going to tell her anything."

"Right." The half smile got bigger and wickeder. In fact, he bore a distinct resemblance to the Big, Bad Wolf. If a wolf could wear Armani.

"Good night, Rome."

"Good night, Lexie." He finally said the words that would let her escape. She turned and bolted for her car.

But it wasn't as easy to stop thinking about him. During the drive to her own apartment Lexie called herself every kind of fool for enjoying his kiss so much. She should have known better than to let herself be tempted.

One thing she had learned: under the right circumstances, men like Rome Lockwood could be irresistible. She had reacted like a moth drawn to a flame, a black flame. Her wings had been singed but she was still ca-

pable of flying away, thank God. Tonight was one night
she was going to block out of her memory.

But on Saturday morning Ginger plied her with questions, demanding to know everything that had happened.

"The evening was truly weird." Lexie sat at the small
breakfast table, dressed in her rumpled robe. She wished
the cup of coffee she was drinking could erase the bad
taste in her mouth from the previous night's fiasco.
"Rome Lockwood found it all very amusing. As for
me—I'm broke."

"It couldn't have been as terrible as you say," Ginger
insisted. "Didn't he kiss you or anything?"

"Yeah." The instant she admitted it, Lexie glanced
sharply at her roommate's beaming face. "Don't look at
me like that," she snapped. "It was just a kiss, nothing
special."

"Oh, come on now," Ginger murmured skeptically,
determined to find a happy ending.

"You're as taken in by his Don Juan image as he is,"
Lexie retorted. "One kiss isn't going to change my opinion of him. And I'm certainly not going to fall in love
with him. I know what kind of merry hell he would put
me through. I've seen it before and it's not going to
happen to me."

"You've seen it before? When? With whom?" Ginger
asked curiously.

"It doesn't matter." Lexie clammed up and took a sip
of her coffee.

"Did he ask you out again?"

She set her coffee cup on the table with abrupt impatience. "What does it take to convince you that we
were both *trapped* into going out together last night,"
Lexie demanded. "Rome Lockwood was just as glad to
see the back side of me as I was to walk away. If we never
see each other again, it will be too soon."

"You don't have to bite my head off. I just asked a simple question," Ginger protested.

"All right." Lexie struggled to control her irritation. "To answer your simple question—no, Rome Lockwood did not ask me out again. Do you mind if we change the subject?"

"No," Ginger agreed reluctantly, finally accepting the fact that Lexie had not been on a dream date the night before.

Lexie had barely convinced Ginger when the phone rang. It was Shari Sullivan, and Lexie had to answer almost the same questions all over again, and parry them with the same noncommittal replies.

On Sunday morning Ginger was quick to wake Lexie up and show her the newspaper, specifically Shari's column. As Shari had said, Lexie and Rome were her headlines. Lexie wasn't surprised by that, but the photograph that accompanied the column did surprise her.

It took an instant for her to realize that it was a Photoshopped image. Someone had used two separate pictures—one of Rome and one of Lexie—and fitted them to make it appear as if they were together. She knew the dress she had on in the photo wasn't the one she'd been wearing last night, although you could barely see it.

When she went to work on Monday, it was just as bad. Everyone wanted to know about her date with Rome Lockwood; every detail from what they wore to what they ate and drank. Their obsession with his name began exasperating.

Stepping into the elevator, Lexie punched the numbered button for her floor and waited for the doors to close. She'd had her Wednesday lunch at a little delicatessen some distance from the newspaper office. She had chosen it because there she wouldn't have to endure the endless comments about Rome Lockwood from her coworkers.

"Going up? Wait!" a familiar voice called. The elevator doors closed on a folded newspaper that was thrust between them. Soundlessly they slid open to let Gary Dunbar inside. "Hi," he said, smiling self-consciously at the sight of Lexie.

"Hi yourself."

"Just coming back from lunch?" At her nod, he said, "Me too. Where did you eat? I didn't see you at the restaurant next door."

"I got a sandwich at a deli," Lexie explained. The elevator doors finally slid shut again.

"Are you doing anything Saturday night?" Before Lexie could answer, Gary rushed on. "I'm doing an article on a neighborhood drama club. They're, uh, giving a performance Saturday night and I've got a couple of free tickets. I wondered if you'd like to come along."

"Sounds like fun," she agreed, not sure if a date like that was preferable to spending an evening alone.

"I don't know how much fun it will be," he said with a disparaging shrug. "It's just one of those amateur things. I'm not in Rome Lockwood's league."

"If I hear his name one more time, I swear I'll scream."

"I didn't mean to upset you—" Gary began an immediate apology.

"Let's make a deal. I'll go out with you Saturday night on the condition that his name never comes up."

"Agreed." Gary smiled and looked somewhat relieved.

It wasn't as easy to persuade others to drop the subject.

The Saturday night date with Gary was like a breath of fresh air. She was able to relax, knowing that she wouldn't have to defend herself against a lot of curious questions the following morning.

As in all things the interest gradually died out. After two weeks her life had begun to return to normal. Even

Shari had stopped being so resentful at Lexie's lack of newsworthy details about the date.

Lexie paused at the door of the columnist's office. "You wouldn't by any chance have a cup of coffee to spare for me?" she asked, glancing at the steaming cups both Shari and Ginger were holding.

"Of course. Got the brew that is true right here. None of Mike Farragut's sludge for me." Shari turned her swivel chair around to fill a Styrofoam cup with coffee from the glass carafe on the coffeemaker behind her.

Lexie accepted it gratefully, set it down for a moment, and flopped into a straight-backed chair. "What a morning!" She picked up the cup and nearly scalded her tongue when she tried to sip the hot coffee.

"Hectic, huh?" Shari offered sympathetically.

"You can say that again," sighed Lexie.

"I was just asking Shari what she thought I could buy Meg for her wedding shower. What did you get her?"

"An electric blanket with his-'n-hers controls. I found one on sale last week." Lexie blew into the cup to cool its contents. "This seems to be the year for weddings around here. Any single women left in the company?"

"Three of them in this room," Shari replied.

"I suppose I could always buy her some sheets or towels. She must be registered at Bath & Bed." Ginger was mulling over the shower gift. "I have to buy something on my lunch hour today. It's going to be too late when I get off work and the shower is at seven."

"Tonight?" Lexie said.

"Yes, tonight," Ginger nodded.

"I can't make it," Lexie declared with a resigned sigh. "You'll have to take my gift, Ginger, and apologize to Meg."

"Why can't you go?"

"Mike just told me that Mac and I have to cover that

fund-raising dinner tonight. The senator is flying in from Washington to attend and a couple of other political VIPs will be there," she explained.

"You mean you have to work tonight?" Ginger asked.

"Surely you know by now that a reporter doesn't have a nine-to-five job," Shari said.

"That's why they pay us the big bucks," Lexie said. At Ginger's wide-eyed look, she continued, "Not. Just kidding. But the glamour of the job more than makes up for the slave wages."

"Okay, I get it." Ginger made a face, going along with the self-deprecating mood. "But it's a shame you're going to miss the shower tonight. It'll be fun."

"You've been putting in a lot of extra hours lately," Shari observed. "Your vacation is coming up, though, isn't it?"

"Next month," Lexie replied without enthusiasm.

"And you're off to London," Shari said, smiling.

"Not this year." Lexie flashed a quelling look at Ginger not to reveal the reason.

"Why not?" Shari frowned. "That's all you've been talking about for the last six months."

"I really can't afford it." Lexie shrugged. "I want to see London in style when I go and it's an expensive city to stay in."

"What will you do on your vacation?" asked Shari.

"Sleep." Lexie laughed away her answer.

"Seriously," Shari protested. "You aren't going to stay around here, are you?"

"I imagine so." Lexie took a drink of her coffee, cooled now. "I don't have anywhere else to go."

"Yes, you do," Ginger said. "In that postcard you got from your father last week, he asked you to come out and visit him." She blushed at Lexie's look. "I wasn't really reading your mail, Lexie," she apologized. "It's just that, well, a postcard is so open."

"It's okay." Lexie wasn't offended.

"Your father lives in California, doesn't he?" Shari frowned as she tried to recall.

"Palm Springs," Lexie said.

"There's your solution. Spend your vacation in sunny California," Shari offered. "You can stay with your father and it won't be all that expensive."

"No, thanks." Lexie finished her coffee and rose. "Dad and I don't get along all that well without a continent between us. The less we see of each other, the more we like each other. You know the old saying: familiarity breeds contempt. That's us."

"Seems like a shame for you to spend your vacation sitting around your apartment," Shari persisted.

"That's the way it goes sometimes." Lexie turned to her roommate. "I probably won't have a chance to see you again before tonight, so don't forget to take my gift with you tonight to Meg's shower. It's wrapped and everything, inside my closet."

"I won't forget," Ginger promised. "Have fun."

"Ha!" was Lexie's scornful response.

In her experience, these fund-raising dinners always seemed like a three-ring circus with something going on somewhere all the time. She often wished for another pair of eyes and ears, or possibly three or four sets.

The dinner that evening in the huge banquet hall proved to be no exception. For Lexie there was more involved than just listening to the speeches and making notes. There was always behind-the-scenes maneuvering going on and it was prudent to pay attention to who was sitting with whom.

Mac, the photographer who had drawn the assignment with her, was a definite distraction. When he wasn't darting around getting a picture of one noteworthy person or another, he was sitting beside her at the press table munching on a cold hamburger and French fries. His on-the-run meal was becoming increasingly unappetizing to Lexie with each passing minute she had to look at it.

"Can't you wait until this is over to eat?" she whispered in protest.

"I'm starved," Mac hissed. "I haven't eaten since yesterday noon and that was a cold hot dog."

Lexie shrugged expressively and tried to concentrate on the current speech. The paper bag rattled as Mac dived into it for more fries.

"What happened to last night's meal?" she asked, keeping her voice down, trying not to distract the others. "And this morning's breakfast?"

"I was up all night covering that fire. I slept through breakfast and caught hell from Mike for coming in late. Then I missed lunch." He listed his woes. "For sure I'm not going to sit her while all these fat cats stuff themselves on steak and I'm fainting with hunger."

After hearing that, Lexie forced herself to ignore his munching. As she listened to the speaker, her gaze swept over the tables. It hadn't occurred to her that all the moneyed people in the area would have received invitations to the political fund-raising dinner, including Rome Lockwood.

She realized it when she saw him sitting at one of the tables. She hadn't noticed him there before and wondered if he had just arrived. To her knowledge he had never actively campaigned for anyone, although his support had often been courted, as it was now. One of the campaign chairmen for this year's election was leaning over talking to Rome in hushed tones.

Had he noticed she was there? Was he aware she might have been assigned to cover the dinner? Lexie wondered, and immediately banished that thought from her mind.

What did she care? Rome Lockwood was nothing to her and vice versa.

Her gaze strayed often to his table after that. Strictly in the course of reporting, Lexie rationalized. If Rome did decide to back a particular candidate, that would be news, her purpose for being there. If Rome ever glanced her way, it wasn't when she was looking at him.

It was just as well, she convinced herself. She wasn't interested in having Rome acknowledge her presence—she'd had enough of that. There was one good thing about his attendance at the dinner: she had forgotten about Mac's noisy meal in the interim. He had finally finished it, and only the ketchup-and-mustard-stained paper was left to remind her.

CHAPTER FIVE

When the dinner and speechmaking were finished, people began mingling and the atmosphere became informal. Mac, who had a knack for remembering faces, was snapping shots of VIPs, while Lexie cornered one of the mayor's aides to pin him down about the mayor's stand on a current tax issue.

There had been a time when she was first starting out that it had been difficult to get people to talk seriously to her, although with her striking coloring, she had never been overlooked. Even now there were times when her questions were answered with indulgence. But more and more people were beginning to respect the reputation she was building for herself. The mayor's aide was quite anxious that she understand the mayor's position.

He had her undivided attention until she happened to catch a glimpse of Rome Lockwood over the man's shoulder. Rome was talking to two men whom Lexie recognized as being politically active in the state. She also noticed that Stella Van Wyck was with him, and a second woman, a brunette, also seemed a part of the group.

Unfortunately, as far as Lexie was concerned, Stella chose that moment to glance in her direction. She felt the blonde's gaze narrow on her. Then with a melodic laugh that carried to Lexie's ears, Stella turned back to Rome, catching on his arm and nodding toward Lexie.

"Look," she said, "there's that redheaded reporter you were with the other night. Is she here to check up on you?"

Rome turned, a white smile flashing across his tanned features. Despite the distance between them, Lexie felt the magnetic power of his charm as his dark gaze caught her look and held it. Then he said something to the others she couldn't hear. They laughed, all eyes focusing on her.

Her cheeks burned as she quickly tore her gaze from his. It required all her strength to center her attention on the man standing before her, talking earnestly.

"It's a confusing issue," he was saying, " with points on both sides. But the mayor feels his stand is right for the community as a whole. You do understand?"

Lexie glanced at her notes. They were sheer gibberish. She hadn't heard a single word the man had said, except for the last few sentences. She had missed it all. How could she lose her concentration like that, simply because Rome Lockwood looked at her?

"Yes, of course, I understand," she lied. She would ask the mayor's press secretary to send her confirming documents later. "Thank you for explaining it."

"My pleasure, Lexie." He knew her name but for the life of her, she couldn't remember his.

"Excuse me." Smiling, she moved away, her steps taking her in the opposite direction from both the aide and Rome Lockwood.

Her throat felt dry. She slipped her notepad and pen into her shoulder bag and headed toward the massive coffee urn sitting on one of the long tables. She poured herself a cup of coffee and turned. Rome was standing in front of her.

"Hello, Lexie," he said quietly, a warm smile on his sexy mouth.

"Goodbye." She pivoted at a right angle to walk away from him.

"Hey!" Rome laughed. "Not so fast. I came over here to talk to you."

A fiery look lit up her blue eyes. "Don't you think I've provided enough laughs for you and your friends?"

His expression was indulgently curious. "Did you think we were laughing at you a minute ago?"

"Weren't you?" she countered.

The overhead lights made his hair seem darker than ebony. "No," said Rome, "but I can see you aren't going to believe that."

"I'm not."

"I've been thinking about you." There was an intimate quality to his low voice.

"You must have better things to do. Why don't you go back to Stella?"

"Jealous?" Rome shot her a mocking look.

"Of course not!" she snapped.

"Good, because if it was Stella I was interested in I'd be over there talking to her now. Since I'm here, it's obvious that it's you I'm interested in."

"I thought I made it clear the last time I saw you that I wasn't interested in you," she retorted.

"That's what you told me," he conceded, "but your kiss said something different."

Lexie looked away. "I wouldn't put too much stock in a kiss, Rome. A woman has to kiss a lot of toads before she finds a prince."

Rome chuckled. "You enjoy trying to put me down, don't you?"

"Yes."

With that teasing gleam in his eye, Rome could be just trying to bait her. Before she could make up her mind, Mac came up to her unexpectedly.

"Hey, Lexie, there you are! I've been looking all over for you."

"I stopped for a cup of coffee."

"Listen, I gotta run. I have all the pictures Mike's gonna need," he said, lifting his camera as if she could see inside it. "If I'm late getting home again, my wife's going to have my hide. I know I promised to give you a ride but you can find somebody else to take you home, can't you? Or catch a cab maybe? Put it on your expense account."

Lexie opened her mouth to say she was ready to leave right now, but Rome stepped forward. "I'll see that Lexie gets home."

Mac wasn't even surprised to see Rome with her—not after all the gossip at the office. "Cool. Thanks, Mr. Lockwood. Got some good shots of you, by the way." He started moving off. "See you tomorrow, Lex!"

He was gone, trotting off toward the exit door. Lexie would have had to run to catch up with him. She glared at Rome. Why did he have to butt in?

"Whenever you're ready to leave, let me know," he said. "I'll be somewhere around."

Lexie decided not to argue. "Thanks," she said instead, and was rewarded by the glimmer of surprise in his look. "There're a couple of other people I want to interview before I leave, so it will be a while yet. I'll find you when I'm ready."

"All right." Rome moved away.

Lexie finished her coffee, waiting until she saw where Rome had stopped, then she began mingling with the various reporters and dignitaries on the opposite side of the room. She picked up pertinent bits and pieces from various sources but when her opportunity came to slip out a side door, she took off.

She hurried down the deserted hallway toward the main entrance of the building. There were always plenty of cabs in this area; with luck, she would find one waiting outside. As the large doors came into view, she saw Rome standing beside them. Her steps slowed.

"Ready?" he asked politely when she reached him.

"Yes." Not for anything would Lexie admit that she had been trying to give him the slip.

"My car is just outside." He reached for the entrance door, holding it open for her.

Thwarted in her attempt to escape, she simply went with Rome to his car. Once inside the luxury sedan she gave him her address and relaxed against the cushioned seat. Maybe if she ignored him . . . The thought formed hopefully.

"I expected more of an argument," Rome commented as the car purred into the traffic.

"About what?" Lexie deliberately pretended innocence.

"About letting me drive you home." His sidelong look said she knew very well what he meant.

"Why should I?" She ran a caressing hand over the butter-soft leather upholstery of the seat. "Talk about the lap of luxury. I'm riding in it." She laughed lightly.

"You mean a man like me does come in handy sometimes?"

"Sometimes, yeah." Lexie gazed out through the windshield, faking an indifference to him that she was far from feeling. "I was surprised to see you at the dinner tonight. I didn't think you attended such functions as a rule."

"As a rule, I don't," he admitted.

"Why did you tonight? Are you planning to become involved in politics? Offer your support to one of the candidates or the party?" Being a reporter was a lot easier than being his date.

"No, my family has made it a practice not to be actively involved in government," Rome answered.

"Then why were you there?" Lexie repeated her first question.

"I know you'll find this hard to believe, considering what you think of me, but I'm interested in finding out about the people who might be representing me in government, local, state, or federal."

"You were just being a public-spirited citizen, is that it?"

"See?" He swung a lazy glance at her. "You just don't trust me. Is that why you accepted the ride? To discover my motives?"

Lexie shrugged and stared out the side window. "Your name is always news. If Rome Lockwood is behind a candidate, it's even bigger news." If that was what he wanted to believe, that suited her.

"Will you have dinner with me on Saturday night?"

Her first startled reaction was "What?" followed immediately by "No."

"Why not?" Rome spared a glance from the busy Boston traffic, his manner calm and expectant.

"Because I don't like you. I've told you that before," Lexie answered flatly. "You're only interested in me because I haven't fallen at your feet. You expect every woman to adore you, and I don't."

"Shucks. I hate it when that happens."

His ego seemed to be just about bulletproof, Lexie thought. But she'd told him how she honestly felt and there wasn't anything else she could do. Nonetheless, she was dismayed by the disappointment she felt that Rome hadn't tried to get her to say yes.

"By the way, what happened to your car?" he said, changing the subject with disgusting ease. "Or did you arrange to ride with the photographer to save money on a parking garage?"

"My car is in the shop. Being repaired, I hope," Lexie replied. "It refused to start tonight and I had to call Mac to pick me up."

"Is it anything major?"

"I hope not. I can't afford a whopping repair bill." That slipped out before Lexie could stop it, her mind immediately flitting to the expensive night out with Rome. "The mechanic thought it wouldn't cost too much," she added hastily.

"What are you doing for a car in the meantime?"

"I can ride back and forth with Ginger, my roommate. She works for the paper too."

"What about your assignments?"

"Until I get my car back, I'll cab it or ride with the photographers Mike assigns. They do reimburse for cab fare but it takes a while to show up in my paycheck." Damn. She'd said the wrong thing again.

"You're welcome to use one of my cars," Rome offered.

"No thanks, I'll manage somehow."

"Sure?"

"I'm sure," she nodded. "My father taught me never to owe anybody favors."

"In case you don't want to pay what they want to collect?"

"That's the idea," she admitted.

"So you're afraid that if you accept the loan of my car you might not like the favor I would ask from you in return?" He was laughing at her, however silently.

"Do you blame me?" countered Lexie.

"No," Rome chuckled, "considering my reputation. I'm a real bad boy, as far you're concerned."

"Oh, knock it off," Lexie said, exasperated.

"Sorry, Lexie. But do you think we could be friends? Just friends—not lovers," Rome argued gently. "But they do say opposites attract. You and I sure as hell qualify in that category."

Lovers. Attract. They were heady words, the kind that disrupted Lexie's pulse. The car turned around a street corner onto the block where her apartment building stood and she was saved from having to respond.

"It's the second building on the right," she directed him. "You can actually park in front—what a miracle. Too bad you're not staying." When he had stopped the car, she shifted the strap of her shoulder bag a little higher and reached for the door handle. "Thanks for the ride," she offered as she pushed the door open and stepped quickly out.

Before she could swing the door shut, Rome was turning off the engine and sliding out from behind the wheel. Their gazes locked across the top of the car.

"It isn't necessary," Lexie started to protest.

"Objection overruled," he replied. "This isn't the safest neighborhood."

With a sigh of resignation she turned away from the car. Rome's long strides soon brought him beside her. Lexie was supremely conscious of the last date and the parting kiss. Even now the imprint of his mouth was on her lips and she couldn't shake away the memory. Damn him. He was just too sexy to resist for very long.

In the narrow and dimly lit hallway outside the door, she was aware of her breath coming quickly. She rummaged through her bag for the key, trying not to show how desperate she was. Rome would wait there until she had it in her hand, an inner sense told her that. At last she came up with the key ring, but Rome took it from her, inserted the key in the lock, and turned it.

He didn't open the door nor did he move out of her

way. A dangerous feeling of intimacy raced through her, yet there was nothing seductive or threatening in Rome's manner. It was just his charm having its usual effect on stupid her.

"Are you going to invite me in for coffee?" He held the keys in his hand and gave her a teasing look.

"No," she said abruptly. "It's late and my roommate is probably asleep."

"Wouldn't be a good idea anyway, I guess." The statement was accompanied by an easygoing smile.

"No," Lexie agreed and held out her hand. "My keys."

"You sure you don't want to have dinner on Saturday?"

"I'm sure. Meaning the answer is still no."

Her legs were beginning to feel shaky. He was much too close, overpowering her with his sensual attractiveness. He offered her the keys and she took them, but before she could draw her hand away, his had closed around it.

"My turn to make the move," he said.

Her mind protested but her pliant body had a will of its own, allowing her to be drawn into his embrace, her head tipping back to receive his kiss. Her arms wound around his neck, as she was caught in the enchantment of his warm mouth.

Surrender quivered through her limbs, ignited a sexual fire that melted her from within. His mouth hardened in its claim on hers, seeking and demanding pleasure. Lexie knew she should kick herself for enjoying this so much, but all she wanted to feel was the heady glory of his kiss.

Weightless in his arms, she experienced a sensation of floating, yet she was bound to him, if only by her own need. His strong hands forced her softer shape to fit the hard contours of his very male body. The pressure of his mouth was as intensely sensual as his caresses. His hand slid up to her arm to draw it tighter around his neck. Her fingers curled into the thickness of his black hair.

His hand moved down to cup her breast, lightly curving over it. Lexie trembled at the intimacy, aroused by it. She didn't want to react this way, respond this way, but a strong instinct was driving her.

Rome seemed driven by it too, but he was stronger than she. Or maybe it was a part of the spell he seemed to be able to cast upon her. Lexie only knew that the force of her own desire made her essentially helpless. Tears moistened her lashes. It was so beautiful and so intense.

When Rome released her lips to press his mouth to her cheek, his breath was as ragged as her own. Her lips throbbed with the passion he had made them feel and give. Her heart seemed to stop, and then start again.

"Why can't we be lovers, Lexie?"

She didn't answer.

"Let me show you what I'm really all about," he said. "Don't say no. Have dinner with me on Saturday," he commanded. "At my place. I'll cook. All you have to do is show up."

She was powerless to deny him anything. "Yes."

"Seven o'clock on Saturday. You'll be there?"

"Yes."

He pulled her arms from around his neck, letting her hands rest lightly on his chest. His dark gaze blazed possessively over her face, and Lexie marveled at the way eyes that were so dark could seem so incredibly bright.

Cupping her cheek with his hand, Rome traced the porcelain-smooth line of her jaw with his thumb. Then he let it seek the curves of her soft lips, outlining them. His thumb forced them apart to feel the white edge of her teeth. Her tongue touched the tip. With a stifled groan, Rome slid his thumb under her chin and let his mouth take its former place.

Lexie was pressed against the wall by the unchecked force of his kiss, aroused still more by the thrusting weight of steel-hard thighs and hips. With a bent arm braced against the wall for support, Rome arched her to him.

His mouth blazed an erotic path to her neck and the lobe of her ear. The moist warmth of his breath blowing unevenly against her skin sent shivers of passionate ecstasy racing down her spine. Lexie clung to his jacket, overwhelmed by emotions too powerful to deny.

"Invite me in, Lexie." There was a husky, deliciously rough note in his voice.

"I . . . can't." She knew better than to explain. He wouldn't accept any of her very good reasons.

She heard the deep, self-controlling breath Rome took as he lifted his head, relieving the pressure that held her to the wall. His rueful smile held more than a trace of frustration.

"Then you'd better go in," he told her. "Before I make love to you in the damned hall."

Lexie found it difficult to move, even after Rome had levered himself away from her. Weak and shaken, she managed to reach the door by not looking at him.

"Lexie." She turned at the quiet sound of her name, the door ajar. His hand lightly caressed her cheek, a fingertip trailing across her lips. "Dream of me?" Rome asked.

In the blink of an eye, it seemed, his hand was withdrawn and he was striding down the hallway. Dazed, Lexie entered the apartment.

As she locked the door she remembered that she had agreed to see him again, have dinner at his apartment. How had he talked her into that? Well, he hadn't talked very much, had he? The misty fog of raw passion began to dissipate in the brightly lit living room. Ginger had left a lamp on, thank God. Senses previously controlled by Lexie's desire surrendered to her ability to reason.

Then, from somewhere in the darkened apartment, Lexie heard the sound of muffled sobs. It was obviously Ginger. More than anything, Lexie wanted to steal into her room and solve the problems of her own love life, but she couldn't just ignore the weeping girl. She made her way to the other tiny bedroom.

"Ginger?" She paused in the doorway. The sobs didn't stop. "Are you all right?"

"Yes," was the sniffling answer.

As much as she wanted to, Lexie couldn't accept that. "Do you want to tell me what's happened?"

There was more sniffling and the creaking of the bedsprings as Ginger sat up. "Yes, but don't . . . don't turn on the light, please."

Lexie walked to the bed and sat on the edge. "What's wrong?"

"It's Bob." Ginger choked out the two little words, her voice constricted with pain.

"I might have known," Lexie murmured. Wasn't it always a man?

"We . . . we had a fight," her roommate hiccuped out the explanation, scrubbing the tears from her eyes.

"What about?" Lexie prompted.

"He wanted me to go out with him tonight but I told him I couldn't because I had to go to Meg's shower. Bob thought I could just go over there and drop the presents off and . . . and go out with him. When I wouldn't do that, he got mad. He said if a . . . if a bunch of girls meant more to me than he did, then maybe we should call it quits." Tears began streaming down her cheeks again. "When I got home from the shower I called him but he didn't answer. I've called and called and called but he isn't there. Oh, Lexie, he really meant it." Her shoulders began shaking. "He's out with somebody else—I just know it!"

"Are you familiar with the signs of abusive behavior?" Lexie asked sternly. "Those guys start with the small stuff, like expecting you to give up your friends for them and getting mad when you don't. He's too controlling, Ginger—"

"You don't understand," Ginger wailed. "I love him!"

"He doesn't deserve it," Lexie argued. "There's nothing loving about emotional manipulation and you're just wasting your love on him. All he wants is—"

"No!" Ginger's strident cry wouldn't let Lexie complete the sentence. "You never did like Bob and—and you think you know it all—well, you don't! Just go away and leave me alone!"

With a sigh Lexie rose from the bed and left Ginger to her misery. It was true enough that she hadn't trusted Bob. But Ginger wasn't the only fool for love. Who was Lexie to give well-meaning advice about not letting a man manipulate your emotions? Rome Lockwood could control her with a snap of his fingers.

Her heart constricted. *Dream of me*, Rome had said. That would be all too easy. His touch, his kiss, his image haunted her. Yes, she would dream of him. All night long.

CHAPTER SIX

Lexie knew she couldn't keep the dinner invitation. She didn't dare. At her desk the next morning, she went online to see if she could find a phone number for Rome. She located a number for Lockwood Enterprises but not a personal one—she didn't expect that to be listed anywhere.

Well, if she got through to someone who could pass her message along to him, that would have to do. She was reaching for a pencil to jot down the number when a shadow fell across her desk. Lexie glanced up and gave a guilty flinch. Shari was staring down at her.

"Am I interrupting something?" the columnist inquired.

Lexie quickly closed the screen. "No, nothing." Her voice was thin in her rush to assure. "I was just going to call the garage to see if my car was fixed yet."

"You took your car into Sam's, didn't you?" Shari had an amazing memory. "You won't find him under the L's but you might find a number for Rome Lockwood."

"How clever of you to notice," Lexi remarked, and smiled a tight, false smile.

"What happened? Did you leave your notebook in his car last night?" Shari asked in a voice that reminded Lexie of a cat's purr.

"How did you know about that?"

"Oh, I have my own private grapevine," came the throaty reply, filled with deliberate mystery.

"Only one person knows about last night, besides my self and Rome. Mac told you, I suppose," Lexie guessed "I sometimes think that man never knows when to keep his mouth shut."

"Was it a secret, honey?" Shari's eyes widened with false innocence.

"Of course it wasn't a secret," she answered impa tiently, not wanting to make the incident seem too im portant and increase Shari's interest. Shari might be a friend, but as a reporter, Lexie didn't trust her to keep anything quiet. "But I can just imagine the way Mac made it sound when he mentioned it to you."

"Lexie, honey, please don't try to convince me that Rome Lockwood gave a lowly junior reporter a ride home simply out of the goodness of his heart." There was something a little too shrewd in the smile she gave Lexie. "Knowing his reputation, I'll never believe chiv alry had anything to do with his motive. So what gives?"

"Nothing." Lexie stubbornly tried to make light of the incident. "Rome happened to be talking to me when Mac said he had to leave and asked if I could wangle a ride home with someone else. Rome offered, I accepted That's all there was to it."

"How many times have you seen him these last cou ple of weeks?" Shari changed her tactics, switching from sly innuendo to direct questions.

"I haven't seen him at all. Except for last night." Lexie could truthfully answer Shari's prying question.

"Haven't you?" A finely drawn eyebrow was delicately arched to dispute Lexie's statement. "I suppose it was pure coincidence that Rome was attending that particular political function."

"I told you before that I'd seen him at similar occasions," Lexie reminded her.

"So you did," Shari admitted. "But the two of you could just as easily have planned to meet there. Your car was conveniently in the shop, and Mac is notorious for disappearing once his part of an assignment is finished."

"Your two and two are adding up to five," Lexie declared.

"You can't blame me for being suspicious. It all looks very arranged." The columnist put suggestive emphasis on the last word.

"Well, it wasn't. It was purely accidental." Considering the unexpected results of the meeting, accidental seemed the appropriate word.

"When will you be seeing him again?" Shari wanted to know, watching her closely.

"I don't know," she replied, knowing that there was still the dinner engagement to be canceled. "Probably the next time Rome hobnobs with the politicians."

"Do you mean that he hasn't asked you out?" The question was asked as if the columnist already knew the answer, which was impossible.

"If he did, Shari, I wouldn't tell you," Lexie retorted. "As a matter of fact, I would hope you'd be the last to know. You've ferreted out all the information from me that you're going to get."

"Is that any way to talk to a friend?" Shari looked offended.

"If you are my friend, you'll let the subject of Rome Lockwood drop and not use me to claw your way to the top," Lexie challenged.

A coldness swept over the older woman's face. "We're both in the business of news, Lexie."

"Then go find your news someplace else instead of rehashing old gossip." A sigh of irritation took much of the steam out of Lexie's reply.

After Shari had walked stiffly away, she tried the number for Lockwood Enterprises. A receptionist informed her that he was not available at the moment. She tried several more times over the next few days but got the same runaround. But she never left a message or asked that he return her call, or even identified herself. She didn't want her name joining a long, long list of other female callers.

She was almost shocked when Rome called her at the newspaper on Friday. She held the receiver in her hand, too stunned by the voice on the other end of the line to speak.

"Lexie, are you there?" His question held a hint of amusement.

It prodded her into answering. "Yes, I am. Sorry. I'm glad you called, I—"

"You know, I was thinking that your car might still be in the shop," Rome interrupted her. "Is it?"

"Yes. I—"

"Templeton!" Mike barked behind her. "How come you're still here? I thought I told you to get over to City Hall!"

"Just a second." She cupped her hand over the mouthpiece and glanced impatiently at Mike. "I'm leaving in a second," she promised.

"See that you do," he warned but despite his gruffness, he wasn't really angry.

Lexie removed her hand. "Sorry," she said to Rome, "I—"

"You're busy. I'll see you tomorrow night at seven, my place."

"No! Wait!" Lexie protested. "No, I can't . . . make it." The last part of the sentence trailed off lamely as a dial tone buzzed in her ear.

"All right, let's get going, Templeton!" Mike urged behind her.

Lexie stared at the telephone in frustration. Its small screen didn't list the digits of the last incoming call—his—but showed the number as blocked. Grabbing her shoulder bag and note pad, she headed for the exit. She knew she had missed her one and only chance to tell Rome her decision.

By Saturday night, Lexie was of two minds about the date. One insisted that she simply ignore the invitation she had accepted and not show up at Rome's apartment. The second wanted her to go, tell him she couldn't stay, and leave.

As she was dressing, she kept searching for a third choice and found none. The door to the apartment opened and closed, and a few seconds later Ginger called to her.

"Lexie, I'm home. Where are you?" The rattle of paper bags indicated that her roommate's shopping expedition had been successful.

"In the bedroom." The taut state of her nerves made Lexie's voice sound shrill. She ran a smoothing hand over her hair before turning away from the mirror to walk to the doorway into the living room.

Ginger's back was to the door as Lexie entered. "I didn't realize it was so late. I hope you haven't eaten. I picked up some Chinese food on the way back and got a bit carried away. There's plenty here, more than I can eat."

"I'm not really hungry."

Ginger turned. "Are you going somewhere? I don't remember you mentioning that you had a date tonight."

"I don't." Lexie hadn't confided in Ginger about her

meeting with Rome or the invitation to dinner she had foolishly accepted. There was too much risk that Ginger would blab to Shari Sullivan. And then, too, Lexie had expressed her opinion of Bob in no uncertain terms. She might have jumped to conclusions about the guy, but she still wasn't going to take back what she'd said about him.

"What are you all dressed up for?" her roommate persisted.

"I'm . . . just going out for a little while," she said evasively. "When is Bob coming over?"

"Eight. That's why I bought all this Chinese food, so I wouldn't have to cook," Ginger explained. "Do you want me to put some of it in the refrigerator so you can have it when you come back? You might be hungry by then."

"Maybe," Lexie replied. Once this meeting or date or whatever it was with Rome was over, her nerves might settle down. "Thanks."

"Where are you going? Shopping?" Ginger started toward the kitchen.

"No place special. Just out for a while," she lied.

Ginger stopped and flipped her long corn-silk hair over a shoulder. She stared curiously at Lexie, a puzzled frown knitting her forehead.

"Are you sure you don't have a date?" she asked again.

"I told you I'm just going out for a while." Lexie didn't meet the other girl's eyes.

"You *are* going on a date," Ginger said in a breathless rush. "I'll bet it's with Rome Lockwood, isn't it?"

"Whatever gave you that idea?" She tried to laugh it away, but ended up sounding guilty.

"Shari said the other day that she was positive there was something going on between the two of you. I didn't believe her, but it's true."

"No, it isn't."

"Hmph. You never said a word to me." Ginger directed the full force of her spaniel eyes at Lexie. "You wouldn't have told me if I hadn't guessed."

Lexie threw up her hands in a gesture of futility. "Okay, okay, you win. I do have a date with him but I'm breaking it. For dinner. At his place. Unfortunately his phone number isn't listed and I couldn't track it down. As much as I'd like to, I just can't stand him up. So I'm going over to his place to tell him the dinner is off."

"That's why didn't you want any of the Chinese food I bought—because you're going to have dinner with him. Why didn't you say so?" Ginger asked in a confused voice.

"I'm not going to have dinner with him," Lexie repeated. "I'm not eating with you because I'm too nervous."

"Nervous? Why?"

"Because I know he's going to argue with me, that's why." And Rome could be oh-so-persuasive, she thought. But she didn't tell Ginger that, not after all the preaching she had done. "And don't you dare breathe a word of this to Shari. I had all the comments I could stand from everybody in the building the last time I went out with Rome. It's finally been forgotten, and I don't want Shari churning things up again by printing something in her column."

"If you feel that way, then why did you say you'd go with him tonight?"

Lexie could understand why it didn't make any sense to Ginger, who was generally clueless about most things anyway. "I think I was out of my mind at the time," she admitted. "Promise me on your mother's life that you won't tell Shari, though."

"I won't. You can trust me, Lexie," her roommate promised.

Lexie glanced at her watch. The hands pointed to a few minutes past six-thirty. "I'd better leave. Unless I get caught in traffic, I should be back before Bob gets here."

"Good luck."

By the time she'd driven to Rome's apartment she was shivering. Her toes felt like ice cubes. She took several deep breaths to warm herself up and entered the building. A different doorman told her that she was expected, words that made her blush.

She paused in front of Rome's door. Before she could retreat she pushed the doorbell. This time there was no waiting, no time to think. The door opened and Rome was there, so casually male, so devastatingly handsome, a satyr with his dark, knowing eyes and that black mane of hair.

She could only stare, speechless, her heart beating faster. The lightning touch of his gaze licked over her body, setting fire to her skin right through her clothes.

"You're right on time." As he reached for her hand, it fluttered quite naturally into his and Lexie was drawn into the apartment, not against her will, because she had no will.

Once inside, Rome brought her effortlessly into the circle of his arm. There was a mesmerizing intensity in his look as his strong hand cupped the side of her face, fingers tangling in the flame gold of her hair.

"I thought you might not come," he murmured. A mixture of delight and triumph was in his soft laugh. "Does it give you any satisfaction to know that I'm not very sure of you, Lexie?"

"None." Was that her voice, so clear and calm? His gaze dwelt on her lips a warning instant before his mouth moved toward them. But she pulled back just in time. "I shouldn't have come," she said.

"Don't . . ." The word came out sharply, and his fingers tightened along her face. Just as suddenly, Rome relaxed, smiling and changing his demeanor from that of a demanding lover. "Don't you trust my cooking?" he mocked.

"It isn't that." Lexie moved out of his arms and he didn't attempt to stop her. She pretended to brush the hair away from her cheek but she was really trying to erase the tingling of her skin where he had touched her. "I didn't plan on coming here tonight. I tried to get hold of you to tell you that, but you have an unlisted number and the receptionist at Lockwood Enterprises never put me through to your office. When you called me yesterday you hung up before I could tell you that I'd changed my mind and wouldn't be here."

"Why did you come then?" Rome eyed her steadily.

"I don't like people who break appointments without warning,' she defended herself. "I think it's inconsiderate and horribly rude, so I couldn't just not show up."

"I see." Rome turned and walked across the room to the liquor cabinet. "You agreed to come the other night."

"The other night was a mistake." His back was to her and she found it easier to talk without his dark gaze leveled at her. "I don't want to become involved with you."

There was the rattle of ice cubes and the splashing of liquid. When Rome turned, he held two glasses in his hand. He crossed the room and handed one to Lexie, who accepted it rather absently.

"I'm sure you have a good reason. You probably made a list of them."

"Uh, no." Lexie stared at her drink. Gin and tonic—he had remembered.

"I had the impression the other night that you wanted me to make love to you. Everything happened kind of fast—maybe too fast."

"Look,"—she bit her lower lip in agitation—"I'm not going to try to deny that I find you very attractive sexually, but I don't think I really like you or respect you, and those are two essential ingredients of a healthy relationship."

"That says it all." Rome lifted his glass and took a quick swallow. He gave her a piercing look. "Now that you've told me, I suppose you intend to leave without finding out whether I can cook."

"I can't stay now—you must see that," Lexie insisted.

His mouth twisted wryly. "All I know is that I have two expensive steaks marinating in the kitchen. In fact, I have an entire meal for two that you expect me to eat alone."

"I can't help that."

"Yes, you can. There's no need for all that food to go to waste. Since you're here, you might as well stay for dinner."

"I . . ." Lexie hesitated, uncertain, torn by what she wanted and what was wise.

"I promise I won't force myself on you," Rome said with a grin, and lifted his glass in a toast. "We'll just be two friends sharing dinner."

She was twenty-four; she was supposed to be an adult. And he really was being nice about it. What was she going to do? Run from his apartment like a scared little bunny?

"Two friends," she agreed, and touched the rim of her glass to his.

She had been truthful when she said she didn't trust him, any more than she trusted herself in his company. As she lifted the glass to her lips she studied him over the rim, looking for any sign that his suggestion masked an ulterior motive, but there seemed to be none.

"Bring your drink out to the kitchen," said Rome. "You can watch me cook the steaks, and you can fix the salad. Unless you would prefer to sit around the living room and wait."

"No, I'll come with you."

To get to the kitchen they had to go through the dining room. It was a small, informal space. Obviously Rome didn't do any large-scale entertaining in his home.

An intimate table for two was beautifully set with an ivory linen tablecloth, crystal and sterling silver. Two silver candle holders flanked a bowl of fresh fruit. The succulent cluster of grapes reminded Lexie of something out of a Greek orgy scene. She could easily visualize Rome plucking a grape and carrying it to her lips. Her body tightened at the sensuous thought.

The kitchen was also relatively small but with top-of-the-line stainless steel everything for the guy chef. Rome moved familiarly around it, setting the steaks in a pan resting on the stove. Lexie stood uncertainly in front of the refrigerator and had to step away when Rome walked to it.

"All you have to do is supervise," he told her. "I'll do all the work."

"That will be a change," was the fake-perky response Lexie offered.

He began placing various ingredients on the counter. The bacon was in the refrigerator; he took two strips and put them in a skillet. While it was frying, he added sugar, water, oil, vinegar, ketchup, and an assortment of spices to a container. As he turned the sizzling bacon in the skillet, he darted a glance sideways at Lexie. "How do you like the picture of a man slaving over a hot stove?"

"I like it." She smiled faintly.

"You would."

"Is there anything I can do?" It wasn't easy standing around watching him. The freedom of looking at him was too unnerving.

"No." Then Rome reconsidered. "You could take the candles off the table, since it's not going to be a romantic evening."

"I'll do that." Lexie turned to the dining room, then stopped. "Where do you want me to put them?"

"On the sideboard along the wall."

Lexie experienced a twinge of regret as she removed the candles from the table, which was silly. She didn't want to share a candlelight dinner with Rome Lockwood. The bowl of fruit remained as the sole centerpiece, the pale green grapes contrasting with the red ripeness of apples—the fruit of temptation—and the burgundy and yellow skin of the peach.

When Lexie returned to the kitchen, Rome was adding chopped eggs and crumbled bacon to the dressing and expertly tossing it all together with fresh spinach leaves in a bowl. Never once did he seem uncertain about the next step.

"You are a good cook, aren't you?" she commented.

"Mm," he agreed without false modesty. "My parents taught me how to be self-sufficient."

"My parents taught me to use a microwave."

Rome shook his head. "I never liked nuked food much. Fresh is best. But I don't always have the time. Do you like to cook?"

"Sometimes," Lexie said. "I'm not all that domestic. I guess I'd rather cook than do laundry, though. I hate sitting around laundromats more than anything. What a waste of time."

"Bring your laundry over here and do it. My socks can get tangled up with your socks." He laughed at her shocked look. "What's the matter? Are you afraid my socks won't respect your socks in the morning?"

"Very funny."

He picked up the salad bowl, missing the blush that brought a high color to Lexie's cheeks. "You're in for a treat tonight, fresh spinach salad with dressing à la Rome, my speciality," he said.

"It looks good," she admitted.

"It is. A few minutes in the refrigerator to let it all chill together and you'll be begging for my recipe when you taste it." With the salad in the refrigerator, Rome turned to the grill. "How do you like your steak?"

"Medium rare."

When they finally sat down at the table, Lexie couldn't find fault with either the meal or the company. The food was delicious. She wasn't sure she could have done as well. The conversation didn't drag painfully the way it had in the fancy restaurant but Rome was directing it. Lexie responded naturally to his easy wit and the interesting topics he picked to talk about. And, of course, there was no awkwardness about ordering wine or paying the bill.

Halfway through the meal, Rome offered, "More wine?"

"Please." She raised her glass for him to fill. "Did you have any idea how embarrassed I was trying to choose from that wine list, knowing I was with a man who was a connoisseur?"

"I picked up on that," he admitted, the grooves around his mouth deepening. "Your eyes are incredibly expressive. I remember they were almost electric blue, shooting sparks when you looked at me across the table."

"You weren't any help," Lexie said. "You wouldn't give me a hint."

"I know." Rome filled her glass, then his own. "The restaurant's wine list was impeccable. It was impossible for you to make a bad choice."

"That's what I was hoping," she said, smiling.

By the time the meal was finished, the bottle of wine was empty. Lexie was sipping the last of it, enveloped in a rosy afterglow of good food, good wine, and good company.

"That was delicious," she sighed and lifted her glass in a salute to Rome. "My compliments to the chef."

He returned her salute with cheerful formality, inclining his dark head in acceptance of her praise. With their glasses drained, he said, "We'll have coffee in the living room."

Lexie was almost too comfortable to move. Reluctantly she pushed her chair away from the table and agreed, "Okay, but first I'll help you with the dishes." She started gathering them to carry to the kitchen.

"No," Rome said. "We'll take them to the kitchen and stack them on the counter next to the dishwasher. The maid can run them through when she comes. I cook but I draw the line at standing in front of a sinkful of dirty dishes."

Together they took care of the chore, and Rome got the coffee going, sending her out minutes later to the living room with a handsome silver coffee service on a tray.

Lexie set the coffee service on the low table in front of a long sofa. She sat near one end and poured coffee from the pot into two china cups. When Rome appeared seconds later, Lexie continued her task without looking up.

"Cream or sugar?" she asked.

"Neither." He walked to the sofa where she sat. "My kitchen talents don't extend to rich desserts, so I decided we would end with cheese and fruit. Is that all right?"

Lexie stared at the bowl of fruit he set on the table, a touch of panic momentarily blinding her to the plate of cheeses and crackers. Her thoughts returned to her previous erotic fantasies with uncomfortable swiftness. Rome joined her on the sofa, but kept a friendly distance between them.

She swallowed and answered in what she hoped would be her previously carefree tone, "That's fine." But she reached for the cheese. "This has almost as many calories as a rich dessert. Maybe more."

His gaze raked her body, his expression indicating that he liked what he saw. "You counting calories? Have some fruit. Would you like a peach?"

He took one from the bowl as relief swept through Lexie that he hadn't said "grape." "Sounds good," she admitted.

Instead of handing it to her, Rome took a knife and completely circled the ripe peach with a deft, lengthwise cut. He split it open and lifted out the pit with a knife point, then handed the two halves to Lexie.

"Thank you." She set one half down and took a bite of the other.

Juice squirted from the ripe, pulpy flesh. Lexie swallowed and laughed self-consciously as it trickled down her chin. She quickly wiped it away with her fingers and started to lick the juice from her lips, aware of Rome's narrowing gaze on her.

"No," he said.

Her heart thumped against her ribs as he leaned forward and kissed the juice from her lips with sensual sweetness. The breath left her lungs and her head was swimming when he pulled back.

"You shouldn't have done that," she protested weakly, looking away so he couldn't see how deeply affected she was by his kiss.

"Sorry,"—he didn't sound it—"but your lips looked so delectable that I couldn't resist."

The rest of the peach remained on the table. Lexie couldn't risk a repeat of what had just happened.

"What were we talking about?" he asked nonchalantly.

"I don't exactly remember," she said, unable to make the transition back to after-dinner conversation as effortlessly as he did.

"Okay. I guess we need a safe topic. I've never asked you where you're from," Rome said.

"Originally from Massachusetts—Salem. But we moved around a lot when I was growing up," she answered.

"From Salem? I knew you were a witch." He laughed, then asked, "What brought you back?" He sounded interested, mildly curious. "Did you attend college here?"

"No, I graduated from U.S.C. Southern California, but I always wanted to come back east and work. So when I graduated, that's just what I did."

"How do you like your job as a reporter?"

"I must like it. I'm sure as hell not in for the money, because there isn't any."

"Where's your family now?" Rome asked.

Yes, Lexie thought, let's talk about my family. It was just the subject she needed to get a grip on herself. Or maybe she was just fuddled because of all the wine. Maybe she needed to sober up. She picked up her coffee, balancing the cup and saucer on her lap.

"My mother died when I was eight. I don't have any brothers or sisters," Lexie answered his question. "There's only my father and me. He lives in California."

"You must have been close," Rome commented. "I can't imagine that your father likes you living so far away."

"Dad realizes that every little girl has to grow up and leave the nest," Lexie shrugged, not bothering to deny his first remark, but there was a wry twist to her lips.

"Daughters do that, don't they?" He smiled and sipped his coffee. "I didn't ask if you'd like some brandy in your coffee. Would you?"

"No." She was almost convinced the wine had been too much.

Rome got up from the sofa. "I think I will." He crossed the room to the liquor cabinet and added a dash of brandy to his cup. Before returning he paused beside a built-in sound system. "How about some music?"

Lexie was about to nod her agreement when he went ahead and put on some sensual hybrid of slow jazz and blues. Suddenly it was all too much—the wine, the sultry music, the intimate atmosphere. She set her cup down and rose.

"It's time I was leaving," she announced decisively. At least she hoped she sounded decisive.

Rome stopped on his way back, looking at her with a raised brow. "So soon?"

"Yes," Lexie insisted. He set his cup down and walked over to her. "Thank you for dinner. I enjoyed it very much." Trite . . . but true.

"Are you busy tomorrow?" he asked.

"Yes," she lied. She would have the whole day to herself. Bob was back on speaking terms with Ginger again and her roommate had been starry-eyed all day with her glorious plans for the weekend with Bob.

"Doing what?"

"Things." Like doing the laundry, cleaning the apartment, trying not to be bored.

"Why are you running out, Lexie?" His question was as direct as his gaze.

"I'm not running. I'm walking," she insisted, unwilling to admit that she felt the need to escape from him.

"Why? Do you think the time has come for the seduction scene?" he asked acidly.

"Hasn't it?" Lexie retorted. "You've wined and dined me. Now there's dreamy background music. When are you going to turn the lights down low?"

"And what if I don't try to seduce you?" The look in his eyes was intense, difficult to hold and impossible to break away from. "What will you do? Will you think I'm waiting to lull you into a false sense of security before I make my move? Would it ever occur to you that I might want you to stay because I want your company?"

"Oh, please, don't start that friendship stuff again," she cried. "You don't want friendship from me."

There was something ruthless in the set of his jaw. "It seems to be a case of damned if I do and damned if I don't. What have I got to lose?"

Her backward step was never completed as he caught her arms and pulled her to him. Lexie turned her head and eluded his mouth but she didn't say no. She didn't want to. Rome brushed his lips very briefly and tenderly on her lips, then found that particularly sensitive spot below her ear and nibbled at the lobe.

In the end it was she who sought the fulfillment of his kiss, indulging in an erotic exploration of his mouth, which Rome matched with practiced ease. He seemed to know just how to stoke a sensual fire and make it burn hotter and hotter, until it was nearly out of control.

When he swept her into his arms and carried her back to the sofa, Lexie's arms curled around his neck with artless abandon. Her senses ruled supreme. She was all too aware of the feel of his rippling muscles, and the intoxicating taste of his warm mouth with its traces of brandy and coffee were a heady aphrodisiac.

Seated on his lap, Lexie felt the roaming caress of his hands stop only to unbutton her blouse with a speed that should have alarmed her. But it didn't.

When he pushed aside the gauzy material, his hands spanned the bareness of her waist, lifting and arching her up to give his lips free access to the swelling curves of her breasts and the tantalizing valley between them. Lexie gasped at the raw sexuality of his intimate touch, and slid her fingers into the black mane of his hair.

Then Rome was moving her backward onto the sofa

cushions, his weight pinning her to them as he followed her down. She was molded to his length as his mouth returned to the ready surrender of her lips. Their body heat fused them together. Lexie only knew that she wanted to touch every inch of him, to find that promised, mindless glory of total knowledge.

CHAPTER SEVEN

She could feel the hammering of his heartbeat, the raggedness of his breathing. There was satisfaction in knowing she had aroused him as fully as he had aroused her. It gave her a sense of power, however uncertainly she wielded it. The hot moistness of his breath touched her cheek as his mouth moved to the vulnerable point along the cord of her neck.

"One of us is crazy," Rome muttered near her ear.

The sound of his voice compelled her to speak at last. Her flesh might have surrendered totally to his will, but her mind still controlled her voice. And her mind still knew how hopeless it was to love him.

"It's me," she cried softly. "I don't want to do this."

"Yes, you do," Rome insisted. "You've wanted it as much as I have from the minute you walked in the door."

"That's not true."

"It is." He kissed the corner of her mouth and she turned her head to one side, dodging his kiss.

"No," she repeated her denial, adding, "I didn't even want to come here tonight."

"Yes, you did, or you wouldn't be here." Rome kissed

her on the temple and the wing of her brow, not deterred by her soft denials or the sudden elusiveness of
her lips.

"That isn't true," she protested. "I tried . . ."

"Stop pretending." He cut her short. Rome lifted his
head and cradled her face in his hand, forcing her to
look at him. "All you had to do was write me a note and
get it to my office."

"I couldn't just show up. And the mail would've
taken too long."

"Two words: bike messenger. You work for a newspaper. They use them all the time."

Lexie was silent.

"If you wanted me to know that you'd changed your
mind, you would've found a way. The only reason you
wanted to reach me by phone was that you wanted me
to talk you into coming."

"No," Lexie breathed.

"Yes." The black fire of his gaze smoldered. "You're
here because it's where you want to be. You want to be
talked into staying. You want me to make love to you as
much as I want to make love to you. Admit it, Lexie."

"No." She had to swallow back the sob that rose in
her throat. "I don't!"

Abruptly Rome pushed away from her, rising from
the sofa and taking a step away, all in one liquid move-
ment that left her suddenly very cold and alone. Startled,
shattered by his statement, Lexie was slower to move, rising shakily, trying to ignore the stinging truth of his
claim.

She stared at his handsome, aggressively male profile. A distant part of her mind registered the fact that
the gray silk of his shirt was unbuttoned, exposing the
bronze of his naked chest and the raw animal virility it
conveyed. But her thoughts were focused on trying to
explain somehow.

He was aloof and withdrawn, seemingly miles away. She rose, her hand reached out to touch his arm and draw him back. The instant her fingers came in contact with the hard muscles, her touch became a gliding caress.

"Rome, I—" she began.

He brushed her hand away in one swift motion.

"Stay away from me, Lexie."

She flinched at the barely controlled anger in his voice and stood motionless. She knew she deserved that. Rome was fighting to control all the passion she had aroused in him.

"Sorry." He said no more and looked as if he regretted that solitary word of apology.

Lifting a hand, he raked it through his hair, rumpling it more than Lexie's fingers had. He crossed the room to the liquor cabinet, putting distance between them, and splashed a healthy slug of brandy in his glass.

"I'll leave," Lexie said quietly.

There was no more point in staying. Rome had made her face the truth. She couldn't pretend anymore. If she stayed, it was for no other reason than to be in his arms and to make love with him.

"Not yet." There was a rough edge in his voice that brought her up short. He tossed down a swallow of brandy. "We need to talk."

There was a brooding quality in his expression that made him look almost dangerous. It surprised Lexie. She'd expected Rome to use his considerable charm as he had in the past, or react with thwarted anger. Certainly she hadn't expected this inwardness. It confused her because it seemed so out of character.

"There isn't anything left to say, Rome," she replied. "It's all been said."

"No, it hasn't. And for God's sake, button your blouse!" he said harshly.

Blushing scarlet under the gaze that touched so decisively on the exposed swell of her breasts, Lexie hurriedly pulled the front of her blouse together and began fastening the buttons.

"Look, I'm not going to pretend that I didn't want . . ." What use was it to state the obvious? She sliced the rest of the sentence away and got straight to the point. "I'm not cut out to be a one-night stand—I want more than that."

"Is that all you think you are?" he demanded.

"Isn't it true?" Tears sprang to her eyes and she had to blink them back. "Maybe you want me for your lover, your mistress, but once the newness wears off I'd be just another pretty face in a long line of pretty faces."

"How can someone as young and beautiful as you have so little confidence in your ability to make a man love you?" The muscles along his jaw flexed, revealing the tautness of his control.

"There's always going to be someone who's younger, prettier and smarter," Lexie retorted. "And I'm going to grow old, wrinkled, and not remember much."

"So will I."

"No," she disagreed, "Men like you acquire character lines and experience and more women chasing after you." She gathered up her things, making sure she had her car keys.

The tears in her eyes were welling up to the point where she couldn't see. Any minute she was going to start crying and that would be the final humiliation. She had already made a big enough fool of herself. With a quick turn she walked swiftly to the door.

"Lexie!" Rome impatiently called her back but she didn't listen.

Before she could turn the doorknob, his hand was there holding the door shut. Summoning all her pride, she turned her liquid blue eyes to him.

"Let me go, Rome," she said. "I can't handle an affair with you."

Although her tears made everything blurry, she felt his silent look. Rome let out a long breath and withdrew his hand from the door.

"Okay. I can't force you to stay and I can't persuade you."

She shook her head.

"But I am going to walk you to your car."

Lexie yanked the door open. "Skip the gallant gestures, Rome."

"Damn it!" He struggled to control his temper. "Listen to me. It's night. Boston is a big city and things happen. If you want to get out of my life, at least let me see that you get out of it safely!"

She choked out, "Have it your way, then."

It seemed like the longest walk Lexie had ever taken—with Rome walking at her side, not touching her—and her heart wanting to burst with each step. She missed the curb and stumbled, but she recovered quickly and avoided Rome's attempt to steady her with his hand.

Without glancing at him, she unlocked the car door and opened it. "Good-bye, Rome," she mumbled and slid behind the wheel.

"See you."

It was just a parting phrase but if Lexie could help it, she was going to see that it never came true. Or at least not for a very long time.

The following Monday around midmorning, Lexi found herself gravitating to Shari's office for an impromptu meeting with the columnist and Ginger. It was an unconscious attempt to avoid being alone with her thoughts, which invariably swung to Rome. As long as she was surrounded by work or people, the ache inside didn't seem as intense. She did little of the talking, but with Ginger around, it didn't matter.

"Don't you just love this outfit?" The question was directed at Shari as Ginger did a pirouette. Lace trimmed the snug-fitting denim jeans she wore, as well as the denim vest.

"It's definitely you, my dear," Shari agreed with a trace of slyness. A tiny smile touched Lexie's mouth. With its old-fashioned, ragbag charm, the outfit did seem to match Ginger's perky Midwestern personality.

"We were walking by this store and I saw it in the window," Ginger explained excitedly. "I showed it to Bob and said isn't it pretty. He asked me if I wanted it. I said sure and he walked right in and bought it for me just like that." She snapped her fingers.

"And I suppose you were properly grateful," Shari said suggestively.

Ginger blushed. "Who wouldn't be? It's beautiful. I love it."

"I'm sure he counted on that," Lexie said with a noticeable edge in her voice, feeling a sudden surge of bitterness at the selfish motives of men.

Her roommate darted her a resentful glance. "You're just upset because"—she stopped herself from blurting out something—"you don't have anybody to buy you presents."

But Lexie knew something about Rome had been on the tip of Ginger's tongue. She felt herself tense and wondered if Shari was thinking along the same lines. She stole a sideways glance at the columnist, who had been watching Lexie, although now her gaze was swinging lazily to Ginger.

"Lexie and I are in the same boat there, but your love life seems to be sailing right along," she said. "While I'm on that subject, Rome Lockwood seems to have dropped out of circulation. You wouldn't know anything about that, would you, Lexie?"

"Me?" She pretended surprise but didn't know how successful she was. "Why should I?"

"I don't know," Shari said with a little shrug. "It was just an idea I had."

"You and your ideas," Lexie murmured.

"Hey, Lexie!" Gary Dunbar paused in the opening to the office. "You're being paged for a phone call that came into the main switchboard. What are you doing Friday night?"

"Nothing," she answered. Her attempt to sound eager was more for Shari's benefit than a desire to spend the evening with Gary.

"We'll go to a movie or something," he suggested.

"Fine," Lexie agreed.

"Around seven then." He started to retreat, then reminded her, "Don't forget that phone call."

"Do you want me to have it transferred here?" the columnist asked as Lexie started to rise from her chair.

"Why not," she said. "I'll probably need paper and a pencil. Can you spare some?"

"Right there." Shari tossed her a notebook and picked up the phone, calling the switchboard to have the phone call transferred to her extension. "Who's calling, please?" she asked. Her eyes widened at the answer and she handed the phone to Lexie. "Rome Lockwood for you. And you have nothing to do with him being out of circulation," she mocked.

Lexie's stomach tied itself into knots as she reached for the telephone receiver. She silently cursed the lethargy that had made her take the call here instead of her own desk. Alone, she could have hung up or refused to take the call. But with Shari Sullivan looking on and listening, she didn't dare.

"Lexie Templeton here." Miraculously her voice had no nervous tremor.

"Lexie, it's Rome." The familiar pitch of his voice reached across the distance and made her heart skip a beat.

"What a surprise," she murmured and heard the faint sarcasm threaded into the words.

"Is it?" Rome said dryly. "I've had time to think over what you said Saturday night. I'd like you to have dinner with me on Friday. My family is giving a party for some friends that night, and I'd like you to—"

"A party!" Lexie interrupted him, her tone artificially bright. "I'm flattered that you thought of me, but it really isn't my line. You should speak to the society editor. Would you like me to connect you?"

"That isn't what I want at all and you know it!" Rome's voice was low and angry. He didn't know that she'd blown him off mostly for Shari's benefit.

"I'm sorry. Th . . . there isn't any way I can help you." Why did she have to stammer like a silly schoolgirl, Lexie railed inwardly.

She heard him swearing under his breath. "Is it so much to ask that I want to see you again?" he demanded.

"I'm afraid it is," she insisted. "Goodbye, Rome."

Lexie hung up the phone before he could say something that might change her mind. She felt drained but there was still Shari to be faced.

"What was he calling about?" the columnist asked. "Was there a party he wanted you to attend?"

"Yes." Lexie swallowed hard, trying to get rid of the lump in her throat. "His parents are having a dinner party. He seemed to think the paper might find it newsworthy." She made a show of looking at her watch. "I'd better run." She started for the door. "Maybe you'll be covering the party, Shari. Nothing the Lockwoods do would ever be of interest to me."

* * *

Within a week, Lexie had cause to contradict that statement as she sat at her desk listening to Mike explain her day's assignment, covering the arrival and activities of a visiting foreign dignitary.

"Officially he's here on an unofficial visit to see his old friends, the Lockwoods. He'll be staying at their home in Marblehead. But unofficially—" Mike paused to give his seeming doubletalk importance—"rumor is it's a cover-up for a secret State meeting. I want you to stick to his party like glue. Follow him into the men's john if you have to."

"I don't think I can do it," Lexie protested.

"The men's john was an exaggeration," Mike frowned impatiently. "His plane arrives—"

"No, I mean, I don't think I can cover the story." There was only one Lockwood family in Boston and that was Rome's.

"Why?" he demanded gruffly.

"Because . . ." But Lexie couldn't think of a reason that she wanted to tell him.

Mike took one look at her face and guessed the truth. "Oh, brother. Must be Rome Lockwood. What happened on that date, anyway? I suppose you slapped his face or pulled some equally stupid stunt."

"I'd rather you find somebody else to take this assignment." How in the world could she explain?

"You would, would you?"

"If you don't mind, I'd really appreciate it," Lexie said hopefully.

"It so happens that I do mind. This assignment is yours and as a professional, you're going to accept it." His toughness softened a little at the strained look on her face. "Besides, I don't have anyone else qualified to cover it." It was the best Mike could do for an apology and he gave her a sympathetic glance before he moved away from her cubicle.

Mac had drawn the assignment along with Lexie. Together they went to Logan International Airport to be on hand for the arrival. As Lexie had guessed, Rome was there with an older couple whom she presumed were his parents. His mother was a dark, vivacious woman and Lexie realized that Rome had inherited his coloring from her. His father had passed along his striking good looks—he was as tall and masculine as Rome. Even at his age, the man was handsome enough to warrant being chased by women.

When the European dignitary—Lexie had to check her notes to recall his name, Edmond Martineau—departed from his private jet, he was accompanied by a small entourage, and Lexie suspected that Mike had cause to believe there was more to the visit than had been made public.

"Wow!" Mike whistled under his breath. "Check her out!"

Jealousy twisted through Lexie at the sight of the woman coming into view. Gorgeous, chic as only a Frenchwoman can be, sophisticated to the bone, the petite brunette in her designer suit glided forward to be at Edmond Martineau's side as he greeted the Lockwoods.

"The next question is," Mac murmured in an aside, "is she his daughter, his wife, or his mistress?"

When the woman kissed Rome on both cheeks and clung to his arm, looking up at him with a flirty smile, Lexie wanted to die. Rome seemed to be not only enjoying the attention but also encouraging it, that male charm and breathtaking smile directed at the woman at his side. Lexie had known that seeing him again was going to be difficult but she hadn't realized it would be so painful.

Security kept the press away from the initial exchange, allowing them only to witness it at a distance. It soon became clear that they were not going to be allowed to question Martineau about his visit nor was he going to give them any statement before he left the airport. They had all waited for nothing. Lexie heard the disgruntled mutterings from the other reporters, but they made little impression.

As Rome and his party started to make their way to a private lounge, Mac grumbled to Lexie, "We're not leaving with nothing. Come on." He grabbed her hand and pulled her behind him as he shouldered his way as close as he could get. "Hey, Rome!" he shouted, lifting his camera high over his head. "How about letting us get a picture?"

Rome glanced over his shoulder in Mac's direction. His gaze lingered for a scant second on Lexie's red-gold hair. She knew he'd recognized her but he didn't pause, continuing with his party to the private lounge. Her heart sank.

A slow exodus of reporters began. The general consensus seemed to be that they would have a better chance when the party went to get into the waiting limousines. Lexie was eager to leave, but Mac kept a firm clasp on her hand.

"The others . . ." she started to protest.

"We're going to wait here." There was a shrewd gleam in his eye as he stared at the closed door. "I've got a hunch and I'm betting that I'm right."

Lexie looked out the door with an apprehensive frown just as it opened. The man who stepped out had been part of the arriving Martineau entourage.

He looked at her and said in a faintly accented voice, "Miss Templeton? Please come in."

She was frozen but Mac wasn't. "I knew it!" he crowed and pushed her ahead of him to the door.

The entire party was seated in the lounge: Edmond Martineau, the brunette, half a dozen aides and embassy officials, Rome's parents, and Rome. All looked up when Lexie and Mac entered the lounge but it was only Rome that Lexie saw.

His gaze held nothing for her. Neither warm nor cold, it was merely different. He stepped forward at their approach, his smile minus the devastating charm she knew so well.

"Mr. Martineau has agreed to answer a few questions and be photographed," Rome announced quietly.

"Terrific!" Mac was enthusiastic but Lexie could only nod.

Rome turned and walked beside her to the chair where his family's important guest was seated. Edmond Martineau rose, smiling widely at Lexie. Before Rome could make the formal introduction, Martineau sent him a twinkling look. "Now I understand why you asked this favor of me, Rome. She is a very beautiful lady."

"Thank you," Lexie said, too self-conscious to derive much pleasure from the compliment.

There was an awkward moment when Rome introduced her, his mother piping up, "That Miss Templeton?"

"The one and only," Rome assured her dryly, using the same identifying words Lexie herself had once used.

The continuing introductions cleared up one minor mystery: the brunette was Martineau's daughter Claudine. Her interest in Rome was even more apparent with Lexie looking on.

The formalities taken care of, it was time to begin the questions. Lexie began by asking what was expected of her—the reason for his visit, et cetera—and received the expected answer: to see his old friends, the Lockwoods. Edmond Martineau had been a Harvard classmate of Rome's father while taking part in an exchange student program, and they had been close friends ever since, although it had been many years since Martineau had paid them a visit.

When Lexie asked, "When will you be meeting with the representatives from the State Department?" a fine tension crackled through the room.

It was perhaps only a second or two before Martineau laughed politely. "This is purely a social visit, Miss Templeton—a few restful days with my old friends and a chance for my daughter to see the picturesque city of Boston."

"Of course, my mistake." Lexie smiled but she was quite aware of Rome's gaze piercing her. She turned away. "Mac? Would you get the rest of your pictures?"

She would have been happy to fade into the wallpaper while Mac snapped the rest of his photographs, but Rome didn't seem to want her to, drifting to her side while Mac took pictures of Martineau and his daughter. Lexie tried to pretend he wasn't there, which was ridiculous, considering every nerve ending in her body tingled the closer he got.

"When we leave the airport," Rome said, "we'll be taking Mademoiselle Martineau on a tour of some of Boston's historic points. Would you like to accompany us?"

Mac's hearing was exceptional because it was he who answered. "You bet!"

Lexie hesitated. With Mike's admonition to both of them to stick with Martineau until they had discovered the actual reason for his visit, it was impossible to refuse this chance.

"It's kind of you to offer," she said stiffly.

"Not kind, Lexie. Not kind at all." Rome's reply was low and sarcastic, meant only for her to hear.

*   *   *

They took the Freedom Trail tour of Boston, starting out at Christ Church, also known as Old North Church, where two lanterns were hung in the steeple in 1775 to signify that the British were coming by sea. From there they moved on to Paul Revere's house, the oldest standing structure in downtown Boston, past a statue of Samuel Adams to Faneuill Hall, the Cradle of Liberty, and then made a stop at the site of the Boston Massacre, by the Old State House, seat of the Colonial government.

At every place Lexie was forced to watch Rome escorting the beautiful Claudine, explaining the historic significance of it all to her and laughing at her comments. Lexie knew she should have taken advantage of the situation to question Edmond Martineau more closely but she didn't have the heart for it. It seemed so unimportant.

She stared into the window of the Old Corner Bookstore, seeing her strained features in its indistinct reflection. There was no feeling of history there for her, no thought that once the literary greats such as Emerson, Hawthorne, and Holmes had possibly looked in the very same window when they had made it their meeting place and made Boston "the Athens of America."

Another reflection joined hers in the glass pane and Lexie stiffened. A further glance saw none of the others in the party, only Rome standing alone behind her. She knew she couldn't risk a personal discussion. She had long ago discovered that when you can't defend you should attack.

She turned. "I thought you told me that your family made it a rule not to become actively involved in politics."

"We don't become involved, and certainly not on an international level," Rome said.

"And Mr. Martineau's visit is . . . ?"

He studied her carefully for a long moment before replying. "His visit is exactly what he claims it to be—a reunion of friends."

"There's more to it than that," Lexie insisted.

"Is that why you were at the airport? And why you came along with us?"

"Of course. It's my assignment. I wouldn't be here otherwise." And that was the absolute truth.

"I see." His eyes were expressionless.

"I'm glad you do." She looked away. Where was Mac? No doubt with the beautiful Claudine.

"You're right. There is more to Martineau's visit than just the reunion," Rome said unexpectedly. Lexie stared at him, surprised that he should suddenly admit it. "Within the next forty-eight hours it will be officially announced that he's been invited to the White House to meet with the Secretary of State."

"Then this is all a cover-up?"

"His visit to my parents came to the attention of the State Department, and the invitation to meet with the Secretary of State followed."

"If what you're saying is true, then why all the secrecy?" Lexie was skeptical.

Rome seemed not to care whether she believed him or not. "As I understand it, it's a matter of diplomacy. Until the invitation is officially issued, Edmond doesn't acknowledge its existence. You should be familiar with protocol, you're a political reporter."

Frowning, she looked away. His answer was logical enough. Now she wondered what his motive was in telling her.

"Why have you told me?" she asked, unable to come up with a reason on her own.

There was an arrogant glitter in his look. "Oh, it's in

the way of a reward. After all that legwork, I wouldn't like to see you report back with nothing."

Lexie would have questioned him further but Martineau and his daughter and Rome's parents came around the corner of the building. And her chance was gone.

She heard them say that the Old South Meeting House, where the Boston Tea Party was launched, was their next stop. Claudine Martineau locked her hands possessively on Rome's arm and Lexie knew she could endure no more of seeing them together. Mac was trailing the group, trying not to drop his professional-grade digital camera, lenses, and its other high-tech accessories. She led him aside.

"This is where we leave," Lexie told him.

"But—" He cast a protesting look at the disappearing group.

"We have our story. Now let's get back to the paper," she insisted as though she was certain she had a story.

When she related it to Mike Farragut at the office, she downplayed its authenticity and avoided naming the person who had given her the inside information: Rome Lockwood.

"What about your source?" Mike asked.

"I don't know how reliable he is," she admitted.

"It's Rome Lockwood, that's who it is," Mac declared from his perch on the edge of Mike's desk. "I tell ya, Mike, we've got ourselves an exclusive! Rome's the one who got us invited along. Lexie won't admit he gave her the information, but they were off by themselves talking and right afterward she tells me we're heading back to the office. It has to be him."

"Lockwood, huh?" Mike eyed her, remembering her

unwillingness to take the assignment because of Rome "Do you think he might be feeding you false information to make you look incompetent?"

"He's trying to make points with her," the photographer said breezily.

Lexie stuck to her story. "As I said, I don't know how reliable my source is. But I do know that Edmond Martineau isn't going to let anything slip. Keeping tabs on him will be a waste of time."

Mike considered the problem for a minute. "It'll be announced within forty-eight hours, you say?"

She nodded.

"Shari Sullivan tells me that the Lockwoods are throwing a big dinner party for Martineau on Friday night—the forty-eight hours you were saying—and it would be the perfect opportunity to make the announcement." He seemed to be speaking his thoughts aloud, for he suddenly took a deep breath and glanced at them both. "I have a few old connections in the State Department. If I get even a hint of verification, we'll run your story on Friday morning, Lex. With your byline."

She didn't feel any sense of elation at the news.

CHAPTER EIGHT

"That's great news, Mike," Lexie said to the man standing in front of her desk. She should have been more elated than she was by his announcement. Instead her enthusiasm was forced.

"My connections at the State Department tried to be close-mouthed about Martineau's visit. But after I reminded them of the favors they owed me, they finally confirmed your story," he said with a smug smile.

"I'm glad to hear it," she lied again.

"You'd better get in gear and get the story written up if you want your byline on the front page on Friday morning," Mike ordered. "You did a helluva job, Lexie. Which proves, I guess, that it pays to know the right people."

"I suppose," she nodded, concealing a sigh.

Mac, the photographer, had convinced Mike that she had used her persuasive powers on Rome to get the admission from him. Mike thought she had wheedled the information from him like any good reporter. But Lexie knew that the story had been handed to her on a platter. So Mike's announcement gave her no satisfaction.

"You suppose?" he retorted with a snort. "We'll break the story twenty-four hours before any other paper in town and you *suppose* it pays to know the right people?"

"I was using your words, Mike," she reminded him.

"Hmph," he said. "It doesn't matter how you got the story. Everybody is going to notice you when you show up at the dinner party tomorrow night."

"The dinner party?" Lexie swiveled her chair toward him. "There's no need for me to attend that. I've already got the story."

"You got the advance story. Now you've got to cover the official announcement, which should be made at this shindig," Mike said. "You can cover that and whatever else develops out of it."

"No." She couldn't do it. She couldn't face Rome again. "Let somebody else go. It's just routine from here on."

"What are you?" Placing his hands on her desk, he leaned across it to emphasize his words. "A reporter? Or a glory-hunting headline seeker?"

"I'm not sure what you mean by the second question," she said cautiously. "But I don't think it's a compliment. So let's just say I'm a reporter."

"Are you sure?" he persisted. "Maybe you've fallen in love with seeing your name in print. Is that why you let Sullivan put all those quotes from you about Lockwood in her column? You got your fifteen minutes of fame and now you think you're too good to cover routine stuff, is that it?"

"No," she said. "It just so happens that I have a date Friday night."

"With who?" Mike wanted to know. The pastrami sandwich on his breath was enough to make her turn her face away.

"Gary Dunbar, from Features. Not that my social life is any of your business," she added.

"It is if it conflicts with the work you were hired to do. Break the date," he said.

"I don't want to and I don't have to."

"All right." He straightened and turned to bark, "Dunbar! Somebody get me Dunbar on the double!"

"What are you doing?" Lexi demanded and guessed that her editor intended to throw his weight around by ordering Gary to break the date. "So help me, Mike, if you—"

"Just shut up, Lexie, and let me handle this." His gruff retort sliced off her powerless threat. There wasn't any more time to argue as Gary came rushing toward them.

"You wanted to see me, Mr. Farragut?" he asked nervously.

"Lexie tells me the two of you have a date tomorrow night." The statement sounded like an accusation.

Gary looked momentarily flustered. "Uh, yeah. We do." He darted a sheepish look at Lexie.

"Where are you going?" Mike wanted to know.

"Well, I . . . uh . . ." Gary quailed under the editor's glowering look. "To a movie. I got a couple of free tickets from Stan over in movie reviews."

"Forget it!" Mike barked. "You're going with Lexie to a dinner party the Lockwoods are giving tomorrow night for Edmond Martineau. Okay?" It wasn't really a question of Gary's agreeing, not as far as Mike was concerned. It was more of a dare to disagree. "Lexie is covering the event for the paper."

"Sure. Fine. That's all right with me." Gary practically fell all over himself in his hurry to agree with the change of plans. Only at the last second did he think to consult Lexie. "It'll be okay, won't it, Lexie?"

It seemed she had as little choice as Gary did. He wouldn't be a very adequate shield against Rome, but he was better than none. Since she had to go to the dinner party, she'd rather attend with an escort in tow.

"As long as you don't mind, it's fine with me," she agreed with a forced smile.

"I don't mind," he assured her.

"Then that's settled," Mike declared, glancing at Lexie to see if she intended to argue.

She took a deep breath and nodded.

"Good." He looked even more smug than he had before. "Get back to whatever you were doing, Dunbar," he ordered gruffly. "And you," he said, his squinty gaze sliding to Lexie, "get busy on that story. I want it on my desk in half an hour."

She turned her swivel chair to face the computer as Gary hustled back to his desk. Mike stayed until he saw her fingers touch the keyboard and begin typing.

As they walked down the plush hotel corridor to the banquet room rented for the occasion, Gary's skittish gaze darted over the guests making their way to the same destination. They were all dressed to the teeth, the men in black tie and the women in gowns and jewelry. Gary cleared his throat nervously and adjusted his brown-striped tie.

"Next time give me fair warning," he whispered to Lexie. "I could've rented something formal."

"Don't worry. We're reporters. We're supposed to look conspicuous so no one will blab any secrets, mistaking us for one of them," she answered.

The butterflies in her stomach had nothing to do with her own less than elegant clothes. They came from anticipation and apprehension about seeing Rome again. Against her better judgment, she had effectively allowed Mike to bully her into this.

It wasn't any use telling herself that she'd done it to protect her job, but it made a pretty good excuse.

At the doorway to the banquet room, they were stopped. Lexie showed the guard her press card as she looked around the crowded room for a glimpse of Rome. Her initial sweep didn't find him. A crazy mixture of disappointment and relief quivered through her as they stepped into the room.

"There's the queen bee herself, Shari Sullivan," Gary said. "Somebody forgot to tell her about the unwritten dress code for journalists."

Lexie admired the designer gown Shari was wearing, then looked down at her own midnight-blue tailored suit. Well, at least the color set off the lighter blue of her eyes. But that was about all her outfit did for her.

"Columnists get to dress up," Lexie sighed. "It's a form of camouflage at a party like this."

"Makes sense." Gary grinned. "But I wonder if she'll talk to us."

"I think we're about to get lucky."

Shari happened to glance their way and saw them standing near the outer wall of the room. She excused herself to the couple with whom she was chatting and made her way toward them.

"Hello, Shari," Lexie greeted her. "You look fabulous."

The columnist preened and patted her freshly highlighted hair. "Thank you," she said. "What brings you here? I thought you said once that the Lockwoods weren't newsworthy."

"They aren't," Lexie countered the little dig. "But Edmond Martineau is."

"And oh-so-eligible," Shari said, turning so that she could look toward the center of the room without being obvious. "When he said *bon soir* to me in that gorgeous

French accent, I wanted to melt like an éclair in the July sun. He has that effect on every woman in the room, married or single."

The crowd of people seemed to part to give Lexie an unobstructed view of the guest of honor. But it was the tall, raven-haired man beside him who captured her attention. When that dark head bent to catch the comment of the chic brunette beside him, Lexie felt a flash of jealousy.

"Everyone is whispering about Rome and the Martineau girl. They've been practically inseparable since she arrived," Shari informed Lexie with deliberate insensitivity. "Have you noticed the way she clings to Rome as though he were her security blanket?"

Lexie only shrugged. "Maybe she's the reason he's been out of circulation lately." Her offhand comment was tinged with bitterness.

Shari's bright eyes glittered with triumph as her arrow found its target. "You've had your chance, darling," she reminded Lexie.

"Chance at what?" Lexie retorted. "I've outgrown merry-go-rounds."

"Gary must be relieved to know that." Shari glanced at him. "I presume you're accompanying Lexie merely as her escort. Or did Features assign you to do a story on tonight's fabulous fete?"

"No, I'm just here with Lexie," he admitted. "We had a date tonight and Mike Farragut just chose the place we were going." Gary laughed as if he had made a joke, but Lexie didn't get it.

"When will they be shooing the reporters out?" Lexie changed the subject.

"Hors d'oeuvres and drinks are being served until eight-thirty," Shari replied. "Dinner won't be until nine. I imagine they'll let the reporters stay until the cocktail hour is over. Of course, I'll be staying for the whole affair."

"Of course," Lexi murmured. Personally she wanted to leave right now. The sight of Rome with the elegant Claudine was tearing her apart.

"You'll never learn anything by standing here, darling," Shari insisted. "All the action is over by the bar. Shall we wander over and help ourselves to the refreshments?"

"Sounds like a plan." Gary was more than willing to tag along. All of this was outside his sphere of experience.

They had to cross the full width of the room to reach the bar. It was the first time in her life that Lexie could ever remember wanting to be a wallflower.

Her nervous stomach could not tolerate the thought of alcohol or food. At her request, the bartender filled a glass for her from the soft drink nozzle and handed it over without comment.

She had barely stepped away when she heard Rome's familiar voice inquire, "What would you like, Claudine?" A tremor of awareness quaked through Lexie at how close he stood to her.

A feather-soft voice responded, "Some white wine, *s'il vous plaît*." The English words were spoken with a delightful French accent.

Lexie couldn't help turning to look at them as Rome gave the bartender their order. Her gaze was met by a pair of brown eyes as soft as the voice of their owner. Recognition was instant.

"Ms. Templeton, it is a pleasure to see you again," Claudine Martineau declared. The tone of her voice always seemed to be barely above a whisper, which enhanced her aura of fragility and conveyed the impression of youthful innocence, as chic as she was.

To make matters worse, as far as Lexie was concerned, the words sounded sincere. It was impossible to make a caustic response.

"Thank you, Ms. Martineau." The words were stiff but at least they weren't tinged with sarcasm.

"I enjoyed so much the tour of your city the other day," the brunette continued. "Rome had told me many things about it." At the moment, Rome returned to her side and handed her a glass of wine. "It was all that you said it would be, *chéri*," Claudine told him

"I'm glad." The smile disappeared from his mouth when he looked at Lexie, all expression leaving his face. "How are you, Ms. Templeton?"

The question was so impersonal, so distant, that she wanted to scream. More than that, she wanted to take the wine glass from Claudine and spill the contents all over her designer gown. She wanted to do anything that would dim the petite Frenchwoman's attractiveness in Rome's eyes. But her fingers curled more tightly around her own glass as she held her temper.

"Fine, thank you, Mr. Lockwood." The heat of her frustration simmered in her voice.

Gary politely made his way through the crowd to reach Lexie. "Whew, I almost lost you," he laughed self-consciously. "Did you get your drink?"

"Yes."

"Good. I—" He saw Rome standing there and seemed to redden. "Hello, Mr. Lockwood."

"Hello. You have the advantage on me. I'm afraid I don't know your name." Rome's black gaze flicked to Lexie, silently demanding an introduction.

"This is Gary Dunbar." She smiled tightly. "Mr. Lockwood you know, and this is Mademoiselle Claudine Martineau, Edmond Martineau's daughter."

"It is a pleasure, *m' sieu*." Claudine offered Gary her hand.

"The pleasure is all mine, *mam'selle*." He awkwardly attempted to kiss the back of her hand in the continental fashion.

He was so plainly fascinated and awed by the stunning French female that he was falling all over himself trying to be suave. Lexie felt sorry for him, and also defensive, especially when she saw the derisive look Rome gave him.

"You two are here together tonight, no?" Claudine asked, wide-eyed.

Lexie began to realize what allure the woman's soft tone had. It invited a person to lean closer. Lexie doubted that there was a man in the room who didn't enjoy that.

"No—that is, yes, we came together," Gary admitted.

"Gary is also a reporter?" Claudine glanced at Lexie for confirmation.

"Yes," she nodded, aware of Rome's black gaze watching her and trying to avoid it.

"It is convenient that he works for your newspaper," the woman commented.

"We work for the same newspaper, it's hardly mine," Lexie said, not wanting to convey the impression that she was anything more than a reporter.

"It must be fascinating work," Claudine insisted. "It is certain that you meet many interesting people."

"I do," Gary assured her. "I enjoy my work tremendously. I would like to travel more than I do, see more of the world, but you can't have everything."

"Ah, yes, travel," Claudine nodded. "Men seem to be born with a wish to travel. Me, I am a 'keep-at-home.' "

"Stay-at-home," Rome corrected her.

Claudine laughed at her own mistake. It reminded Lexie of the soft tinkling of silver bells, and Gary seemed enraptured by it. There was warmth in Rome's look, too, when he gazed at the petite Frenchwoman. The delicate laugh irritated Lexie.

"Rome knows me so well!" Claudine smiled. "He even knows what I mean when it isn't what I say."

"Lexie mentioned that your families are very close," Gary remarked.

"*C'est vrai.* It is true. Rome's papa and mine are very close, like brothers," she explained. A light danced in her eyes as she peeked up at Rome through naturally long lashes. "Rome has known me since I was an *enfant.*"

"Thank heavens, you aren't an infant anymore," he mocked.

"When I was younger, I had a—how do you say it—a crush on Rome," confided Claudine, smiling at him. "I followed him around like a puppy dog."

"And now?" Shari Sullivan spoke from behind Lexie, having unobtrusively joined the group. "Have you managed to snare Rome Lockwood?"

"*Pardon?* Snare?" Claudine repeated the word with a puzzled look.

Shari rephrased the question. "Is there a romance between the two of you?"

Lexie wanted to push her way out of the group before Claudine answered, but she was hemmed in to the point where it was impossible. She somehow managed to control the almost overwhelming sensation of panic.

"Claudine, may I introduce Shari Sullivan," Rome interrupted before his companion could respond to the nosy question. "She has a society column."

"For the same newspaper as Ms. Templeton?" Claudine asked.

"Yes," Shari admitted.

"There will be no one left to print the newspaper," Claudine joked. "Are you all here tonight?"

"Not quite," Shari said dryly, aware of Rome's ploy.

"As I was—"

"To answer your previous question, Ms. Sullivan,"

Rome said smoothly, "Claudine and I are"—his pause seemed deliberate—"just good friends."

"*Oui*," Claudine agreed with a bright smile. "We are good friends."

Lexie felt sick. Good friends. Seeing them together, looking into each other's eyes, she could well imagine that they were a lot more than that.

"I am sure you regret your visit is such a short one," Shari was saying. "I heard you're leaving the day after tomorrow. You've hardly had time to see your friend, what with the tour of Boston and the reception tonight."

"The dinner tonight is necessary in order to meet everyone." Claudine didn't seem unhappy about it. "Tomorrow we'll have a quiet evening with just our two families." A manicured hand touched Rome's sleeve as Claudine glanced beyond them through the throng of people. "Look, *chéri*. Papa is about to propose a toast. Your mama and papa are there, too. Perhaps we should join them."

Rome nodded, encompassing them all in a look. "Excuse us, please."

As he shouldered a path through the crowd, protectively drawing the petite Frenchwoman along with him, Lexie didn't feel any less nervous. More than anything she wanted to sit down. Her knees had begun to tremble until she wondered how much longer they would support her.

"Come on." Shari's gaze hadn't left the departing couple and her expression hardened with purpose. "Let's find out what's going on. I want a closer look."

As she started forward, Gary automatically followed. Lexie was caught in the middle and swept along with them. When she was able to stop, she found herself on the inner ring of a semicircle around the host family and their guests of honor. Edmond Martineau raised his glass in a toast.

"To my friends, the Lockwoods. May our visits be more frequent in future." As he sipped from his glass, others did likewise.

There was a hush in the room while everyone, the reporters especially, waited for another announcement. It was several seconds before they began to realize nothing more was forthcoming.

A reporter from a competitive newspaper spoke up. "Excuse me. Were the Lockwoods the only reason for your visiting the United States at this time, Mr. Martineau?"

With a stricken look, Lexie glanced at Rome. What if the information he'd given her was wrong? Mike Farragut had said he'd confirmed it, but—

"Perhaps . . ." Edmond Martineau paused, drawing Lexie's gaze. His eyes twinkled brightly back at her. "Perhaps you should put the question to Ms. Templeton." An amused murmur ran through the crowd. "She claims to know a great deal about my reasons for coming to your country."

She swallowed once and tried to find her voice. "Isn't it true that when you leave here Sunday, you will be flying to Washington, D.C.?"

Edmond Martineau glanced around the room and lifted his hand in a Gallic gesture. "How can I, a Frenchman, deny a beautiful lady anything? Yes, I can confirm what she says. It is true that I fly to Washington where I will meet with members of your State Department."

Rome hadn't lied to her. Her gaze swung back to him in relief, but he was looking at her with contempt. The statement by Martineau prompted a flurry of questions from the other reporters. As they rushed forward to vie for his attention, Lexie allowed them to close around her and force her into the background. She felt sick and cold, and must have looked it. Gary frowned at her with concern.

"Are you all right, Lexie?"

"No." She didn't lie. "I don't feel very well, Gary. Would you mind taking me home?"

"No, I don't mind," he assured her and curved an arm around her waist to escort her out of the room.

"I'm sorry to spoil the evening this way," she said once they were in the car.

"Hey, it's all right," he shrugged. "I understand."

"I'll get over it." Lexie meant Rome, and knew it wasn't going to be easy.

Saturday night the phone rang while Lexie was in the bathtub. Her first inclination was to let it ring, but common sense drove her out of the bubbly water. It might be an important call. She quickly wrapped a bath towel around her as she hurried into the living room.

"Hello." Her voice sounded strained even to her own ears.

"Hi, could I speak to Carla?" a bright female voice asked.

"You must have the wrong number. There isn't anyone here by that name," Lexie sighed.

"Are you sure? This is the number she gave me."

"Well, it's the wrong one."

"Is this—" the voice reeled off a number that was one digit off from Lexie's own.

"No."

"Sorry."

The line clicked dead.

Retracing her watery trail to the bathroom, Lexie found the bubbles had all dissipated and the bathwater was tepid. Her skin was already dry so there was little need for the towel wrapped around her. She unwound it and slipped on her quilted robe, using the towel to mop up her wet footprints from the floor.

Hanging the damp towel on a rack, she wandered

into the small living room. The apartment seemed so silent and empty. Ginger was out with Bob again and Lexie was alone. It wasn't a night when she wanted to be alone. But then was any night? She wouldn't admit the real reason. She felt so empty and lonely. She picked up a book and put it back down.

There was a knock at the apartment door. Lexie stared at it, wondering who would be visiting at this late hour. Not for the first time she wished the door had a peephole. She slipped the heavy security chain into place and opened the door the few inches the chain permitted.

"Hello, Lexie." Rome stood outside, resplendent in black-tie evening wear.

"What are you doing here?" she breathed. She had the oddest feeling that he would vanish any second. But he didn't. He just stood there.

There was a trace of his old teasing mockery when he spoke. "I thought it was obvious. May I come in?"

"No." Her answer was abrupt as she recovered from her initial surprise. "I don't want to see you."

"I want to talk to you, Lexie."

"I think I've heard that line before."

His mouth straightened. "I give you my word, Lexie. We'll talk. That's all."

She started to close the door without answering him, but his hand slipped into the opening to stop her. Maybe crushing his fingers wouldn't be such a good idea, she thought. On the other hand, *I don't want to see you* meant just that.

"Shut the door if you want," Rome told her. "I can talk loudly enough for you to hear me, even through a closed door. But either way, Lexie, you're going to listen to me."

He removed his hand from the door. Lexie closed it, hesitated, then slipped off the chain. Rome was capable of doing exactly what he said, and she didn't want that type of discussion carried on in a public hallway. She opened the door for him to enter and walked away.

"I thought you were giving a big important party for the Martineaus tonight," she commented.

"I'm not. My parents are." At her pointed glance at his formal attire, Rome added, "I put in an appearance and left."

"Why are you here?" Lexi's nerves were as charged as a high-voltage wire. They stood in the center of the small room, facing each other.

"I saw the article in this morning's paper."

"Did you come to congratulate me? Or to collect your due?" she snapped. "I should've known you had some devious reason for telling me. You gave me a scoop and you expect me to be suitably grateful. Well, I'm sorry but your word wasn't good enough. We confirmed the information through other sources. I don't owe you anything."

"I didn't say you did."

"So why are you here? Spiffy cummerbund, by the way. You look great," she said sarcastically.

"We have to talk," he declared again.

"Look, Rome, I told you I didn't want to become involved with you. I don't even want to see you." Which was a lie. She was drinking in the sight of him, so formidably male.

"Oh, hell," he sighed. "But I've discovered that I want to see you again, Lexie, while you claim that you don't want to see me. How do you suppose I can solve that?"

"I don't know." Lexie turned away in agitation. "That's your problem, not mine."

"Can't we compromise?"

"Can't I change my mind, is what you mean," she retorted. "Why don't you go back to your parents' party? I'm sure Claudine can come up with a solution."

"Were you jealous?" Rome asked blandly. "I hope so. I hope you were miserable."

Lexie whirled to face him. "Is that why you singled Mac and me out from all the others at the airport? Why you invited us along on the tour? So I'd have to watch you with her?"

"I had so many reasons for inviting you along that I doubt if I can remember them all." There was a troubled look in his dark eyes and Lexie's breath caught at his answer. "When I saw you standing there with all those other reporters, I knew I had to be near you again. And I was willing to use whatever means I had at hand to accomplish it—even if it included trading on my parents' friendship with Edmond Martineau. Does that give you an idea of the way I feel about you?"

"Don't." She didn't want to hear any more. She was much too susceptible.

"I've barely thought of anything else but you since you walked out of my apartment," Rome told her. "I've picked up the phone a hundred times to call you, but you looked so damned vulnerable when you begged me to leave you alone."

"Why didn't you?" Lexie moaned.

Rome ignored that. "So, at the airport, when I had the chance to single you out, I did. I wanted you to see that you were someone special to me, but I didn't even get a thank-you for it. I paid a lot of attention to Claudine, hoping you would be jealous."

"Very grown-up of you."

He let out a long breath. "Do I get points for honesty?"

"Maybe."

"I can't help how I feel about you, Lexie. Anyway, when I finally got you alone that night, the first thing out of your mouth was politics—reporting."

"What did you expect me to say?" she cried.

"Anything but that," he retorted. "So I gave you the information you wanted, partly out of anger because you said it was the only reason you were there, partly out of selfishness because I wanted to show you again that you were special—and yes, partly because I wanted you to feel grateful to me. What did I get in return? Your doubts. Your questions. You still didn't trust me."

"Is it any wonder," Lexie protested, "considering the kind of man you are?"

His mouth thinned in exasperation. "Are we back to my bad-boy reputation again?"

"Looks that way, doesn't it."

"Has it ever occurred to you that I might be looking for the right woman?"

"You'll never find her."

"Maybe I have," he challenged.

"For men like you, there never is a right one. And I don't want to be part of a plurality in any man's life."

"You haven't listened to anything I've said," Rome sighed, and let his hands settle on her shoulders to knead the taut muscles. "I want to see you again and go on seeing you. I don't know where you got these ideas about me, but I want to show you they aren't true."

He was quite capable of persuading her. His voice, his touch, his nearness were all working on her fragile defenses. "Forget it," Lexi continued to hold out. "We're very different. I don't fit in your social circle. I can't afford the clothes, for one thing."

"You looked better than ninety-nine per cent of the women there tonight," he said patiently.

"And the other one per cent would be Claudine, who looks better than anybody." She couldn't resist the jab.

"Lexie . . ."

"I don't even like those people anyway," she said stubbornly.

"Snob. You don't know them."

"I know you. Sort of. Look at you, Rome. You're vichyssoise and I'm split-pea soup."

"Not split-pea soup," Rome smiled. "Spicy minestrone, maybe, but not split pea. Besides, what is vichyssoise? Nothing but cold potato soup."

"You don't understand," argued Lexie.

"Why don't you explain it to me?" He glanced behind her to the tiny kitchen. "Do you have any coffee on?"

"No."

"Why don't you make some and we'll sit down and talk about the way we're different," he suggested, turning her around and giving her a little push toward the kitchen.

"It isn't a difference I can explain." Mechanically Lexie went about doing what she was told, filling the coffee maker with water and reaching for the coffee canister. "How can you explain feelings?" The canister was empty and she opened the cupboard door to get the new can of coffee on the top shelf. "They're there. They simply exist." Stretched up on tiptoe, she could barely reach the can with her fingertips.

"I'll get it."

Rome was beside her, reaching over her head for the can, his tallness enabling him to reach it easily. As he lifted it down, his other hand slid in a more or less automatic caress down her spine to the small of her back, his touch sensually familiar.

"Whoa," he said under his breath. "You don't have any clothes on under that robe, do you? Don't tempt me, Lexie—"

"You know, that was about the last thing on my mind," she snapped. "I generally find it easier to take a bath without clothes. It's not as if I was expecting you!"

Rome pulled away from her, setting the coffee can

on the counter. "Okay. You have a point. But you oughta put some clothes on."

She looked down at what she had on. "It's hard to believe that a quilted robe could drive a man wild with desire."

"Oh, Lexie . . . do I have to explain?"

She shook her head and left the room. The cream linen pantsuit she had worn that day was still lying on her bed, along with a print blouse. Stubbornly she avoided it, going into her closet to take an old pair of Levis off the hook and a shapeless gray T-shirt, to point out with her choice of clothes, another of their differences.

"Where are the cups?" Rome asked when she retuned.

"In the cabinet to your left." She walked into the kitchen.

His dark gaze took in her attire. "What are you trying to prove now, Lexie? That I'm too old for you?" he chuckled. "What is there? Eleven years between us?"

"Yes," she said.

"Eleven years," he mused. "No big deal."

"I know I'm not a big deal to you, that's for sure."

He shook his head. "Actually, you are. I'm in love with you." His seriously gentle tone alarmed her. "I don't know if it was a case of love at first sight. Maybe it was the second, third, or fourth. But I love you, Lexie."

"No!" Her heart constricted painfully.

"What do I have to do to convince you I'm sincere?" Rome's expression was intent and concerned. "Do you want me to get down on one knee and propose? I'm prepared to do that too."

From his jacket pocket he took out a ring box and snapped it open. A diamond solitaire winked at Lexie, bright and sparkling, a rainbow of colors, flashing in the overhead light.

"Okay," she said warily, "this can't be happening."

"I assure you it's the real thing," he said with teasing gentleness.

"I can see that." Her voice trembled. "But I hardly know you. And you're handing me an engagement ring? How many others have tried it on?"

He seemed annoyed that his grand gesture hadn't gone over too well. "You can check with anyone you like—gossip columns, social register, my old girlfriends, my parents. You'll find that I never asked any woman to marry me."

"That may be," she said slowly. "But that doesn't change the fact that we have had exactly two dates, neither of which were particularly successful. You don't build a lifetime on a beginning like that." She raked a hand through her hair. "What am I saying? This is just so unreal. Put that thing away, please. I think the little sparkly lights it makes are doing something to my brain."

He snapped the ring box shut and replaced it in his jacket pocket. "Sorry. I just thought—"

"What were you thinking when you bought that? I really am curious, Rome."

"That I loved you," he said simply. "Do you want me to?"

She just gaped at him. For a moment, she felt as if she were standing outside herself, looking at this scene rather than being in it. Her, in grubby T-shirt and jeans. Him, in evening wear. Talking about love and working up to another spectacular quarrel, most likely. Lexie shook her head to clear it.

"Does that mean no?" Rome asked.

Lexie hesitated. "I can't take your ring. This is happening too fast. Way too fast."

"Then let's take it slow. I'll wait as long as you like."

"Okay. Maybe we could, uh, go somewhere for starters. Somewhere peaceful."

"No more parties. I don't want that creepy columnist slithering up behind me and asking a lot of questions. And as for Jimmy Olsen, cub reporter—"

"Shari and Gary, respectively," Lexie said.

"I assume you're not serious about him."

"Ah, no. I'm not."

Rome managed a slight smile. "Good. Just give me a chance to prove that what I said is true. Look, we really got off on the wrong foot when I walked into the office and dared you to ask me out."

"Ever done that before?"

He shook his head. "No. At first I just wanted to see who was ruining my reputation, but the second I saw you I wanted to go out with you. I was surprised when you agreed to it, especially on my terms. In retrospect, it was a dumb idea. And when you came over to my place for dinner, I got a little carried away."

"You got a lot carried away," she said, "and so did I, come to think of it." She gave him a guilty smile, re-membering just how much pleasure they'd given each other.

He reached out to her then and she didn't even feel like resisting. He buried his face in the silken tangle of her hair. "Come with me tomorrow," he said softly. "We can drive to Cape Cod late in the afternoon. My parents have a place there. We can . . ."

"Maybe not," said Lexie. "That might be too peace-ful." The truth was that she didn't trust herself to be alone with him.

"It isn't what you're thinking. My parents will be there. They're driving down tomorrow after the Martineaus leave. It's all going to be perfectly respectable."

"Oh." Her voice was small as he swept aside her reason for objecting. "Your mother," Lexie hesitated, remembering the reaction at the airport. "I don't think she likes me."

"What makes you think that?" Rome frowned.

"She knows who I am—I mean, she knows the things I said about you in Shari's column."

"Yes," he agreed with a nod.

"She was the reason you came to see me at the newspaper. She was upset by them."

"Well, she did mention the column once or twice," Rome admitted. "But believe me, she doesn't dislike you."

"She gave me a very odd look at the airport," Lexie insisted.

"I think her womanly intuition has already warned her about the way I feel toward you. She was probably taking a good look at her future daughter-in-law."

"Maybe." She qualified his statement.

"As far as I'm concerned, there are no maybes about it."

"You can say that now." Lexie was determined to be the voice of reason, even if it drove her crazy.

"You haven't given me your answer about tomorrow," Rome reminded her.

Lexie hesitated, then asked. "What time should I be ready?" Her foolish heart did a somersault when he smiled at her.

"Three o'clock."

A smoldering light suddenly burned in his eyes and the smile faded from his face. "Am I allowed to touch you at all, Lexie?"

"You're touching me right now," she answered uneasily. "This is called a hug."

"You know what I mean," he whispered.

She glanced at his well-shaped mouth, knowing the sensual rapture she would find in his kiss. She ached to feel it. And a kiss was only a kiss. But an inner sense of doubt drove her to deny what both of them ultimately wanted.

"Not that way. Not yet."

Held so closely to him, Lexie felt his muscles tense. Yet Rome didn't argue as he slowly withdrew his arms from around her. The smile he gave her showed the strain of control.

"I'll be here at three tomorrow," he promised, and she nodded in agreement. Rome gave her another long look. "Good night, Lexie."

He walked past her into the living room to the door. His hand was on the doorknob. In another second he would be gone.

"No," Lexie said softly.

Rome turned and she went into his arms. Hungrily they kissed, the fire of their passionate love leaping into full flame. It would have raged into an inferno, but Rome pulled her arms from around his neck and reluctantly dragged his mouth from hers.

"I want you, Lexie," he told her. "But I want you without doubts. I won't settle for less." It was a warning, accompanied by a hard, sure kiss. "Tomorrow at three," he said, pushing her away from him and opening the door.

"I'll be waiting."

The weekend with Rome was more perfect than Lexie had dreamed it could be. After an initial feeling of self-consciousness around his parents, Lexie relaxed and just let herself enjoy their company. They treated her like one of the family without ever commenting on her relationship with Rome.

They did practically everything as a group—boating, cooking, walking along the beach, although she and Rome

did steal a few delicious moments alone. Lexie found
herself covertly studying his parents now and then, trying to figure out if they were truly happy. There seemed
to be a genuinely warm affection between them, but
she couldn't be sure.

Cape Cod, as always, was beautiful. On Lexie's previous visits she had been part of the thick stream of summer visitors, which meant crowded motels, chain
restaurants, and endless traffic. With Rome she saw a
different view.

The large but cozy Lockwood cottage was on a winding road in a quiet residential area where rambler roses
grew along the lanes. There were miles of silver-gilt
beaches and breezes carried the salt tang of the ocean.
Time seemed to stand still on that leisurely weekend,
blessed by the magic of the sun and the sea—and Rome's
company.

The following week she saw him often, having lunch
with him one day and dinner with him the next. She realized he was courting her in an endearingly old-fashioned way.

On Saturday they were to have spent the entire day
together until Mike Farragut called at the crack of dawn
with an assignment for Lexie. It wasn't supposed to take
long, so she'd called Rome and postponed their date
until later that morning.

Assignment completed, Lexie walked briskly from
her parked car to her apartment building. She had just
enough time to change her clothes and do a makeup
check before he came.

Sweeping into the apartment on the airy cloud she
had been traveling on, she glimpsed her roommate's pale
blond hair as she turned to close the door. "Hi, Ginger!
Why are you still here? I thought it was a Bob day."

Miracle of miracles, she had even begun to look

kindly on Bob. Maybe love did mellow a person, Lexie thought as the door clicked shut.

"Not yet," Ginger answered.

"Hello, Sunshine," another, very familiar voice said to Lexie.

When she turned she saw the man rising to meet her. Tall and agelessly handsome, he smiled, carving deep grooves in his tanned face. His red hair was darker than hers and going gray, but the vivid blue of his eyes was identical to hers.

Her lips were dry, threatening to crack when she smiled. "Hello, Dad," Lexie returned his greeting and forced herself to cross the room to receive the customary kiss and bear hug.

"It's good to see you again," Clark Templeton declared. "I've missed you."

Lexie skipped the rote response that he seemed to be expecting. "Guess you met my roommate."

"Ginger?" Her father beamed at the blonde, who blushed under his look and Lexie knew that he had made another conquest. "I certainly have. How come you never mentioned you were sharing your apartment with a gorgeous girl like this?"

Careful, Ginger, Lexie wanted to warn. *Don't listen to his lines.* Not that Ginger would pay the slightest attention to her.

Lexie disentangled herself from his arms but he kept hold of her hand. She knew they made a striking father-daughter combination. She had been told that often enough when she was growing up.

"This really is a surprise," she declared. "Why didn't you let me know you were coming?"

"Then it wouldn't have been a surprise," he reasoned with a chuckle.

"When did you arrive?"

"We caught a very early flight this morning and go[ ] in a little while ago."

"We?" Lexie repeated. "Did Mary-Anne come with you?"

There was only the slightest flicker of discomfort in his expression but Clark Templeton covered it well. "It['] been longer than I thought. Mary-Anne and I broke up months ago."

"But you e-mailed me a few weeks back. You didn['t] mention Mary-Anne so I assumed things were still the same between you," she said evenly, not all that surprised by the news. "Who is the new 'we'?"

Her father didn't seem to notice the false brightness of her tone. "Teresa Hall. She's part of the reason I flew here to see you. I want you to meet her, Sunshine. I've asked her to marry me and she's accepted."

"Well, well. Congratulations," Lexie offered. "When['] the happy day?"

"We haven't set a date yet. I wanted you to meet her. After all, she is going to be your stepmother. You'll like her. I know you will."

"Of course," she agreed.

"I thought we could all have dinner tonight—you me, and Teresa. It'll give the two of you a chance to get acquainted."

"I'd love to, Dad, but I already have plans for tonight," Lexie explained with pretended regret.

"Are you going to a party or what?" He glanced from Lexi to Ginger, as if asking her roommate for the answer.

"Lexie has a date," Ginger explained helpfully.

"No problem," her father declared. "Bring your date along too. We'll make it a foursome."

Great. Just great, Lexie thought. Double dating with dad. That was about the last thing she wanted to do. " [I] don't know," she stalled. "I'll have to ask him."

"You do that," he agreed. "I'd like to meet him and see what kind of guy you're dating."

"You'd like him, Dad," Lexie said with a hint of irony in her voice that was entirely lost on her self-absorbed father and the adoring Ginger. "He's a lot like you."

"Is he now?" He looked delighted, smiling broadly as if he had received the highest possible compliment. "Then I definitely want to meet him."

"I'll have to ask," she said again.

"I'm counting on seeing you tonight and so is Teresa. I know you'll do your best to make it. In the meantime"—he reached into his pocket—"I want you to go and buy yourself a new dress. Something blue to match your beautiful eyes." He pressed some bills into her hand.

"No, Dad," Lexie tried to refuse.

"Take it," her father insisted. "A working girl can't always afford a new dress. Consider it a birthday present from me. Tonight's going to be a celebration and I want you to look your best!"

Her fingers curled around the money in her palm as she died a little inside. "Okay," she agreed.

"It's time I was going back to the hotel before Teresa thinks I've forgotten her," he joked.

After making arrangements with Lexie for her to call once she'd talked to Rome, her father left with his usual charming disregard for the way he had disrupted her life.

"Honestly, Lexie, I don't see why you said you couldn't get along with your father!" Ginger declared. "He's an absolute doll! I wish my father was like him."

"Be careful what you wish for," Lexie said dryly.

"Are you going to call Rome?" At Lexie's nod, Ginger asked, "Don't talk too long, okay? The battery on my cell phone died. I forgot to recharge it."

Typical. Lexie said nothing, waiting for the rest.

"I haven't heard from Bob yet," Ginger continued. "If he doesn't call me pretty soon, I'm going over to his place and find out what's wrong."

Lexie absently heard the closing of a bedroom door and turned to find that Ginger had left the room. She stared at the unwanted money in her hand, then at the telephone.

CHAPTER NINE

After two rings, the phone was answered and Lexie recognized Rome's voice on the other end of the line. "Hello, Rome. It's me, Lexie."

"That didn't take long." The warmth in his voice reached across the distance to her. "When do you want me to pick you up?"

She hesitated. "Something has come up."

"Not another assignment, I hope."

"No, it isn't that. My . . . my father has flown in from California." Her fingers curled into a fist, wadding the money in her hand.

"Okay, I can deal with that," Rome said. "I mean, I'd like to meet him. Perhaps the three of us could have dinner together this evening."

"No. That is . . ." The first tear slipped from her lashes and her throat constricted.

"Lexie, what's wrong? Don't you want me to meet your father?" Rome sounded puzzled.

"No—I mean yes." Lexie realized she wasn't making any sense.

"What's the matter?"

"You see, my father's getting married. He's brough❚ his fiancée along," she explained.

"Are you upset by the idea of your father marrying? Is that it?" Rome questioned.

"Not really. Actually, my father invited you to dinner tonight, but since it's going to be in the way of a celebration, I wasn't sure if you'd want to come." At first she had wanted to keep the two men apart, but now she realized that she would be able to show Rome what she hadn't been able to explain in words.

"You met my family, Lexie," he reminded her. "I have an obligation to meet yours. That includes your father and prospective stepmother."

"Yes, of course," she agreed, somewhat numbly. Was it just her or was it really that easy for people to fall in love, get engaged and get married? Hey, seemed like some people could do it just like that. What was the trendy term for it? *Serial monogamy.* The thought depressed her.

"Are you spending the afternoon with them or are our plans still on?"

Lexie wiped a tear from her lip. "Daddy wants me to buy a new dress for tonight." She didn't want to spend the rest of the day with Rome, so she clung to the excuse her father had unknowingly given her.

Rome caught the tremor in her voice. "You're upset," he accused. "The idea of your father getting married again does bother you. I'll come over and we'll talk about it."

"No, please," she said. "It's all right."

"Lexie, are you sure?"

"I'd rather be alone this afternoon," she admitted. "I'll work it out."

"I'll be here all afternoon. If you want me, just call."

"I will," Lexie promised. "About dinner—we're supposed to meet my father at his hotel at seven-thirty."

"I'll pick you up at seven."

"See you then, Rome. Bye."

Hanging up the phone, Lexie slipped into her own room and cried softly so that her roommate wouldn't hear her. She didn't want to make the explanations that nobody had ever understood. Later, the closing of the front door signaling Ginger's departure acted as a signal to shut off the flow of tears. At last Lexie washed her face and splashed cold water on her swollen eyes.

With her father's money, she went out and bought a new blue dress, per his suggestion. It was beautiful. The sales associate raved over the combination of Lexie's flame-colored hair and the unusual blue of the material. Lexie took no pleasure in it. She was fulfilling a duty as she had done so many times in the past. This time the color of the dress happened to match her mood, a deep, dark blue.

Picking out the dress took quite a while and it was several hours before Lexie returned to the apartment to walk lethargically to her door. The evening stretched ominously before her like a long tunnel with no light at the end. Lexie walked on blindly because it was what she had to do.

Tucking the dress bag under her arm, she unlocked the door and pushed it open. A red-eyed Ginger glanced up, sniffling once before resuming the task Lexie had interrupted.

Oh, no. Not more drama. Between her and Ginger, they were crying enough tears to flood the Charles River. But Lexie supposed that couldn't be helped. All part of being a modern girl.

She stared blankly at the suitcase at Ginger's feet and the one her roommate was locking.

"I'm glad you're back, Lexie," Ginger declared in a voice that threatened to break into a sob at any moment. "I didn't want to leave without saying goodbye."

"Huh?"

"I'm going home." Ginger set her suitcase on the floor with others.

Lexie closed the door and leaned against it, bewildered. "What's happened?" she asked. "What do you mean?"

"When . . . when Bob didn't call me and I couldn't get any answer, I . . . went over to his place." Her roommate looked so forlorn, so shattered. "Oh, Lexie," she broke into a sob, "he had another girl with him!"

"Ginger, no," Lexie protested sympathetically, feeling the pain as if it was her own.

"Yes. He . . . told me to get lost. You were right, Lexie," Ginger hiccupped. "Bob never loved me—he told me so. In front of her." She hung her head, letting her pale blond hair fall to the side. "So I'm going home. These big city guys just think they can do whatever they want."

"It's not the city, Ginger," Lexie murmured, scarcely knowing what to say that might comfort her. "I mean, men are the same everywhere. Some are bad, and some are good."

Ginger shook her head obstinately, as if convinced that Boston, and only Boston, was a hotbed for losers, jerks, and commitment-phobes. "Whatever. I'm leaving."

"I'm . . . sorry," Lexie offered, knowing how inadequate it sounded.

"You tried to warn me about Bob, but I wouldn't listen. I thought I knew it all." There was a wealth of youthful bitterness in the declaration. "Anyway, I'm going home where I belong—where a guy still treats a girl with some respect." She struggled to compose herself. "A cab is coming to take me to the bus station. I called my parents and they're expecting me."

"Ginger, are you sure this is what you want to do?"

"Yes." The answer was decisive. Then Ginger remembered something. "I forgot—there's an envelope in your bedroom with a letter telling you what happened because I wasn't sure I would see you before I left. My share of the rent is in it too."

"You'd . . ." Lexie started to protest.

"It's the least I could do. With the first of the month coming up, I didn't want to put you in a bind and you may not find someone right away that you'll want to share the apartment with. Of course"—Ginger gave her a brave but teary smile—"the way things are going with you and Rome, you may not be wanting the apartment yourself."

"Don't be too sure," Lexie sighed.

"I don't care what you tell them at the newspaper on Monday," Ginger rushed on. "You can tell them the truth if you like. It doesn't matter." A horn tooted outside. "There's my cab."

Lexie set the bag with her blue dress aside. She'd forgotten that she was holding it. "I'll help you with the luggage."

The phone was ringing when Lexie returned to the apartment from seeing Ginger off amidst tears and hugs and promises to keep in touch. It was Rome.

"Are you all right, Lexie?" he asked.

"Yes, I'm fine," she lied. "I was just going to get in the tub to get ready for tonight."

Rome didn't sound satisfied with her answer but he accepted it. "I'll see you at seven."

He arrived a few minutes early, inspecting her closely, but Lexie was acting out a part she had rehearsed well, and her mask was firmly in place.

"You look a little pale," was all he said.

"Nerves," Lexie smiled away the reason. "I'm a little anxious about this evening." She left Rome to draw his own conclusion from that.

Her father was waiting in the hotel lobby when they arrived. One look at the woman with him and Lexie's suspicions were confirmed. Teresa Hall was Lexie's age, a tawny-haired creature with a gorgeous California tan.

Lexie was prepared for it. Her father's girlfriends had been getting younger as she got older. As the introductions were made, she stole a glance at Rome. If he was surprised by how young her father's fiancée was, he didn't show it.

Clark Templeton had chosen the restaurant that Lexie had taken Rome to that first time. "I was told it was one of the best in the city," he said.

"It is," Rome agreed and sent Lexie a twinkling look of remembrance, but when she said nothing, neither did he.

"I didn't have any problem getting a reservation," her father said, as if he felt he should have. "But then, I did call early."

Rome suggested that they all ride in his car—even though her father had rented one—explaining that he was more familiar with the city than Clark. Her father readily agreed.

On the drive to the restaurant, Lexi felt sick at the quiet murmur of voices from the backseat where her father and his fiancée sat. Rome reached over and held her hand but she found no comfort in his touch.

Following the other couple into the restaurant, Lexie saw the maitre d' look at her father first and then Teresa. Then he looked at Rome and finally saw Lexie, remembering her from the previous time.

"A reservation for four for Templeton," the maitre d' said before her father had an opportunity.

"Yes." Clark Templeton was plainly stunned. "How did you know?"

"Lexie and I have been here before," Rome explained. "As a matter of fact, on our very first date."

"What a coincidence!" her father declared. "It's almost prophetic that I chose this place, isn't it?"

Remembering how disastrous the previous time had been, Lexie thought that it probably was, but she offered no comment. They were shown to their table and ordered drinks. Although she said little, Lexie made a show of entering into the spirit of the evening, smiling and drinking to the toasts her father proposed.

During the meal, Rome made a reference to their weekend visit to Cape Cod. Her father smiled and shot a teasing glance at Lexie.

"Did you go boating?" he asked.

"Yes." It was natural to return his smile. "And we didn't sink. How about that."

"Clark loves boats," Teresa spoke up, sending an adoring look at the man whose ring she wore. "He has a cruiser at the local marina and we spend almost every weekend out on the water."

Lexie had only to close her eyes to picture her father in white ducks with a yachting cap on his head. He would look like an ad for men's cologne, she knew, with his face to the salt spray and the sun glinting on the ocean waves.

Clark reached for his fiancée's hand, carrying her fingertips to his lips. "Teresa loves the water as much as I do."

Lexie wanted to gag. As far as she was concerned, Teresa could jump overboard whenever she liked.

"It's one of the many things we have in common," her father blathered on. "We both love to snorkel and go deep-sea fishing. Two weeks ago she landed a shark. I'm having it mounted for her to hang in our den. She's quite a girl, my Mary-Anne."

"Her name is Teresa," Lexie said quietly and smiled at the young woman, who gave her an uncertain look. "You'll have to forgive my father—he has trouble with names. He remembers them but he puts them with the wrong faces. I've learned to answer to anything."

Neither her father nor Teresa seemed embarrassed by his error, although Lexie felt Rome's quizzical look. It had obviously happened before.

"It's all right," Teresa exclaimed, giving Clark a dopey, loving smile. "I know I've had a lot of competition, but all those others are in the past now."

Honey, you ain't seen nothing' yet, Lexie thought, but she just smiled and murmured some suitable response. She had wanted Rome to meet her father and understand her feelings. But when had understanding ever changed anything?

"Talking about boating," her father continued brightly, "we had a terrible time with Lexie when she was a kid. She used to get seasick at the sight of water. Fortunately, she outgrew it." He laughed. "Remember the time Angela took you to Disneyland and you got sick on the Jungle Cruise?"

"That was Beth," she corrected and felt a lump rising in her throat. "Angela took me to the museums."

"Was it Angela? I thought it was Doreen," he said, frowning.

"No, Doreen liked sports," Lexie reminded him and took a sip of wine to try to wash down the lump in her throat.

"Is that right?" Her father sounded skeptical. "I always thought . . . oh, well, it doesn't matter. As Teresa said, it's all in the past." *But the past has a way of repeating itself,* Lexie thought. "But it certainly was a wonderful day when Lexie stopped being seasick," he reiterated.

A comment seemed to be expected from Rome and he made it. "I'm sure it was." As if sensing the need to change the subject, he picked up the bottle and offered, "More wine?"

But Lexie had had enough—enough wine, enough talk, enough of everything. All that remained was a desperate need to escape. There had been nothing to gain by enduring this evening. She realized that now. She had lost all that mattered to her before it started.

But it was difficult to lose something that had never been hers, even if she had pretended it was possible for a little while. She knew better now. Her father's visit was actually opportune, because she needed to be reminded of a few unpleasant facts of life.

Lexie pushed her chair from the table and rose, trying to mask her haste with an air of nonchalance. "Would you excuse me, please?" she asked, knowing they would all assume she was going to the powder room.

Rome half rose from his chair, his eyes sharp and questioning, but she touched his shoulder lightly as if to assure him that everything was all right.

She paused at the maitre d's desk, glancing back to make sure she couldn't be seen from the table.

"Yes, Ms. Templeton. What can I do for you?" the maitre d' inquired solicitously.

"Would you call me a cab, please?"

"A cab, miss?" He raised an eyebrow, his glance straying in the direction of her table.

"Yes, please," Lexie repeated. She guessed his curiosity and tried to allay it. "After I've left, would you take a message to Mr. Lockwood?"

"Of course."

"Tell him that I wasn't feeling well. I have a headache and decided to cab it home and for him not to worry. Tonight's dinner is something of a celebration for the others," she explained, "and I don't want to rain on their parade."

"Of course, Ms. Templeton, I understand," he nodded. "I'll have a cab brought around to the door in a few moments."

"Thank you." And she fervently hoped it would be only a few moments.

True to his word, he returned in a very short time to

tell her a taxi was waiting out front. After giving the driver her address, Lexie leaned back in the seat and closed her eyes against the stabbing rush of pain.

It seemed that they had barely left the restaurant when the cab pulled up to the curb in front of her apartment. Lexie fumbled in a blind haze through her bag for the fare, paid him, and hurried to her empty apartment.

Inside she turned on a light and walked no farther than the lumpy cushions of the sofa. She stared dry-eyed at the ceiling. The mask that had been in place all evening was abandoned. Her features showed the mark of emotional strain.

Love. What good was it and what was it good for? As far as she knew, absolutely nothing. She felt a grim pleasure in not having accepted Rome's engagement ring and sparing herself the torture of returning it.

She vaguely heard the sound of someone in the hall-way but it made no particular impression on her consciousness. The world could have come to an end and Lexie wouldn't have cared. Not that the world was going to cooperate, of course. Her bleak mood made the white walls she looked at seem gray.

There was an imperative knock on the door that made her entire body tense. "Lexie?" Rome called her name and knocked again. She didn't move. "Lexie?" The pounding on the door hammered at her head. "Lexie, I know you're in there. Answer me!"

His commanding voice prodded her into speaking. "Go away!"

"Lexie, unlock this door," Rome ordered.

"Please, just go away and leave me alone," she moaned.

"I'm not going anywhere until I see you. Now open this door!"

"If you don't leave, I'll call the police, I swear!" Lexie

sobbed. "I don't want to see you. Just go away and leave me alone!"

There was silence, the knocking ended, then there was the sound of footsteps echoing down the hallway. Lexie had won. She rolled face down onto the couch and began crying; racking sobs heaved her slender body. Denying him was heartbreak.

Lexie knew she would have to do it again because she knew Rome wouldn't give up. Eventually she would have to explain that she wasn't going to see him anymore, and this time she would be steadfast in her decision.

The clink of metal and the rattle of the doorknob pierced the foglike pain of her consciousness. She gulped back the sobs and lifted her head. Her hair clung to her tear-moistened cheeks and she pushed it away in time to see the door open and Rome walk in.

"How . . ." she mumbled, and struggled upright, a disheveled mess.

"I told you I wasn't leaving until I saw for myself that you were all right," he told her and turned back to the door.

Her blurred vision had a glimpse of a figure behind him. Confused, Lexie saw the flash of something bright in his hand outstretched to the other person. It took her a full second to realize that it was a key ring.

"Thank you, Mrs. McNulty," said Rome. "Sorry to bother you."

Mrs. McNulty, her landlady from downstairs. She had let him in with her passkey. Lexie supposed he would have kicked down the door otherwise.

" 'Tis no trouble," the landlady insisted.

Never mind kicking down the door, she thought dully. Rome Lockwood's charm was enough to persuade a tough Irish landlady who most definitely did not have a heart of gold, to do what he wanted.

"Go away!" Lexie cried, and started forward. "I don't want to see you!"

So desperate was she to have Rome leave that she didn't pay attention to where she was going. Her knee bumped the wooden coffee table and she nearly fell over it. Before she could recover on her own, Rome was there, his hands imprisoning her arms, holding her upright and steadying her.

"I'm sorry," he offered over his shoulder, the apology directed to the landlady. "I know Lexie doesn't want you to see her like this. I'm afraid she had too much to drink tonight."

"I'm not drunk!" How dare he. She had barely tasted her wine.

She tried to twist out of his hold but his strength was too much. With the slightest exertion of pressure he caused her to stagger forward against his chest, as if to prove his claim.

Mrs. McNulty clicked her tongue in reproof. "That's what my late husband used to say, God rest his soul. He never drew a sober breath in his life," she sighed.

Lexie sobbed at the comment. The stupid woman was obviously convinced and Lexie was too overwrought to try and correct the impression. She lowered her head and tried to ignore the exquisite pressure of Rome's touch.

"There's some coffee in the kitchen," Rome said, still talking to the landlady. "I'll get some down her. Maybe that will help."

"It's the best thing," the woman nodded.

"If she needs assistance getting to bed, may I call on you, Mrs. McNulty?" In effect, he was dismissing the woman from the apartment.

"Aren't you the gentleman. And handsomer than your picture in the paper, too. I recognized you right away."

That was why Rome had persuaded her so easily. Lexie was overwhelmed by a fresh wave of despair. Men got away with everything.

"I'll be right downstairs if you need me," Mrs. McNulty was saying.

"Thank you."

Lexie laughed with faint hysteria at the way he had coaxed another woman to do something she shouldn't have done, pulling her strings and directing her to do his bidding. The door closed and he set Lexie firmly down on the couch. As he walked away, Lexie turned to see where he was going. In the kitchen he put some coffee on to reheat.

"I don't need any coffee. I am not drunk," Lexie insisted. Did he think she was?

"I know that." He took a cup from the cabinet. "But you could use some strong hot coffee just the same."

Lexie didn't argue about such a trivial thing. She needed to conserve her strength for what was to come. Her hope of putting off this dreary discussion wasn't going to come true.

CHAPTER TEN

Lexie had dried her eyes by the time Rome entered the living room with the cup of hot coffee. There was a determined set to her chin as she glanced up at him, towering beside the couch, and accepted the cup from his hand.

"Why did you come here?" It was more of a bitter protest than a question.

"Did you expect me to believe that excuse about a headache?" Rome countered.

"It's real. It's a doozy." Her temples were throbbing, a thousand snare drums beating in her head.

"Whatever. I wasn't going to let you run away like that without an explanation."

"Do you need one?" Lexie stared at the shining black surface of the liquid in the cup, wishing she could sink beneath it into oblivion. "Wasn't it obvious?"

"I can imagine how you felt when you met your father's fiancée." He chose his words carefully. "I know it's probably difficult to adjust to the idea of your father remarrying. Evidently he failed to mention the fact that his prospective bride was no older than you."

Lexie just stared at him. His handsome face was grim, a troubled darkness in his eyes lit by a spark of compassion.

"Running out like that didn't solve anything," Rome said, tempering his criticism with a gentle voice. "You still have to face the fact that he's going to marry her."

"No," she mocked.

"You're just making it harder on yourself," he said. "I want to help you but you have to let me."

"Didn't you listen to anything that was said tonight?"

Rome frowned, not really following her question. "What do you mean?"

"Teresa isn't the first girlfriend my father's had who could pass for my sister," she declared in agitation. "Angela, Beth, Doreen, Cynthia, Mary-Anne—he's practically gone through the alphabet. He's all the way up to the T's!"

"Girlfriends, yes, but he's marrying this one," he reminded her. "There is a difference."

"Is there? You don't know the whole story," snapped Lexie. "Since my mother died, I've had three stepmothers. My father finally got wise and stopped marrying before he was financially destroyed by divorce settlements. I've lost track of how many times he's been engaged. He always insists each time that this is the right one. Give him a year and he'll be accidentally calling some new girl by Teresa's name."

"You aren't making a whole lot of sense." Impatience edged Rome's voice. "Drink your coffee."

"I'm making a lot of sense." Absently she took a sip and felt the hot liquid burn down her throat. "You just don't want to understand."

"You know you can't change him. This has been going on for years, according to what you say. So why are you so emotional about it?"

"Don't you see?" she pleaded. "You and my father

share a few traits that I just don't trust. You're both handsome and exceptionally charming men. Look at the way you just persuaded Mrs. McNulty to let you into my apartment!"

"And you think—" he began angrily.

"I don't think, I know," Lexie interrupted. "Ever since my mother died and even before that, there's been a steady stream of gorgeous women in my father's life. At first when he brought one of them home and announced that so-and-so was going to be my new stepmother, I used to try to like her, to be friends with her. But they never stayed around long enough. Someone else always took their place. I always had to compete with someone for my father's attention. I can still remember hearing my mother cry because he didn't come home until late at night."

Rome sat down on the couch beside her, resting his elbows on his knees and clasping his hands in front of him. He stared for a silent minute at his intertwined fingers, his jaw hard, his mouth grimly straight.

"Why didn't you tell me all this before?"

"Would it have done any good?" she whispered, her heart aching. "Would it have made any difference?"

"At least I would have understood why you were so reluctant to trust me," Rome stated and let his mouth twist into a smile. "But you didn't trust me enough to tell me."

"Sometimes words aren't convincing. You wouldn't have believed me. You had to be shown." Her voice was barely a murmur. "And in your social circles, what he does is commonplace."

Rome shook his head. "My parents are happily married and so are most of their friends. But I do know what you mean."

"I don't think so, Rome. It's just too easy for you and it always will be. You don't have to work at relationships if there's always going to be another woman—or women—panting after you, begging to be next."

"Is that what that noise I keep hearing is?" he asked wryly. "I thought my air conditioner needed a new filter. But it was actually gorgeous babes, panting after me. Doggone it. I was too busy falling in love with you to sleep with them all."

"Shut up. It isn't funny, Rome."

He shook his head. "No, it isn't. But you've got to get some perspective on it, Lexie. I'm not your father. I'm not like him at all. Give me a chance, would you?"

"It's no use." Her heart splintered as his persuasive words were spoken. "Rome, I've seen you look at beautiful women—like Claudine—when you were with me, admiring them—"

"Guilty as charged," he said. "Yes, I look at beautiful women. I admire them the way I would a painting. That doesn't mean I want them in my life, or that I want to make love to them. If you see a good-looking man, do you pretend that he doesn't exist?" he challenged.

"I . . ." Lexie fumbled for an answer and couldn't find one.

"Don't expect more from me than you do from yourself. I'm not a saint, Lexie," Rome warned.

"I don't expect you to be a saint," she said.

"Don't you?" For an instant he sounded really angry. "Tell me, what do you expect of me?"

Lexie trembled. "I just want you to love me." Her eyes were a luminous blue, shimmering with unshed tears.

His expression softened as his hand cupped her face in a caress. "I do. I've asked for the chance to spend the rest of my life proving it, Lexie."

Her lashes fluttered down, letting the warmth of his touch steal over her skin. She let herself be drawn into his arms.

"I can't begin to explain why your father is the way he is," Rome told her. "Maybe he's afraid of growing old. Maybe he's just vain, and shallow, and stupid—"

"You forgot heartless," she said. "And egotistical. And a few other things."

"Lexie, I'm sure it's a long list. And I get that you don't love him very much. But are you going to let him keep you from being happy? I want to make you happy. Let me. For me there's only you. I haven't known you long but I know that for a fact."

"Why?" she whispered.

"Because you're gorgeous and smart and sexy. Because you're really good at what you do and you work incredibly hard." He took a deep breath. "Because you're funny and you're fierce. Because—because there's only one Lexie Templeton. If I let you go, I'd never forgive myself. And I'd never be happy."

"Really?" Her voice seemed to be coming from very, very far away.

"Yeah. Really."

Lexie lifted her head a few inches to see his face. His look was so earnest, so determined, so compelling. There was so much strength of character in his face. And the burning flame of love in his dark eyes simply could not be faked.

"I believe you," she whispered, and it was the sweet glorious truth.

His hand was at the back of her neck stroking her hair and drawing her upward to his mouth. The moaning sigh that escaped from her lips an instant before she felt the heady sensation of his kiss carried with it the last doubts, banishing them forever from her mind. Her arms slid inside his jacket, curving around his waist to spread her hands over the sinewy muscles of his back.

Rome pulled her onto his lap, touching her, caressing her, needing the reassurance of her responses.

As he bent his head down, imprinting tender kisses on her throat, Lexie murmured, "You'll have to teach me to trust, Rome. It's something I didn't learn very well when I was growing up."

"There are a few other areas of your education that have been sadly neglected," he said, his mouth moving against her silken skin.

"Such as?" She smiled with dreamy pleasure just imagining what he could teach her.

"Such as learning when to stop talking."

Lexie didn't mind being quiet. It was enough to be in his arms and knowing that he truly loved her. The erratic beat of his heart beneath her hand was the most beautiful sound she had ever heard—perhaps second only to his low voice saying "I love you."

"My ring—" Rome teased her lips with his own. "Will you wear it?"

"Yes," she agreed in a voice choked by the depth of her emotions.

"I've been carrying it with me," he said softly, "just in case you changed your mind. Remember, you can still change your mind. I rushed out and bought it, thinking you'd be so impressed and all I managed to do was scare you."

"I'm not scared anymore."

"It's gonna be all right. You'll see. I love you, Lexie," he said, smiling. "Let me be your hero, okay?" He wiped away the tear that trickled down her cheek.

"Okay," she sniffled. "I think I need one."

He nodded. "Now where were we?"

She arched into him, demanding his caress and giving equal time to him. Her arms wound around his neck. Rome stiffened and tried to pull back a little.

"When will your roommate be home?" he said thickly.

"She won't." Lexie pulled him back.

"What do you mean?" His lips hovered above hers.

"She's left for good, moved out. Gone back home to East Corndog, where there aren't any evil Bobs."

"Huh?"

"Never mind. We're alone. Trust me."

With a stifled groan he covered her mouth and pressed her backward onto the cushions. The time for words had come to an end.

KONA WINDS

CHAPTER ONE

The car tires crunched over the narrow, snow-packed street, empty of traffic after midnight. Warm air blasted from the heating vents but it wasn't enough to keep out the bitter cold.

Julie Lancaster clenched her teeth to keep them from chattering. "Wish I was back in sunny California. I'll never get used to Boston winters."

"Rule number one. Wear your woollies," Marilyn said, letting the steering wheel slide through her mittened hands.

"I am, but I'm still freezing."

Marilyn grinned. "Rule number two. Prepare for worse weather. It's January. Winter has just begun."

"No need to remind me." Julie snuggled deeper into her hooded parka and moved her feet directly under the passenger side vent. The fake-fur lining of her boots wasn't enough to keep them warm. "After five years I guess I should know that."

Marilyn looked at her sideways. "Have you been in Boston that long?"

Julie shivered. "Yes."

"Wow. I thought you said you planned to go back to California after you graduated from high school. How come you didn't?"

Julie sighed and looked out the window at the falling snow. "I fell in love with that Boston College guy, remember?"

"Uh, no. I missed that part of your life story."

The two of them hadn't had much time to talk since they'd met at the small, family-style restaurant where they worked part time for not much more than minimum wage and tips. But they'd quickly become good friends.

"You just don't pay attention, Marilyn," Julie teased.

"Hey, what with the weirdo who wanted mustard instead of ketchup on his fried clams and the lady who said the coffee was too hot, I got a little distracted. What did she want me to do, blow on it for her? Puh-leeze."

It was Julie's turn to grin.

"So what happened with the guy?" Marilyn slowed the car, looking for a parking space.

"Nothing much," Julie said. "I fell out of love."

"Were you heartbroken?"

"Um, no. Not exactly."

Marilyn spotted a space, realized it was a hydrant, and drove a little further. "Rule number three. You have to break the law to find a place to park in Boston. But I draw the line at hydrants. So then what happened?"

"I stayed in college and got a BA and my teaching certificate."

"Excellent. I'm proud of ya."

Julie smiled and continued. "Anyway, while I was doing that, I tutored a teenage girl with a learning disability. Nice kid. We really bonded. Her parents wrote a great letter of recommendation to the school district for me."

"Everything helps. Did you apply anywhere yet?"

Julie shrugged. "Yes, for substitute teaching, but I've only been called twice."

"At least you have a degree."

"For what it's worth." Julie looked out the window again as Marilyn drove past her building and then put the car in reverse to end up in front of it.

"Okay, I give up," Marilyn announced. "You're here."

"Home sweet home," said Julie wryly. "Thanks for the ride. And you have to let me pay for the gas next time."

"Nah. Your place is on my way home."

"Maybe so, but it's worth something to me not to have to stand out in the cold waiting for a bus," Julie argued.

Marilyn waved her concern away. "We can talk about it another time."

Julie was so tired that she didn't argue. "Okay. Take care. Thanks again, Mar." She pushed the door open and stepped onto the shoveled walkway.

The house was dark as she approached, except for a flickering square of light coming through the sheer curtains of the front windows. She put the house key in the lock, turned it, and pushed the door open. Standing in the doorway, she turned and waved to Marilyn, who had waited at the curb to make sure she got safely into the house.

Marilyn waved back and drove slowly away.

Over the low rumble of the old car's engine, Julie could hear the sound of a blaring TV. It was what she always heard when she came into the closed-off entryway with its staircase to the second floor. Mrs. Kelly, her landlady, had ninety-nine channels on her cable service and seemed determined to watch them all. Right now she was probably glued to her favorite news show from Ireland. The announcer's soft brogue echoed in the hall.

Julie took off her gloves and looked up the stairs. No one was there. The second floor of the old house had been converted into three studio rentals, but because of her working hours, Julie rarely saw her fellow lodgers. Both had day jobs. The two other women seemed nice, but Julie didn't know either of them well.

With a last glance at the front door to be sure the night lock was bolted, she moved to the stairs. The second step creaked under her foot. Before she reached the third step, a door opened, and the Irish news announcer's brogue grew louder.

"There you are, Julie. I thought I heard a car," Mrs. Kelly said. She spoke with a flat *a* and no *r* at all. *Theah you ah.* The way she said *cah* always made Julie smile. It had taken a while for her to get used to Boston accents.

"I'm sorry, Mrs. Kelly," Julie said. "I didn't mean to disturb you." She paused on the stairs.

Her landlady was in her sixties, widowed, with an abundance of pearl-gray hair piled in a straggling bun on top of her head. Mrs. Kelly claimed to be five feet tall but Julie doubted it. From her position on the staircase, she thought that the older woman looked even shorter. There was something about her landlady that reminded Julie of a leprechaun. Maybe it was the constant twinkling in her eyes.

"You didn't disturb me." Mrs. Kelly waved the apology aside. "I've been listening for you."

"You have?" Julie murmured, hoping her kind landlady wasn't going to invite her in for hot chocolate. Julie had accepted such invitations in the past but tonight she was just too tired.

"Yes, someone called for you, said it was very important. Good thing you gave her my number just in case. She said she tried your cell."

Julie smiled politely. To save on expenses, Mrs. Kelly

had never had the upstairs wired for phone service, knowing that her renters seldom stayed longer than a year. Like them, Julie relied on a cell phone. She looked in her purse for it. There it was, to one side, its little screen blank and dark. "Oops. Forgot to charge it."

"Just a minute and I'll get it for you. I wrote it all down on a piece of paper." Mrs. Kelly disappeared into her front room.

A phone call that was important. Obviously it wasn't from her parents, since her landlady had met both of them and passed along a few messages when they hadn't been able to reach her. That left one possibility: the school district. They probably needed a substitute for tomorrow.

Julie leaned against the stairwell wall. If that were the case, she desperately needed to get to bed. She didn't want to arrive at a classroom tomorrow groggy from lack of sleep.

"Here it is." Mrs. Kelly reappeared, waving a torn piece of paper in her hand.

"Thank you." Julie descended two steps to take it. What with a forty-watt bulb overhead, another economy on her landlady's part, the light in the stairwell wasn't good. Neither was Mrs. Kelly's handwriting. She didn't attempt to decipher it there. "Good night, Mrs. Kelly."

"Good night." The door was closed and the latest news from Dublin faded away.

In her one-room studio, Julie switched on a big, bright lamp and bolted the door. Unbuttoning her parka and pushing back the hood, she read the note. A Ms. Grayson wanted her to call first thing in the morning.

Julie frowned. She couldn't remember any Ms. Grayson with the school. It took her tired mind several seconds to place the name. Ms. Grayson was the director of a posh employment agency where Julie had interviewed, although Julie had talked to her assistant and not Ms. Grayson. She had hoped to find a teaching position in a private school but the only job available had been the tutoring one.

After all this time, she had given up. But maybe there was an opening. Releasing a sigh, Julie draped her parka over the back of a chair. She didn't have the energy to get excited by the possibility. Tomorrow morning would be soon enough.

Sitting on the same chair that held her parka, she untied the knots that held up the cuffs of her fake-fur boots. She slipped the boots off, curling her toes and rubbing her aching arches. The boots were comfortable but the restaurant owner expected the waitresses to wear dressy shoes and change after their shifts. Her feet hadn't had a chance to recover.

She caught a glimpse of herself in the wall mirror. Uh-oh. Hat hair. Or should she call it hood hair? Whatever. It was another thing about cold winters that she hated. Fine wisps escaped from the bun at the nape of her neck and floated up.

She unpinned the bun and shook her straight hair free. Its color was not exactly light brown or dark blond, but fell somewhere in between. Back home in California, the sun usually bleached it naturally to an unusual shade of platinum-gilded blond.

Since she had moved East, the color had changed. Tan was the closest description, Julie thought, but whoever heard of tan hair? But it was still sleek and shiny. It framed her oval face from a center part, its indefinite color at least helping to bring out the soft brown of her eyes.

At the moment, she was too weary to think about her appearance for another second. Sleep would put back the roses in her cheeks, but nothing short of a major makeover would restore the sun-kissed look she'd taken for granted in California. The thought was depressing.

Sighing, Julie rose. Her bed looked inviting, even more so than a soak in the tub, no matter how sore and tired she was from waiting tables. Her movements were automatic as she undressed and got ready for bed.

The small studio was sparsely furnished. A single bed, a chest of drawers, and a narrow drop leaf table with two chairs were about all she had in the way of furniture. Half of one wall was taken up by makeshift wooden cabinets that held her kitchenware and a coffeemaker. Next to the cabinets was a tiny gas stove, and a small refrigerator.

She'd brightened up the place with a colorful poppy-motif cloth covering the table and a coordinating reddish-orange spread on the bed. Lemon and lime toss pillows were mounded on top of it.

An assortment of sunny posters and appliquéd cloth pictures were a lively contrast to the sun-yellow walls, and the woodwork was painted a pristine white. Even the refrigerator and the stove had been decorated with magnets of butterflies and flowers and colorful, hand-loomed potholders for a homey look.

The décor was a touch of sunny California in winter Massachusetts. But as Julie piled the pillows onto the floor and pulled back the bedspread, she didn't notice the cheerfulness of the room. Sleep was the only thing on her mind.

The alarm seemed to go off too soon. Padding about in a robe and slippers—and avoiding her bleary-eyed reflection in the wall mirror—Julie treated herself to a restoring pot of coffee. The fragrance filled the room.

After the first sip, Julie realized that she had been

too tired to remember to charge her cell phone. She would have to call Ms. Grayson from her landlady's phone.

She dressed and went downstairs. Mrs. Kelly was in her favorite green coat and pixie boots, looking more than ever like a leprechaun, and on her way out to do her grocery shopping. But she was happy to help, bringing the phone to Julie and telling her to lock the inner door when she left.

Julie punched in the number on the torn piece of paper she'd brought downstairs, and asked for Ms. Grayson. The director of the employment agency was courteous enough, but seemed reluctant to give details over the phone, sparking Julie's curiosity.

"Do you have an interview for me?" Julie asked the point-blank question after Ms. Grayson requested that she come in.

"I do have a job offer that might be just right for you," the woman said without further explanation. "But I'd like you to come in so we can discuss it."

"A job offer?" Julie repeated. "Teaching?"

"Yes, teaching," Ms. Grayson assured her. "How soon can you get to the office?"

"I'll leave now."

Julie hung up, feeling excited and wondering what it was all about. She decided to splurge and call a taxi. Only now would she admit to herself that she'd been afraid of never finding a permanent teaching position. Her few stints as a sub hadn't been very encouraging.

By the time she was seated in Ms. Grayson's office, she was having a hard time staying calm. The sparkle in her eyes was a dead giveaway, but the employment agency director didn't seem to notice.

"So. Tell me about the offer," Julie said. *Might as well get to the point.*

Ms. Grayson sifted through the papers on her desk and withdrew one halfway down a stack. "I got a phone call yesterday from a Ms. Harmon. She wants to hire you to tutor her niece, and she's offering—"

"Tutoring?" Julie said with disappointment. "I thought this was a teaching post."

"Tutoring is teaching," the other woman pointed out. "Besides, I think you'll find this offer very attractive."

"Perhaps." But Julie felt misled. She couldn't summon up much enthusiasm for it.

"You see, Ms. Harmon and her niece live in Hawaii." A faint smile edged her mouth at Julie's startled glance. "I thought that might get your attention."

"How did she know about me?" Dazed, Julie tried to recall whether Ms. Grayson had actually said she had been requested for the job. She was certain she had.

"From your work with the Rifkins' daughter last summer. Apparently she was just accepted at Vassar and they're very grateful to you. Anyway, they know Ms. Harmon and gave you a very positive recommendation. I pulled up your files and e-mailed them to her."

Julie gave her a doubtful look. "There must be someone in Hawaii they could hire."

Ms. Grayson shrugged. "The Rifkins vacation there and they think the world of you. They know you're from California. Maybe you said something to them about missing all the sunshine? I don't know. You could call the Rifkins and ask."

Julie nodded. She couldn't remember what she'd offered in the way of personal information after so much time, but she was glad that the Rifkin family thought so highly of her.

"There's more. Ready for the details?"

"Yes."

"Ms. Harmon's niece was injured in a car accident just before Christmas, as I understand. She's out of the hospital now but her recovery is going to keep her out of school a lot longer, possibly for the rest of this school year. The girl is sixteen, a junior in high school. She really wants to graduate with her class."

"So I would be tutoring her for about five months," said Julie, going over a mental picture of a school calendar.

"Ms. Harmon will guarantee six months' salary to persuade you to leave whatever job you have now. And your airfare and all other expenses are covered as well." Ms. Grayson smiled. Then she named a salary that made Julie's eyes widen. More and more, this was looking like an offer she couldn't refuse—and didn't want to refuse.

"You'll live with Ms. Harmon and her niece. She also wanted me to assure you that there is a nurse and you would not be required to do any sickroom care. Evenings and weekends you're totally free to do as you please."

Julie shook her head. "This sounds too good to be true—a paid vacation in Hawaii in the dead of winter—wow!" A faint laugh escaped her throat. "Where do I sign? When do they want me?"

"Immediately."

"Okay." Julie gulped. "At least I think it's okay. Probably I should say yes. I mean, I have to think about it."

"Don't think too long. Ms. Harmon expects you to come when it's convenient for her, Julie. These are rich people, and they're used to having things their way. But here's the good news: she's prepared to wire an advance on that salary to cover your relocation expenses. And she'll reserve a first-class e-ticket. You could be on your way to Hawaii day after tomorrow. I can call her this afternoon with your answer."

"The day after tomorrow. That isn't much time," Julie murmured. She made a mental list and did some swift arithmetic while she was at it. *Do laundry. Shop for clothes. Pack. Call the restaurant owner, call the school district, and quit.*

She didn't have time to move out, though. She decided to give Mrs. Kelly a check for five months' rent and have her keep an eye on things. Just in case the job didn't work out, Julie would have someplace to come home to. Finding inexpensive rentals in Boston wasn't easy, and besides, she liked Mrs. Kelly.

"So what's your answer?"

"What else can I say?" Julie's shoulders lifted in an expressive shrug. "Yes. Tell Ms. Harmon yes."

A few minutes later, she rose to leave. The agency director promised to handle the business of the wire transfer into Julie's bank account, and gave her the address of her new, if temporary, place of residence in Hawaii, an unpronounceable town on the island of Oahu.

She still felt a bit dazed by her good fortune. She added a few more thing to her mental list. *Call Marilyn. Scream with joy. Jump up and down.*

Ms. Grayson rose to see her out. "Send us a postcard. Or an e-mail. I'm sure you'll have your own computer and everything else you need. But I'd like to hear from you. Let us know how you're getting along, Julie."

"I will," she promised.

"Aloha. I understand it means good-bye and also good luck."

"Thank you. Aloha." Julie grinned.

Outside, she succeeded in flagging down a taxi for the ride back to her apartment. Bundled up in her winter parka, an itchy wool scarf around her neck, she gazed out of the window at the bleak, gray skies and snow-packed streets. In two more days, she would be looking at palm trees and sandy beaches. It seemed impossible.

A ridiculous mental picture popped up of herself in a grass skirt. On a surfboard. Shooting the curl of a gigantic blue wave while bronzed beach boys cheered. She wanted to laugh out loud but the grim-faced taxi driver would probably think she was nuts.

Mrs. Kelly was at the door to meet her when she arrived. "Did you get the job?"

"Yes!" Julie pulled off her gloves; she was bursting with the news. "Mrs. Kelly, it's in Hawaii!"

The little old lady's blue eyes grew round. "Hawaii!"

"Yes, can you believe it?" Julie explained everything in a happy rush and added that she would like to keep the apartment. Just as happily, Mrs. Kelly agreed to the offer of five months' rent in advance and promised to look after everything. She even offered to dust.

"But promise me one thing, dear. Send me scenic postcards. I've always wanted to go to Hawaii. Ever since Elvis was in that movie—I loved that movie—what was it called?"

"*Blue Hawaii*." Who didn't love Elvis Presley, Julie thought. Listening to classic Elvis songs and watching old Elvis movies was a guilty pleasure that she shared with Marilyn. Although Julie had never seen *Blue Hawaii*, come to think of it.

"And that scene with the hula dancers . . ." Mrs. Kelly waved her arms to the side and wriggled her ample hips. "I always wanted to learn to hula."

"You could take a class," Julie suggested.

"In Boston? I don't think so, dear. But you can. Do you think you might want to stay in Hawaii?"

"I don't know," Julie admitted. "That's why I'm covering my bases here. But Boston winters are a little much for me."

"Yes, I can see that. Well, the job sounds wonderful."

"It's only temporary. The girl I'll be tutoring was in an auto accident." Julie explained as much as she knew of that.

"Oh, dear."

"She's facing a long recovery but she wants to graduate with her classmates. I'll be following the curriculum set by the school she attends."

"I understand. I'm sure you're a very good teacher." Mrs. Kelly gave her a twinkly look.

"It's what I really want to do, Mrs. Kelly. But since the job isn't permanent, I don't know if I'll be staying on there. Depends on whether I can find another position."

"A smart girl like you? You will. Never fear."

Julie blushed. "Okay. I have to get organized and make some calls. Oh, shoot! I still haven't charged my cell phone."

"Just be sure to call your parents. Do it now, before you forget. Use my phone, dear."

"I wouldn't forget them, Mrs. Kelly," Julie said, laughing. "But I'll call them tonight. Right now I have a million things to do, starting with the laundry."

"You bring your dirty clothes downstairs. I'll wash them for you," Mrs. Kelly offered.

"Would you? You are so sweet, Mrs. Kelly. I'm going to miss you" Julie gave her diminutive landlady a big hug. "I'll bring down the basket right now."

With her purse and her hooded parka clutched in her arms, she took the stairs two at a time to the second floor. She could just hear Mrs. Kelly singing below and caught the words "heavenly flower."

Julie knew she would be much too busy in the next thirty-six hours to do much singing, but Mrs. Kell could do it for her. Her to-do list was growing by th minute.

CHAPTER TWO

"Ladies and gentlemen, we are beginning our descent into the Honolulu airport. Please make sure that your seats are forward and your tray tables stowed in the upright position . . ." The flight attendant droned on until the captain took over.

"Welcome to paradise, folks."

Julie smiled and looked out the window as he went on.

"Hope you all had a pleasant flight. The weather service is reporting . . . a breezy day . . . and it's a balmy seventy-two degrees, with overcast skies and occasional light showers. Those of you on the right side of the aircraft should have an excellent view of Diamond Head and Waikiki beach when we break through the clouds."

Julie leaned closer to the thick glass. The jumbo jet was engulfed in a cloud, and she saw nothing but a gray-white mist outside the window. Although she was exhausted from the frantic schedule of the past forty-eight hours, including more than eight hours of flying, Julie was determined not to miss her first glimpse of the island of Oahu.

The cloud dissipated into wispy trails and then nothing. Etched against the oyster-gray backdrop of the sky was Diamond Head, jutting into the sea. Directly below, the wind churned up whitecaps on the Pacific, sending rows of foaming white to the shore. Towers of every size rose behind the pale sand of Waikiki Beach—a mass of skyscraper hotels and office buildings formed a city in miniature from this elevation. Houses climbed the slopes of the mountains behind the beach as Honolulu seemed to tumble over itself in search of room. It was much bigger than Julie had expected.

She tightened her seat belt and took one last look. Her tiredness was chased away by a curious anticipation of what was before her, not just for the job, but for the people and the place. The aircraft wheels seemed to thud onto the runway and seconds later the powerful thrust of the jet engines reversed itself. The plane slowed to taxi to the terminal.

Having a first-class ticket gave Julie the advantage of being one of the first to leave. She emerged from the long tunnel of the jet way into a glassed boarding concourse. The instructions from Ms. Grayson had said she would be met at the airport and Julie simply assumed that someone would hold up a placard with her name on it. She took a deep breath and walked forward.

She was right.

A Hawaiian man was holding up a sign with her first initial and last name clearly spelled out. He scanned the people exiting the plane as if he had been told what she looked like. Julie waved to him.

"I'm Julie Lancaster."

The man smiled. He looked to be in his late thirties, of medium height, with a waistline that had begun to thicken. His hair was the same jet-black as his eyes. "Aloha, Julie." He took the lei he held and placed it

around her neck. In the same motion he gently kissed
her cheek. "Welcome to Hawaii."

Like his smile, the kiss on her cheek was totally friendly.
She gave him a big smile right back. She touched a finger to the pale yellow petal of one of the tubular flowers
strung one after another into the lei. The blossoms'
spicy fragrance reminded her of ginger. She guessed
that that was what the flowers were.

"Thank you." She meant the words sincerely.

"In Hawaii, we say mahalo." The man smiled again,
warmth and gentleness radiating from his face.

"Mahalo," Julie repeated.

"You're welcome." The dark head bobbed in acceptance of her gratitude. "This way, please. Miss Emily is
waiting for you over here."

Miss Emily? Julie supposed he meant her employer,
whom she knew as Ms. Harmon. She followed her
guide to one side of an exit. Standing there was a fairly
tall and very erect woman.

A hat of natural straw was on her head, the white
band around the crown almost matching the woman's
hair. She wore a navy blue suit with a knee-covering
skirt, and sensible navy blue shoes. The cotton blouse
beneath the navy blue suit jacket was buttoned all the
way to the throat. Julie got the overall impression of
someone starched and prim. She didn't feel nervous
about meeting her employer, only curious.

"Ms. Lancaster, I'm Emily Harmon." The older woman
greeted her with a smile that, while it wasn't as all encompassing as the man's had been, was certainly friendly.

"Hello, Ms. Harmon." This time Julie was greeted
with a plain handshake. "And thank you for the lei."

"We couldn't overlook the Hawaiian custom of greeting halihinis."

"Newcomers," the man said. "Or tourists."

"Dan has the car waiting outside," Emily Harmon said. "Dan is actually our mechanic. He doubles as a chauffeur when I have to come into Honolulu. I can't stand the traffic."

Julie found herself being escorted out the exit door but not before she noticed the stream of passengers heading for the baggage claim area. "What about my luggage?"

"Give your claim tickets to Dan. He'll collect it for you," the woman commanded. Julie did as she was told, thanking Dan in advance. She hurried to catch up to Emily Harmon, who was headed for a silver-gray Mercedes parked not far from the door. As they walked toward it, Emily issued another order. "Breathe in. Tell me what you smell."

Julie did. There was an elusive quality to the air she breathed, something soft and gentle but she couldn't identify it. Emily's alert blue eyes read her puzzled expression and the older woman smiled faintly.

"It's clean air," she explained. "It's been washed by thousands of miles of ocean, kept cool by the water while acquiring the softness of rain. That first breath will be etched on your memory."

Julie's lips parted in astonishment that the explanation could be as simple as clean air. "It's wonderful!" she exclaimed.

"Yes, isn't it?" Emily Harmon replied, a trifle smugly. Dan held the rear door of the Mercedes open for them. Julie climbed in first, sliding to the far side behind the driver. When Emily Harmon was safely inside, Dan closed the door. "He's going to drive around to the baggage claim area," Emily said, as if to reassure Julie that they weren't leaving without her luggage.

"Of course," she nodded.

"Were you able to see Honolulu and Waikiki when you landed?" the older woman asked.

"Yes, I did and Diamond Head too."

"What did you think?" It wasn't an idle question; Emily Harmon was interested in her reaction. Dan got behind the wheel and the engine purred into action.

"It's a much larger city than I imagined, and there were a lot more skyscrapers than I thought there would be," Julie admitted.

"My family once had a beach house on Waikiki. That was when the only hotel was the Royal Hawaiian. It's difficult to believe, isn't it? Of course, that was very long ago. Now there are so many hotels all up and down the beach that the Royal Hawaiian is practically lost in their shadows. Ruel says it's progress."

"I suppose so." Julie wondered who Ruel was. It was an unusual name. But she didn't have a chance to ask as her employer continued. "You'd be surprised at how many tourists come here, stay on Waikiki for a week, and believe they've seen Hawaii. They go home with their Hawaiian shirts and a crate of pineapples and good riddance." She paused for a considering moment. "When Captain Cook landed here, he called the chain the Sandwich Isles after his sponsor, the Earl of Sandwich. Did you know that?"

"No," Julie admitted.

"Then the whalers came and the missionaries. When I see women on the beach wearing microscopic bikinis, I find it difficult to believe that my forebears taught the Hawaiians to put on clothes." The remark amused Julie, who ventured a smile.

The car rolled to a quiet stop in front of the baggage area and Dan stepped out. "Don't be too long in there, Dan," Emily Harmon admonished. "I don't want to arrive home after dark."

"Yes, Miss Emily."

With the instruction given, the woman returned her attention to Julie. "You have a pleasant voice, Julie. May I call you Julie?"

"Please do," Julie said eagerly. She had been a little put off by the older woman's formality. First names were fine with her.

"What part of New England are you from? My ancestors came from New England. They were among the early missionaries here."

Looking at the proper and fastidious Emily Harmon, Julie found it easy to believe that. "Actually, I'm not from New England. I was born and raised in California, but I attended college in Boston."

"Oh." There was a wealth of meaning in the simple word. Julie was positive that she had just fallen several notches in Emily Harmon's esteem. "California, eh? Then I misunderstood."

"Does it matter?" Julie couldn't resist asking. She didn't quite understand the older woman's frosty tone.

"No, not really, I suppose," the woman sighed regretfully. "It's just that New Englanders tend to be more reserved and controlled. Less exuberant, if you will. I felt that Deborah needed someone of that type right now."

"Deborah is your niece?"

"Yes. She is a very active, outgoing girl. Her confinement during her recovery may prove to be a problem. I had hoped for someone who would project a calming influence." Emily Harmon looked thoughtful. "But your youthfulness could be an advantage."

"How old is she?" asked Julie.

"Sixteen. She'll be seventeen in March. How old are you?"

Surely she had seen Julie's date of birth on the e-mailed files. Julie had the feeling the older woman was simply trying to get the upper hand.

"Twenty-two," she answered.

"So young!"

Julie felt that she had dropped another notch in the

woman's estimation. "I graduated from high school when I was only seventeen."

"I see. Well, you do seem mature and levelheaded."

Julie was positive that Emily Harmon had mentally tacked on the qualification *even if you are from California.* She swallowed a smile and decided to change the subject.

"I know Deborah was in a car accident. How badly injured was she?"

"We expect a full recovery, no permanent injuries. She's in a body cast—for a broken pelvis, among other things. I won't bore you with the gory details. A live-in nurse sees to Deborah's medical care, as you know. Ah, here's Dan with your luggage."

The trunk popped open and Julie could hear the stocky Hawaiian stowing her suitcases.

"We'll soon be home," the older woman said with a sigh.

"How far do you live from here?" Julie asked.

"It's about an hour's drive. We live near the north shore, one of the last bastions against progress on Oahu." There was disdain in the sweeping look Emily Harmon gave the buses and taxis and cars zipping in and out of the terminal complex.

Dan opened the front door and slid behind the wheel, driving the luxurious car over the airport roads into the mainstream of traffic. Within minutes they were on a freeway and crawling along in bumper-to-bumper traffic three lanes wide. The skies were still overcast, but darkening to slate with the approach of a hidden sunset.

"I've made an appointment for you to meet Deborah's teacher late tomorrow afternoon," Emily told her. "After traveling all day and adjusting to the time zone changes, I know you'll need to sleep late in the morning."

"That's thoughtful of you," Julie said. "I am tired, but a good night's rest will take care of that." She hesitated. "I was wondering about Deborah's parents. I had the impression from Mrs. Grayson that they'd died."

Emily leaned forward and tapped Dan on the shoulder. "You're speeding!"

The car slowed perceptibly. Julie hadn't been paying enough attention to realize that they were out of the traffic jam. She noticed how Emily Harmon craned her neck to read the speedometer before she sat back in her seat. Julie's glance caught Dan's gaze in the rear-view mirror and he winked. The gesture seemed to say that he and Emily Harmon were constantly at odds over the pace he drove.

"About Deborah's parents," the woman returned to the question Julie had asked, "they were both lost at sea when she was five. They'd gone sailing and apparently encountered a sudden squall. The coast guard found the wreckage of their boat on a reef a couple of days later."

The tight line of her mouth indicated that she found the subject painful even after all this time. Julie decided not to pursue it further. She began studying the road signs and was confronted with a mass of unpronounceable words—Waipahu, Aiea, Wahiawa, Wailua, Haleiwa, Waianae. Her tongue couldn't seem to roll over all those vowels.

"Are those the names of towns?" She pointed to a sign.

"Waipahu and Waianae—yes, they are," Emily Harmon pronounced them effortlessly.

"I'll never be able to pronounce them," Julie laughed a little self-consciously.

"It can be a bit confusing at first. The Hawaiian language only consists of seven consonants—w, p, h, l, k, m, and n—and the five vowels. With only twelve letters, we make use of them all. I believe we have a book on Hawaiian for beginners in our library. Remind me to give it to you."

"I'm sure I'll need it," Julie sighed.

Within minutes after the car had climbed away from the coast onto a broad, flat plateau flanked by two mountain ranges, they were in darkness. The headlights illuminated little of the open country on either side of the road and they seemed to have run out of freeway.

As they drove past a U.S. army base, Emily Harmon identified it. "That's Schofield Barracks. When the Japanese attacked Pearl Harbor, they made their first strike here, bombing and strafing the base."

"I didn't realize it was so far inland," commented Julie. Although she knew a lot about American history, she was not that up on the World War II years and much of what she knew about Pearl Harbor had been gleaned from the recent movie. But she wasn't going to tell Emily Harmon that.

"Most people don't. They think it was somehow adjacent to the naval base at Pearl Harbor, which, of course, it isn't." As they passed the last entrance gate to the base, the car was again in darkness, the lights of town left behind.

"As I mentioned to Ms. Grayson," the older woman continued, "your evenings and your weekends are your free time. You're young and attractive, and I am sure you will want to enjoy yourself now and then. I wouldn't presume to dictate what you should do or whom you should see when you are out. However, I must caution you. We have a lot of military personnel stationed on this island, and then there are the surfers on the north shore."

Emily Harmon said *military personnel* and *surfers* in the same frosty tone of voice she'd said *California*. Julie suppressed a sigh.

"I am talking about the men, of course. Most of them are interested in only one thing," the older woman continued, "and that's sex."

Julie was surprised by the blunt statement. For all her prissiness, Emily Harmon said what she meant.

"Oh. That's what most of the men back in the States are interested in, too," she offered dryly.

"The mainland—always refer to the other forty-nine states as the mainland. Hawaii is in the United States. We kamaainas are a bit touchy about that. So if you don't want to offend us, use the term mainland."

"A kamaaina is a native or old-timer," Dan explained helpfully.

"Watch the road and slow down!"

Julie didn't know what to think. Between the imperious old lady and Dan the Dictionary, she wasn't sure what she'd gotten herself into. But their sparring seemed friendly enough.

Emily Harmon turned to Julie, her tone quiet and reasonable once more. "Now, as I was saying, I wouldn't presume to dictate to you, but I think you should be careful about whom you date."

"Thanks, Ms. Harmon. I'll keep that in mind," Julie said. Despite her employer's old-fashioned way of putting things, Julie found her concern somewhat touching. And she suspected that it had to be genuine. Julie just didn't see how any indiscretion on her part could possibly make the prim and oh-so-proper Miss Emily look bad.

Conversation lapsed for the rest of the drive. Julie felt the accumulated tiredness of the last two days overcoming her. The wintry streets of Boston seemed very, very far away.

She fought to stay awake and not become mesmerized by the inky black world outside the windows of the luxury car. They passed through another small community and took a road that paralleled the shoreline for a while. Here and there, Julie glimpsed the almost iridescent white of the swelling ocean waves rushing to shore. Finally Dan took a turn onto a side road, taking the Mercedes up a switchback onto a tree-lined lane.

"Here we are," Emily Harmon declared when Dan stopped in the circular drive.

Lights gleamed a welcome from the windows. It was too dark for Julie to see the details of the outside of the house. Trees seemed to hover about it to keep it hidden and secluded. It was white and two-story, and gave the impression of being large. Dan came around to open the door and assist her out of the car. Then he did the same for Miss Emily.

The front door of the house was opened before Julie and Emily had climbed the short flight of steps to the wide veranda. Again Julie found herself looking into a friendly Hawaiian face, only this time it belonged to a woman in her forties, trim and attractive.

"Julie, this is Malia. She takes care of us," Emily Harmon announced. "Malia, this is Julie Lancaster."

"Aloha," the woman smiled.

"Aloha." Julie found it amazingly natural to return the same greeting.

The white walls of the interior added to the feeling of spaciousness. The large entryway was furnished with white wicker pieces with bright green cushions. To continue the tropical theme, numerous potted and hanging plants adorned the large room. The atmosphere suggested that the rest of the house was equally spacious and casually elegant, but, more important, warm and inviting. At the far end of the room, a staircase built of light polished wood climbed in a series of three tiers to the second floor.

"I fixed a snack, if you would like?" Malia said.

Julie hated to refuse when the woman had gone to

the trouble but she knew she didn't want it. "No, but
thank you, Malia," she said. "I just couldn't. They gave us
so much to eat on the plane."

"I think Julie would like to be shown to her room,"
Emily Harmon stated. "After traveling all day, I'm sure
she would prefer to bathe and make it an early night."

"I would, yes," Julie admitted.

"I generally have breakfast at nine o'clock on the
lanai. If you're awake at that time, perhaps you would
like to join me," Emily said.

"Thanks very much. I'll do that." Julie stifled a yawn.

"I'll show you to your room," said Malia in her soft
melodic voice. "Dan will bring up your luggage soon."

"Good night, then, Julie," Emily Harmon said.

"Good night," she replied. "I'll see you in the morning."

"Sleep as late as you wish," the older woman insisted
and moved away through an open archway.

Julie followed Malia up the staircase, silently admiring the innate grace of the woman's posture. At the
head of the stairs, Malia turned to the right down a win-
dowed hallway. At the second door she stopped and
opened it. Walking into the room, she turned on a
switch to flood the room with light, and Julie entered.

The white walls here were offset by a bold combination of coral and sunny yellow. The color combination
was repeated in the quilted spread on the bed, the full-
length curtains, and the area rug on the floor. Besides
the bed, dresser, and a chest of drawers, there was a
writing desk and chair, and a small divan, its thick plush
cushions covered in a print that incorporated the two
main colors with a dark green.

"It's a beautiful room," Julie declared.

"I'm glad you like it. Your private bath is through this
door." Malia showed her, then walked to the curtains,
pulling them apart to reveal French doors, paneled with

sheers. With a flick of a wrist she opened them and moved aside as Julie came forward.

As she stepped into the warm night air, Julie saw that the balcony ran the full length of the house, the roof reaching out to shelter it. It overlooked a swimming pool, its shape barely discernible in the flickering light of two flame torches. Beyond were shrubbery and more trees.

"Awesome. My own balcony!" It seemed like a dream. It lacked only a moon and a canopy of stars.

Julie turned to share the delight she felt with Malia, but Dan had entered the bedroom with her luggage and Malia was telling him where to set it. Julie put aside her pleasure for the business at hand and returned to the bedroom, closing the French doors.

"Aloha ahiahi," Dan smiled to Julie as he withdrew from the room.

Uncertain how to respond to that, Julie simply nodded and smiled. When the door closed, she turned to Malia, unable to keep the puzzled look out of her eyes. "What did he say?"

"It means 'good evening,'" Malia explained with a beaming smile. "Now you just show me which of these bags has your night things and I'll unpack it for you while you bathe."

"No, you don't need to do that," Julie said. "I can take care of it."

"Of course you can, but I'm going to. Now you tell me which one and go relax in the tub."

"No, please, I can't let you. Besides, maybe Miss Harmon will want you for something," Julie argued.

Malia shook her head. "Miss Emily knows there's a cold tray of food on the table and her tea is hot on the warmer." Her sparkling black eyes surveyed Julie. "Now, you're tired—you've got circles under your eyes. You go take that bath and tell me which of these suitcases has your night things, otherwise I'll open every one of them."

Julie knew when she had been defeated by a superior force and pointed to the small weekend case. "But you leave the rest of the unpacking to me. I work here, too, Malia." A thought occurred to her. "I should have met Deborah tonight, but I was so tired that I never thought about it."

"Debbie will understand. She's a good girl."

Running a hand over the carved headboard of the bed, Julie began wondering about her private student. What if she was spoiled or filled with self-pity? Well, somebody in a body cast had good reason to feel sorry for themselves, Julie reasoned. But it would be awful if she had to spend five months tutoring an unhappy teenager who was too miserable to pay attention.

"What's she like, Malia?"

"She's a wonderful girl—happy, generous. She loves everybody!" The light that had been shining in her expression faded as Malia sighed and lifted the suitcase onto a folding rack that had been left open. "That's why it so awful to see her lying in that bed."

"She was in a car accident," Julie prompted.

"Yes. Debbie and some of her friends went to a rock concert in Honolulu. They were on their way home when one car tried to pass another on a curve. They nearly crashed head-on but the boy who was driving swerved into a ditch."

"Were any of the others hurt?"

"One had a broken leg and another a broken arm. Otherwise, it was just cuts and bruises. Debbie was the one who was the most seriously hurt. Luckily all the doctors have said there isn't any permanent damage. It's just going to take a long time for her to heal and—" Malia glanced up just as Julie yawned. She hadn't meant to be rude, but she was so tired she couldn't help it. "Go take your bath before you fall asleep leaning against the bed."

"I guess you're right," Julie conceded. As she straightened up, the lei around her neck brushed her chin. "What about my lei? Do you suppose it will keep?"

Malia shook her head slightly. "Ginger? No, they're very short-lived."

"Oh, well." Julie sighed with resignation and took the lei from around her neck to drape it over the bedstead.

A half hour later, when she slipped beneath the covers, bathed and refreshed but even more exhausted, the spicy fragrance of the blossoms scented the air she breathed. As she closed her eyes, she decided it was an excellent way to go to sleep on her first night in Hawaii.

CHAPTER THREE

Julie awoke early the next morning. Of course, by Boston time, it was late. She stretched away her sleepiness and sat down in front of the mirror, where she fluffed her long hair with the brush. By the time she picked out clothes to wear and dressed, the clock on the dresser said 9:35. Emily had said to join her for breakfast at nine on the lanai.

Of course, she had forgotten to ask what that was or where it was. She inspected her reflection and decided she wouldn't scare anybody.

She walked out of the door into the hallway. There was bound to be someone around who could point her in the right direction. If not, she'd find the lanai thing somehow.

Rain beat against the windowpanes in the corridor. Hawaii was anything but sunny today, she observed. She peered out one of the windows but saw little beside lush, dripping greenery. Still, it was preferable to snow and sleet and bare, skeletal trees.

Her shoes made almost no sound on the stairs, thanks to their soft soles. With two tiers behind her, she turned down the last one. At the sound of male voices approaching the entryway at the base of the stairs where she had come in last night, her foot hovered on the next step.

She glanced up as two men entered the area from another part of the house. One of the men was tall, towering over his shorter and stockier companion. It was the tall one who caught Julie's interest.

His hair had the color and sheen of rich mahogany, curling thickly over his collar. The white material of his shirt stretched with ease across his broad shoulders, then tapered to the waistband of his dark jeans. He looked really, really . . . *fit* was the polite word, Julie thought. But if she had to describe him to a girlfriend, she would just say *built*.

The short guy spoke. "Ain't no work to do on a day like dis. Dem Kona winds are bad."

"Tell me about it, Al. Those Kona winds never bring anything good." As if sensing her presence, the tall, dark-haired man made a leisurely turn and looked directly at Julie.

Even though she had been caught accidentally eavesdropping, she decided there was no use in feeling shy or acting self-conscious. Since she had been noticed, she continued down the stairs.

Might as well make an entrance. She was dressed for one. Her narrow-cut white pants gave her a long and leggy look. Her lemon-yellow top had three white bands at the waistline, which actually didn't make her look fat. She could see by the expression in the tall man's eyes that she had made an impression.

"Maybe dem Kona winds will blow all away by tomorrow," the short guy went on.

"Maybe. I hope so, Al." His gaze never left Julie.

"I'll be goin' now. See ya tomorrow."

"Right."

Now that she was alone with the other man, Julie could see his face was hard and vital, browned by long hours in the tropical sun. But he didn't look like he'd gotten that tan sitting around in a chaise longue.

His arresting blue eyes were making a cool and thorough appraisal of her. The line of his mouth held no gentleness—in fact, she would have to describe it as having a cynical look. It didn't curve into a smile as she came closer.

"You must be Julie Lancaster."

Okay, every member of the household was probably aware of her late-night arrival. But who was he? The man didn't seem inclined to introduce himself, which she found rather annoying.

"Yes, I am. But I don't know who you are." She softened her tone with a smile.

"I'm Ruel Chandler."

The unusual name clicked in her memory. Emily Harmon had mentioned him yesterday at the airport. Despite his lack of friendliness, this Ruel Chandler intrigued her. The fascination she felt must have registered in her look, because she noticed the shrewd and sexy gleam that lit up his eyes.

"Nice to meet you." She gave him a demure nod. He wasn't that much older than she and she wasn't going to insult him by calling him Mr. Chandler. On the other hand, calling him by his first name seemed a little too casual. She wondered what his position was in the house. "You are . . . ?"

"I'm Debbie's brother," he stated, slight amusement in his voice.

Julie didn't have to feign surprise. "Oh. I didn't know Debbie had a brother. Her last name is Chandler?"

"Yes."

"Then Emily Harmon is—"

"My mother's sister."

"I had it all mixed up. I never bothered to ask. I just assumed that Debbie's last name was the same as your aunt's."

"Doesn't matter." The hard set of his features didn't change, but Julie thought she detected a note of boredom in his voice.

In another minute he would walk away. Not good. "Maybe you can help me."

"What's the problem?"

"Your aunt asked me to join her for breakfast this morning on the lanai. My problem is I don't know where or what a lanai is."

"It's a porch or balcony. Emily usually has her breakfast on the ground floor lanai," he explained. He gestured toward the rain coming down the windows. "But as you can see, the weather isn't cooperating. Breakfast is in the dining room. Right through that archway." He pointed in the direction from which he had just come. "You can't miss it."

"Thank you."

He gave her a nod before he walked off. She watched him for a couple of seconds. The back view was every bit as good as the front. Then she walked through the archway he'd indicated. A living room led into a dining room where Emily Harmon was seated.

"Ah, Julie." She glanced up. "Did you have a good night's rest?"

"Yes, I did, thank you."

"Sit wherever you like," Emily instructed. "What will you have? Juice? Fresh fruit? Pineapple? Papaya? Malia will fix you some eggs."

"Fruit and toast is fine. I've never been able to eat a large breakfast." Julie took the chair across from Emily.

"Pineapple or papaya?" Malia asked.

"Hm. Papaya. Thank you."

As Malia disappeared through a door, Emily offered, "Coffee?"

"Yes, please. Black." Julie noticed a place setting at the end of the table. It hadn't been used. She supposed it was for Ruel Chandler.

Malia returned carrying half a papaya in a bowl, a green tinge to its ripely yellow skin. A lemon wedge was nestled in its hollowed-out center.

"Squeeze the lemon juice over the fruit," Emily Harmon instructed. "It tones down the sweetness and gives it a tangy flavor."

Julie didn't want to tell Emily that she'd eaten plenty of papayas. The older woman seemed determined to teach her things that everybody knew. She squeezed the lemon wedge and scooped out a spoonful. It was deliciously sweet.

Emily was waiting for her opinion. "It's very good," Julie assured her.

The older woman nodded her approval and turned to Malia. "Would you please find out if Ruel intends to join us this morning? I'm not even sure he's up yet. I know he came in very late last night."

"He's up." Julie offered the information and met Emily's questioning gaze with a bland smile. "He was walking through the entryway when I came down. He was talking to someone named Al."

"You met him, then?" It wasn't exactly a question.

"Yes, he introduced himself. I didn't know that he was Debbie's brother."

"Never mind, Malia. If he's going to join us, he'll be along. He probably went to see Deborah," Emily said.

"Very well." Malia glanced at Julie. "I'll bring you some toast."

"Actually, Ruel is Deborah's half-brother," Emily said

as the housekeeper left the room. Her tone was matter-of-fact. "Deborah is the daughter of Ruel's father's second wife."

"Oh." Julie thought that over for an instant. "Then you aren't really related to Deborah."

"Not by blood but I consider that an unimportant detail."

Julie believed her. Emily Harmon seemed genuinely devoted to the young girl Julie had not yet met. "What does Ruel do?" she asked.

"He manages this place and he has business interests in Honolulu and Waikiki." The last was admitted very grudgingly.

The statement that Emily had made yesterday at the airport about Ruel came back to Julie. The older woman had been talking about the proliferation of hotels and skyscrapers and said that Ruel called it progress. Julie understood that it was a touchy subject with Emily Harmon, so she avoided it.

"It was too dark for me to see much last night and with the rain this morning, I really don't know all of what you have here," she commented.

"The usual. Sugar fields. Cattle. But it's unusual now on Oahu, what with all the development," Emily said. "Of course, Ruel spends most of the time in Honolulu with his other . . . projects. Al oversees most of the work around here." The tone of her voice left little doubt that it was a situation Emily Harmon didn't like.

When Malia returned with the toast, Julie let the conversation lag. Ruel and his business interests seemed to be a sore subject with Emily. Maybe it was best to get busy with the butter and guava jam before attempting to discuss anything else.

After breakfast was finished, Emily suggested, "Let me take you to Deborah. I know she's eager to meet you."

"Sure," Julie said. The two of them left the dining room together. Rain continued to come down outside, but it wasn't the deluge it had been. The air in the house was muggy and warm.

"Deborah's room is here on the ground floor. It used to be Ruel's bedroom, so his comings and goings at odd hours wouldn't disturb the rest of us. After Deborah's accident, it was much easier to move his things to a guest room on the second floor than to try to get a hospital bed upstairs. And"—a smile briefly touched the older woman's mouth—"when Deborah starts walking again, we won't have to worry about her falling down the stairs."

They were crossing the entryway and Julie glanced at the stairwell, understanding Emily's concern. It would have been next to impossible to get a hospital bed up and around those stairs, and dangerous for anyone on crutches to negotiate the polished wooden treads.

Entering the second, smaller wing of the house, they passed a room that was a combination study and library. The door stood open to reveal an unoccupied room. A second door was also open. Emily went ahead through it and Julie followed.

The room was dominated by the stark serviceability of a large hospital bed. A dark-haired, dark-eyed girl lay framed by the white sheet. A rolling table that fit over the bed held the usual teenage paraphernalia: cell phone, magazines, an iPod with a custom cover, and a set of headphones with earbuds.

A very expensive flat-screen computer took up another table that had been adapted for Debbie's use. Julie saw a game box and a CD/DVD burner beside it, bristling with knobs and wires, and CD cases scattered on top of both.

Okay, so maybe Debbie was a little spoiled. But a lot of kids owned that much gear. Julie noticed the warmth in the girl's smile and was reassured. Malia had not been exaggerating.

"Hi, Auntie Em," Debbie Chandler greeted her aunt first, but her interested gaze was centered on Julie.

"Hello, dear. This is Julie Lancaster," Emily said. "We got in rather late last night and I sent her to bed right away."

Deborah gave Julie a look of conspiratorial amusement when her aunt turned to open the curtains a little more. Julie smiled at her. It was clear that everyone was used to Emily Harmon's bossiness and didn't take it too seriously.

"Hello, Ms. Lancaster," Debbie said politely. "How was your flight? It takes forever but you get, like, a million packets of macadamia nuts and stuff."

Julie nodded. "Yeah, I ate a lot of them. They're pretty good. You can call me Julie, by the way." She approached the bed. One side of the girl's face was faintly discolored but the bruises had practically faded. Julie felt a flash of pity for her. Being confined to bed couldn't be easy.

"This is Sue Ling, my nurse." Debbie introduced a slender Asian woman, uniformed in a white pantsuit, as she lifted a tray from a service cart.

"Glad to have you with us, Julie." The nurse smiled.

Again Julie felt thoroughly welcomed. "I'm glad to be here." Of all the people she had met since she arrived, only Ruel Chandler had held himself aloof. But it was foolish to think about him. He wasn't the reason she was here. The girl in the hospital bed was.

"Yeah, I'm glad too," Debbie said. "My right arm and my head are the only two things that I can move." She rapped on her body cast. "I hate being Plaster Girl. Sue won't let me draw on it."

Sue Ling tsk-tsked. "I have to keep it clean. You know that, Debbie."

"Yeah, I guess so. But it would be something to do."

Emily Harmon stood by, smiling without speaking. Julie realized that the older woman was giving her a chance to get to know Debbie a little without interfering, and she was grateful.

"So anyway, I actually want to study, Julie. I'm totally bored," the girl said.

"Okay, great," Julie laughed. Not many people would joke about being in a body cast, especially a sixteen-year-old. "Good for you. We'll get you up to speed by the time you're ready to go back to school."

"She's nice, Auntie Em," Debbie declared suddenly. "Thank you for bringing her over."

"You're welcome, Deborah." Emily Harmon's face softened with tenderness. "I'll leave you two alone now. I have other work to do."

"I'll take the breakfast tray back to the kitchen. I won't be long." Sue Ling exited the room with Emily.

"Ruel told me he met you this morning," Debbie said.

"Yes, I was lost. This is a big house. I had to ask him for directions," Julie admitted.

"I know. He told me," was the smiling response.

Julie could just imagine what he told her—*your new teacher didn't know what a lanai was.*

"Did you like him?" Debbie asked eagerly. "My friends think he's hot. But he's my brother, so what can I say?"

Evidently an answer wasn't required. "He is handsome." The edges of Julie's mouth twitched with a smile. She couldn't help wondering how a super-serious guy like Ruel Chandler reacted to giggly teenage adulation.

"Not really. Well, maybe he is. For a brother."

"I know what you mean," Julie laughed.

"Do you have one?"

"Yeah. He's older. I really like him now but I didn't always."

"Does he live in Boston?" Debbie asked. "Auntie Em said you were from Boston."

"Actually, I'm not. No, he lives in Michigan with his wife and two little girls. I haven't seen him in quite a while."

"Cool. You're an aunt."

"That's right."

"And we both have big brothers so we have something in common."

"I guess we do, Deborah." Julie smiled.

Laughter sparkled in the girl's dark eyes. "Um, call me Debbie, okay? Deborah sounds like I did something wrong and you just found out."

"Debbie it is."

"What's your favorite subject?" Debbie seemed determined to find something else in common with her new teacher.

"American history."

"Mine's English. What about math?"

"It's my weak spot," Julie admitted.

"Mine too."

"Then we're both in trouble!" They shared a laugh and talked for a while longer. Julie kept the conversation centered on Debbie's schoolwork, finding out how far along she was and what interested her. Most of it was information she would confirm later with Debbie's teacher when they met. But she wanted to get a feel for her new student's abilities. The girl seemed really positive about learning.

When Sue Ling came back, Julie was ready to leave. "Okay, that gives me a good idea of what you like and what you don't like. Thanks for talking to me, Debbie."

Debbie looked a little put out. "Do you have to go?"

"Hey, I haven't unpacked yet." For a few seconds Julie watched Sue Ling begin to tidy up the clutter on her patient's bed table and then she waved good-bye. "See you later."

It was still raining when the time came to keep the appointment with Debbie's schoolteacher. Emily Harmon went with Julie, although she didn't really participate in the discussion.

Julie couldn't make up her mind whether her employer was merely being polite or wanted to find out how Julie would talk to a fellow professional. Either way, Julie felt the discussion went well, and she returned to the house with an armload of books, school records, and subject study schedules.

"Dinner is at seven," Emily told her on their arrival at the house. "Please be prompt. I change for it but you don't have to."

Julie decided that she would, just to be polite. Besides, the clothes she had on were damp from dashing around in the rain. She chose an ocher skirt and a matching blouse in gorgeous silk, and came downstairs a little before seven to join Emily in the living room. There was no sign of Ruel Chandler.

At seven on the dot, Emily rose from her chair. "Shall we go in to dinner?"

"But," Julie hesitated, "aren't you going to wait for your . . . nephew?"

"He knows what time we have dinner. If he isn't here, we start without him," was the uncompromising answer.

"With the rain and all, he might be delayed by the weather." Julie didn't understand why she felt she had to make excuses for him.

"I've learned to expect Ruel when he arrives," Emily explained. "He's thirty-five and he doesn't seem inclined to tell me his schedule."

"Does he drive into Honolulu every day?" Julie asked, hoping she didn't sound too curious.

"Practically." Emily Harmon led the way into the dining room.

"Long commute."

"He has an apartment in the city. If it's too late, he simply stays there."

Somehow Julie doubted that he always spent the night alone. She glanced around the dining room, so welcoming and elegant with its rich woods and glassed doorway, to the courtyard and swimming pool outside.

Ruel Chandler not only had all the comforts of a big house, but a bachelor pad as well, she thought ruefully.

Emily Harmon had noticed Julie's gaze stray outdoors. "I often have my evening meal on the lanai, especially if I'm alone." Her lips thinned. "I hope this Kona weather doesn't last long."

"It has something to do with the winds, doesn't it?" asked Julie.

"The trade winds come from the northeast," the older woman began. "They're our dominant winds."

Julie suppressed a smile. Emily Harmon seemed to be incapable of a simple explanation.

"As you will see, the trade winds bring fair skies and sunshine. When the winds are from the south, it means rain and high humidity. No one likes the Kona winds."

"And why are they called that?"

"They take their name from the big island of Hawaii and its Kona coast. Since the big island lies south of Oahu, the winds coming from that direction are also coming from Kona, hence Kona winds."

"I see," Julie murmured politely.

Malia came in with the soup course and the discussion of the weather was put aside. Fresh fruit and good cheese were served for dessert. Ruel Chandler still had not made an appearance. They had tea in the living room while Malia cleared the dining room table.

"I think I'll go see Debbie," said Julie when she had finished her tea. "Do you mind?"

Emily Harmon glanced up from the magazine she was reading. "No, go right ahead."

The television set in the bedroom was on when Julie knocked and walked in. Debbie seemed surprised to see her but gave her a big smile.

"Ready to hit the books tomorrow?" Julie asked teasingly.

"Yeah. I really am bored."

"What are you watching?" She glanced at the screen as a commercial flashed on.

"*American Idol.* Don't you hate Simon? He's so mean. Paula Abdul is nice, though."

Julie settled herself cross-legged in a chair by Debbie's bed while they discussed the merits of the latest round of contestants. They talked for a while, about music and many other things. Julie found more to like in the girl. At times she seemed oddly mature, and at others she was innocent and vulnerable. In all respects, she was a typical teenager, interested in music, boys, school, and the future.

They were halfway through the show when Debbie's cell phone rang. Debbie flipped it open and looked at the caller ID. "Mm. It's Cathy. Do I want to talk to Cathy?"

Julie shrugged. "I'll see you in the morning," she whispered as she uncoiled her legs from the chair.

"You don't have to go, Julie. I can watch TV and talk to her and you at the same time. She's watching the show too."

"You don't really want your teacher listening in on your conversation," Julie insisted with a knowing smile. Debbie started to argue as she finally picked up Cathy's call. But she was soon distracted by her friend's chatter.

"Good night, Debbie," Julie said.

"Good night."

When Julie didn't find Emily Harmon in the living room, she went on upstairs to her bedroom. She looked over the work sheet she had filled in for the next day's subjects and got ready for bed somewhere around ten. The house was quiet. It occurred to her that she hadn't heard Ruel Chandler come home.

CHAPTER FOUR

During her first week, Ruel Chandler only had dinner with them twice. He was pleasant and courteous to Julie, but he didn't go out of his way to make her feel like part of the family. His attitude was such a contrast to everyone else's that she sometimes let it bother her. Wanting everybody to like her had always been one of her faults. So she tried to ignore her pointless frustration.

Her first free weekend she decided against doing any sightseeing. She would have time to tour the whole island in the next few months. Wearing a swimsuit beneath her jeans and top, she thought she would get a little sun and shop for souvenirs for her friends and family.

Emily suggested that she do both in the town of Haleiwa and offered to let her use one of the old cars that Dan had fixed up in his spare hours. Julie visited the big garage that held the family's cars, took one look at it, and decided to go by bus, even though it meant a long walk down the switchback road to the highway.

Haleiwa was quaint, with old storefronts and roadside fruit and shell stands. A small shopping center, recently expanded, had kept the rustic motif of the older stores, complete with board sidewalks. It was a peaceful seaside community.

After exploring a general store and a neighborhood art gallery, she had lunch outdoors at a sandwich shop. Then she wandered down to the small harbor. Applying sunscreen liberally, per Emily Harmon's inevitable instructions, she lay out for a couple of hours in the sun and watched the sailboats and other small craft going in and out. Later she returned to the town proper, purchased some souvenirs that weren't too tacky, and caught the bus back.

After walking for so much of the day, she found the road leading to the house much longer, plus she had the added burden of the things she'd bought. She began to wish she'd taken the beater car after all as she eyed the steep switchback road to the upper part of the estate.

A car roared toward her from behind and Julie moved to the grassy shoulder. Instead of swerving past her, it slowed to a stop. At first she saw only the sleek, black sports car with the passenger door opening before she realized that Ruel Chandler was behind the wheel.

"Hop in," he said.

With the daunting prospect of climbing that hill, Julie didn't need a second invitation. "Thanks." She slid into the bucket seat, juggled her packages, and closed the door.

Immediately the car was shifted into gear and it shot forward. "Been shopping, I see." His blue gaze flicked to the assortment of bags on her lap.

"I went into Haleiwa," she offered in explanation.

"Nothing more ambitious than that?" He sounded as if he were mocking her but Julie couldn't be sure. She was determined not to let his condescending attitude get under her skin.

"No," she said. "Not this weekend." The low-slung

car seemed to snake around the tight curves up the hill. "I thought I'd go to the beach tomorrow, swim, just take it easy."

"If it's swimming and sun you want, you're better off in the pool at the house," he told her. "We have strong currents here on the north shore and powerful undertows. And you can get pretty banged up on the coral reefs if you can't swim clear."

"Sounds awful," she murmured.

"The beaches at Haleiwa or Waimea are about the only places for what you have in mind. If there aren't any breakers, you can feel safe swimming at Waimea."

"I'll remember that. Thanks." Within seconds he was braking the car to a stop in the circular drive of the house. "Thanks for the lift too. It would have been a long, hard walk." She was determined to be pleasant, and properly but not overly appreciative.

"No problem."

Leaving the black sports car parked in the drive, Ruel walked up to the house with her and opened the door, since her hands were full of packages.

"Thanks again." Julie smiled. His nod of acknowledgment was courteous and nothing more. He returned to the car.

"Ruel?" she heard Debbie call from her bedroom.

"It's me—Julie."

"You're back already!" came the loud reply.

It was silly to keep shouting back and forth. Julie walked to the girl's bedroom and appeared in the doorway.

"Wow, you got a lot of stuff. Can I see?" Debbie asked. "Did you find something for your landlady?"

"I think so." Julie set her armload of plastic bags on a chair and tried to keep them from slithering off. "I told you she loves old movies and Elvis. Check this out. Mrs. Kelly will look like an extra in *Blue Hawaii*."

From one of the bags she took out a muumuu. The flowered material was mostly scarlet with splashes of orange and yellow. She held up the shapeless garment in front of her for Debbie to see. "What do you think?"

"The color is all wrong. Too bright," Ruel commented from the doorway.

Julie turned to him, startled. "It isn't for me."

"It's for her landlady, Mrs. Kelly," Debbie added.

"Do you hate her that much?" He lifted a doubtful eyebrow when he looked at Julie.

"No." Julie glanced at the audaciously bold material. "I think this is what she would expect."

"Yes," Debbie agreed. "It's a muumuu for a leprechaun. It's so awful it's cool," she giggled.

Ruel glanced from one to the other. "This must be a private joke."

Julie didn't feel like explaining it to him. She folded the long dress and returned it to the bag, gathering the rest of them together.

"It is a private joke. So don't ask questions."

Julie looked at Ruel to see how he would react to Debbie's rather rude answer. He only grinned at his sister. Then she changed the subject.

"I thought I heard your car in the driveway just before Julie arrived."

"You did. I gave her a ride from the highway."

"At least you didn't have to climb our miniature Matterhorn," Debbie teased.

"That's what I thought," Julie agreed. "Okay, I'm going back to my room. Talk to you later, Debbie."

"Okay."

Ruel stepped to one side to let Julie past. Being under his gaze made her skin prickle. It was an odd sensation that didn't go away until she was in her room.

*   *   *

Wearing a ladylike wraparound skirt that Emily Harmon would have approved and a shell-pink blouse over her swimsuit, Julie attended Sunday service the next day at one of the little churches along the highway.

Afterward she took the bus to Sunset Beach where there were as many surfers as tourists. One group was on the sand dunes watching, the other was bobbing in the ocean with their brightly colored surfboards.

She slipped off her sandals and walked barefoot on the beach. She found a peaceful spot, took a towel from her beach bag, and spread it over the sand. The tugging trade winds flipped up the corner, and she anchored all four with her shoes, bottle of sunscreen, and her beach bag.

Stretching out her long legs, she began applying the sunscreen to her exposed skin. Luckily she tanned easily but she knew about the deceptive tropic sun of the islands and didn't want to risk a burn.

Leaning back on her elbows, Julie watched the surfers. The waves seemed awesome when compared with the California sun she knew. Here they looked as if they were ten feet high. A surfer on a red board caught her eye as she watched him paddle out. He was a powerful swimmer and a good surfer, and rode the big wave effortlessly, with graceful twists of his body. Julie held her breath when she saw him disappear into the curl, but he shot out the other side, crouched on his board.

In triumph, the surfer rode the wave into shore, getting the most out of the collapsing wave before it carried him to the beach. Breathless, ecstatic, he picked up his board and looked back at the ocean that he had conquered for a few moments. Julie couldn't resist applauding.

He turned, suntanned and golden, and flashed that happy, triumphant smile at her.

"Great ride," Julie called.

He trotted up the sand to where she sat and dropped on his knees beside her. "That wave was perfect," he said. "Like a dream."

"I saw it," she nodded.

He was still trying to catch his breath, panting from the exertion of the ride. His shining brown eyes looked her over with obvious appreciation.

"Do you surf?" he asked.

"I have," Julie admitted. "But that was a long time ago. These waves are out of my league."

He set his board upright in the sand and sat down beside her. "Where are you from?"

"California."

"I'm Frank Smythe from Virginia." He offered her his hand.

"Julie Lancaster." His grip was firm but he didn't attempt to hold her hand too long.

"What are you doing here?"

"Like everybody else, I'm here to watch," she answered, glancing toward the tourists on the beach.

"No, I meant what are you doing here in Hawaii? Are you on vacation?"

"I'm working. How about you?" she returned his question.

"I'm working too, at night. Got a job as a waiter in a restaurant up the road. I came here, like, two years ago to see if the surf was as great as everybody said it was. I'm still here."

"I've only been here a week myself, but I already like it," Julie said. She looked down at her pale skin, comparing it mentally to his deep tan.

"Your back is beginning to look a little red. Want me to put some lotion on it?" Frank Smythe offered.

Julie hesitated, then agreed with a nod. "Okay. Thanks." As he worked the cool lotion over her shoulders and spine, she noticed the caressing quality to his touch. Julie knew he was waiting for a reaction from her, but she waited a little while, enjoying the pampering.

"That's great," she said at last. "Thanks again."

He stopped rubbing her back and gave her a long look. "A bunch of us are getting together for a party tonight. Want to hang out?"

"No, I have to work tomorrow," she replied. "Maybe another time."

"Remember you said that," he smiled. For another fifteen minutes or so, he sat and talked to her. His gaze kept moving between her and the waves swelling in the sea.

Rising, he lifted his surfboard. "I guess I'll go back out. Sure you don't want to come along?"

"No, thanks. Catch a good one," she wished him.

With a last wave to her, he waded into the water and lay on his board to paddle out to where the other surfers were bobbing. Julie stayed for another hour, enjoying the glorious beauty of the scene. Sometimes she saw Frank trying to wave, but most of the time she had his red surfboard mixed up with one belonging to another surfer. After spending another hour in the hot sun, she decided to leave.

This time she took the bus to Waimea Bay. The water was glass smooth. There weren't any of the breakers that Ruel had warned her about. After a cooling swim in the clear turquoise waters, Julie chose to avoid baking in the sun and relaxed in the shade of the trees in the park.

It was almost five before she caught the bus to take her back. She enjoyed the ride, even if the bus driver acted as if he owned the road where other traffic was concerned. She was free to look at the countryside.

Horses grazed in small pastures and an odd cow or two was staked out in a vacant lot. There were stands of trees she didn't recognize crowding the beaches and green hills rising away from the road. There were sugar-cane fields and, oddly enough, cornfields. A flowering shrub of some sort seemed to be blooming in almost every yard the bus passed.

Julie was so intent on the scenery that she almost missed her stop. Luckily she didn't. This time, though, Ruel didn't drive up behind her once she was off the bus. She had to walk all the way to the house, including up the switchback road, and the calves of her legs were aching when she finally entered the house.

The pace of the first week set the routine for the second week. The better part of the day was spent with Debbie and her schoolwork. Then, sometimes, Julie would swim in the pool in the late afternoon. But she liked to get out of the house when she could. On her next two free days, she took the bus to the Polynesian Cultural Center at Laie where the crafts and culture of the various Polynesian tribes were kept alive.

The third week began much the same as the first two. The trade winds blew and the skies remained clear. Invariably there was a small shower or two at some time during each day, often when the sun was out. Liquid sunshine, it was called by the natives. Generally it was blown by the winds from rain clouds hooked by the mountain peaks. Julie didn't mind it. To her it was like walking under a soft spray of warm water.

On Thursday, she had taken a quick dip in the pool, showered, and dried her hair. Over the last two and a half weeks, her skin had taken on a golden cast and her hair had lightened a shade. She took a pale green sundress from her closet and slipped it on.

It was too early yet for dinner, but the weather was too nice to stay indoors. Julie wandered onto the lanai

off her bedroom. She had learned the first week that at
the end of the lanai there were stairs leading to the
ground. It was perfect for swimming. She never had to
track through the house in a wet suit; she could use the
outside stairs to her bedroom.

Now she descended them to wander through the ex-
pansive garden surrounding the pool. It was a favorite
place of hers, a private tropical paradise lined with palm
trees. A massive banyan tree dominated the grounds.
To support its spreading growth, the tree sent shoots
downward that would ultimately form new roots and
trunks. As Julie wandered among its pillars; she was
glad it wasn't carnivorous.

An autograph tree carried Debbie's name on one
side of its large ovate leaves. Julie touched a pink-shaded
petal of one of its large white flowers. Emily had told
her that in the West Indies, the leaves of the autograph
tree were marked and used as playing cards.

The feathery leaves of the gray-barked jacaranda tree
waved gently in the breeze. Violet-blue flowers were
scattered over its limbs. A magnificent Royal Poinciana
flamed like a scarlet umbrella in the garden, rivaled
only by the peculiar tiger's-claw tree. Bare of leaves, the
tips of its branches were painted crimson by its claw-
shaped blossoms.

Closer to the ground were the flowering shrubs. The
delicate blossoms of the spider lily seemed lost in a clus-
tered spray of long, wide leaves. The yellow blossoms of
the plumeria were a favorite choice for leis. The anthuri-
ums never looked real to her. The single, circular petal
of brilliant red was so shiny, it looked artificial.

As Julie strolled past a hybrid hibiscus bush that hadn't
been in bloom before, she saw a flower had blossomed.
The other hibiscus were scarlet or deep pink, but this
one was a golden yellow. She cupped it in her hand to
draw it down and sniff the fragrance. The stem snapped

KONA WINDS   225

in her fingers. After a moment's hesitation, she tucked
it behind her ear.

The sun was sinking behind the Waianae range. Its
lengthening rays cast scarlet-pink hues on the puffy
white clouds and set fire to the serrated outline of the
mountain peaks. It was a beautiful and quiet display put
on by nature.

Julie's slow pace brought her to the lanai, with a hazy
idea in mind of watching the sunset from the wicker
chair there.

"Enjoying the sunset?"

Julie glanced toward the shadows of the lanai where
Ruel's voice had come from, and saw his familiar tall
form leaning against a pillar.

"Yes. It's beautiful."

Straightening, he walked leisurely toward her and
stopped. The dimming light accented the masculine
angularity of his features while the slanting rays of the
flaming sun did wonderful things for the mahogany
sheen of his hair. Dressed in a white linen shirt with
small shell buttons that were mostly unbuttoned, and
clean, faded jeans, he looked casually sexy and somehow elegant at the same time.

Nice, she thought nervously. Very nice.

His gaze centered on the flower behind her right
ear. "Looking for a lover?"

"What?"

"You're wearing a flower on the right side. That's
what it means."

"Oh. Well, I didn't know that."

He grinned at her.

"I accidentally picked it, and it was so pretty I decided it was a shame to throw it away, so I stuck it in my
hair." She knew she was rattling on but it was hard to
stop.

"Come to think of it, maybe that's not what it signifies," he mused. "That's just what floated into my head. You look really pretty, by the way."

His blunt statement made her even more nervous. He studied her mouth. Her lips felt dry. She wanted to lick them but that would only make things worse.

"You kind of look like a flower yourself," he went on, "in that dress, I mean. Better watch out for bees."

She shot him a look. She was definitely not interested in a birds-and-the-bees conversation. Next they would be talking about something really dangerous . . . like pistils and stamens and pollination. Basic biology. Male and female.

Julie told herself mentally to snap out of it. "Right."

His mouth quirked at her obvious embarrassment.

"Ruel?" Malia called to him from the dining room door to the lanai. "Phone for you."

"Thanks, Malia, I'll be right in," he answered, never taking his eyes from Julie. "See you around," he said softly and went inside.

When he had gone, Julie discovered she was trembling. How ridiculous. She scolded herself for getting so worked up over some stupid flirting. Surely she was more mature than that. But it was several minutes before she felt calm enough to go in to dinner.

Emily Harmon was at the table when Julie entered through the French doors. A place was set for Ruel but he wasn't in the room. She took her regular chair. Malia entered the dining room and Emily gave her a sharp look.

"He's still on the phone, Miss Emily."

"Then go ahead and serve the soup," the older woman said.

The housekeeper left and returned with a tureen of delectable bisque. Julie was half-finished with hers when Ruel came striding into the room. He looked not in the least concerned that he was late, or that they had begun without him.

"Your soup is getting cold," Emily informed him.

Instead of walking to his chair at the head of the table, Ruel stopped at his aunt's. "Something's come up. I won't be able to have dinner with you tonight after all."

Disappointment made the older woman's mouth droop for an instant but it was banished quickly by what could only be described as a stiff upper lip, Julie noticed.

"Why?" Emily demanded.

"I have to go into the city." He bent and lightly kissed the woman's forehead. "Don't wait up for me, Em."

The lines at the corners of his eyes crinkled when he smiled at his aunt. Julie thought she detected an affectionate tone in his voice even as he gently mocked her.

Emily sniffed with disdain. "I haven't waited up for you in years, Ruel."

"Good night." It was an all-encompassing farewell. Ruel walked out of the room.

Julie thought it best not to comment on his departure unless Emily mentioned it. Minutes later, the quiet of the evening was broken by the roar of the sports car as it accelerated from the house.

"Why does he have to drive so fast?" Emily muttered, masking her concern with anger. She caught Julie's glance and added, "I wouldn't have been surprised if Ruel had been in an accident instead of Deborah."

Julia waited until Malia had taken away the soup dishes, then tried to introduce a different topic. "Deborah said that the cast on her left arm is to be removed next week."

As she'd hoped, the conversation turned to Emily's niece—her schoolwork and health in general. By the end of the meal, Emily seemed more relaxed. Julie had felt the tension that had existed at the start of dinner.

The strange part was that the tension seemed to transfer to her. She was restless all evening. She tried to watch a documentary on TV, but it didn't hold her interest. She knew it would be hopeless to try to concentrate on a book as Emily was doing. She wandered into Debbie's room, thinking she might go online, but Debbie was talking to her boyfriend on her cell phone.

Finally Julie went to her own room. She wrote a short letter to her parents and a longer one to Marilyn, and answered the one from Mrs. Kelly, who had loved the muumuu. For a long time she sat in one of the wicker chairs on her balcony. At half past eleven, she got ready for bed even though she wasn't sleepy.

When she switched off the light and climbed into bed, the luminous digital clock kept her company. Unwillingly she watched the numbers change as the hours passed. It was after two o'clock when she heard the sports car quietly drive up. She rolled on her side and fell asleep at last.

CHAPTER FIVE

Time had gone by so swiftly. It seemed impossible to Julie that she had been in Hawaii for more than a month. Still, it was another weekend again—Saturday. She leaned against the balcony railing, enjoying her view of the garden. It was a riot of color: hibiscus, bougainvillea, oleanders, poinciana.

The sun was well up in the morning sky and the air was warm. Her plans for the day were still fairly open. She wanted to start with a swim in the pool, for which she was already wearing her orange bikini and beach jacket. Then, breakfast . . . and maybe a trip to the Kahuku Sugar Mill. Julie lifted her gaze to the hills where thick stands of pine trees would randomly give way to open meadows.

As her gaze ran over the rising hills, it was stopped by the ominous billowing of smoke. She stared for a long, heart-stopping minute. It seemed to be coming from just over the next rise. Julie raced into her bedroom, out the door, and down the stairs. As she rounded the corner into the living room where one of the telephones was, she collided with a rock-solid object. She would

have careened off it like a billiard ball, but her upper
arms were clamped by a pair of strong hands.

"Where are you going in such a hurry?" Ruel de
manded.

The collision had knocked the breath out of her. It
was a couple of seconds before she could manage to say,
"Fire! There's a . . . fire!"

She became conscious of the well-muscled body
inches from hers, aggressively male and sexually strong.
He smelled clean and fresh with an individual scent of
his own that was faintly musky. His mouth set in a line
when he heard what she said.

"Where?" He didn't let go of her.

"Just over the next hill." Julie gulped in a breath. "I
saw the smoke from the balcony."

He hesitated, as if not believing her. "Show me."

"There isn't time!" she protested. "We've got to call
the fire department!"

"Show me where it is first."

"Are you crazy?"

"Most days, no." He kept a firm hold on her arm as
he propelled her toward the doors of the lower lanai.
Julie resisted briefly, looking frantically at the telephone
just out of her reach, before going along for the sake of
speed.

Outside the smoke was plainly visible beyond the
fronds of the palm trees.

"Do you see it?" she pointed.

"Yeah. It's coming from our cane fields," Ruel said.

"We'd better call the fire department right away," she
said decisively.

Instead of letting her go, Ruel kept his grip on her
arm, and her exasperated look caught the amused slant
of his mouth.

"I said it was the cane field," he repeated.

"I know what you said," she began. "Now let go of me."

He finally did.

"Would you mind telling me what's going on?"

"It's being deliberately burned off." He seemed to enjoy knowing something she didn't. "The fire was set on purpose. The men are keeping an eye on it. There's no need to call the fire department."

"Oh. Well, I didn't know that. I was concerned for Debbie—and all of us."

"I appreciate your concern," Ruel said gravely. "But there's nothing to worry about. Obviously you've never seen a cane field burned." He gave her a considering look. "Can you ride a horse?"

"Pretty well, yeah."

"Go and change into some jeans and I'll have a horse saddled for you. We'll ride over so you can see firsthand how it's done."

"Give me a minute," Julie said, sure that her rush of enthusiasm was for a new experience and nothing more.

Again she raced through the house for the stairs. In record time, she changed into a tan blouse and jeans, and a pair of flat-heeled boots. She hurried back down the stairs. Her foot was on the last step as Ruel walked through the front door.

"Ready?" He gave her an approving once-over.

"Yes." She was slightly out of breath but it didn't interfere with the eagerness of her smile.

"The horses are saddled and waiting." He held the door open for her and followed her out. "You can ride the gray. He's well trained and docile."

Ruel held the bridle while Julie mounted, and the horse stood quietly. It was an unusual experience to be looking down at Ruel. His superior height demanded that she always look up.

"How are the stirrups? Are they short enough?"

Julie shifted a bit in the saddle, checking the length "Fine."

A blaze-faced chestnut snorted softly at Ruel when he looped the reins around its neck. It stood as quietly as her horse had when he mounted. Reining his horse around, Ruel started toward the trees and Julie followed.

She soon saw that a barely visible trail wound through the trees. On the other side was a stable with two more horses in the corral. They came whinnying to the fence as they rode by. Once they were out of the trees, onto rolling but relatively flat terrain, Ruel urged his horse into a canter.

The smoke was clearly visible now. Julie expected the cane field to appear any minute over the next rise as Ruel angled toward it. But it was farther away than it looked. Julie didn't mind. It was an exhilarating ride. Her gray horse had a comfortable gait and kept up easily with Ruel's.

Finally they topped a hill and she saw the burning cane field below. Ruel reined in his horse and stopped it on a small knoll overlooking the field, and Julie halted her mount beside his.

"This is close enough for the horses," he said. "If we get any nearer to the fire, it might spook them."

Julie nodded. She noticed the way the gray's ears were pricked toward the crackling sound of the flames. Its head was held alert and high. The trade wind was blowing the smoke away from them.

Half of a green field of sugarcane was blackened by the fire. Where the flames ate into new areas, it glowed orange red. Julie frowned at the sight. Towering stalks of cane with their mauve tassels were being destroyed by the fire.

"What's wrong with the field that you have to burn it?" she asked.

"We burn our fields before we harvest the cane," Ruel explained.

"I know this is probably a dumb question," Julie said, feeling awkward, "but why?"

"There are several reasons. The fire destroys the debris and excess plant life. At the same time, it seals sugar juice in the stalk. Plus it gets rid of all the insects and vermin that have been living in the field."

"You mean rats and snakes and things like that?" Julie was glad they watching from the knoll and weren't down where the creatures would come scurrying out.

"Not snakes. Well, not many. Non-native snakes have been introduced, but Hawaii used not to have any."

"Do you mean this was once an Eden without serpents?" she asked.

"Yes."

"It's still beautiful."

"Yes, it is. But we stand to lose a lot of rare species found only in Hawaii. Introduced species are a big problem."

"Debbie was doing a report on that," Julie said thoughtfully. She returned her attention to the scene below. "It seems so old-fashioned somehow. The burning, I mean."

"It is," Ruel agreed. "Sugarcane is a labor intensive crop and not very profitable. Most sugar comes from beets now. But these people are the children and grandchildren and great-grandchildren of men and women who worked the Hawaii cane fields. This is what they know and what they do. I'm not going to ask them to quit."

Julie respected him for sticking to tradition—and for his love of the land he'd grown up on. Then she heard a faint crackling sound in the grass near her horse's hooves and looked apprehensively at Ruel.

"Anything else I should know about in the way of interesting critters?" she asked.

"Well, there are scorpions in the cane fields. Lots of 'em. Probably as many as the rats."

"I don't suppose there's much you can do about either of them." Her gaze was drawn to his face, liking the look of it now that his mood was not so withdrawn and cynical.

"A plantation owner some time back tried to do something about eradicating the rats. He imported mongoose from India but it was a dismal failure. The mongoose sleeps at night when the rats are out. Now the island has another pest—the mongoose." An ironic smile came to his lips. His gaze locked onto hers in quiet contemplation.

The gray stamped a restless foot. Julie smoothed a hand over its neck and glanced toward the burning field. "How long does it take to grow sugar?"

"From eighteen to twenty-four months, depending on the amount of rainfall. It take two thousand pounds of water to make one pound of sugar. Tourists are usually fascinated by statistics like that," he observed dryly.

"Is it true?"

"Would I lie to you?" Resting an arm on the saddle horn, he looked at her with those cool blue eyes. "Did I tell you about the shadowless days?"

"No."

"The Hawaiian islands are officially located in the tropics, specifically, the Tropic of Cancer. Since we're so near to the equator, there are days in the summer when the sun is so directly overhead that an object—building, tree, or person—doesn't cast a shadow."

"Interesting," she said, not entirely sure that he wasn't pulling her leg.

Ruel glanced at his watch. "We'd better start back or you'll miss your breakfast."

Julie started to say that she didn't care, but she realized that he probably had more important things to do than explain fascinating facts about Hawaii, so she turned her horse around and pointed it back toward the house.

Her tour of the Kahuku Sugar Mill that afternoon reinforced what Ruel had told her and she learned more. The restored mill had displays that explained everything about processing sugarcane. She spent a while just watching its colorfully painted giant flywheels turning and grinding.

After church on Sunday, Julie went to the Waimea Park. It was a lush, green valley with a rippling stream and exotic plant growth. There were several historic sites being excavated—ancient, moss-covered formations offering clues of the past. The singing water of the falls itself was worth the trip, with its natural swimming pool at the base.

It was a short walk from the falls entrance to Waimea Bay Beach Park. Julie had crossed the road and was walking in that direction when a van went by. She heard somebody shout, "California! Hey, California!"

Brakes squealed and she turned to see what was going on. The van had stopped on the shoulder and Frank Smythe, the surfer she had met at Sunset Beach, was climbing out. Someone handed him his red board and a duffel bag before the van took off. With his surfboard under his arm, he dashed across the highway to where Julie stood.

"Hey, California, where'd you run off to the other day? I thought you were going to wait for me. I got out of the water and you were gone," he accused.

"I don't remember saying I was going to wait for you." Julie was positive the subject hadn't even been raised.

"Maybe not, but I thought you would." He grinned at his own conceit. "You can't imagine what I've gone through. I don't know where you live or where you work."

"I bet you were really upset," she said mockingly. "You don't even remember my name."

"Jane? No. Jeannie?"

"Oh, please." She turned to walk away.

"Julie! That's it. Julie Lancaster." He laughed out loud. "Lighten up. I remembered it. I was just kiddin' ya."

Julie found his goofiness a little unnerving. He wasn't as grown-up as he looked, despite his fabulous physique. "Nobody ever called me California before."

"That's what you look like to me. All sunny and golden, like California." He fell into step beside her.

"That description would fit Hawaiians too," she countered.

"No, Hawaii is dark hair and dark eyes," Frank assured her with an engaging smile.

"I see." She couldn't help smiling back. Lean and muscular with a swimmer's broad shoulders, he was a perfect piece of eye candy, that was for sure.

"Where are you going?"

"For a slow swim in the shallow part of the bay. Where there aren't any waves. Then I'll probably laze around in the sun for a couple of hours." Her answer was deliberately candid. With that surfboard under his arm, she doubted if Frank would settle for such a tame afternoon.

"I'll come with you."

"It's a free beach." The shrug of her shoulders said she couldn't stop him.

"Hey, California," he frowned, "are you playing hard

to get or don't you really care whether I come along? What I really mean is, do you like me or not?"

His demand put her on the spot. She didn't really know what she felt. "I guess I like what I know about you, but—"

"If I was just playing you, I wouldn't remember your name after three weeks," he stated.

"Maybe not. Sorry, Frank." She wondered why she was apologizing, and then she wondered why she was taking this so seriously. He was a good-looking guy and he wanted to hang out with her. Big deal. She reminded herself that sunny, laid-back Hawaii was a much more relaxed place than Boston.

"See? You even remember mine. That's a good sign."

"I suppose so." Julie laughed without really knowing why. It didn't make any sense but then it didn't have to. It was a beautiful day and it seemed right to share it with someone.

When they reached the long, wide stretch of white coral sand, Frank covered her beach bag and his duffel with his surfboard before they both waded into the water. They swam and floated and played around for more than an hour before Julie finally pleaded exhaustion.

"Do you know what I miss?" he said, sinking to his knees on a corner of her beach towel. "The seagulls," he said, answering his own question.

"Seagulls." Julie suddenly realized that she hadn't seen any. "Why aren't there seagulls?"

"Something to do with the fact that there's hardly any difference between high and low tide here, I think. So it doesn't give them any place to find food."

"I thought they ate garbage. No shortage of that, even in Hawaii."

"Well, that's what I heard. But I could be wrong." He grinned at her and shook his wet hair like a puppy, covering her with cold droplets. She squealed and he looked pleased.

"I'd ask you to come out with me tonight, but I have to work," Frank said suddenly.

"So do I," she said.

"What do you do?"

"I'm a teacher." She swept the wet length of her hair behind her neck, letting the water trickle down her back.

"No kidding! Which school? Maybe we can have lunch together at noon," he suggested.

"I'm not teaching at a school. I'm a private tutor for a young girl who was injured in a car crash and won't be able to go back to school for a while. She doesn't want to fall back a grade in the meantime," Julie explained.

"Sounds like you've got it made."

"It's a good job," she agreed. "I work five days and have Saturday and Sunday off."

"Where do you live?" Frank noticed her hesitation. "Hey, California, I'm not going to let you get away from me without knowing where to find you again."

"It isn't a secret." Julie wondered whether she should share the information with a guy who was essentially a stranger, and hesitated once more. She told herself that Ruel was big enough and strong enough to rip Frank's head off—and Dan lived on the property—and somewhere, so did a small army of field hands. She decided telling him where she lived wouldn't be a problem. "Emily Harmon hired me to tutor her niece Debbie Chandler. I live there."

"Chandler," Frank repeated. "The same Chandler that has that sugar plantation about a mile or so back up the highway?"

"Yes, that's the place."

He whistled. "Rich people. Must be a comedown for you to hang out with a beach bum like me."

"Don't be silly. They're really nice. Besides, I only work

for them." Julie found herself becoming defensive. But in the last month, she had begun to feel very close to Debbie and her aunt. She avoided thinking about Ruel; what made him tick was a puzzle to her still.

"Okay. Chalk it up to envy." Frank shrugged away his previous comment. "Well, your job rules out noon lunch dates. So how about next Friday night? There's always a party going on somewhere. And I don't have to work."

"All right," Julie agreed, taking a deep breath. "Friday night. What time?"

"Eight o'clock? Is that too early or too late?"

"It's fine."

"Wait until the dudes find out I have a date with my California girl." He grinned at her. "They were beginning to think I made you up—but you're real." He cupped her chin in his hand as if to reassure himself, then leaned over and kissed her.

It was a warm, exploring first kiss, like many others Julie had had, and she returned it in the same unaffected way. But when Frank started to deepen the kiss, Julie placed a checking hand against the muscled hardness of his tanned shoulder.

His mouth lifted an inch from hers, his breath warm against the faint dampness of the seawater cooling her cheek. "You're beautiful, California," he murmured.

"Don't rush it, Frank." She liked the casualness of their present relationship. She didn't want to plunge into something more serious until she tested the water.

Reluctantly Frank resumed his former position on the towel. The expression on his boyishly handsome face said he was prepared to wait and not rush it, just as she'd asked. With relative ease, he began talking about himself, telling Julie of the places he'd been and the things he'd done. He'd spent some time in Boston and they began exchanging stories about the city.

Not surprisingly, neither of them missed the awful winters.

By the time the afternoon drew to a close, Julie wasn't really eager to go. She enjoyed Frank's company, it was that simple. She slowly began gathering her things to catch the bus home.

Just as she was ready to go, Frank said, "Watch my board, California. There's one of my buddies down the beach. I'm going to see if I can borrow his wheels."

Before she could respond, he was running off across the sun-bleached sand. The gusting winds carried the name he called away from Julie's hearing. Thirty yards away, a pudgy young man turned and waited for Frank to reach him. After a brief conversation, Frank ran back, his tanned feet kicking up small sprays of sand. A set of keys jingled from the key ring in his hand.

"I've got it. It's parked in the lot," he told her and hoisted his surfboard under his arm. Grinning, he added, "We haoles stick together."

"Haoles?"

"White people," he explained, and slipped a hand under her arm. "There are so many good-looking Hawaiians—you know, dark and handsome—that when one of us gets a girl, we close ranks."

For some reason, Julie thought of Ruel Chandler when she heard *good-looking Hawaiian*, despite the fact that his hair was a burnt shade of brown and his eyes were blue—neither were the gleaming black of a real Hawaiian. So she simply smiled at Frank's comment and said nothing.

The borrowed car was an aging dune buggy. Its yellow sides were splashed with red mud. The yellow stripes on its canopied top had been bleached to a cream color by the strong sun. After stowing his surfboard in the back, Frank hopped into the driver's seat. He glanced at Julie to make sure she was safely in and started the motor. It rumbled quickly into a deafening roar. Julie suspected there was a hole in the muffler or no muffler at all.

"It's no Mercedes!" Frank shouted above the din, and shifted it into gear.

"Who cares?" Julie retorted at equal volume.

The dune buggy rattled and roared onto the highway. Since the vehicle possessed only a front windshield, the wind whipped through the open sides, churning Julie's long hair like an eggbeater. She pushed the whirling strands away from her eyes and leaned back to enjoy the wild sense of freedom.

She felt a moment of misgiving when the dune buggy roared up the circular drive. Julie could just imagine Emily Harmon's reaction when she heard the noise outside. After her frosty warnings about horny surfers, not that the older woman had or ever would use that word, this vehicle and its driver weren't going to make a good first impression. In spite of that, Julie smiled.

"Here you are, all in one piece," Frank declared above the earsplitting idle of the dune buggy.

"Surprise, surprise," she laughed.

His expression turned serious. "Don't forget, Friday night at eight sharp."

"Eight o'clock," Julie agreed.

His hand cupped the back of her neck and drew her toward him. His mouth settled onto hers, warmed by the sun and tasting of the sea. It was a hard kiss, a little possessive but definitely pleasurable. When it ended, she felt quite satisfied. But she didn't linger for a repeat.

Stepping out of the vehicle, she offered in good-bye, "I'll see you Friday."

As the dune buggy rumbled and clattered away, she descended the short flight of steps to the front door. Turning, she waved to Frank. In answer, he pushed the horn. *A-oogah! A-oogah!* The strident sound made Julie wince and then laugh. That would really impress Emily Harmon.

Upon entering the house, Julie saw her standing there. The older woman's mouth was drawn in a disapproving line, although she tried to conceal it. Meanwhile, Julie was trying to look serious, without much success.

"Someone gave you a ride home." Emily's observation was more in the order of a question.

"Yes. His name is Frank Smythe. I met him a couple of weeks ago," Julie explained, well aware that it wasn't much of an explanation.

"At the beach?"

She nodded. "He was surfing. He, um, works nights," she added to assure her employer that he wasn't a total loser or just a beach bum. "He has his Friday nights free and he asked me out."

"Did you accept?" Emily was still hesitant.

"Yes. I like him. He's a lot of fun, and he seems nice, and he's really intelligent." Although it sounded like it, Julie wasn't really defending her decision. "I think I'll go shower away this salt water. It makes my hair really stiff and strange."

As she glanced toward the stairs, she saw Ruel on the lower landing and something told her he had been listening to the entire conversation. Until that moment, Julie hadn't minded Emily's interrogation.

But looking into his strongly cast features, she felt a rush of antagonism. His brilliant blue eyes regarded her with an aloof amusement that was both challenging and insolent. After the ride in the dune buggy, she knew she looked tousled and windblown. But did she look *kissed?* Ruel's expression said so.

"I do hope you're right about him," Emily remarked, "for your own sake."

"I am." Julie's response was impatient and short.

She crossed the entryway to the stairs, trying desperately to ignore the man who started down. Her walk
lacked its usual free and easy grace. She was too conscious of the tension fluttering over her nerve ends.
Forced to acknowledge his presence, she met his gaze
but it was indifferent, and that fact seemed to irritate
her all the more.

Tight-lipped, she passed him and hurried up the
stairs. It was no use telling herself that her reaction was
absurd. It was there and she couldn't change it. She
swept into her room and dropped her beach bag on the
floor, not caring about the grains of sand it scattered.

She marched straight into the bathroom and stripped
off her clothes and the bikini underneath. Without taking the time to adjust the water temperature, she stepped
into the shower and was blasted with cold water. Gradually it warmed to a bearable degree and she stayed
beneath the hammering jets until she felt her muscles
relax.

CHAPTER SIX

"Do you have any difficulty with the third quantitative problem?" When her question went unanswered, Julie looked up from her papers to see her student staring vacantly into space. "Debbie?"

Debbie seemed to come back to the present with difficulty. "What did you say? I'm sorry I wasn't listening."

Julie observed a suggestion of strain in the young girl's face. She was usually so cheerful. But the last couple of days Debbie seemed unable to concentrate on her schoolwork. Julie wondered if they had been overdoing it.

"It doesn't matter." She didn't really need an answer to the quantitative problem. Julie smiled. "It's Friday, so why don't we end our class an hour early?'

"Okay." It was an enthusiastic response.

Nibbling at the edge of her lower lip, Julie hesitated, then jumped in. "Is something bothering you, Deb?"

"No, nothing." The reply was too quick to be the truth. As if sensing that, Debbie plucked at the binding of the blanket. A misty film of tears darkened her eyes and there was the faintest quivering of her chin. "I'm just so sick of being in this bed." Her young voice was low and tight to keep out any tremor.

In the past, Debbie had made an occasional joke about her situation but never once had she seemed to feel sorry for herself. Compassion surged through Julie. The kid was having a very tough time and she was being unbelievably brave about it.

"It won't be for much longer," Julie said, knowing how inadequate that sounded.

"I guess." Furtively, Debbie wiped at a tear that had trickled from the corner of her eye, as if ashamed of it. "I mean, I know I'm lucky in a lot of ways. And I'm going to be all right. Thanks to you, I'm not going to fall behind in school. And my friends come to see me as often as they can. It's just that—"

Julie thought she understood. "It's just that it's Friday night, right?"

Debbie managed a tremulous smile and nodded. "Yeah. All my friends have a date tonight. Ruel has a date tonight. Even you do, Julie."

Something hardened inside of Julie. For some reason, she didn't want to know how Ruel Chandler intended to spend his evening. She tried not to let it show.

"Is that the worst?" she teased. "I mean, your teacher having a date, that is."

"No-o-o! Why shouldn't you go out with a guy? I didn't mean to make you feel guilty," Debbie insisted, her face reddening.

"I know you didn't, Debbie." Julie smiled her understanding. "I wish I could be your fairy godmother and wave my magic wand and get you out of this cast tonight."

"I think you have to be a fairy orthopedist to do that," Debbie said.

Julie really laughed. "You have a great sense of humor, Deb. Don't ever lose it."

Debbie managed a smile.

Setting the schoolwork aside, Julie tried to think of a way to cheer the girl up. She had worked so closely with Debbie in the last month and a half that it was impossible not to be emotionally involved. Over the last two weeks or so, she had realized that she'd begun to think of Debbie more as a younger sister than a student. She wasn't sure that was a good thing, but it was too late to do anything about it now.

Later, when Emily looked in on her niece at half past four, the depressed mood had vanished and Debbie was her optimistic, smiling self again. Julie left the two of them to chat, as they usually did at the end of school time, and went to her room.

Just before eight, Julie decided what to wear. She chose a pair of white denims and a long-sleeved pullover in midnight blue velour.

Frank arrived right on time. Instead of the dune buggy, this time he was driving a van—a fact of which Emily Harmon took due note.

"I've heard they usually throw old mattresses in the back of those vans," she informed Julie. "With no sheets." Her meaning was clear.

"Well, maybe." It was an effort for Julie to keep from smiling at Emily's motherly concern. "I mean, I wouldn't know."

Emily merely sniffed.

"Besides, I think I can take care of myself," Julie said. "You'll feel better after you meet Frank," she assured her when he knocked at the front door. She hoped and prayed that he hadn't gelled his hair into spikes or worn tattered clothes just in case they were going to a place where grunge was still cool.

Emily looked skeptical but she brightened up when Julie introduced her to Frank. He instinctively turned up the charm, but in a polite, genuine way that seemed to melt most of the older woman's natural reserve.

They said their good-byes, although Emily couldn't resist one last disapproving look at the van in the driveway as she shut the door.

Once they were inside the van with the doors closed, he ran an admiring glance over her. "You look great, California! I like the fuzzy top."

He patted her velour-covered sleeve as if she were a stuffed animal and Julie laughed. "Thanks."

"You won't get cold on the beach."

"Is that where we're going?"

He turned the key in the ignition and Julie was happy to hear that this vehicle had a functioning muffler. "Yup. Friends of mine are having a party. A real walk on the wild side."

"Meaning?"

"Toasting marshmallows. Singing camp songs. Stuff like that."

"Sounds great."

Everyone was there when they arrived. A bonfire was blazing on the otherwise deserted beach. Overhead, the sky was studded with stars, outshone somewhat by a full moon that glistened on the waves. The trade winds rustled through the needles of a stand of ironwood trees and made the palm trees sway. Classic rock played softly from a boom box perched on a piece of driftwood.

"Okay, I was lying about the camp songs."

"Thank God," Julie said.

After some good-natured jokes about the mathematical improbability of Frank's dating a beautiful California girl, they were drawn into the circle seated around the fire on the sand. One couple was managing to half-pop and half-burn popcorn in a metal mesh popper. A bag of marshmallows and sticks were making the circuit around the fire, with each person helping themselves and toasting their own. The flameouts were tossed back into the fire. And there was an ice chest filled with beer.

It was a fun-loving group with a lot of laughing and talking and storytelling going on simultaneously. Julie found herself liking Frank's friends as much as she liked him. At first she had been apprehensive that as the evening wore on couples would begin to drift into the privacy of the night's darkness, but it didn't happen. The hour grew late, but no one wandered into the trees behind the stretch of beach.

The mood grew more mellow. Like other couples, Julie was leaning against Frank, her shoulders resting against his chest while his arms circled her waist. Occasionally he would nuzzle her neck, or, when she'd turn to say something to him, he would steal a kiss from her. But it never got too hot.

A little after midnight, they ran out of firewood and beer, and the party began breaking up. Frank didn't suggest that they go elsewhere when they left, as if sensing that Julie would've refused anyway.

In the driveway, they sat in the van and talked for a while, separated by the bucket seats. Finally Julie said it was time she went inside and Frank walked her to the steps. There they stopped to say their good nights.

"I don't remember the last time I had this much fun," Frank said. "Must be the company."

"Maybe it was the beer," Julie teased.

"I'm not drunk," he said quietly.

"No," she agreed.

"Um . . . mind if I kiss you again?"

"No. Please do."

When his head bent toward her, she lifted her chin expectantly, her hands sliding around his muscular middle. His mouth was firm and eager against her parted lips. Julie relaxed, letting his arms engulf her in a warmly sensual hug. It was a long, lingering kiss, sweet in its intensity.

Frank continued to hold her close, murmuring against her cheek, "I wish the evening was just getting started."

"Mmm, no. I think it's morning already," she breathed, and made an attempt to move out of his arms.

"Don't go in, Julie." His hold tightened. "Not yet."

When she lifted her head to insist, his kiss silenced the words on her lips. At first, Julie submitted to his demands, not resisting when he pushed the silken length of her hair away from her neck and explored its curve. Instead of satisfying his ardor, she was fueling it. As his hands attempted to mold her to him, she strained to get a little breathing room.

"Frank, I have to go in." Her protest was gentle but definite.

"Not yet, babe," he insisted, and attempted to sweep her resistance aside with another passionate kiss, but this time Julie turned her face away.

She wedged her arms against his chest. Frank continued in his attempt to change her mind. Denied her lips, he satisfied himself with the hollow below her ear. Julie didn't feel threatened by his persistence. She had warded off more determined advances in the past and felt perfectly capable of doing so now.

"That's enough, Frank." As she arched away from him, drawing her head back so that he could see from her expression that she meant it, a car entered the circular drive. They were bathed in the glare of its headlights and Julie was momentarily blinded.

She recognized the sleek black sports car Ruel Chandler drove. It growled softly up the drive, looking like a prowling jungle creature with shining eyes. By the time it stopped behind the van, Frank had let her go. He shifted guiltily as if they had been caught doing something they shouldn't, and Julie could tell that he was suddenly very anxious to be gone.

Which was okay with her. He had definitely overstepped a line.

"It's getting late. I'd better go," he said as he heard the car door open." He kept his voice low as if he didn't want to risk being overheard. "I'll call you."

"Sure," she agreed tightly, then remembered with relief that she had not given him the phone number. But Frank was already moving toward the van. Julie doubted if he had even heard her answer.

Ruel was approaching the steps where she stood. As badly as Frank had behaved, she was determined to stand her ground. She controlled her emotions and put on a calm face. After the briefest look at her, Ruel paused beside her and turned to watch the van driving away.

"Seems like I arrived just in time," he said in a low voice.

He stood so tall beside her and seemed so reserved that Julie felt a shiver of intimidation. She stood up very straight and confronted him.

"I don't know what you mean by that," she retorted.

There was a hint of steel in his gaze. "Really? You looked like you were about to fight him off."

"No," she said coldly. "Not at all."

"Maybe you'll be a little more selective in your choice next time. Beach boys go for hookups. Not just kisses."

His attitude fired her temper. "Gee, what about you? Bet you're looking for more than just kisses," she challenged him. "You had a date tonight. Did you get lucky?"

His eyes narrowed to cold blue slits. "I'm not going to answer that."

"Hypocrite," Julie declared. "You see two people sharing a kiss and you jump to conclusions. What's on your mind? I think I can guess."

"Maybe not," Ruel said slowly. "But I was thinking about you, whether you like it or not. Your safety. Your reputation. You do live under my roof, Julie. And you're only twenty-one."

"I'm not a kid," Julie snapped. "And a kiss is no big deal."

"I think I'm finally beginning to understand what you're really saying." Ruel eyed her complacently.

"Are you? I doubt it!"

"Your ego is bruised."

His response so astounded her that Julie could only laugh out a startled "What?"

"I haven't asked you out, pretty as you are. Don't tell me you don't know it, Julie." He gave her a mocking smile. "So you let the first guy who came sniffing around get a little too close for your comfort, and you're ashamed that I saw it happen."

"I didn't *let* him, he just—" She held up a hand. "Wait a minute. I resent what you just said about asking me out."

Ruel shrugged. "That guy wanted one thing. I think you deserve to be treated with a lot more respect than that."

"Back it up. I also resent the term 'sniffing around.' "

"Sorry. He doesn't look like someone I want within a mile of my house."

For a moment, Julie was so incensed that she could hardly speak. She was trembling with the force of her anger. Her long fingers curled into the palms of her hands.

"Are you going to tell me who I can and can't date?"

"No."

"And were you implying that I want to be one of the women that you date?"

"I wasn't implying it. I was saying it."

"If that weren't so pathetic, it would be funny." Julie

started up the steps, not trusting herself a minute longer in his company. The urge to slap his face was just too strong. Before her foot touched the third step, his strong hand clasped her wrist.

"Maybe not," he said quietly. "I see something in your eyes when I look at you."

"Yeah. Your own reflection. What a thrill."

He didn't let go. "No. It's more than that. Whether you want to admit it or not, I think you sometimes wonder what it would be like if I kissed you."

"Don't flatter yourself."

He studied her face for a long moment. "Am I wrong, Julie?"

Her gaze was drawn to the tense line of his mouth. She felt a heady excitement—and a sense of danger. Even with her limited experience, she knew instinctively that he would be a hard, demanding lover and altogether satisfying.

The gleam in his blue eyes mocked her, as if he were capable of reading her thoughts. "Tell me you aren't interested in being kissed by me."

"I'm not. Not at all." But her words were breathless and held little conviction.

She could almost hear his silent amusement. His fingers tightened on her arm, giving her only a second's warning of his intention. Her hands came up to spread across his chest but were trapped there as Ruel gathered her inside the steel band of his arms.

Julie made no attempt to fight, nor did she avoid the mouth seeking out the softness of her lips. His kiss was far more tender than she had imagined and she knew that he was holding back because of her, not wanting to frighten or intimidate her. Yet the fierce sensuality that emanated from him was a force to be reckoned with . . . and in less than a minute, she had forgotten about Frank entirely. Ruel knew what he was doing.

The hard pressure of his body against hers, his muscular arms that held her so close to his heart, melted her into pliancy. Passion became a living thing that flamed between them.

Her fingers inched up his shirt as she worked her arms free to encircle his neck. She tried to arch closer still, loving the feel of her breasts pressed against the solid wall of his chest, but she lost her balance on the step.

Held by him as she was, there wasn't any real risk of falling. But the few inches she moved was enough to break the kiss. When she opened her dazed eyes, her feet were on the same level with his and her head tilted back. His chiseled male face was above hers. Satisfaction at being proved right glittered in his eyes as well as the fire of desire.

When his head bent toward hers, Julie rose on tiptoe to meet him halfway. It seemed impossible, but the second kiss was more electrifying than the one before.

Her lips parted under the probing pressure of his tongue. The caress of his hands was creating an urgency within her that she had never experienced before. She clung to him, her fingers sliding into his thick hair, pressing his mouth more firmly against her own, finding ecstasy in the nearly unbearable wanting.

An uncontrollable shudder of need hammered through her when his hand slipped under her sweater and encountered her bare flesh. It was fire against fire—their body heat consuming each other. His hand sought and found her breast, cupping it in his palm. Her heart beat fast, then faster . . .

"Ruel? Ruel, is that you?" Emily Harmon's imperious voice broke the stillness of the night. It came from somewhere above them and ripped their kiss. "Ruel?"

His hand pressed Julie's face against his shirt as if to silence any outcry from her. She seized the opportunity to close her eyes and inhale his very masculine scent. He looked down at her, dropped a light kiss on the top of her head, and then looked up. "Yes, Em, it's me," he replied.

The part of her mind that could think marveled at his control. She doubted if she had the strength to speak. She was aware of the way her body was trembling against his—not from fear, but she wondered if he thought so.

"I thought I heard you drive in a little while ago. What are you doing out there?" his aunt demanded.

With her senses coming back to reality, Julie was able to tell that Emily Harmon was speaking from a second floor window. The shadows of the front lanai concealed the two of them from her view.

"Just thinking. Watching the moon," Ruel answered. "It's late, Em. You should be in bed. You need your rest."

"So do you," was the snappish reply, followed almost immediately by a sigh. "Julie hasn't come home yet. I'm worried about her. We don't know anything about that young man she went out with. He—"

"Julie is here," he interrupted.

"Julie is here?" There was disbelief in the older woman's voice.

"Yes, she came back the same time I did," Ruel said truthfully and slowly loosened his hold on Julie. "She's here on the steps with me."

"Julie?"

"Yes . . ." Julie's voice was uncertain.

"You're home!" Emily declared.

"Yes, I got back a little while ago." Julie stole a glance at Ruel, who was now standing a full step away from her. The moon had sunk lower into a gap between two trees and it illuminated his face, which showed no emotion.

The torrid embrace did not seem to have shattered him the way it had her.

"Good," Emily said finally. A long pause followed, as if she was about to say something more, but she didn't. "I'll turn in now. Don't you two stay out there too long. It's late."

"We'll . . . we'll be in directly," Julie promised.

Her words were followed by a silence—a tense silence. Ruel showed no inclination to take her in his arms again.

"I owe you an apology, Julie," he said softly. "I never become involved with any woman who works for me, directly or indirectly. I won't make any excuses." He didn't sound remorseful. "You were so self-righteous that I kissed you the first time just to prove you were wrong."

"And the second time?" Julie didn't know why she was asking.

"The second time was because you were so damned passionate the first time." His voice was tinged with controlled amusement.

Julie wished she could deny it but she was fully aware of her abandoned response. There was a proud lift to her chin as she turned to meet his gaze. His eyes were watchful, studying her reaction.

"I have no excuse, either," she said. "It's not like—I mean, we can't—let's just forget it."

"I agree," Ruel said.

"If that's settled, then, I think I'll go in," she said stiffly.

He shrugged and looked away. "There isn't anything more to keep you out here."

"No, there isn't." And she felt sick inside.

Her legs were trembling as she walked to the front door. Any second, she expected him to say . . . What did she want him to say? That he loved her? No. There was undeniably a powerful physical attraction between them but mere chemistry was not love.

Closing the door, she leaned weakly against it. She understood his reason for not wanting to let the mutual desire they had experienced turn into anything more. Sooner or later it would become awkward for both of them. It was sensible and logical to end it now.

"Julie? Julie?"

Someone was whispering her name. For a heart-stopping minute she thought it might be Ruel but the voice had been female and young. It was Debbie. For a second, Julie toyed with the idea of ignoring it, but that was too cowardly. Glancing briefly toward the stairs, she moved silently across the entryway to the girl's bedroom.

"How was your date?" Debbie whispered when she appeared in the doorway.

"It was fine," Julie answered and immediately changed the subject. "Why aren't you asleep?"

"I don't know. Insomnia, I guess." The indifference in her voice told Julie that Debbie was concerned about something. "Ruel came home the same time you did, didn't he?"

"Yes." Julie was relieved there was no light on.

"I thought I heard the two of you arguing."

"Huh?" Julie said. "No. You must have heard—I don't know what you heard."

The vague answer seemed to satisfy Debbie. "Where did you go on your date?"

"To a beach party." That seemed such a long time ago. So much had happened since then.

"That must have been fun—and romantic," Debbie said hopefully.

"It was. But I'm pretty tired. You may not be sleepy but I am. I'll tell you all about it in the morning," Julie said.

"Are you going to see him tomorrow?"

Did she mean Ruel? That was Julie's first thought. Then she realized Debbie meant Frank. Tomorrow was Saturday, her day off. She suddenly wondered how she was going to fill the hours. The last thing she wanted to do was think about it.

"No, not tomorrow," she said. "I'll talk to you in the morning. Good night, Debbie." She slipped out the door before Debbie could ask more questions that Julie didn't want to answer.

Upstairs, she lay in her bed another hour before she heard Ruel walk down the hallway to his room. Sue Ling, Debbie's nurse, had the next bedroom to Julie's. It separated her room from Ruel's. But the little distance between them only made her want him more.

It wouldn't last, Julie assured herself. She would forget.

CHAPTER SEVEN

A month later, Julie was able to congratulate herself for dealing with the aftermath of the kiss. Or, as she had come to think of it, The Kiss. It had taken on the aspect of a dream that seemed real enough at the time, but had faded into a distant memory with the passage of days.

It helped that there were so few occasions when she had to be in Ruel's company. Even during those times there was always someone around, either his aunt or Debbie, to keep any mention of the incident from cropping up. Ruel treated her in the same distant fashion that he had before it happened.

If there were times when she looked at him and had the sudden, vivid memory of his sensual mouth on hers, or the feel of his tautly muscled body imprinting itself on hers, or the intimate caress of his hands finding the places that excited her, Julie never consciously admitted it.

When she walked into the dining room that evening and saw Ruel seated at the head of the table, she gave him a cool smile and took her usual chair on his left. The beat of her heart remained steady. There wasn't the slightest tremor in her hands as she spread the cloth dinner napkin across her lap.

"You look pretty this evening, Julie," Emily Harmon commented from across the table. "Is that caftan new? I don't recall seeing you wear it before."

"Yes, it's new. I bought it in one of those shops at the Kuilima resort." The delicate pastel shades of yellow and pink in a Hawaiian print had caught her eye.

"The color suits you. Don't you think so, Ruel?" Emily asked him.

"Sure. Yeah."

"Thank you." Julie wanted to applaud herself for replying calmly.

"It's so good to have you with us, Julie," said Emily, the statement seeming to come out of the blue. "You've almost become one of the family since you arrived—you fit in so well."

Without realizing it, Julie darted a glance sideways at Ruel, but he appeared not to have heard what his aunt said. Immediately she curved her mouth into a smile and directed it at the older woman.

"Well, you make it easy. You and your family are so nice."

Emily smiled back. "I don't know why I haven't said it before but I feel we're truly fortunate to have you to tutor Debbie," Emily added. "Of course, the Rifkins recommended you so highly and you did so much good for their daughter. I heard she was accepted at Vassar."

Julie nodded. "Yes. I was so happy for her."

"At the time I was worried that you wouldn't be able to finagle a leave of absence from your teaching job. You taught at the high school level, isn't that right? I'm relieved they were able to find a replacement for you on such short notice."

Somehow the conversation had never got around to what Julie had been doing before she arrived in Hawaii.

They had talked of her family and her college years and of life in Boston. Julie had always presumed Emily Harmon knew she had been available for this job. Now she was at a loss as to how to explain the chain of events that had brought her here.

"Did you have a special field of interest?" Ruel changed the subject as if to cover Julie's silence.

"I . . . I majored in American history, yes." She hesitated. "But after college, I wasn't able to find a teaching job, except for tutoring Carla Rifkin."

Emily's soup spoon was halfway to her mouth. It stayed there for a second before she returned it to the soup bowl. Julie was uncomfortably aware of Ruel's shrewd gaze.

"I thought you were actually teaching," Emily commented.

"I was employed as a substitute teacher," Julie explained. "You know how it is when you're fresh out of college—I had the degree but no experience."

"What were you doing?" Ruel asked with casual interest.

Julie directed her answer to Emily, trying not to sound defensive. "I was working as a waitress. Ms. Grayson knew—I thought she'd told you."

Out of the corner of her eye, she saw Ruel's mouth quirk and resolutely kept from looking at him. He could think what he liked. Waiting on tables had paid her rent.

"What a deplorable waste of your education," was Emily Harmon's reaction. "Everyone has to start somewhere. Did the school administrators ever give you an explanation?"

"Not really. They were fairly vague—they have to be. But I had a hunch that it had a lot to do with how young I looked. And how young I was. They probably thought I couldn't control a high school classroom," Julie answered frankly.

"Yes, especially the boys," Ruel said dryly.

"The girls can be just as rowdy," she retorted.

"That's not what I meant. Boys have a habit of falling in love with pretty teachers. I know I did."

"Oh, really? Well, I guess there's just something about teachers. We're irresistible." Julie seethed inwardly and struggled to control her emotions. It didn't work. Their eyes clashed and locked, charging the air with volatile tension. All pretense that their kiss on the lanai hadn't happened was dissolved in seconds.

"Julie, I—" Emily Harmon's hesitant and confused voice made Julie sharply aware of what she had said and how sarcastic it had sounded.

"I'm sorry," she said, breaking the electric contact with Ruel's eyes. "I don't know why I said that."

"I'm sure it's been very frustrating for you," Emily agreed. "I know Ruel understands that you didn't mean it personally."

"Of course." Ruel quietly seconded his aunt's comment. Julie wondered if she were the only one who picked up on the suppressed emotions in his calm tone. The phone rang and he pushed his chair away from the table. "I'll get it . . . it's probably the call I've been expecting. Excuse me."

"Don't be long," Emily admonished, but received no response from Ruel as he left the room.

From experience, Emily didn't hold up the meal for him. They were halfway through the main course when he returned to his seat at the head of the table. Malia was there almost instantly to serve him his meal.

"Mahi mahi," Ruel identified the broiled fish on his plate. "It looks excellent, Malia."

"It is," Emily stated and looked at Julie. "Do you like it, dear?"

"It's delicious," she agreed. "Is it a tropical species?"

"It's a dolphin," Ruel told her.

"A dolphin?" Her eyes rounded in startled dismay,

"Relax," he mocked. "It's the fish dolphin, not the mammal. You aren't eating Flipper."

His baiting tone irritated her. She wondered if he were deliberately trying to rile her and pay her back for her remark. That was foolish, of course.

"Don't tease her, Ruel," his aunt reproved.

But Julie didn't want to be defended by Emily. "Mahi mahi is the Hawaiian name for the dolphin, then?" she asked.

"Yes." It was Emily who responded, as Julie expected. It started a discussion of the Hawaiian language and kept the conversation away from personal topics.

By the end of the week, Julie found it hadn't been so easy to forget how she had reacted to his offhand comments when she'd had to explain her employment history. She hadn't become as indifferent to him as she had thought; his opinion of her mattered. Very much.

Finding that he could evoke such strong feelings with such ease was unsettling. She wanted to believe that she had pushed him from her mind and her senses.

A car whizzed by and she stepped quickly back to avoid being splashed by the water on the road. A steady drizzle was falling but the temperature was warm. The sunshine of the morning had been replaced by overcast skies and rain.

Shielding her eyes from the heavy drizzle, Julie peered down the highway for a glimpse of the bus. When she left the house that morning, she hadn't prepared for a change in the weather.

Her hair was plastered to her head, a gleaming dark honey shade. She was almost soaked to the skin and her wet clothes clung to her. But at least she was warm.

There was more than half the afternoon left. Since

the weather showed no sign of improving, Julie had decided she might as well spend the rest of her Saturday back at the house. Unfortunately, there was no sign of the bus. She debated whether or not to take shelter in the grocery store behind her, but she was afraid she wouldn't see the bus coming and would miss it.

A convoy of military trucks and jeeps went by. A few of the soldiers whistled and waved when they saw her standing at the bus stop. Sighing, Julie hunched her shoulders against the light rain. The burnt-red volcanic soil at her feet was turning into mud.

A honking horn made her look up, and the sight of a glistening black sports car slowing to a stop made her tense up. She saw Ruel lean across and open the passenger door, his strong face looking out at her, elemental and raw.

"Get in," he ordered.

Julie took a step backward. "I'm all wet."

"I don't care." Impatience thinned the line of his mouth. "Come on. Get in. I'm not going to beg you to ride with me. I'm holding up traffic."

She glanced down the road and saw the cars behind him. The bus still wasn't in sight. After only a second's hesitation, she slid into the passenger seat and closed the door. Ruel put the car in gear and accelerated forward.

"Thanks for stopping." Courtesy demanded that she say that much, regardless of what his motivation might have been.

He made no response. Her face was beaded with raindrops. She wiped at it with a wet hand and he offered her a bandanna that had been left in the car. She glanced at him as she accepted it. He faced the road, his bold profile expressionless.

The windshield wipers swish-swished back and forth in a hypnotic rhythm. Julie wiped her face dry with the bandanna. He must have used it for a similar reason after a ride in the hot sun. The tantalizing scent of his aftershave clung to the cotton material, a musky fragrance that evoked his masculinity.

Not that Julie wanted to be reminded of that—especially not in the close quarters of the car.

"Are you cold? Want me to turn the heater on?" Ruel asked, distantly polite.

"No, that's not necessary. I'm just wet." She was nervous, disturbed by his nearness and unwilling to admit it.

The bandanna was damp as she wadded it into her hands and held it on her lap, reluctant to return it to him in its present sodden condition. The heavy silence between them was unnerving. Julie longed to end it but she was afraid she would begin chattering like a nervous teenager. She felt irritated and wished she had waited for the bus despite the drizzle.

Directly ahead of them, a shaft of sunlight pierced the clouds and created a rainbow in the sky. She tried to concentrate on the way the colors faded into each other, instead of the man behind the wheel.

It didn't work. She fidgeted.

"Damn! Would you relax?" Ruel asked brusquely.

"I am relaxed," she lied.

"Just sit still."

Julie composed herself. "If I seem uncomfortable, it's because I am," she retorted. "Who wouldn't be if they were sitting around in wet clothes?"

His gaze moved over her, taking swift note of the way her knit top stuck to the shapely roundness of her breasts.

Heat coursed through her veins, warming her skin, but almost immediately his attention was back on the rain-slick highway in front of him.

"We'll be at the house soon and you'll be able to

change into dry clothes." Once again his voice and expression were smooth and emotionless.

As far as Julie was concerned, they couldn't get there soon enough. She made some meaningless comment to him and stared out of the side window. She didn't draw an easy breath until Ruel stopped the car in the circular drive in front of the house.

"Thanks for the ride." She didn't even glance at him as she said it, pushing open the door and using the excuse of the rain to bolt into the house.

In the entryway, she heard a trio of laughing voices from Debbie's room and guessed her girlfriends were visiting her. She didn't see either Emily or Malia as she hurried up the stairs to her room.

Stripping out of her wet clothes, she put on a short terry cloth beach jacket. She was shaking, but she didn't know whether it was from nerves or because she was chilled from her wet clothes. The first seemed the most likely. Angry with herself, she began toweling her hair dry with a roughness that hurt.

A knock at her bedroom door brought an automatic response, "Come in."

Julie turned as it opened. Ruel walked in and she dropped the towel.

Why didn't he leave her alone, she thought wildly, and demanded, "What do you want?" Her voice was sharp to the point of rudeness.

His gaze traveled down the length of her tanned legs before meeting the challenging directness of her eyes. She had nothing on underneath the jacket, which he obviously guessed. She was grateful it came down over her hips.

She was surprised to see what he was holding: a small tray with a cup and saucer and teapot on it.

"I asked Malia to fix you jasmine tea," he answered evenly, and walked into the room to set it on the desk.

"Aren't you sweet." Her tone indicated that she thought he was anything but sweet. "Tell her I said thank you on your way out."

He nodded but didn't move.

"Should you be in my bedroom? I thought you didn't want to become involved with women who worked for you." Julie couldn't keep the sarcasm out of her voice.

Ruel treated himself to a long, lazy look at her. His slow smile irked her more than anything. "That's right, I don't." He shoved his hands in the pockets of his jeans.

Julie couldn't help remembering how warm and strong those hands had felt under her shirt—but she wasn't prepared to admit how much she wanted him to caress her again. She turned her back and lifted the lid off the teapot, letting the fragrance waft upward in a thin curl of steam.

He took a few steps to stand just behind her, his hands on her shoulders for a few dangerous seconds. Julie trembled but she didn't turn around. He let his hands drop and left, slamming the door behind him. Waves of disappointment rushed through her. She slumped into the desk chair and buried her face in her hands. The tea was lukewarm before she got around to drinking it.

After dinner that evening, Julie sat in the living room with Emily, painfully aware of Ruel's presence. It was a strain to concentrate on what the older woman was saying and appear interested, but she tried.

"You look pale, Julie," the woman observed. "Are you feeling all right?"

"Fine," she insisted with a tense smile. The narrowed glance of skepticism she received made her add, "I have a slight headache, that's all."

"Ruel mentioned to Malia that you were caught in

the shower this afternoon. Maybe you're coming down with something," Emily suggested.

"I don't think so," Julie said. "It's just a common headache, not the common cold."

"Maybe fresh air will help," said Ruel. He stood beside the French doors that led onto the ground floor lanai. "It isn't raining anymore. Take a stroll outside."

"Okay. Good idea," she agreed eagerly, glad to escape the stifling atmosphere of the house.

Rising from the sofa, she crossed the room to the double doors Ruel held open for her. It wasn't until she had stepped onto the veranda that she realized he intended to accompany her, and she glanced back into the room at Emily. There was nothing in the woman's expression to indicate that she found anything wrong with the situation.

As soon as they were out of earshot, Julie said, "I want to apologize for what I said and the way I behaved today. You didn't deserve it, and I'm sorry."

"Apology accepted," he said simply. "Although it doesn't solve our problem, does it?"

She wasn't quite able to meet his eyes. "Problem? I don't know what you mean."

"Don't you?"

"No. Do we have to play guessing games?" Annoyed with him again, Julie walked a little ahead. She was glad of the darkness and the concealing shadows.

The touch of Ruel's hand on her upper back halted her. Applying slight pressure, he turned her to face him. She forced herself to breathe evenly and not pay any attention to the fluttering of her pulse. As long as his touch remained impersonal, she wasn't going to make a fool of herself by resisting.

"Pretending hasn't made it go away, Kulie," he said.

His hands moved down to lightly span her waist but he didn't make any attempt to lessen the distance be-

tween them. Julie felt herself relax a little too much at
his touch and she turned away from him while she still
had some backbone. Ruel let her turn away, but he didn't
release her.

"I don't know what you're talking about," she repeated. "What was that you called me?"

"Kulie. That's your name in Hawaiian," Ruel answered.

"How fascinating." There was a faint tremor in her
voice as she attempted to change the subject. "What is
yours?"

"Ruel is an old family name. There is no Hawaiian
equivalent."

"I see," she murmured.

An awkward silence fell between them.

"Okay," he sighed. "Like I said, we're going to have
to come up with a solution to our problem."

Here we go again, she thought. "As far as I'm concerned, we don't have a problem." She took a quick
step forward, moving out of his unresisting hold, and
staying out of his reach. "I'm going in. I, um, have some
letters to write." It was lame, but it was the best excuse
she could come up with. She started toward the outside
set of stairs that led to the upper lanai and her bedroom. "Good night."

"Running isn't the answer, Julie." His voice carried
quietly to her, but he didn't try to stop her. "You'll have
to face it sooner or later."

Julie infinitely preferred later. Tonight she couldn't
cope with the potency of his attraction. She sure as hell
couldn't be as calm and reasonable about it as Ruel
sounded.

The French doors to her bedroom were unlocked.
She opened them and paused. Glancing over her shoulder, she saw Ruel walk around the perimeter of the

pool. His strides were fast and angry and he didn't look up.

Julie could only guess at the cause of his anger. This physical thing between them didn't please him any-more than it pleased her. He was probably irritated with himself for even mentioning it. As for a solution . . . she went into her bedroom and closed the doors. An affair was the obvious answer. But if it burned itself out before Debbie was better, how would she able to stay here in the same house with him?

CHAPTER EIGHT

Ruel was seldom at the house during the week that followed. On the one evening he did spend at home, he made no attempt to speak to Julie or draw her aside. She kept telling herself she was relieved that he had decided not to pursue the matter. If she wasn't convinced, she didn't admit it.

On Saturday morning she joined Emily for breakfast at nine o'clock on the lanai. The sun was warming the cobblestone floor and the air was fragrant with the scents of many tropical flowers blooming in the garden. Julie helped herself to the slices of fresh pineapple on the table and sat in a rattan chair next to Emily.

"It's a gorgeous day, isn't it?" Julie remarked.

"It couldn't be better," Emily agreed. "What are your plans for today?"

"I thought I'd go into Honolulu. I haven't been there yet and—"—she lifted her shoulders in an expressive shrug and laughed—"what would my friends say if I never got to Waikiki?"

"I don't know. But personally I don't think you're missing anything." Emily's opinion hadn't changed.

"Besides, there are a lot of things I want to see in Honolulu," Julie said.

"You're welcome to take the car," Emily said doubtfully.

Julie wasn't sure which car she meant. She didn't want to risk the Mercedes in an unfamiliar city and she didn't want to drive the beater.

"Thanks. I'll take the bus. That way I don't have to worry about parking and I can really see the city on foot."

"It's quite a long bus ride," the older woman cautioned.

"I don't mind. It will give me time to look at the countryside."

"What will?" Ruel walked onto the lanai.

"Good morning, Ruel." Emily offered him a cheek, which he bent to dutifully kiss before helping himself to the coffee.

Dressed in a loose-fitting shirt of white cotton and his usual blue jeans, Ruel walked behind Julie to sit in a chair beside her. Setting his cup on the table, he buttered a slice of sweet bread.

"Julie is taking the bus into Honolulu this morning," his aunt explained. "I was just warning her that it would be a long ride, what with all the stops it has to make along the way."

"I'm going downtown this morning. You're welcome to ride with me," he offered indifferently.

Julie hesitated, about to say no, but Emily was speaking before she had the chance to respond.

"How thoughtful of you, Ruel!" she exclaimed. "It's the perfect answer."

"You don't have to go to the trouble. I know you have business in the city and—" Julie tried delicately to get out of accepting.

"It wouldn't be any trouble," Ruel assured her, a glint

of challenge in his blue eyes. "I have to drive to Honolulu anyway. I can drop you wherever you like."

"Of course he can," Emily said. "It would certainly be more comfortable than riding on a crowded bus. And Ruel can give you the scenic tour." She beamed at both of them, having figured things out to her satisfaction.

Julie couldn't very well say no.

After breakfast, she went upstairs to collect her purse while Ruel brought the low-slung car around to the front. Emily waved good-bye to them from the house. It was an hour's drive into the city and she tried to think of what they could talk about for that length of time.

The commute. Everyone liked to gripe about their commute. Ruel wasn't any different from other people.

"You make this drive every day, don't you?"

"Yeah."

"Ever get tired of it?"

"Sometimes," he said, "especially if the traffic is heavy. But it gives me time to think and sort out various projects and problems. Views like that"—he indicated the one ahead of them—"keep it from becoming too monotonous."

They had just started down the switchback road that led to the highway and the height provided a panoramic view of the coastline. The ocean was a pale blue near the shore where the reefs were and a deep, rich blue beyond—the color of lapis lazuli. White strips of beach were broken by clumps of rust-black lava rock rising from the golden sands. The vivid green of the abundant tropical foliage provided a brilliant contrast. Jutting out to sea was the headland of the Waiainae range of mountains.

"It is spectacular," Julie agreed. Even that seemed an understatement. Before she could take it all in, the car had made the last curve and the road was leveling out toward the highway.

At the intersection, Ruel waited for a lull in the traffic before turning onto the road. Not wanting to distract him, Julie kept silent. As they drove along the coast a few minutes later, she couldn't think of anything to say again. They passed a small beach with surfers bobbing in the waves.

"What happened to your friend?" Ruel slid her an inquiring look.

"Frank? He's around." Her answer was carefully nonspecific.

"Don't you see him anymore?"

"Yes." Which was true. She had simply avoided going out with Frank—mainly because she knew his feelings were stronger than hers. She liked him but she didn't want it to go any further than that.

"You haven't gone out with him lately," Ruel said.

"He works nights," she said as if that was the explanation. "I usually see him sometime during the weekend, like on Sunday."

"Are you meeting him in town today?" Ruel circled the cloverleaf to the Honolulu turnoff.

"No." Julie looked out of the window. Short stands of grass punctuated a field of plowed earth in a semblance of rows. "Is that sugarcane?"

"Yes, a new field. As it grows, it'll spread out until it's as thick as that." He indicated the cane just ahead, towering thick and green close to the road, tassels waving over the top. "When you see tassels on a field, the cane stalks are usually sweet. This particular field is about ready to be fired."

"I enjoyed seeing that the day we rode out to your field," she said without thinking, a look of pleasure lighting her eyes.

She remembered the interlude vividly—the two of them riding across the meadow toward the smoke, pausing on the knoll to watch the red wall of fire creep through the field. There had been an easiness between them that Julie suddenly wished she could recapture.

"Have you been riding lately?" Ruel asked.

"No. I wasn't aware I could just take out a horse."

"You're welcome to ride the gray whenever you like, take him down for a run on the beach sometime. Tell Malia and she'll have Al saddle him for you."

"Thanks," Julie said. "I might do that some weekend." Even if it might be a little lonely riding without him. She quickly put that thought out of her mind.

Abruptly, the cane field was behind them. Now on either side of the road grew low, spiky plants. It took Julie a second to recognize them as pineapples. The fields were geometrically designed with rounded corners and straight rows.

Ruel noticed her rapt expression as she gazed out of the window. "You haven't seen pineapple growing before? It's a thrill."

"No," she admitted.

"I guess they don't have excitement like that in Boston," he teased. "Got a minute?" He smiled at her.

"Sure."

The car began to slow perceptibly. Julie thought it was to give her a better view but instead Ruel pulled onto the shoulder and stopped the car. In the rows paralleling the highway, she could see hundreds of pineapple, growing as offshoots of the parent plants.

"They're harvesting over there." Ruel pointed to a machine farther down the field straddling the rows with a conveyor belt, complete with lights for nighttime picking, stuck out from its side like a long arm. The field hands walked behind the arm, dropping the pineapples on the belt where they rode to the machine.

"You'll notice the pickers are wearing a lot of clothes—

long-sleeved shirts and jackets, pants, and boots and gloves. Pineapple plants are wickedly sharp, so the pickers need a lot of protection."

Julie watched the process for several minutes before realizing with a flash of guilt that this was all very old to Ruel, who had seen it a thousand times or more before. She gave him a rueful look.

"I'm sorry. You should have said something rather than let me hold you up like this," she protested.

"It was my idea to stop in the first place." His mouth slanted into a brief smile. "If I weren't willing to be delayed, I wouldn't have done that. We'll leave when you're done looking."

"I am," Julie insisted.

"Besides"—Ruel paused to check the oncoming traffic, drove back onto the highway, and then continued his sentence—"I couldn't let my sister's teacher be ignorant about pineapples."

"That would be bad, wouldn't it?" she smiled.

"I get something out of it too," he said.

"What?" She was curious.

"Looking at Hawaii through your eyes, it becomes something new for me. I stop taking it for granted."

The traffic became heavier as they passed Schofield Barracks and the town of Wahiawa. The pineapple fields were left behind and the terrain became rolling and wooded. There were dozens of monkeypod trees—Julie recognized those.

Just as suddenly, it seemed, the open country gave way to a mass of towns running together. Highway signs pointed to Pearl Harbor, Honolulu, and Waikiki.

"Where would you like me to take you?" Ruel asked.

"Wherever it would be most convenient." Julie had no specific destination in mind. She had the whole day to see the downtown area.

"How about the yacht harbor? It's not far from the center of Waikiki," he told her.

"Perfect."

Seconds later, he was stopping the car on a side street near the curb. The tall masts of sailboats rose in the distance, crowded together. For all that the ride had begun with misgivings on Julie's part, she was sorry to have it end.

"Thanks for bringing me," she said.

"Enjoy your day," was his parting remark. He made no mention of seeing her later or possibly giving her a ride back.

She stepped onto the sidewalk and waved as Ruel drove away. She had a decidedly let-down feeling as she started down the street alone. Resolutely, she told herself it was the way she wanted it.

After more than an hour of wandering through the tourist shops, she picked up sightseeing brochures at the visitors' center. From the luxury hotels along the beach she journeyed to the Punchbowl, an extinct crater that had become the cemetery of the Pacific. From there she traveled to downtown Honolulu and walked through Chinatown, then on to the State Capitol building and Iolani Palace where the native Hawaiian monarchs had lived. The palace was now a museum. A visitor there suggested to Julie that she would enjoy the Bishop Museum, where there were exhibits on Polynesian cultures and their contribution to Hawaii.

It was afternoon when Julie arrived at the Bishop Museum on the mountainside of Honolulu. With her admission paid, she went to the snack bar in the center of the courtyard before touring the place.

The old, massive stone building had been a summer palace of the Hawaiian monarchy years ago. Its beauty was evident in the carved wooden panels lining the stairway, and the banisters and woodwork. Most impressive was the main room with a ceiling that rose several floors high.

Hanging from the ceiling was the skeleton of a whale, one side exposed and the other sculpted out of fiberglass to embody the vast bulk of the creature. On each floor were exhibits of various cultures and eras. From the wrought iron railings around each floor she could see the whale and the typical Hawaiian hut built on the main floor.

A magnificent display was devoted to the feathered cloaks once worn by Hawaiian royalty. The rich yellow and red and black designs were created by taking single feathers from exotic birds and weaving them into a solid fabric. It had taken years to make one robe, according to the signs, but the brilliant colors had not faded with the passage of time.

Julie worked her way to the main floor. As she started down the last staircase, she happened to glance up from the steps. Waiting at the bottom was Ruel, a hand resting on the curved banister, a half-smile curving his mouth. Her heart skipped a beat.

"How—how did you know I was here?" she stammered.

"I asked myself where a history major would go sightseeing. The only logical answer was a museum. I simply had to go around until I found the right one," he answered smoothly.

"You haven't been to every museum," Julie protested.

"Only the three obvious choices—Iolani Palace, the mission house, and here." He glanced around the main floor. "Have you seen it all?"

"Yes," she nodded. "It was wonderful."

"Would you like a ride home?" Ruel asked, studying her with a sideways tilt to his dark head.

For the first time Julie glanced at her watch, surprised to find she had spent more than three hours in the museum. It was a few minutes before four o'clock.

"Yes, I would." It seemed like an unnecessary answer to an unnecessary question.

Ruel walked beside her to the exit. In the parking lot was his sports car. "What did you think of the city?" He unlocked the door and held it open for her.

"I liked it." Her answer was automatic, given before she thought about what had prompted his question. "Were you wondering if Emily ruined it for me?" she laughed as he slid behind the wheel.

"Did she?" His amused glance told her she was right. "Em is convinced Waikiki is one step away from Coney Island."

"Oh, I admit all the tall buildings didn't seem to fit my idea of Hawaii, but it has a lot of redeeming qualities."

"Such as?" Ruel wanted to know as he left the parking lot and maneuvered his way into the traffic.

"The people," Julie decided. "There's such a mixture."

"Oahu, the Gathering Place. That's the island's nickname," he explained. "It's true. People watching is the most popular pastime in Honolulu."

"I can believe that," she laughed softly.

"So where haven't you been?"

"I haven't been to Pearl Harbor yet, or the Arizona Memorial," Julie answered.

"Have you been to the Pali lookout?" Instead of making the turn toward the ocean and the highway home, Ruel turned the car toward the mountain range rising above Honolulu.

Her glance was quizzical. "Pali? Is that the goddess of volcanoes?"

"No, that's Pele. Pali is the Hawaiian word for cliff. The Pali is the gap through the Koolau range of mountains that takes you from Honolulu and the leeward side of Oahu to the windward side. There's a scenic lookout at the top of the pass," Ruel told her. "Want to go?"

"It isn't on the way home, though." Julie was positive of that.

"It isn't that far out of our way," he assured her.

"In other words, you're taking me there whether I want to go or not?" She laughed as she made the accusation.

"That's right," he admitted.

The highway that they traveled climbed toward the mountains with their steep, fluted cliffs forming a long serrated ridge. Clouds drifted near the peak of the range.

"The Pali highway is closed occasionally," Ruel said. "The mountain gap sometimes focuses and concentrates the trade winds into hurricane force. Local joke is that if a suicide jumped off the cliffs the winds would blow him right back up."

"That's an exaggeration."

"Ya think?" Ruel grinned at her.

"I think."

"Okay, here's a fact. The waterfalls in Nuuanu Valley on the windward side have been known to flow upside down."

"Really?"

"It's the truth." He took the exit to the lookout and parked the car. The cities and coastline of the windward side spread out before them, the vivid blue of the ocean outlining the island. "Here, at the Pali, is where Kamehameha the Great, the first of the Hawaiian monarchs to rule all of the Hawaiian islands, conquered the Oahuans.

He drove them up Nuuanu Valley to the Pali, and finally over the cliffs. People still find the bones of these warriors from time to time around the foot of the cliff."

Julie shuddered. It was difficult to imagine that such a beautiful place could have been a setting for bloodshed. The cliffs were steep. It was a very long way to the bottom.

"How is your geography, teacher?" Ruel asked.

"Pop quiz? Not my strongest subject, but try me." She turned from the view to study him instead.

His roughly hewn features were very male—compellingly so. Her heartbeat quickened in response to the powerful attraction she felt for this man. It caught at her breath, making it shallow.

"Are you aware that the Hawaiian island chain consists of some of the tallest mountains in the world?" he asked.

"No," Julie confessed.

"The Pacific Ocean is from sixteen to eighteen thousand feet deep off these islands. Mauna Kea on the big island is over thirteen thousand feet above the sea. From its base on the ocean floor, it's somewhere over thirty thousand feet."

"I'm impressed," she said, and meant it.

"Good. I wanted to impress you." His relaxed attitude seemed to change subtly to a more brooding mood. Julie became aware of his right arm stretched along the back of the seat with his hand resting on the leather upholstery very near her shoulder.

With her long hair swept into a honey-colored coil, the curve of her neck was exposed. His forefinger traced the sensitive cord that ran the length of her neck. Julie's lashes fluttered closed in reaction to his deliberately sensual caress.

"You're beautiful." It was a flat statement, spoken quietly. "And you have a delectable neck."

Julie imagined Ruel nibbling on that sensitive place. Her skin tingled from the light contact of his hand, igniting a fire of longing within her. The fact that Ruel had an apartment in Honolulu kept running through her mind. Opening her eyes, she stared straight ahead.

"It's getting late. I think it's time we started home." She kept her voice low, hoping it wouldn't quiver.

"There's another full hour of sunlight left," Ruel said. "I thought we'd drive over by Koko Head. You haven't seen the blowhole."

"Um, maybe another time?" Julie was unable to meet the penetrating intensity of his gaze. "I'd rather go back so I have time to relax before dinner."

"Whatever you say." The light touch of his fingertips on her neck ended as he withdrew his arm from the back of the seat and started the car.

Retracing the route to the lookout, they rejoined Pali Highway. Instead of returning to Honolulu, Ruel continued across the pass. The tropical rain forest of eucalyptus and native trees, thick ferns and philodendrons was left behind on the leeward side as the highway tunneled through the cliffs.

Ruel switched on the radio. It was tuned to a station that played traditional Hawaiian songs. Julie couldn't understand the words and had never heard some of the melodies, but that didn't diminish her enjoyment of the music. It was a double blessing since it filled the silence and eliminated the need to talk.

On previous excursions around the island, Julie had traveled as far south on the windward side as the Valley of the Temples. It wasn't long before she was in familiar territory. Shortly after Ruel had turned onto the Kamehameha Highway along the coastline, she saw the small, cone-shaped island called Chinaman's Hat for obvious reasons, sitting in the bay.

Farther on, the road cut through a banana grove. The

short, stocky trees with their wide fronds resembled shaggy palm trees in a constant state of molt. Heavy stalks of green bananas drooped from the fronds. After passing the Polynesian Cultural Center at Laie and the Kahuku Sugar Mill, they drove by the excavations for an aqua farm where seafood would be cultivated. Square ponds were being formed by bulldozers to raise prawns once the squares were flooded.

Rounding Kuilima Point, they were on the north shore of Oahu. It wouldn't be long before they reached the private road leading to the house. Julie stole a glance at Ruel. There was something uncompromising in the set of his features.

The sun had dipped so that it was shining directly in their eyes when she looked back at the highway. She covered her eyes against its blinding light. The car slowed to make the turn into Waimea Bay and the sun was temporarily blocked by the opposite headland. The car didn't follow the highway around the bay. Ruel turned off at the entrance to Waimea Falls.

"Where are we going?"

"You said you wanted to relax before dinner. I decided we would stop here for a drink," he said, unconcerned that she hadn't been consulted.

CHAPTER NINE

Almost immediately the narrow walls of the verdant valley began closing in on them, blocking out the setting sun. The thick tropical growth kept the valley floor shaded and cool. Julie looked straight ahead, her arms folded over her chest.

Ruel lifted an eyebrow at her. "Any objections?"

"You could have asked me."

"You would have said no. I would have insisted." He shrugged. "So we skipped all that." He swung into the parking lot and half turned in his seat to face her. "This is a great place. Am I going to drink alone or are you coming with me?"

Julie realized she could either sit in the car and wait for him or catch the bus. Both sounded a little childish.

"I'll come with you," she agreed, trying to sound offhand.

"Good." A smile crinkled his tanned face and sent Julie's heart knocking against her ribs. The smile was directed at her only briefly as Ruel turned to open his door and step out.

Julie followed suit, not waiting for him to walk around

to open her door. Together they crossed the parking lo
to the park's rustic buildings. A rooster strutted out o
their way.

Ruel's hand rested on the back of her waist as they
climbed the steps to the wooden-floored breezeway be
tween the buildings. His touch was warm and vital, and
it seemed to spread right through her. He guided her
down the length of the buildings to the outdoor stair
case and then to the second floor.

On the upstairs lanai, they sat at a table near the rail
ing. It overlooked a grassy clearing where peacocks were
parading, their eerie cries at odds with their beauty
The sky had turned golden and the birds began finding
their favorite roosts in the tall monkeypod trees.

A waiter came to their table to take their order
"Would you folks like a drink before dinner?"

Ruel glanced at Julie, saw her hesitation, and or
dered, "A Blue Hawaii for the lady, and I'll have a
whiskey. Macallan's, if you have it. Straight up."

"Yes, sir."

Julie opened her mouth to protest but the waiter was
gone. She looked at Ruel and saw the complacent curve
of his mouth. "Don't you like Blue Hawaiis?"

"I don't know. I've never had one," she answered
with faint exasperation.

"I thought you'd like to try an exotic drink."

"Thanks for asking what I wanted."

"You seemed like the Blue Hawaii type. But you
could have a Mai Tai or a Chi Chi if you don't like it."

She held up a hand. "Whoa. I won't be able to walk.

Amusement lurked in the depths of his eyes at her
response. The waiter returned and set a tall, stemmed
glass in front of Julie. The liquid inside the glass was a
vivid blue, topped with a wedge of pineapple and a
maraschino cherry.

"That looks . . . colorful," she murmured. Ruel grinned at her and sipped his whisky. She stirred the strange concoction with the straw and tried it. It was sweet but not overly so. With a little luck, all that food coloring wouldn't turn her tongue blue.

"How do you like it?" Ruel asked.

"It's good," she admitted. "What's in it?"

"Rum and pineapple juice with blue Curacao. So are you sorry we stopped here?"

"No." Julie wasn't sure what she was admitting when she said that, but it was the truth. The setting was serenely beautiful with dusk stealing gently over the valley. From the open lanai, Julie saw the glimmering light of the evening star.

"I thought this place would appeal to you after spending your day in those musty, dusty museums," said Ruel.

"I enjoyed them," Julie said. "I'm still surprised that you went to so much trouble to find me."

"Why were you surprised?" came his quiet challenge.

She wanted to ignore the implication of his question. "I appreciate the effort you made to find me." She sipped at her drink and swirled the blue liquid. "I didn't expect the ride home."

"I didn't suggest it this morning because I didn't know what time I would be finished with my appointments today," Ruel explained. "And because I thought you would dream up some excuse not to accept."

Julie thought he was probably right and tried to defend herself. "Hey. I don't expect you to act as my chauffeur."

"Is that the reason?" His mouth quirked. "I thought you were just trying to avoid me." He signaled the waiter to come to their table, then glanced at Julie. "In that case, will you have dinner with me? The food here

is very good." The waiter arrived before Julie could re
spond. "We'd like to look at your menu now," Ruel re
quested.

"Yes, sir."

As the waiter walked away, Julie protested, "We can
stay for dinner. It's getting late."

Darkness had settled quickly in the valley. She couldn
even make out the shapes of the peacocks nesting i
the trees. Their table was lit by a candle flame protecte
by a colored glass container.

"Do you have a date this evening?" Ruel took th
menus the waiter handed him and passed one to Julie

Automatically she reached for it. "I don't have a date,
she admitted, "but your aunt will be expecting me."

"You have Saturdays and Sundays off. Why shoul
she be expecting you?" He opened his menu and bega
looking at the fare.

"But I'm always back in time for dinner," she tol
him. "Emily will be worried if I'm not there by seven."

He gave her a disbelieving look and reached in hi
jeans pocket. He took out a small cell phone and place
it on the table in front of Julie. "The house number i
on speed dial. Hit three. I'm going back to the car for
minute, so you can say whatever you want."

"Why are you going back to the car?"

"I forgot something."

"What?"

"My pride. Would you quit working me over, Julie?
just want to take you out to a nice dinner. Go ahead an
call Em." He pushed back his chair and left.

Julie hit three and waited for the connection. Emil
answered on the third ring.

"Hello. This is Julie."

"Julie—I was just wondering where you were." Th
nervous wobble in the older woman's voice confirme
what Julie had suspected.

"I thought I'd better call to let you know I won't be home for dinner," she said.

"Oh." The one word was followed by a long pause. "Will you be home very late tonight?"

"No." Julie glanced toward the staircase that Ruel had gone down. "No. I don't expect to be late." Since Emily hadn't asked who she was with, Julie didn't volunteer the information.

"Very well. Enjoy yourself."

She wasn't sure if she wanted to do that. "Thank you, Emily. See you later." She flipped the phone shut as Ruel returned.

"Is Em satisfied that you're safe?"

She sipped her drink. "Yes, I think so."

"Want another one?" He gestured to her drink.

"No, thanks. I'm turning blue already."

He took a swallow of his whisky and studied her face. "Did you tell her you were with me?"

"No."

"Why?"

"Because I thought you didn't want her to know," she replied crisply.

"Why should I care if Em knows? She isn't likely to object. What made you think I didn't want her to know?"

Julie shrugged. "Probably because of your policy of not getting involved with the hired help."

He leaned back. "Wow. We're off to a great start. I can tell this is going to be a memorable evening."

She glared at him. "I don't have to provide you with beautiful memories, you know. Not in my job description."

Ruel laughed despite his annoyance. "Actually, you already have."

"What are you talking about?" she asked uneasily.

"I can't forget what it was like to hold you in my arms," answered Ruel without hesitation.

The breath seemed to stop in her lungs. She stared at her drink, unable to look at him yet riveted by the blue color of the liquid, its shade not that different from the arresting blue of his eyes. Her heart pounded in her chest.

"No comment?" Ruel asked.

"No." She swallowed to ease the tightness in her throat and nervously smoothed one side of her hair back. "No comment." She was a poor liar. She never would have been able to convince him she had forgotten what it was like.

"Would you prefer to dine inside or out here?" His change of subject was a godsend for Julie.

"Inside," she said, hoping the well-lit interior of the restaurant would dispel the feeling of intimacy the darkened lanai provided.

Rising, he took her hand. "Leave it," he said of the drink.

Julie didn't argue. The last sip had been watery. She walked through the wide opening into the restaurant while Ruel followed, carrying his whisky. She paused inside the room with its planked walls and board floor. Its turn-of-the-century décor was enhanced with stained glass and expensive antiques.

"California! What are you doing here?" The enthusiastic greeting from Frank Smythe brought Julie up short.

He came hustling toward her, his boyish face wreathed in a smile, dressed with uncharacteristic neatness in dark pants, a white shirt, and a print vest. She realized with dismay that this was where he worked.

"Hi, Frank." Conscious of Ruel behind her, Julie's greeting was much more subdued. She had a vague feeling of dread. She wished now that she had been interested enough to ask Frank where he worked before now.

"Why didn't you let me know you were coming?" Frank stopped in front of her, his eyes seeing only her.

"I didn't know," she answered truthfully, and would have drawn his attention to Ruel, but Frank didn't give her a chance.

"Listen, I have to work until closing, but we booked a pretty good band for tonight. If you can stay—"

"The lady is with me." Ruel towered beside her. "And we won't be staying."

Frank's head jerked toward him. He glanced from Ruel to Julie and back to Ruel again.

"I didn't realize Julie was with you, Mr. Chandler." It was more of a challenge than an apology.

"Obviously," was Ruel's dry response. "Excuse us."

Frank stepped aside, flashing Julie a look that demanded to know what she was doing with Ruel. An answer was impossible under the circumstances.

The host came forward and led them to a booth. Its floor-to-ceiling partition guaranteed privacy for its occupants. Sitting on the cushioned booth seat, Julie glanced across the table at Ruel.

"I didn't know Frank worked here," she said, just in case he thought she had.

"Neither did I," he retorted.

She managed a nervous smile. "We don't have to eat here." Ruel didn't seem to hear.

"Good evening." Frank appeared at their table, his expression polite, regarding them as strangers.

Julie turned pale as she realized he was their waiter.

"Both the mahi mahi and opakapaka are fresh this evening. The pork ribs are always excellent." He filled their goblets with ice water. "Would you care to see the wine list, sir?"

"No, thank you."

Irritation darkened Ruel's eyes to the color of deep water.

"I'll be back in a few minutes to take your order." Frank nodded and moved away.

Julie glanced at Ruel, expecting a comment, but he made none. The menu was in front of her; she hadn't looked at it when she was on the lanai. There was a full range of dishes, from glazed mandarin duck to prime rib.

"What would you like?" Ruel asked.

"I don't know." She couldn't decide. "What is this Hawaiian platter like? What's lomi lomi salmon? Or this kalua pig?"

"Okay. Hawaiian Cuisine 101. Take notes. The lomi lomi salmon is raw salmon that's been massaged for tenderness."

Julie gave him a disbelieving look. "How do you massage a salmon? Never mind, I don't even want to know."

Ruel had to laugh. "Then I won't tell you. The kalua pig is pork that's been baked in an earth oven. I wouldn't actually recommend the Hawaiian platter. Comes with poi."

"Which is?"

"A starchy vegetable, kind of like potato, that's been pounded into a pulp, diluted with water, and allowed to ferment."

"I'll pass," Julie said decisively. "What should I have?"

"Do you like fish?"

"Yes, but I've already had mahi mahi. I'd like to try something different." Julie studied the menu.

"Why not have the opakapaka?" Ruel suggested.

"What is it?" She was wary after his explanation.

"Red snapper," he smiled.

"I'll have that," she decided immediately and joined in when Ruel chuckled softly.

The moment of shared laughter ended the instant

Frank returned. Ruel gave him their order in a precise, clipped tone. He stayed irritable after Frank left, and the situation wasn't helped by the way Frank kept checking their table and asking if everything was all right. Julie suspected that he was deliberately trying to spoil their evening.

"Shall I take your plate, sir?" Frank appeared the minute Ruel had finished. At a nod, he gathered the plate and silverware. "More coffee, sir? Dessert?"

"Nothing right now." Ruel flashed him a dismissing look.

"You may take my plate, Frank. I'm done," Julie told him. He stacked her dishes on the tray with Ruel's. Before Frank could ask any more annoying questions, she added, "Nothing more for me."

As Frank carried the dishes away, Ruel glared at his back. There was a hint of impatience in his face when he turned to look at Julie. "Your boyfriend is making a jealous pest of himself."

"It isn't my fault," Julie replied.

"Meaning it's mine?"

"Meaning it's his. I have no control over the way he behaved, anymore than you would if one of your girl-friends were waiting on us."

A cold smile twitched the corners of his mouth. "They probably wouldn't be so civilized about it."

He appeared to be fascinated by the sugar packets in a white ceramic box on the table, arranging them neatly and not looking at her. Julie studied him. His expression was unhappy.

Was it because of her remark about his girlfriends? Why had she put it in the plural—and why had she assumed he wouldn't be satisfied with one girl? He had never been married, as far as she knew. How he had escaped for so long?

"If you don't mind my asking . . ." Julie began.

"That's a sentence that never ends well," he observed sourly.

She decided to go for it. "How come you never married?"

"Maybe," he slowly lifted his gaze to hers, "because I haven't found a woman who didn't bore me either out of bed or in it." His voice was as serious as his face. With a sinking heart, Julie was forced to believe what he said.

"Your check, sir." Frank placed a small tray on the table beside Ruel and began refilling the water goblets.

After glancing at the amount, Ruel placed a bill on the tray. "Keep the change."

"Thank you, sir." Frank picked up the tray with the money.

Each time Frank said "sir" in that ingratiating way, Julie saw Ruel's jaw tighten. His irritation was turning into an anger that tested his control. She could see it in the sharpness of his gaze as it sliced across the table to her.

"Are you ready to leave?" It was meant to be a polite question, but it was a little too abrupt for that.

Julie nodded. To get to the stairs, they had to pass the cash register. Frank was there, and his gaze sought Julie as they approached. She held her breath, hoping he wouldn't say any more to Ruel. Frank didn't, but the host who was behind the cash register did.

"Good night, Mr. Chandler. Was everything satisfactory?"

The remark forced Ruel to slow his stride to respond. When he did, Frank was at Julie's side. She tried to warn him away with a shake of her head, but he paid no attention.

As Ruel said, "Everything was fine, thank you," to the host, Frank was whispering, "Will I see you tomorrow at the beach, Julie?"

Before she could draw a breath, Ruel had a hand on her elbow. "No, you won't!" he snapped at Frank, and propelled her toward the staircase.

"Dude, you don't own her!" Frank hurled after him.

By then they were halfway down the first flight of steps. "What did you mean telling Frank that?" Julie demanded, her temper flaring.

"Exactly what I said." They had reached the ground floor and Ruel directed her to the parking lot. His grip didn't permit her to slow down.

"Sunday happens to be my day off, as you pointed out earlier this evening," she reminded him.

"You aren't going to see that punk kid," Ruel stated.

"Don't tell me what I can and can't do!" Julie retorted.

He flashed her an angry look and unlocked the passenger door of the car. He more or less pushed her inside and slammed the door. Julie sat in the richly upholstered leather seats and fumed. He had gone too far this time.

Ruel slid behind the wheel and started the motor. "Fasten your seat belt."

She did, casting an apprehensive look at him when she heard his clip.

The sleek sports car had been built for speed, maneuverability, and acceleration. As the car roared out onto the curving drive to the highway, Ruel seemed intent on testing all three.

The powerful thrust of the engine pushed Julie's shoulders against the back of the seat. At the junction with the highway, the car made a running stop before turning onto the road that was miraculously free of traffic at that moment.

The tires squealed around the corner and spun at the sudden demand for acceleration. The speed that they were traveling had Julie's heart in her throat. They were racing in the opposite direction from the house, but he didn't seem to notice or care.

Traversing the twisting highway that followed the coastline, weaving in and out of traffic, they covered a lot of ground in record time. Julie's gaze was riveted to the road directly ahead of them, illuminated by their headlights. Any second she expected them to miss a turn or overshoot a curve.

Once she forced a look at Ruel. The strong hands on the steering wheel seemed totally in control, firm in their grip yet relaxed. There was nothing in Ruel's expression to indicate that he thought they were going too fast. Neither was there anger. But a glimpse at the speedometer made Julie close her eyes.

It never once occurred to her to say something to Ruel, not even to suggest that he slow down. Possibly she didn't want to distract his steel-blue gaze from the road. It was worse riding with her eyes closed. She couldn't see what was going to happen next. She opened them just as Ruel swept past a slower car.

Suddenly she was staring into an oncoming pair of headlights, and she breathed in a stifled cry. She understood what Emily had said about how dangerously fast Ruel drove. The black sports car swerved easily into its own lane, missing the oncoming car by several yards.

Almost immediately its speed began to decrease. Taking the first really deep breath she'd drawn since leaving the restaurant parking lot, Julie glanced at Ruel.

"Sorry. I didn't mean to frighten you." He flicked her a brief glance.

"It's okay." But her voice sounded shaky.

The shoulder of the highway widened to provide parking on the beach side of the road. Ruel slowed the car and turned onto the shoulder. Switching off the motor, he looked out of the window at the ocean. A thin strip of sandy beach was in front of the car. Julie had no idea where they were or how far they had come.

"I'm going for a walk on the beach," Ruel announced, and opened his door. "You're welcome to come along if you want."

The invitation was so offhand that Julie wasn't sure he meant it. It didn't matter to her. A walk was as fast as she wanted to travel for a while. And she liked the idea of having land under her feet.

When she climbed out of her side of the car, Ruel was already standing on the ribbon of pale sand at the water's edge. His hands were thrust deep in his pockets. Closing the door, Julie walked over the dune. The coolness of the trade winds seemed to fill her lungs, reviving her.

As she walked onto the beach, her shoes sank into the sand. She had stupidly forgotten to take them off, but after a ride like that, she could forgive herself for forgetting a lot of things.

Balancing on one foot, she took off one shoe, then the other, and carried them in her hand. Barefoot, she walked down to where the waves lapped the shore. At night, with only the moon and stars for light, the water seemed to shine.

Farther along the coast, the strip of beach widened. A grove of windswept ironwoods rose on its dunes. Julie wandered in that general direction, aware that Ruel had begun to stroll after her. She lifted her face to the sea air and walked on.

CHAPTER TEN

The waves were stronger near the stand of iron-woods. They crashed onto and over the lava rocks that edged the sand at the shore. Julie stopped to watch the churning white foam lift, plunge, and recede. She heard the soft crunch of Ruel's footsteps in the sand directly behind her.

"Quite a sight, isn't it?" she said over her shoulder, her gaze not straying from the pounding surf.

"Yes." Ruel's voice was calm.

He had stopped closer to her than Julie had first realized. Still she didn't turn from the mesmerizing sight of the sea. Something seemed to slip from her hair. But not until the sensation was repeated did she realize that the pins securing her coiled hair were being pulled out with infinite gentleness.

Letting her shoes fall to the ground, she turned. "Don't do that!"

Ruel ignored her protest and continued to pull out the hairpins, despite her effort to stop him. In a matter of seconds her hair was tumbling about her shoulders as she was powerless to do anything about it.

She sighed with exasperation.

"Indulge me. I like it better this way." Rule slid his fingers into the tangled silk of her hair and cupped her head in both of his hands. "I've wanted to do that ever since I saw you at the breakfast table this morning. That hairdo reminds me of a prim and proper—"

"Schoolteacher," Julie said.

Her face was tilted toward his while her heart raced faster than the sports car had. His hands were so strong, yet so devastatingly gentle. His shadowed eyes seemed to be taking in detail of her face.

"Something like that," he said, and in another second he was covering her mouth with his.

There was no holding back and Julie didn't try. She wound her arms around his middle and pressed herself close to his length. The hard, branding kiss seemed to reach her soul. Ruel wasn't content to take possession of only her lips. Holding her face in his hands, he kissed every inch of it before reclaiming the softness of her waiting mouth.

Releasing her face, he slid her arms around her and gathered her into the fullness of his embrace. Desire quaked through her and erupted to flow like fire through her veins. Ecstasy burned in its wake as she felt the way Ruel trembled against her, as aroused as she was.

Her hands tugged his shirt out of his pants and slipped under it, seeking to feel the bareness of his hard flesh. It was hot to the touch. The skin of his back stretched tautly over his muscles.

He abandoned her mouth to explore the curve of her neck, nibbling at the sensitive skin. His accompanying caresses only created new needs within her. All her senses were dominated by him. He murmured her name over and over again in hungry demand.

When she felt his fingers loosening the buttons of her blouse, she helped him. Ruel left the task to her and unfastened the front closing of her bra. Then his hands were taking her over. But Julie had never felt so deliriously happy in all her life. The light caress of his hands was sweet torment. They were wrapped in each other's arms and it still wasn't close enough for either of them.

Suddenly something drove at their legs, undermining the sand beneath their feet. Ruel staggered forward a step, carrying Julie with him, almost completely losing his balance for a moment. Dazed, she opened her eyes to see a wave receding to the ocean. An object bobbed on its surface.

"My shoes!" she gasped.

Ruel gave her a puzzled frown and looked where she was looking but didn't let her go.

"I dropped them on the sand and the wave got them—the one that hit us," she explained as she tugged at the arm around her waist holding her captive.

Ruel started to let go of her and then held her back. "Stay here, I'll get them." But as he waded into the water, another wave swelled into a curl that drove him back to shore.

"Oh, well," Julie said. "They're gone."

"I'm afraid so."

She looked at him. His shoes were soaked and his pants drenched to a point above his knees. Her shoes had been washed out to sea and the legs of her own pants were wet with seawater. The situation seemed funny somehow and she started to laugh.

"So you think it's funny?" Ruel smiled at her breathless laughter. Then his arms circled her waist to lock his hands behind her back. He drew her hips against his.

"It is," she insisted. "You with squishy shoes and wet pants, and me with no shoes at all."

Despite the half-smile on his mouth, his eyes were serious in their regard of her. "You should be glad it happened."

"Why?"

"That was nature's way of cooling us off. Things were getting too hot," he explained.

Julie sobered. Suddenly aware of the gaping front of her blouse, she pulled it shut with her hands, clutching the ends together. She made no attempt to escape the circle of his arms, but she wasn't totally at ease any more.

"You're right." She couldn't meet the steadiness of his look.

"I want you, Julie," he told her in a remarkably cool tone. "Nothing is going to change that."

He smoothed the hair away from her cheek and rested his hand along the side of her neck, stroking her jaw with his thumb. "I want to make love to you," he went on. A few minutes ago they might have done just that.

"Here's your chance for second thoughts," he told her. "I have an apartment in Honolulu. No waves. Nobody around. Just you and me."

"What about what you said?" she faltered.

"You seem to remember every word I say," he growled. "I don't. "

"But—"

"I want you, Julie." His voice was raw and urgent, controlled but only barely.

Instead of feeling joy at his words, Julie felt chilled. Everything began to freeze up inside her. "Aren't you worried that I might bore you?" It came out flat and cold.

A muscle flexed in his arm as if he was fighting an urge to crush her to his chest and drive that coolness from her body. After a long moment, he let her go and took a step away.

"Let's go back to the car so I can drive you home," he said.

Her mind seemed incapable of focusing on anything that mattered. Only little things registered as they walked silently and apart to the car. Trivial stuff like buying a new pair of shoes to replace the ones she'd lost, and wondering where Ruel had discarded the pins he'd taken from her hair.

In the car, Julie thought about the sand they were tracking onto the carpeted footwells and wondered if the seawater from their wet clothes would damage the leather upholstery.

The lights were on downstairs when they reached the house. Julie had no idea whether it was early or late. The gravel in the driveway bit into the bare soles of her feet as she stepped from the car and she had to pick her way to the steps. Ruel reached the front door ahead of her and opened it for her.

Emily Harmon was coming down the stairs as Julie entered. "You're home, Julie. I was wondering what time to expect you." Her smile seemed relieved. When she saw Ruel walk in behind Julie, her eyes widened in surprise. "You didn't tell me you were with Ruel."

"Didn't I? I thought I had." Julie tossed out the lie with numbed unconcern.

"Where are your shoes?" Emily began to look at them more closely, a thousand puzzled questions in her eyes.

"I took them off to walk on the beach and a wave washed them out to sea. Ruel waded in after them, but he couldn't reach them." Julie felt something begin to splinter inside of her and knew she couldn't keep on answering these questions. "Excuse me, Emily, I'm really a mess. I'll see you in the morning."

She rushed past the older woman and up the stairs, leaving Ruel to handle the explanations. In the safety of her room, she gave in to her shakiness, figuring it was a natural reaction to what had almost happened. But even when she had calmed down, it took effort to simply undress, wash, and climb into bed.

Sunday came and went with Julie venturing no farther from the house than the swimming pool. There were no more questions from Emily about the previous night. And Ruel was nowhere around. Those two factors should have made it easier, but she only felt more tense. She was glad she had work that she liked to keep her grounded in reality and she found herself actually looking forward to its routine demands.

Midafternoon on Monday Julie was in Debbie's room, trying to explain the solution to an algebra problem. "I just don't understand how to do it. Can't we leave it for today?" Debbie pleaded. "I can't concentrate."

"I noticed," Julie sighed.

"Did Auntie Em tell you the news?" Debbie's eyes glowed with excitement, making her look very young.

"What? No, I don't think so."

"I'm going to the hospital on Thursday, for X-rays and to see how I'm healing. If everything's all right, they'll take off this cast and put me in a smaller one. I might even be able to use a wheelchair. Isn't that great?" she burst out.

"Wow! Yes, it is," Julie said with a wide smile. "That's the best news I've heard in ages. I'm happy for you."

"I'm happy for me too," Debbie declared, and glanced toward the window at the sound of a car pulling into the drive. "That's Ruel! I can't wait to tell him."

Too happy to see the tension in Julie's expression, Debbie pushed away her schoolwork. "He's home early today. I wonder why."

Julie heard the car door slam and winced. "I think we should concentrate on finishing up for right now."

"Noooo! Not that algebra problem again!" Debbie wailed.

"It's not that difficult."

"Easy for you to say." Debbie looked past Julie to the door. She broke into an immediate smile. "Hi, Ruel!"

Julie stiffened, well aware of his presence in the room but unwilling to turn around. She stared instead at the page of equations in her hand.

"Hi, Deb. How are you?" His footsteps approached the chair by his younger sister's bed.

"Fine, and guess what—"

Julie broke in. "Would you mind visiting later? Debbie really needs to focus on her work and finish today's assignment."

Debbie gave her an astonished look. "Huh?"

"I came to speak to you," was all Ruel said in reply.

He was standing much too close to her chair. Agitated, she rose and put distance between them, clasping the math papers in front of her as if they offered protection.

"As you can see, I'm busy." She met his narrowed gaze for a second or two before she turned her head away, keeping her chin high.

"This will only take a moment," he said.

Julie didn't want to back down. "Why would you need to speak to me?"

"For one thing"—he crossed the room to where she stood—"I wanted to give you this."

There was no place for Julie to retreat. She couldn't keep running from him anyway. Debbie was already staring at them with rapt fascination, as if they were playing a scene in a soap opera. Julie just stared at the box he offered to her.

"What is it?" She made no move to take it.

"A pair of shoes to replace the ones you lost the other night. Malia looked through your closet and told me your size."

"Oh." The thought that the whole household now knew about the minor incident was very upsetting. Julie told herself not to be so silly but her nervousness did not go away.

"So here you go. Same style." He held out the box again. "It was no trouble. You're welcome."

Julie's eyes widened at his sarcastic tone but she took the box this time. "Thank you," she said stiffly.

Ruel turned to Debbie. "I'll come by to see you later. Get back to work, kid." He didn't wait for a response, and his long strides echoed down the hall after he left.

"What was that all about?" Debbie asked, her eyes bright with curiosity.

"We were walking on the beach. A wave ate my shoes." Julie set the shoebox on a side table.

"Oh. Was that Saturday night? I heard you come home with Ruel. After you went upstairs, he told Em that you two had dinner together." Debbie continued to study her intently. "So what happened? Did you two get into an argument?"

Julie forced a smile. "Why would I be arguing with your brother?"

"I don't know. You tell me. A minute ago the vibration in here was really weird."

"Hey, guess what." Julie took a deep breath, about to tell the teenager it was none of her business, when Debbie interrupted her.

"I mean, if you and Ruel want to hang out together, I think that's great. You're together a lot anyway. Is he, like, your secret crush? He's really cute even if he is kind of obnoxious."

At the moment, Debbie was giving her brother a run

for his money in the obnoxious department, Julie thought with annoyance.

"No, I don't have a crush on him."

"It's okay if you do. Everyone does."

Not exactly what Julie wanted to hear but there was no shutting up a teenager on a roll.

"You can tell me what you fought about. I won't tell anyone."

Right. Julie gave the girl a long look. "Once and for all, Debbie, your brother and I didn't fight. And I'm not going to discuss the subject any further. Is that clear?"

"I was just trying to help." Debbie's dark eyes held a look of wounded dignity.

"You can help by paying attention to your lessons," Julie said quietly.

By the time Thursday arrived, Julie was almost glad to see Debbie leave for the hospital, since it gave her a break from the girl's curiosity.

At almost seventeen, Debbie was too perceptive. She didn't make any more attempts to get her teacher to confide in her, but Julie knew the teenager would love it if she did.

The strain of pretending that absolutely nothing had happened was wearing on Julie. And Ruel's studied politeness didn't make it any easier.

Julie wasn't on hand to welcome Debbie home late Friday afternoon. She had swum laps in the pool, to the point of exhaustion, and was stretched out on one of the lounge chairs when she heard the commotion of Debbie's return. She didn't think she could match the happiness of the voices filtering from the house, so she made no attempt to join them. Besides, Ruel would be there and Julie preferred not to be with Debbie when he was around and vice versa.

Closing her eyes against the glaring sun, she tried to relax. Its warmth didn't ease the tension in her body or her frayed nerves.

The familiar slip-slapping sound of Malia's sandals on the sun deck warned her of the housekeeper's approach. "Miss Emily was wondering where you were, Julie. Debbie's home from the hospital."

"Yes, I heard." She didn't move or open her eyes. "Sorry I didn't come around. I'm not exactly dressed," she murmured.

"You should see her! She's so excited about that wheelchair," Malia declared. "It will be good for her to get out of that room each day."

"Yes, it will," Julie agreed. "Debbie's really been looking forward to that."

"Well, when you change, go see her, Julie," the housekeeper said.

"I will. But I'm sure her brother and Emily want to spend some time with her. I wouldn't want to intrude."

"Miss Emily would never think you were intruding," Malia said warmly. "And Ruel is having dinner in town tonight. He said he just had time to shower and change before he leaves."

"Oh." Julie swallowed the lump that rose in her throat. His dinner date probably was a gorgeous woman who didn't care if she bored him. "Tell Debbie I'll be in to see her later," she repeated at last. "Sometime before dinner."

"Okay." Malia sighed softly, as if she regretted not being able to persuade Julie to come in sooner.

As Julie listened to the woman's footsteps retreating to the house, she heard other footsteps not far away. Overhead.

She opened her eyes and looked up. Ruel was standing on the lanai that overlooked the pool. The doors were open behind him. His shirt was pulled free of his jeans and was unbuttoned most of the way down. He looked as if he had stopped in the act of taking it off. He was staring at her.

Julie felt a little like a sacrificial offering to the sun. Her orange bikini had always seemed to provide enough coverage, but now she felt exposed—almost naked. She had the weird feeling he could see into her head and read her mind. And she didn't even want to admit to herself the thoughts about him that ran through it.

Rising abruptly, she grabbed for her beach jacket and hurriedly stuffed her arms into its sleeves. She wrapped it around her and tied the sash. When she glanced again at the upper lanai where Ruel had been, he wasn't there. The doors to his bedroom were partially shut.

Her shoulders sagged. Julie sighed. Just what was she protecting? He had only been looking at her. She concluded that she was her own worst enemy. She had to get control of herself and her emotions.

As she climbed the outer staircase to the lanai and her bedroom, she felt the beginning of silly tears. She told herself to knock it off. Crying was pointless, and there was nothing to cry about.

Pushing open the French doors to her room, she walked in. Her hair was almost dry from the swim and outdoor shower to get the chlorine out, but it was matted around her shoulders. She lifted it from her neck and let it fall back. Her appearance had ceased to concern her. Untying her beach jacket, she took it off and started to toss it on the chair by the wall.

Something skittered across the white-painted wall and she gave a shriek of alarm before she recognized it as one of the tiny, harmless lizards that usually inhabited the gardens outside.

If she hadn't been so edgy, the little creature would

not have scared her. Shaking nonetheless, she clutched the robe to her stomach. Her heart was attempting to resume its normal beat.

You're losing your mind, she told herself.

The French doors burst open.

She spun around, and saw Ruel, naked to the waist, concern etched in his hard male features.

"What is it? I heard you scream," he demanded.

She fought a wave of foolish panic. "Nothing. One of those . . . lizards or geckos, whatever they are . . . ran across the wall," she explained in a faltering voice. "It scared me for a second before I saw what it was."

Exhaling a breath, he relaxed. His muscles seemed to visibly uncoil. "Okay. I thought you hurt yourself or something."

She shook her head. "No, I'm all right."

It was impossible to take her eyes from him. She had never seen him like this, his chest bared, hard flesh rippled with muscle, his skin deeply tanned all over. His virility shook her senses, assaulting her from every direction.

Her fingers curled into her palms, wanting to thread through that very masculine hair on his chest. She could almost hear the steady pounding of his heart—or was it hers? His natural scent seemed to reach across the room and envelop her.

She looked into his face and saw his eyes move over her body. The beach jacket was a crumpled ball, pressed to her stomach, concealing none of her curves.

When his eyes met hers, she saw the desire blazing there, and elemental hunger trembled through her. She felt exposed all over again, defenseless against the emotion he aroused.

"Get out of my bedroom." It was a hoarse plea not to test her resistance any further. She knew she had none.

He shook his head. "Julie." He held out a hand and took a step toward her.

With a soft, muffled cry she swayed toward him. It was all the answer Ruel needed as he crossed the room to sweep her into his arms. Julie locked her arms around his neck and gave in to her own desire.

CHAPTER ELEVEN

Alive with a nameless joy, she pressed kisses against his jaw and cheek while he buried his mouth in the curve of her neck. "Julie," he moaned.

His lips moved up her neck to seek the parted softness of hers. His sighing breath of satisfaction filled her mouth. She felt his hand moving up her back to the bow of her bikini. One deft pull on the right string and it loosened. She wriggled her shoulders so he could remove the top completely, then it went sailing across the room as naked flesh met naked flesh.

"God, how I want you," Ruel muttered against the hollow of her throat. Carrying her with muscular ease, he brought her to the bed and set her down on the coverlet. The mattress compressed as he followed her down. With the pressure of his body spread half over her and half beside her, Julie felt luxuriously weak. A heady lethargy took hold of her and she surrendered to the sensuous demands he made.

She shuddered with desire when he bent to kiss her

breasts and tease the rosy nipples into hardness. A longing for more warmed her body—and she was overwhelmingly aware that Ruel was equally aroused.

His mouth was back on her lips for a moment, then he whispered, "Kulie." His hand slid down her waist and over her hips. "Ipo, ku'uipo," he said into her ear. "Aloha auia oe." He rubbed his chin and cheek against hers in a rough caress. His eyes were half-closed with passion. "I don't know why it's so much easier to say in Hawaiian," he murmured. "Do you know what I said?"

"No." Words had ceased to matter. "Kiss me. Love me, Ruel," she begged.

His mouth covered hers in urgent possession. His hands were seeking and shaping her body to his. Neither could seem to get close enough to the other. His weight pressed her down on the bed, his body hot against hers.

A succession of sharp raps on the door was followed immediately by Emily calling, "Julie? Are you all right?"

Julie surfaced from his kiss with a rush, but not quickly enough to call out an answer. The knob rattled as she grabbed at the coverlet and pulled it partly over herself. Then the door opened and Emily stepped in.

It all happened in a span of seconds. There wasn't enough time for Julie and Ruel to jump up, let alone make an attempt to look as if they had been doing anything even remotely respectable.

After Julie's initial glimpse of Emily's shocked expression, she turned her face away, burying it in the hard muscle of his upper arm. He shielded her from his aunt's view for a moment.

"What is going on here?' Emily finally breathed out the words.

"Damn! What the hell do you think is going on?" Ruel snapped, and levered himself away from Julie to rise from the bed.

Hot with shame and embarrassment, Julie pulled up more of the comforter. A wave of nausea swamped her. She was sure she was going to be sick. She couldn't bring herself to look at either Emily or Ruel.

"Julie, I—" The shock of disappointment and disapproval was clear in the older woman's voice.

"For God's sake, Em, leave her alone," Ruel muttered,

"You know very well that I can't permit—this," his aunt declared, provoked by his rudeness into real anger.

"If anyone needs to be lectured, it's me," he said with barely controlled fury. "Leave her alone!"

Silent sobs began to shake Julie's body. Her trembling fingers pulled the coverlet around her; she hunched her shoulders beneath it. Despite what Ruel said, she knew she was as much to blame for what happened as he was.

A hand touched her shoulder and she cringed from it. Her tear-filled eyes were aware of Ruel standing beside her, but she couldn't turn to him. He hesitated.

"It was my fault. I'll explain to Em," he promised quietly. "Julie, I have to go now."

She couldn't lift her head to look at him. She wasn't sure if she could look anyone in the face again. She simply nodded to indicate that she'd heard him.

She heard him walk to the door. When it closed, she rolled over into a miserable ball. Okay—this was worth crying over. She let the silent tears flow.

In the hallway she heard Em's voice. " I thought I heard her scream, Ruel."

"You did. And so did I. I just got there faster."

There was a pause. "You certainly did," Emily said sharply.

"Don't start, Em. Just don't." Julie heard him sigh. "She saw a lizard and it scared her. That's why I . . . oh, hell. An explanation is going to make this worse."

Their footsteps retreated down the hall and Julie didn't hear any more of their conversation. She cried—for what she'd done and what she'd lost. It was a long time before the well went dry. She lay on the bed in a stupor after it was over.

She knew she couldn't hide in her room forever. Sooner or later she would have to face the others. Struggling out of the coverlet, she walked to the bathroom and scrubbed her swollen face with cold water. From the closet she took her long house robe and put it on, zipping it all the way up to her throat. Then taking the hairbrush, she began raking it through her tangled hair with punishing force.

There was a knock at the door and she froze. "Who is it?"

"It's me, Emily. May I come in?" This time she waited for permission before entering.

If only she'd done that the last time, Julie wished sadly. At the least the results wouldn't have been so humiliating. Heat flooded her cheeks as she turned away from the door.

"Come in," she said.

When the door opened, Julie didn't turn around. She continued to brush her hair, stroke after stroke. She heard Emily step in and close the door. She kept her back turned to the woman.

"I want you to know, Julie," Emily began quietly, "that coming here is very painful to me, as painful as it is to you. But it's important that we have this talk."

"I understand," Julie said, lowering the brush. She closed a hand around the bristles, letting them dig into her palm. The physical pain was preferable to Emily's gentleness.

"I did cause you a great deal of embarrassment by walking in like I did. For that, I apologize. However, you must know that I will not tolerate a repetition of this afternoon."

"Yes," Julie nodded, "I guessed that would be how you felt. You don't have to worry about asking me to leave. I'll just pack and go. Tonight, if you want."

"Leave? I don't want you to leave, Julie," Emily protested. "That was never my intention."

"Please." Julie turned, trying to salvage some of her pride. "I know what you must think of me and—"

"I think you're a human being, capable of moments of weakness," Emily Harmon interrupted. "I don't condemn you for what happened, but as I said, I can't condone it."

"I don't expect you to." Julie crimsoned, her gaze falling away under the directness of Emily's.

"My nephew is an attractive man. You're a young, beautiful woman. What happened was only natural. But you do understand that it can't continue."

"Yes. Ruel already mentioned that he doesn't generally become involved with hired help." A hint of self-pity crept into her biting reply.

"Hired help? I don't consider you hired help, Julie." The older woman sounded indignant. "You seem practically a member of the family. Whatever faults I may have, I've never looked down on anyone because they worked for a living. In my house or anywhere else."

"I'm sorry, Emily."

With a sigh, Julie replaced the hairbrush on the dressing table and walked to the French doors. The gauzy sheers cast a film over the courtyard view, darkened by the shadows of twilight.

"I seem to be making a mess of this," Emily said. "I think I do understand what happened here. Ruel is a charming and persuasive man when he chooses to be."

"Oh, please!" Julie whirled around in protest. "No matter what he told you, I was a very willing participant."

"I didn't mean to suggest he was forcing himself on you, dear, or seducing you against your will. I'm quite aware that it was mutual."

"That's right." Embarrassment reddened Julie's cheeks even as she admitted the truth.

"I hope you don't think that I reached the age of fifty-nine without having experienced the heat of passion. I do know what it's like to be carried away by emotions," Emily said with gentle patience. "I never married but that doesn't mean I was never in love."

"I know it doesn't," Julie murmured.

"My lover was stationed here in the military. I lived for those hours when he was off duty and could get a pass to see me. The world seemed perfect when I was in his arms. The moments we stole to be together were the most precious." There was a beautifully poignant quality to her voice. "When he was reassigned, he promised he would come back to me, and I believed him."

"What happened?" Julie's own pain was put aside for a moment, replaced by compassion for Emily.

A rueful smile twisted the older woman's mouth. "He went back to Georgia and married his high school sweetheart."

"I'm sorry, Emily."

"It was a very long time ago." Emily shrugged off the sympathy and squared her shoulders. "You and Ruel are adults. If you feel strongly about each other, I can't prevent it. If you wish to see each other, if you wish to go out on dates, I can't stop you—I wouldn't even try. You have my blessing. But I can't permit the two of you to carry on an intimate relationship in this house."

"I promise you it will never happen again," Julie said.

"You do understand why. I have Debbie to consider. She's only sixteen and you do set an example for her. How she decides to live when she's on her own is beyond my control, but in the meantime, you and Ruel are not to . . . you know what I mean."

Julie nodded. A tightness gripped her throat. She was reminded again of how very fond Emily was of her niece. And as for the older woman's extraordinary tact—Julie felt nothing but gratitude and admiration.

"So you understand, Julie, I didn't come here to embarrass you. I care too much about you to do that. But I wanted to make it clear to you why I disapproved so strongly of what happened. I'm not a prude. But I must think of Debbie," Emily concluded with touching simplicity. "I love her very much."

"I understand completely," Julie said. "And I know she loves you too." She was surprised to feel a slight welling of tears in her eyes. Julie had thought they were all gone.

"In that case, why don't you get dressed and join me for dinner?" Emily suggested. "It's five minutes after seven and Malia will think no one is coming down."

Not twenty minutes ago Julie hadn't cared whether she ever had another meal again. The thought of eating made her gag. Now, after being treated with such gentleness by Emily, the idea was not unpleasant.

"Give me a few minutes to dress and I'll be there," she promised.

"I'll give you exactly five minutes to dress before Malia starts serving," was Emily's warning.

Julie believed she meant it. Emily always meant what

she said—that was one of the good things about her. People always knew where they stood.

The private discussion had eliminated any chance of strain between the two women. Their dinner was typical of many they had shared together over the last months. Afterward Malia reminded Julie that she hadn't been in to see Debbie yet.

"I'll go right in," she promised, feeling awfully guilty.

"Hi!" Her cheerfulness was genuine enough as she entered Debbie's bedroom. A wheelchair occupied a corner of the room. "Won't be long before you can have dinner with us."

"I think I've forgotten what it's like to eat at a table. Auntie Em will have to teach me manners all over again," the girl joked.

"How'd all the tests and X-rays go at the hospital?"

Debbie's answer was long and detailed, colored with asides about dumb doctors and cute interns and nice nurses. She wrapped it up by saying that she was progressing faster than anyone thought.

"That's great," Julie smiled.

The girl's dark eyes surveyed her and didn't miss a thing. "Have you been crying? Your eyes look red."

"Chlorine, I guess. I was swimming in the pool this afternoon."

"So that's where you were when I came home."

"Uh, yeah." It was a necessary lie.

"I sure would like to know what's going on around this place," Debbie sighed, "First Malia tells me you'll be in to see me before diner, then Emily comes in to say you have a headache and aren't feeling well. And you say you went swimming."

"Well, it's all true," Julie said. "I was swimming, and I did get a headache from the sun, didn't feel well, and lay down for a while. Now I'm better."

"Oh. Is that why Ruel went slamming through the house, shouting in whispers at Auntie Em? Something about you. I couldn't really hear."

Busted, Julie thought with dismay.

"Well, I did hear one thing."

"What was that?" Julie asked.

"Something about coming back early to talk to you. It was like he was warning Em about something too. I couldn't understand it all. What was it about? Did you have another fight? What does Aunt Em have to do with it?" The teenager's curiosity was almost too much for her to contain.

"Um, I didn't have an argument with your brother." That was true enough. "I don't know any more than you do about the rest of it."

"Why don't you trust me, Julie?" Debbie sighed.

"I trust you," she laughed, "but not totally."

Debbie stuck out her tongue in a friendly way. "I tell you practically everything. That's so totally not fair."

"News flash. Life isn't. You've had a long day, better get some rest."

After exchanging good nights, Julie returned to the living room where Emily was reading. She sat on the sofa and glanced through a magazine. The more she thought about Debbie's comment that Ruel planned to come back early, the more she wasn't ready to see him.

"If you don't mind, Emily, I think I'll go to bed. I'm tired." Julie straightened to her feet.

"Ruel said he would be home in another hour or two. He wanted to speak to you," Emily said. "Perhaps you should wait up for him."

"No." Julie refused with a decisive shake of her head. "I'd rather not see him tonight."

"Is that what you want me to tell him?" Emily studied her thoughtfully.

"It's the truth. It's been a really emotional day," Jul
answered. "And I just don't think I want to discuss
with Ruel."

"I understand," the other woman smiled and nodded. "The morning is soon enough."

CHAPTER TWELVE

A rosy dawn crept softly into the bedroom. Slowly Julie opened her eyes to see the sunrise turning the walls pink. Pushing aside the covers, she climbed out of bed. It looked like a beautiful morning and she didn't feel like missing it. As she started toward the French doors, she saw a piece of paper had been slipped under the door.

Bending down, she picked it up and unfolded it. The bold handwriting said, *"Julie—come riding with me this morning. Meet me at 7:30 in front of the house. Ruel."*

She stared at it, reading the message again. It seemed cold and impersonal. Folding the note, she fingered the crease. She wanted more time to think before she met him.

Today was Saturday. Julie walked to her closet and took out a pair of jeans and a blouse. She slipped into her bikini, put the clothes over it, and folded a clean beach towel to put in her beach bag.

She walked to the French doors and opened them. There was no one in the courtyard below and no sound

of anyone stirring in the house. Stealthily and quietly
she made her way along the lanai to the stairs.

Reaching the circular driveway, she hurried down
the private lane. She didn't pause to admire the panoramic view of the coastline as she made her descent of
the switchback. When she reached the junction with
the highway, the bus that passed Waimea Bay was just
approaching. She waved to the driver to stop, climbed
aboard, and swung breathlessly into a seat.

The beach was deserted at that early morning hour
and Julie had it all to herself. A large volcanic rock rose
from the sand at the water's edge and jutted into the
bay. The rock was often used as a diving board by the
more brave and daring swimmers. But Julie wanted only
a place to sit and think. With her beach towel as a cush-
ion, she settled onto a ledge.

In the sheltered bay, the gentle waves seemed to caress the shore. The air was soft and pure, warmed by the
steadily rising sun and stirred by the breath of the lazy
trade winds. Behind the bay rose the proud cliffs that
had been there for millenia before the first white man
landed on the island.

Losing herself in a silent reverie on nature's beauty,
it was some time before Julie turned her thoughts in-
ward. Emily would be at the breakfast table on the lanai
about now. On occasion, she had sometimes left before
breakfast on Saturdays so it wasn't likely that Emily
would worry about her absence.

Ruel would be expecting her to go riding with him,
but Julie wasn't prepared to face him yet. She wondered
what he thought of her. True, he had defended her and
taken the blame for what happened. Obviously, he de-
sired her but was that the only basis for their relationship? Yesterday, that had been enough for her. Today
Sighing, Julie didn't think she knew.

Laughing, shouting voices came from the beach, and she turned to see a family wading and splashing into the water. Sunbathers were scattered along the golden strand of beach. She no longer had it all to herself. A pair of adventurous boys were clambering over the mound of cinder rock toward her.

Someone came trotting across the sand in her direction but she didn't bother to really look. Someone was always running across the sand—swimmers, children, joggers.

"California? Julie! I thought I recognized you, but I wasn't sure." Frank stopped beside her, his hands at his sides. His expression hovered between glad-to-see-her and a look of betrayal.

"Hi, Frank. What are you doing here?" Sitting up, Julie brushed the sand from her palms in an attempt at nonchalance. She hadn't seen Frank since the night at the restaurant with Ruel.

"I stop at this beach every weekend looking for you," he answered. "You didn't come last Sunday. What happened? Did you and Chandler have such a big night that you slept all next day? Or maybe he told you couldn't." His tone was bitter.

"Stop it, Frank." Her voice was low and stiff with control.

"Where's the big man today?" he jeered.

"Last week you told Ruel that he didn't own me," Julie reminded him, her brown eyes flashing. "Well, neither do you. So maybe you'd better just leave. Take your surfboard and go cool off somewhere."

"Oh, Julie!" His sigh seemed to drain away his anger as he sank to his knees on the sand beside her. "Okay, I was jealous. When I saw you and him at the restaurant, I felt kinda crazy."

"I didn't know you worked there."

"I guessed that after I saw Chandler. Or at least, I didn'
think you would come there with him on purpose, know
ing how I feel about you," Frank qualified. "All along
I've been thinking you were my girl. I didn't realiz
he was beating my time. What were you doing goin;
out with him?" Instead of anger, this time there wa
hurt.

"He asked me to have dinner with him and I sai
yes." She locked her hands around her knees an
looked out to sea.

"But why?"

"Because I wanted to," she admitted. "It's not tha
big a deal."

"Must be really convenient, both of you living in th
same house and all," Frank said with disgust. "Wheneve
ol' Chandler gets bored, you're right there."

"It's not like that at all." Was it? Seeing it from Frank'
perspective was troubling.

"Why didn't you come last Sunday?" The look in hi
dark eyes revealed the rejection he felt.

"Probably because I knew this would happen and
didn't want to discuss Ruel with you. And I don't want t
discuss him with you now." Unclasping her hands, Juli
lay back on the towel and closed her eyes. She hoped h
would take her unsubtle hint and drop the subject.

"Don't you think I have the right to an explanation?
Frank asked in a righteous tone.

"No. We're just friends, Frank," she insisted.

"We're a little more than that," he protested. "You'r
my California girl—everybody knows that."

"I'm not your girl." She kept her voice even.

"Are you his girl?"

A stab of emotion made her wince a little. "I'm no
anybody's girl. And I told you I didn't want to discus
Ruel."

"What happened? Did he dump you already?" Frank jeered.

"Frank!" Opening her eyes, she shot him a warning look.

"Okay, we won't talk about him," he agreed grudgingly. "If that's what you want, we'll forget about him."

"That's what I want." But Julie knew it was impossible. She would never forget about Ruel. He had taken over her thoughts—and her heart.

Frank scooped up some sand and sifted it through his fingers. "One of my buddies is having a luau tonight." He shifted his position to sit cross-legged on the ground. "It's going to be awesome, with roast pig and everything. Should be fun."

"Sounds like it. Are you going?" Julie phrased her question to exclude herself.

"I have to work tonight."

"Too bad," she murmured with indifferent sympathy.

"But I could call in sick." Frank paused. "What I'm trying to say is . . . I'd like to go to the luau with you."

"I don't think it would be a good idea," she said.

"Aw, come on," he coaxed. "We'll have a good time."

"No, Frank."

"You'll change your mind before the day is over." He wouldn't accept her refusal. "It'll be a blast. We can spend the day together swimming and playing in the sand."

He grabbed another handful of sand and held it over her, letting it trickle from his fist into her belly button. Julie wasn't amused. She brushed the sand away. "Will you stop it?" she demanded.

A looming shadow fell across her body. In the same second, Frank was hauled to his feet and set to one side.

"Ruel, you can't—"

"I just did."

"Dude, who do you think you are?" Frank couldn't ge
his balance for a few seconds.

Ruel threw him a contemptuous look and didn't an
swer. He turned to Julie. "You're coming with me," h
ordered.

"No, she's not!" Frank shouted and grabbed him b
the arm.

In a fluid move, Ruel shook him off—and swung, ca
sually ridding himself of an annoying pest. Frank stum
bled and came back, his forward impetus carrying hir
right into the hooking fist. It all happened before Juli
could break the paralysis of surprise and do somethin,
to stop it.

"No!" she protested too late. The blow knocke
Frank backward onto the beach. Afraid he was hur
Julie moved to him. "Frank—"

Her intention went no further than calling his nam
and taking a step before Ruel was pulling her away. Sh
tried to tug free.

"I said you're coming with me." He reached dow
and scooped up her beach bag and towel.

"Let me go! He's hurt!" She looked at Frank, who la
gasping on the sand in a fallen-hero pose.

"He's making the most of it, but he's not hurt." Rue
flicked a merciless glance at his rival and just stoo
there, waiting for Julie to say something.

Julie looked from him to Frank, who kept his eyes o:
Ruel. He sat up halfway, fury in his eyes.

No matter what she did, one of them wasn't going t
like it. And she knew better than to get between tw
guys spoiling for a fight. She grabbed her beach ba
from Ruel and stalked off. Let the cavemen slug it ou
She didn't give a flying fish which one won.

She headed up the beach to the parking lot, not er

tirely surprised when Ruel caught up to her a few minutes later.

He grabbed her arm and she turned around, looking over his shoulder to see if Frank was all right. The surfer was far down the beach, walking away.

"I didn't touch him," Ruel growled. "And the first time was an accident. Looked to me like you needed a little rescuing."

She tossed her hair and looked at him with infinite scorn. "Actually, I didn't."

"I'm sorry."

"No, you're not."

He gave her a wolfish grin. "Okay, I'm not. Let's go. Get in the car."

Julie heard the faint squeal of air brakes and turned to see the Waimea bus pulling out. There wouldn't be another one for an hour and she really didn't want to stick around. If nothing else, Ruel could take her back to the house where she could sunbathe in peace and do a little sulking. The morning had been ruined.

They walked to the black sports car in unbroken silence until he unlocked the doors with the key ring remote.

"Is this going to be another one of your high-speed rides?" she challenged. She opened the door and threw her beach bag in the back. Ruel tossed in the towel. They both got in at almost the same second, slamming the doors with a one-two bang.

He sliced a quelling glance at her and started the car. Like a caged beast, the car prowled onto the highway at a restrained pace. The power of the motor was never called upon to exert its thrust as they traveled sedately over the asphalt.

Then Ruel turned off onto a farm road. Towering stalks of sugarcane closed around them, the red dirt

road tunneling a path through the field. At a wide spot
Ruel drove the car to one side and stopped. A touch of
a button sent the windows rolling down to let the trade
winds blow fresh air though the car.

When he turned off the motor, Julie could hear the
wind swishing through the tall leaves of the sugarcane
swaying the mauve tassels on top. Ruel leaned an elbow
on the steering wheel and rubbed his mouth, staring
resolutely ahead.

He seemed to be waiting for her to say something.
She frowned, wishing they weren't out in the middle of
nowhere. On the other hand, she could really let him
have it if no one was listening.

"That was completely uncalled for," she began. Julie
wasn't ready to forgive him and she wasn't going to let
him distract her with a kiss.

He slammed a hand against the steering wheel.
"What did you expect?" He was almost yelling. "You
knew I wanted to see you! I left a note asking you to
come riding with me this morning. And don't tell me
you didn't get it, because I slipped it under your door
last night. This morning it was on your dressing table. I
found it when I went looking for you."

"You had no right to be in my room," she snapped,
since she couldn't say that she hadn't seen the note.

"Sorry. I seem to be saying that a lot."

"You should be."

Ruel scowled. "When I didn't find you in your room,
I went looking for you."

"Good work, detective. You tracked me down."

"Hey, I have some brains. Not like that stupid surfer
you seem to like so much."

What could she say? *You've got it all wrong, Ruel. Frank
isn't a stupid surfer. He's . . . just a surfer.* Not much of a
defense. Frank wasn't anything to her, she realized. No

really. He was a good-looking guy and they'd shared
some good times. Nothing more than that.

"I don't see why you get so upset over him," she said.
She knew the comment would irritate Ruel but she did-
n't care.

"You really want to know, Julie?"

"Yeah. I do."

He turned to her and suddenly kissed her hard on
the lips, leaving her breathless. He broke off the kiss
and sighed. "Because I love you," he said hoarsely.

He sought her lips again, and all her anger eva-
porated under the demanding possession of his mouth.
Somehow her arms found their way around his neck as
she arched her body to him. The steering wheel got in
the way but Ruel reached out to draw her closer anyway.

"I never guessed . . ." Julie twisted sideways, tipping
her head back to see his face and sliding her fingers inside the buttoned front of his shirt to feel the hair on
his chest and the pounding beat of his heart. "I didn't
know you loved me," she told him.

The invitation of her parted lips was one he couldn't
resist. His next kiss was brief, keeping the fires of passion burning but not letting them blaze out of control.

"I told you I did yesterday." His glowing look seemed
to radiate over her. "Don't you remember?"

"No." She wouldn't have forgotten something as important, not even in the heat of the moment. "Unless—
you said something in Hawaiian."

"Aloha auia oe. I love you," he translated. "Ku'uipo,
my sweetheart, my lover."

He brushed his mouth over her lips. His hand fitted
itself to the curve of her neck, his thumb rubbing the
hollow under her ear in a sensual caress. Julie quivered
under the spell of his potent charm.

"I would have made sure you understood me yester-

day," Ruel told her. "But Em walked in." His jaw tightened. "That really ripped me up—just knowing how hu
miliated and embarrassed you were. All I wanted to do
was comfort you and tell you that it would be all right
But not with Em there. And I knew she wouldn'
leave—she really likes you and she's very protective."

"I know," Julie murmured.

"And then I had that appointment in the city and
then you kept dodging me," he added, pulling her hair
in a gently teasing way. "You crazy little wahine."

Julie giggled. "I love it when you talk Hawaiian."

"Just you wait. I'll talk Hawaiian to you all night
long," he said, giving her a wicked grin.

"It all worked out, though," she reassured him
reaching out to trace the outline of his mouth with her
fingertips. The clean, male smell of him was an aphro
disiac to her senses.

"But it was hell in the meantime." He exhaled a long
breath.

"It's heaven now."

Her head was tipped far back on his shoulder. With a
look of tenderness, Ruel covered her lips. His hand
slipped across her bare belly and slid down to her hip in
an attempt to turn her into his arms, but the steering
wheel blocked them again.

"Damn it," he growled. "I'm going to rip this thing out.'

"Then we'll never get back to civilization."

"Good." He helped himself to another lingering kiss
"Oh, Julie," he whispered, "why didn't you wait up for
me last night? We could have had this whole thing
straightened out by now. I broke every record getting
back from Honolulu, and then found out you'd gone to
bed. But why didn't you meet me this morning?"

"Because I didn't think I could face you. Not yet. I—
I wanted time to think," she admitted. "I didn't run very
far, did I?"

"No," he said.

"I didn't want to, not until I'd made up my mind."

"About what?" He molded his hand to her breast and seemed enchanted with its shape. His erotic touch built the flames again, the heat spreading to other areas.

"Until I'd made up my mind whether I could handle it when you became bored with me."

"Bored with you!" Ruel leaned his head back against the seat and laughed at the ceiling. "Not a problem so far. Not from the moment you came down the stairs that first morning, looking like you owned the place. You walked across the room to me and looked me right straight in the eye."

"You were talking about the Kona winds with Al." Julie remembered it as vividly as he did. "And you knew who I was immediately."

"Yeah, but you didn't seem exactly impressed with my deductive prowess," Ruel said. "Or anything else about me."

If you only knew, Julie thought. "I liked you, I guess," she said diffidently. "But you were hardly ever around. I didn't know if you liked me or not at first."

"Nah, not really. I just thought you were the smartest, sweetest, sexiest female I'd ever met. Other than that, no big deal."

"Thanks a lot," she laughed.

"As if you didn't know I was attracted to you," he mocked. "Running around with flowers in your hair, sunbathing under my balcony, and fooling around with your surfer to make me jealous."

"I really didn't do it on purpose." She cast him a sideways glance. "Were you really jealous of Frank?"

"He's younger than I am. He's built. He's good-looking. I hate his punk guts."

Her hand spread over the solid muscles of his chest

to the firmness of his abs. "But I like your body better
Ruel. It's hard . . . and warm . . ."

"Stop it, Julie." He closed his fingers over her hand
"Keep that up and you'll find out just how hard and
warm it is. This car isn't designed for making love."

"It isn't?" She felt a sense of power in being able to
arouse him and exercised a little of it now.

"No," he repeated firmly, but his gaze wandered
down to the swelling curves of her breasts, exposed by
the cut of her bikini top. "Can't you wait until we get be
hind closed doors? On a bed?"

"Maybe. Maybe not."

He drew in his breath. "Okay." He reached out and
twined his fingers in her hair, drawing her close for an
other lingering, deeply sensual kiss.

A horn honked loudly as a truck rumbled to a
squealing halt. They moved apart as it honked again
Ruel sighed with frustration. "Field hands."

"Hey, boss! It mo' betta if you move dat car!" a male
voice shouted. "We gonna fire dis field wikiwiki."

With a saluting wave, Ruel acknowledged the advice
and information. He set Julie completely in her own
seat and reached behind it for her beach bag.

"Here." He put it in her lap. "Better put some clothe
on."

The cane truck squeezed past them as Ruel started
the car. Fighting the cramped space of the front seat
Julie managed to pull her jeans on and shrug into he
blouse. When the truck was behind them, Ruel re
versed the car and maneuvered it back the way they had
come.

"Was this where you wanted to ride to today?" Julie
asked as they emerged from the dirt road to the drive.

"Probably." He slowed the car to a crawl. "I jus
wanted to get you away from the house where we could

talk. Which reminds me . . ." He reached out to take her hand.

"Of what?" Julie asked.

Ruel turned to study her. "I've been the one who's been doing most of the talking."

"And?" She was puzzled by the intensity of his gaze.

"Your turn."

Another truck rumbled up behind them, its horn blaring. There wasn't enough room for it to pass. Ruel swore under his breath and waved his arm out the window for the truck to wait.

"Hey, boss! Have you gone pupule? You can't park dat car in da road."

"Damn it, Al!" Ruel leaned his head out the window to shout at him. "I'm not moving until she says she loves me! So lay off that damned horn!" Impatience was in his expression when he looked at her. "Well?"

That was what he had been waiting for her to say. Julie laughed in delight. She thought she had told him a hundred times—a thousand times.

"I love you, Ruel Chandler," she declared in a buoyant voice.

"It's about time you said it." His gruffness was the most beautiful sound she had ever heard. His hand cupped the back of her head to draw her mouth to his.

In the truck behind them, the driver leaned on the horn, announcing to the world the answer she had given. It became the second most beautiful sound in the world.

A Behind-the-Scenes Look at
That Boston Man and *Kona Winds*

Dear Reader,

It's impossible for me to remember writing this book without recalling my first visit to the New England area—and how very much I was dreading going there. I know, a statement like that requires an explanation. First, let me remind you that I was born and raised in a small Iowa farming community, small enough that I knew practically everyone in town and many were related to me. Seriously, my great-aunt, Cora, lived next door; a shirttail cousin lived on the other side; two houses down the street were more cousins, who were also my playmates; across the street was my great-uncle, Jack; behind his house on the next street was my great-aunt, Kate; and my grandpa lived on the corner. It was a place of familiar faces with lots of land and sky.

New England, to my way of thinking, was going to be crowded cities full of noise, traffic and people. I based this mostly on my solitary visit to New York when Bill and I flew there to meet with my agent and publisher. Yes, I was awed by the concrete canyons of Manhattan, but the horns and the sirens and the jam-packed sidewalks full of strangers who never looked you in the eye (although a few stared a lot at Bill's cowboy boots)

made me ache for open skies, the whisper of wind
through the cornfields, and the sound of birdsong.

Therefore, I was certain that New England was
going to be full of crowded cities—just like the Gulf
Coast of Florida, where we had spent the winter that
year—and where it was difficult to tell where one
city/town stopped and the next one began; they all just
ran together.

This is what I was expecting in New England, and I
wasn't looking forward to a summer traveling around
it. Thankfully, Bill insisted that I should never write
about an area without first visiting it. I had been wrong
about other places already, so I knew he had a valid
point. Still. . . . Although he didn't exactly drag me
there kicking and screaming, it was close. Wisely, Bill
plotted a course that skirted the major cities and
concentrated on the countrysides of New Jersey and
Connecticut. So before we ever reached Massachusetts, I had begun to warm up to the area.

If our travels through Massachusetts had ended in
Concord, I would have been perfectly happy. I was
positively enchanted by it. But, no, Bill said we were
going to Boston. A city! Oh, but what a city, as I quickly
discovered. Granted, it isn't a place to be toured by
auto. No, you have to walk it, and walk it we did, following history's path—the old North Church, Paul
Revere's home, the harbor, everywhere. And I fell in
love with a city. Later, I read an article that identified
what were believed to be the four unique cities in
the United States—San Francisco, California, San An-
tonio, Texas, New Orleans, Louisiana, and Boston,
Massachusetts. I totally concur with those choices.

From that point, there was no doubt in my mind
that my Massachusetts book would be set in Boston. I
can't tell you how happy I was when my niece (who is
only six plus years younger than me, so more like a

baby sister) moved to Boston several years ago. Her home is in Charlestown; a short walk downhill from her place, Old Ironsides is anchored, and uphill is the Bunker Hill monument.

Boston opened my eyes and showed me that this country girl could become a city lover. From that moment on, I was eager to tour the rest of New England. *That Boston Man* will always hold a special place in my memories, and I hope you will find the story memorable, too.

The worst advice I ever received as a writer came from my high school creative writing teacher; she told me to write what I know. I was horrified. I lived in Iowa, for heaven's sake!!! I couldn't imagine anything more boring than writing about Iowa. The best advice I ever received came from that same high school creative writing teacher who told me to write what I know. Why? Because you can research anything, then write from knowledge.

There are times when research can be dull and time-consuming, with hours spent in libraries, searching for necessary background material for a particular occupation or historical detail or descriptions of native flora and fauna of a given area. But sometimes it can be an absolutely fabulous experience—like the time Bill and I traveled to Hawaii so I could use it as a background for this book. It was truly a workcation.

Obviously, the logistics of attempting to transport the thirty-four-foot travel trailer that was our home at the time were just too daunting, so it was left behind. Fortunately, my agent had a condo on the North Shore of Oahu, which he offered to us for our month's stay on the island. How lucky is that?

I don't think I will ever forget that first glimpse of

Diamond Head and Waikiki Beach from the jet's
porthole windows—the sun was just going down and
everything was bathed in that yellow-pink light of
early sunset. That first visit to Hawaii took place in the
late seventies and, upon landing, we were welcomed
with leis just like out of the old travelogues. Suddenly,
we were enveloped in the fresh scents of the island—
plumier and salt sea air, all languid and heavy. That
wonderful greeting was followed by the usual hassle of
waiting at baggage claim to collect ALL of our luggage, then heading for the car rental counter. It felt as
if we'd signed our life away by the time we finally finished all the paperwork. By then it was dark outside.

Armed with the map my agent had provided with
directions to his condo, we headed out, tired from the
long flight and ready to reach our home for the next
month. Honolulu had long disappeared from the
rearview mirror when we came to our first intersection. That's when I had my first real introduction to
Hawaii. Every single town on the signpost started with
an H followed by a whole bunch of vowels. Bill said,
"Which way?" I had the map, but I couldn't find any of
those towns on it. With cars behind us, there wasn't
time to stop and figure it out, so I told him to stay left.
To my way of thinking, we were on an island—how lost
could we get? As it turned out, we took the long way to
the condo, but we arrived safely.

The very first thing I did the next morning was to
buy a Hawaiian dictionary so I could learn how to pronounce all those words full of vowels. Believe me, I
made good use of it during our month's stay on the
island. By the time we left, I could pronounce Hawaiian words like a native. My mind is full of snapshot
memories of that first trip to Hawaii—lunching on the
veranda of the Royal Hawaiian, cooling myself with a
sandalwood fan, sipping a mai tai while on a dinner

cruise aboard a sailing schooner, wandering through a pineapple field, and watching a field of sugar cane burn. During that late seventies visit to Hawaii, I was struck by one of the building ordinances Honolulu had, which prohibited any building from being taller than a palm tree. When we went back to Hawaii a few years later, that ordinance had been abandoned and the city was stacked with high-rises. There was a new ordinance that mandated every building must receive a certain number of hours of sunshine every day. Hawaii had undergone an explosion, and there were no more fields of sugar cane or pineapple—only a few large gardens to show tourists how they are grown.

But Hawaii is still Hawaii, an island paradise with its ocean-scented air, tropical breezes and lush vegetation. And the Kona wind still blows.

Catch up with the first book
in the Bannon Brothers series,
HONOR!

There was no shortage of gorgeous women at the reception, but not one was in her league, in his opinion. Kenzie was his definition of perfect. Smart. And sexy, with a superfit, petite body that looked fantastic in a plain white T-shirt and camo cargos—her version of fatigues, now that she was no longer a soldier.

A female guest strolled nearby, trilling a hello to a friend a few tables away. Linc looked idly at them as the woman stopped to chat, then realized she was holding a tiny dog wearing a ruffled collar in the crook of her arm. He'd taken it for a purse at first. Her pampered pet blinked and yawned as the woman moved away.

He shook his head, amused. Not Kenzie's kind of dog, that was for sure.

She'd been a K9 trainer for the army, on a fast track right out of basic. Kenzie wasn't one to brag, but Linc had been able to fill in the blanks from the bare facts she'd offered. Her knack for the work had gotten her quickly promoted to a position of critical importance:

training military handlers assigned to new animals and developing new skill sets for the experienced dogs to keep up with what was going on in country.

Then something had happened, she wouldn't say what. She didn't seem to want to reenlist. She didn't seem to want to do anything but work. A lot.

Which was why he was solo on his brother's wedding day.

Two weeks ago he'd stopped by the JB Kennels and seen her out in the field with a half-grown shepherd. Their jumps and leaps looked like pure joy, but he knew she was testing the pup's reflexes and instincts. In time, under her tutelage, the young animal would learn to turn play into power. The sight of the two of them, twisting and turning in midair, was something he would never forget.

Hell, Kenzie looked good even in thick bite sleeves and padded pants. But he let himself imagine her in something close-fitting and classy, her hair brushed to a silken shine and her head tipped back to gaze up at him as they danced to a slow number. Like the one the band was playing right now . . .

"Linc. You with us?"

He snapped out of his reverie and looked up at his younger brother. "Just thinking."

Deke took hold of a bentwood chair, spun it around with one hand and sat on it backward, resting his arms on the curved top and stretching out his long legs.

"About what? Or should I say who?" he asked shrewdly.

"Give me a break, Deke." Linc took a sip of champagne and set the glass aside.

His younger brother wasn't done ribbing him. "You've got someone on your mind. I can see it in your eyes."

"What are you talking about?"

"That moody, distracted look is what I'm talking about."

"You're imagining things, Deke."

His brother only laughed. "Am I? Just so you know, one wedding per year is all I can handle. I'm not ready to see you walk down the aisle."

Linc smiled slightly. "If I found the right woman, why not?"

Deke was tactful enough to quit at that point. He surveyed the crowd. "Look at all these gorgeous babes. How come you're not dancing?"

"I'm waiting for a song I like," Linc parried.

Deke gave up, shaking his head. "Okay. Have it your way." He returned the inviting smile of the brunette on the other side of the dance floor. She brightened, but stayed where she was, smoothing the brilliant folds of her taffeta dress. "There's my girl. I think she likes me."

"Go for it. You're not taken."

"Neither are you."

Linc only shrugged.

Deke turned his head and studied him for a long moment. "C'mon, bro. You can tell me. What don't I know?"

"Nothing."

Deke didn't seem to believe that reply. "Wait a minute—there was someone. Her name was—it's coming back to me—Karen, right?"

"Who?"

For a second, Linc drew a blank. Then he remembered. Months ago Kenzie had used that name when she'd showed up at Bannon's door with a guard dog to loan him as a favor to Linc.

"Karen," Deke said impatiently. "You know who I mean."

Linc smiled. "Oh, yeah. Her. Ah, we're just friends."

Deke shot him a knowing look.

"If that changes, I'll let you know," Linc said calmly.

His brother lost interest when the brunette seized her chance and swept across the dance floor as the band paused. "I do believe she really is interested." Deke ran a hand over his brown locks and asked, "How's the hair?"

"Looks great. Very natural," Linc teased, echoing the photographer's comment.

"Shut up." Deke straightened his lapels.

The two brothers rose at the same time, but Linc turned to go before the brunette arrived. He wandered away down a carpeted corridor, feeling a little lonely. Without intending to, he ended up in the hotel's bar. It was mostly empty. There was only one other customer, an older man having a beer, but no bartender. The distant noise of the reception was barely audible in the dim, luxuriously furnished room.

He slid onto a stool, folding his arms on the counter and looking around idly while he waited to be served. The liquor bottles arrayed in ranks behind the bar reflected blue light coming from an unseen source. The bar was dark otherwise, but he didn't mind.

The bartender appeared from a door at the end of the polished counter and took his order, exchanging a few words with Linc as he set the drink on a napkin. Then he turned away to prepare for the evening rush, setting clean glasses of various types on trays and filling up a compartmented container with slices of lemon and lime and bright red cherries.

Linc barely noticed. He took one sip and set the drink down, intending to make it last. He had nothing to do and nowhere to go except back to the reception.

Later for that. He was truly tired and it was catching up with him. Being the best man was serious work.

Linc had rolled out of bed at six a.m. and barely had a chance to catch his breath since.

Zoning out over a cold drink felt fine. The TV over the bar was tuned to the local news, on low. Good. He didn't really want to listen. The weatherman was saying something about clouds rolling in by nightfall. So be it. The perfect day was over.

Linc undid his black silk bow tie, taking a deep breath or two as he eased the collar button open next. He wasn't made to wear monkey suits.

He half heard the reporter going on and on about an accident on I-95 just outside of a town with a name he wasn't going to remember. Not a pileup, not a jack-knifed semi, just a solitary car.

Filler. News shows made a huge deal out of a fender-bender when there wasn't anything else to yap about.

Then the live feed crackled and filled the screen behind the guy and Linc winced. The accident wasn't minor. It looked like a rollover. Smashed frame, crumpled black chassis scraped to the gray undercoat in a lot of places, back wheels high in the air.

Linc could just make out an ambulance, a red and white blotch in the background, and activity around it, a stretcher being loaded. He got a glimpse of what looked like a head-and-neck stabilizer frame attached to the stretcher.

Fatalities got a body bag, not that rig. He automatically wished the injured person well—he or she was lucky to be alive.

He scowled when the cameraman evaded the highway patrol officer's gaze and moved around for a close-up of the nearly totaled vehicle. The reporter on the scene dogged him, trying to stay in the frame and not always succeeding. They both knew what would get on TV: a dramatic shot, preferably with blood.

Good thing there were a few seconds of lag time

before any broadcast, Linc thought. Imagine the
shock of someone recognizing a victim of a bad accident or identifying detail—

He pushed away his barely touched drink. Linc
knew that license plate. There was only one word on it.
KENZYZ.

Ready for more from Janet Dailey?

Read on for a peek at her new book,
TRIUMPH,
available in June 2013.

Kelly St. Johns smoothed her suit, waiting for the countdown in her earbud mic as a cameraman a block away prepared for a long establishing shot. Seventeen stories of open concrete floors towered behind her, next to a huge crane and flatbed trailers laden with rebar. The construction project had been idled, its dirty-money financing gone and its site locked down by the feds. The deserted streets around it were silent, ideal for taping.

"Three, two, one."

Kelly straightened and spoke the sentences she'd memorized before the shoot, gesturing to the unfinished structure.

"Another scandal-ridden project shut down by the authorities. Millions of dollars—your tax dollars—lost to kickbacks. When will it end?"

"And . . . cut. Back to you in a minute, Kelly," the cameraman said. "We want to see how that looks."

Kelly barely registered Gordon's comment. She could hear Laura, the segment producer, discussing

the footage with him. She turned and looked around
at the building and construction site, searching for a
different visual. They were sure to ask for additiona
takes. There was no point in removing the small wire
less mic clipped to her lapel or the earbud.

Today's tape would be digitally edited at the new
studio and used as an opener for her previous re
portage and interviews on corruption in the buildin;
industries. Not her first feature story, but it was an im
portant one. Atlanta was growing faster than ever
crowded with gleaming skyscrapers and world-clas
hotels that overshadowed the quiet, idyllic neighbor
hoods surrounding the metropolitan hub.

She ignored a faint tremor of unease. Laura ha
decided to film at the end of the day to take advantage
of the dramatic shadows, getting clearance to use th
construction site, abandoned months ago, for a loca
tion and obtaining keys to the padlocked gates. Sup
posedly, there was security somewhere around.

Kelly reached into her pocket and took out her lam
inated press pass. If anyone stopped her, it would
come in handy. She walked through the half-buil
structure, her heels echoing on the dusty concrete
going around pillars and avoiding the deep hole fo
the elevator banks.

No safety cones, no nothing. No graffiti either, and
no signs of squatters, both of which struck her as odd
A management company had to be maintaining th
unfinished building—what there was of it. But th
researcher assigned to the story had it on good au
thority that the owners had fled the United State
without bothering to declare bankruptcy.

She could see clear through to the back of the site
greened by tall weeds growing in the gouges left by
the treads of heavy machinery, now gone. Kelly con
tinued toward the open area, stopping at the edge o

the unfinished floor and looking out, her arms folded over her chest.

"Kelly?" The cameraman's voice crackled in the earbud. "Where'd you go? We can't see you."

"I'm at the back," she answered. "It doesn't look like anyone's been here for months, but it hasn't been trashed. Kind of weird that I don't see any footprints besides my own."

Gordon's reply was cheerful. "Okay, we'll follow them. Laura wants another backdrop, same lines. Anything fabulous where you are?"

"No." Kelly didn't elaborate, noticing a car on the other side of the chain-link fence behind the weeds. It was the sole occupant of the parking lot, a wasteland of cracked asphalt and stomped beer cans.

The car's tinted windows and gleaming black finish seemed out of place in the desolate setting. There was no sign of life that she could see, but maybe that was because of the slanting angle of the late-afternoon light.

She heard Laura and Gordon enter and follow her trail, their sneakered footfalls quiet on the concrete. Kelly turned toward them. The segment producer was carrying Kelly's bag and her own, and some of Gordon's equipment.

Laura, a short brunette in no-nonsense jeans and jacket with the station logo, stopped several feet away beside Gordon. The burly, older man hoisted the camera and looked through the viewfinder. He took his time about focusing and adjusting the lens. Kelly waited, distracted by sounds coming from the parking lot.

Car doors opened and closed softly. So there was someone in that car. Had the three of them been noticed? She didn't like the feeling of not knowing what was behind her.

"Ready for your close-up?" Gordon said finally.

That old line. Always the joker. "Yes," Kelly snapped

"I say we get a shot of you picking weeds and call i a wrap."

Laura was craning her neck to get a glimpse of the viewfinder that jutted out from the side of the video camera. "Gordon, do you want that car in the back ground?"

"The editor can zap it out," he said absently. "Kelly we're rolling. Three, two, one—"

"Who are all those guys?" Laura demanded. "Wait there's a woman, too. In the other car."

Kelly whirled around. A second car, a near twin o the one she'd seen, pulled into the parking lot behind the chain-link fence. Two men had gotten out of the first car and stood behind the open rear doors, as i they were shields. A woman gestured from the rolled down passenger side window of the second car, saying something, not in English.

Instinct made Kelly step back into the shadows.

"Hey," Gordon said. "Not there. We're losing the light. Kelly, move back where you were—"

"Shut up!" she hissed, walking quickly toward him

The cameraman looked up at her, baffled. "What' the matter? Want me to stop?"

Laura's eyes widened, taking in whatever was hap pening on the viewfinder. Something was radicall wrong, Kelly knew that much.

"Get down! *Down!*"

Not Gordon's voice. Deeper. Urgent. Kelly spun too startled to figure out more. She heard a muffle *crack* and the faint, unmistakable *zing* of a bullet.

Someone shoved her behind a pillar and held he there.